MARGOT DURAND COZY MYSTERY BOXED SET

DANIELLE COLLINS

FAIRFIELD PUBLISHING

THANK you so much for buying my book. I am excited to share my stories with you and hope that you are just as thrilled to read them.

If you would like to know about all my new releases and have the opportunity to get free books, make sure you sign up for our Cozy Mystery Newsletter.

FairfieldPublishing.com/cozy-newsletter

CROISSANTS AND CORRUPTION

CHAPTER 1

IT WAS the beginning of a perfect late spring day in North Bank, Virginia, despite the fact that the sun hadn't yet come up. The crisp air coming off the Potomac invigorated Margot Durand as she picked up her pace down the street on the way to her bakery, *The Parisian Pâtisserie.* It sat at the river's edge waiting for lights and the scent of baking pastries to fill the space.

It was a typical early morning—a baker's morning—aside from the fact that, as Margot unlocked the front door and rushed to disarm the alarm, her phone vibrated in her pocket.

Who in the world is calling me at three in the morning?

Depositing her bag on the counter and flipping on the bright halogen lights, she dislodged her phone from her back pocket and jammed her finger against the screen before she lost the call.

"Hello?"

"Heya, sis."

"Renee?" Margot blinked in shock. Her sister lived in California and, with a little mental math, Margot realized it was midnight for her. "Why are you calling me so...late?"

"It's early there, right?"

Margot nodded then remembered her sister couldn't see her. "Yes. I've just made it to the bakery."

"I figured..." Her sister trailed off, but Margot caught the hint of warning in her voice.

"Rae, what is it?"

After a lengthy silence, Renee said one word. "Taylor."

"Oh no." Margot dropped into her desk chair, swiveling her knees under the counter and propping her chin on her palm. "What's she done this time?"

An image of her niece—long blonde hair and the perfect California tan that came from living in Laguna Niguel—filled her mind. She was what, nineteen now? And there was no end to the grief she had given Renee.

"She's all but failed out of her second semester at Coastline Community College and I'm at my wit's end to know what to do with her. She's running around with a bunch of beach bum surfers and I swear she thinks she'll be able to live like that for the rest of her life. She has no idea what hard work means and…" Her sister took in a shuddering breath. "I think she could be into drugs."

"Oh, Renee…" Margot shook her head, sending up a prayer for her sister's daughter as much as for her sister. "What will you do?"

Another long pause. So long, in fact, that Margot began to wonder if her sister was still on the line.

Finally, she spoke again. "I need to ask a huge favor."

A feeling of dread sunk into the pit of Margot's stomach. It was the same feeling she got when trying out a new recipe and knowing for a fact that it wasn't going to turn out.

"What do you mean?"

"Can you *please* take Taylor for the summer?"

"Take…her? What do you mean?"

"I don't care that she's old enough to make her own decisions." Renee's voice steeled as she went on. "I want to send her to live with you for the summer. I want her to work for you. I think showing her how rewarding owning your own business can be will be a really great thing for her. It may even save her life, Marg."

Save her life.

The words echoed through Margot but the terror remained. "Are you crazy?"

Renee laughed. "I've been accused of worse."

"No, I mean, what makes you think she'll want to stay with me?"

"Because we're cutting her off if she doesn't go."

"Cutting her off?" Margot repeated the words, trying to make sense.

"We've been footing the bill for her little escapades, but no longer. We're giving her an ultimatum. She either goes to stay with you *and* work for you for the summer, or she's... out of the house." Her sister's voice broke on the last word.

"I'm so sorry, Rae. That's not something you want to say about your own daughter."

"No." Her sister let out a heavy sigh. "With Dillon working on that oil rig months at a time, I haven't had the strength —or the clout—to deal with this. Am I a bad mother, Marg? You know it was hard for me to step in like this..."

"Of course you're not a bad mother!" Margot was quick to reassure her sister. "You've done a great job with her. It's not your fault she's acting out. She just needs some guidance."

"So..." Her sister's voice was full of hope.

"I'll take her." *God help me.*

"You will?"

"Yes. But she should know there will be strict rules. The life of a baker isn't easy and—"

"She'll do it. Trust me. When her father comes home and conveys our rules, she'll agree. Or, at least I hope so. Thanks, sis. I really want to see this turn her life around."

The weight of what Margot was agreeing to rested squarely on her shoulders as they said their goodbyes.

Shining stainless steel counter tops beckoned for their daily dusting of flour as Margot made her way back into the kitchen. She stretched her fingers and donned her apron, turning the stereo on so that classical music wafted from her mounted speakers.

But, just before she dropped the first ingredients into her mixing bowl, she stopped, resting her hands against the cold metal top of her workstation.

What was she doing? Had she lost her mind, agreeing to take in Taylor? The teen was notorious for being a troublemaker, but it was more than that. There was a lot of hurt for her to deal with having lost her mother at age eleven. When Renee married Dillon, Taylor was thirteen and not looking for another mother. Six years and she still hadn't accepted Renee.

Wiping away a stray hair from her shoulder, Margot dropped eggs one at a time into the sugar and milk concoction in the industrial mixer. Maybe the Lord had a bigger use for Margot's spare bedroom than a place to collect the dusty stacks of paperback mysteries she had collected. Maybe it was time to open up her home and her heart to her niece in a way that could bring healing to them both.

~

"I THOUGHT you were getting that young thing at the airport today."

Margot delivered a steaming caramel pecan cinnamon roll and cup of black coffee to the small, round table where Bentley Anderson, one of her regular customers, sat with newspaper in hand.

"I'm just waiting for Rosie to show up."

"Saw her at the senior center last night," Bentley said taking a sip of his coffee. "She and Betty were tearing it up at the pinochle table."

The corner of Margot's mouth quirked. "Real exciting, I'm sure."

"Hey, watch it, young lady." He stared her down, one bushy eyebrow raised. "Things get exciting over at the senior center. You'd be surprised."

"Don't I know it?" She propped hands on her hips. "I volunteer at least once a month over there. You all are a rambunctious bunch."

"You should bring that niece of yours over."

Margot narrowed her eyes. "You know, that's a good idea."

"I'm full of them." Bentley's laugh was rough and mingled with the sound of bells from the door opening.

"There you are," Margot said, watching as Rosie stepped into the bakery and undid the bright yellow scarf she had tied around her short, gray and black hair.

"It's gusting out there."

"That's not a real word," Bentley said, his gaze fixed on the paper.

"It sure is." Rosie eyed him but turned her attention back to Margot. "Sorry I was late, took a little longer to get going this morning."

Any other morning and Margot wouldn't have even noticed her part-time employee being a few minutes late, but she had at least a thirty-minute drive to Ronald Regan Airport to pick up Taylor and you never knew what traffic was going to be like.

"No problem, but I'm late. You'll be all right?"

Rosie gave her a look. "You *know* I'll be fine, girl. Now go!"

Grinning, Margot grabbed her purse and light jacket from the backroom and rushed out the door to where she'd parked at the end of Main Street in the public parking lot. Pulling onto the freeway, she glanced at her phone, happy to see she hadn't received a text from Taylor yet.

Thankfully, traffic wasn't as bad as she'd expected and she

pulled into the pickup line right on time, her eyes scanning for Taylor's blonde hair and lithe frame.

A waving hand caught her attention and she pulled the car over, recognizing Taylor instantly.

"Hello!" Margot said, slipping out of the car with extended hands.

"Hey, Aunt Margot," Taylor said, thin arms wrapping around her.

"We need to feed you some pastries," Margot said, leaning back with a grin. "You're much too thin."

Taylor blushed, her grin widening. "A girl needs to watch her figure if she's going to the beach every day."

"Good thing you won't be spending much time at the beach then." The girl's expression fell and Margot rushed to explain. "It's freezing, Taylor!"

"It's going to be summer," she said, laughing.

"True, but by that time, you'll be elbow deep in dough."

She sent a look to the side, but Margot read it loud and clear. She was *not* happy about the arrangements.

"Let's get your stuff into the car and head back to North Bank. We'll get you settled in the spare bedroom and then I'll take you out for Italian. You do still like Italian food, right?"

"Yeah." Her response was noncommittal but Margot

decided not to let it affect her. Things were going to change, that was a given, but she would make the most of it.

They drove back down I-365, blessedly going against the flow of traffic, and by the time Margot exited the freeway and pulled into the small parking pad in front of her historic row house, Taylor had loosened up, if only a little.

"I remember visiting here."

"That's right. You were...what, fourteen?"

"Yeah." She pulled her backpack from the backseat and Margot picked up her suitcase, dreading the ascent up the steep steps that climbed to the narrow entry way.

"Want some help?"

Hefting the bag, Margot shook her head. "I've got it. I've been taking Krav Maga classes."

"Seriously?" Taylor's eyebrows disappeared into her fringy blonde bangs.

"Hey, your aunt isn't some old lady. I like to stay active. Hiking, biking, baking, and now, self-defense."

Taylor shook her head as Margot hefted the suitcase up and climbed the stone steps. Breathing heavy, she took the inside stairs more slowly until they stood in front of the small guest bedroom.

"I tried my best to stack the crime novels out of the way. I didn't do such a good job."

The girl peered in the room and her eyes widened. "Wow. Have you read all of those?"

Margot surveyed the wall-to-wall bookshelves stacked with crime novels, mysteries, and thrillers. "Not all. A lot of them were Julian's." Margot caught the saddened expression of her niece. "Your uncle was a great man and he loved to read. It always shocked me, knowing that his job as detective put him *in* something like a crime novel every day, but he couldn't get enough of them for some reason. He said he liked to guess 'whodunit' in real life and fiction."

"I miss him."

Her niece's soft words surprised Margot. She and Julian hadn't been around her sister very often. Living on the opposite side of the country did that to a family, but they had made an effort to get to know Renee's husband and his daughter.

"He really liked you."

Taylor turned surprised eyes upward. "Yeah?"

"He didn't call you *mon canard* for nothing."

Taylor laughed. "I never got why he wanted to call me a little duck."

"It was just his way of showing his affection."

"He used to write me letters."

"He did?" Margot felt a rush of warmth flood her chest.

Her husband had been a wonderful, kind, and caring man. It didn't really surprise her that he would have taken a special interest in his sister-in-law's adopted daughter.

"Yeah. It was after we came to visit here. He started sending letters and cards almost every month. I really looked forward to them. I'm sorry...that he's gone."

"Me too, Tay," Margot said, resting her hand on the girl's shoulder. "Hey, why don't you get settled in then we'll go to dinner? The dresser over there is empty and you can hang anything you want in the closet. We'll have to share the bathroom, but I think we'll manage."

Taylor nodded without saying anything and closed the door behind her, leaving Margot in the hall. Thoughts of her late husband squeezed at Margot's heart, but the ache was different than it had been. Five years had gone a long way to heal the brokenness, though the place he'd filled in her life would never be the same again.

CHAPTER 2

TAYLOR EMERGED from her room forty minutes later looking exhausted but insisting she was hungry. Margot knew the jetlag wouldn't really catch up to her before the morning, but her niece had taken an early flight so she assured her it would be a quick dinner break then to bed for them both.

When they pulled into the small parking lot at the back of *Pane Dolce,* Taylor sent a wary look her way. "Sweet Bread?"

Margot laughed. "I forgot you took Italian in High School. Antonio didn't think anyone would know what it said, at least that's the way he tells it. I always thought he just didn't know what to name his restaurant."

Taylor looked doubtful.

"Despite the name," Margot rushed to assure her, "it's the

best, most authentic Italian cuisine this side of the Atlantic."

"Whatever you say."

They entered through the back door and a large, salt and pepper-haired man rushed up to them with arms held wide. "*Mia bella!*"

"Hello, Antonio," Margot said, kissing both of his cheeks in the traditional greeting. "This is my niece, Taylor. She'll be staying with me for the summer."

"*È molto carina.* She is very pretty. Like her aunt, no?"

Taylor blushed and Margot laughed. "We'd like a table, you old flirt."

"*Sì.* For you, my best table. This way."

They trailed behind him in the busy restaurant and he seated them at a round table in the bay window at the front of the restaurant.

"I feel like we're on display," Taylor muttered under her breath.

"*Sì.* Such beauty cannot be hidden," Antonio said with a devilish grin.

He handed over their menus and promised to return soon to take their order personally. Taylor studied her menu for a moment before putting it down, resting her head in the palm of her hand, eyes on the crowd in the large, dimly lit room.

"You okay?" Margot asked, putting down her own menu.

"Yeah. Missing my friends, I guess."

"Oh?"

Taylor shot her a look. "I know. Renee probably told you that I hang out with a bunch of deadbeats, but they really aren't bad guys. And, no matter what Renee thinks—I'm *not* doing drugs, Aunt Marg."

The words stole Margot's breath. She didn't want to speak against Renee or incite the girl's anger. It was dangerous territory that Margot wanted to tread carefully. Then again, the first night Taylor was in Virginia and during their first meal—in public no less—probably wasn't the time to have a serious conversation with her.

"Your mom cares about you," she said, hoping the use of 'mom' wouldn't offend the girl. "She's just worried."

"Yeah. Whatever."

Margot was about to press the point when a waiter showed up with a pitcher of water. He was young, likely in his early twenties, and had a flashy smile pointed toward Taylor.

"*Buonasera*, lovely ladies. Can I get you something to drink besides water?"

Margot fought the urge to wave a hand in front of his face as if to remind him that she was there as well, but it wasn't worth the effort.

"Water's fine," she said.

"And you?"

Margot imagined she could see the hormones flying between the two and fought the urge to roll her eyes. Ah, to be nineteen again. She cringed at the reality though, knowing she wouldn't wish to go back to that tenuous time.

"Water's good," Taylor said, her smile sliding into place with the perfect amount of flirtation.

Margot cleared her throat and the young man took a step back, his own smile a match to Taylor's, before he disappeared. It was looking like Margot would have her work cut out for her keeping track of Taylor.

Once their order was taken, the over-eager water boy visited their table no less than five times in the span of twenty minutes. Margot was about to call Antonio over to have him say something to his server when Taylor bolted up from the table, her napkin falling to the floor in her haste.

"I'm, uh, going to the bathroom." She forced a smile at Margot then turned toward the back of the restaurant.

Margot watched her go, wondering at her odd behavior, then straightened in her seat when she saw the same server trailing behind her niece.

"It's just a coincidence," she said to herself just as Antonio walked up to the table.

"Is everything *bene*—good?"

"Yes. *Sì.* It is wonderful, as always." Margot hesitated, then, after one more glance toward the back of the restaurant, turned toward Antonio. "Who's the server who's been helping us? Filling our water and such."

"Ack." Antonio rolled his eyes. "He's a friend of my sister's kid. Marco Rossario. Word on the street is that he's bad news, but you know me, *mia bella,* I'm a...what do they say? Softie? He's only just started working here—if you call making eyes at every girl under the age of thirty working."

Margot glanced at her watch. Taylor had been gone too long.

"I—um, excuse me for a moment. The washroom?" she asked, pointing to the back.

Antonio smiled and pointed toward the back where Taylor had disappeared. The thought of Marco being anywhere near Taylor sent a chill down Margot's spine as she rounded the corner that led toward the bathrooms.

"Stop it! Seriously!" Margot instantly knew the firm, somewhat high-pitched voice belonging to Taylor.

But where was she? The hall ended in a door to the men's bathroom and a door to the left to the women's. Then there was—the closet!

"I said I don't have—"

Margot yanked open the door to find Taylor pressed up against the side of a utility closet, Marco holding both of her wrists by the side of her head.

"Hey!" Margot said. "Get away from her!"

Tears filled Taylor's eyes and she took Marco's distracted attention to yank her arms away and shove him against the other side of the wall. In a crash of mops and supplies, he fell backward, not quite catching himself before he fell to the floor.

Margot could tell that Taylor was shaking from head to toe and she wrapped her arm around the girl, directing her back toward the main restaurant area and the back door. Antonio came toward them, his eyes wide at seeing Taylor's tear-streaked face.

"What has happened?" He looked between Taylor and Margot.

"Marco Rossario attacked my niece." Margot felt the anger surge up in her at the thought of him taking advantage of Taylor like he had. Taylor had likely gotten herself into the situation with flirtation, but it didn't excuse the fact that he had tried to force himself on her.

"Shall I call the police?" Antonio looked to Taylor, waiting for her instruction.

"Just—just forget it. I want to go home." Taylor wrapped her arms around her middle.

Antonio looked helplessly to Margot and she nodded. "I think we should leave. Can we take our meal to go?"

"Of course! I will wrap it up personally. And you are not to worry—I will let Marco go this moment!"

Without waiting for their confirmation, he left them to get their meals and Margot turned to Taylor. "I'm sorry, honey. Are you going to be all right? Do you want to talk to the police?"

"Nah." Taylor pushed hair from her face. "I...I don't know what was going on. I just want to go back to your place."

Margot felt the weight of exhaustion and worry taking over. Taking care of Taylor was going to be a lot more challenging than she'd expected. What was the right thing to do in this situation?

"Maybe we *should* call the police."

"No." Taylor met her gaze, eyes fierce. "I seriously just want to go back to your house. I'm so done with today."

Worry still pressing in on her, Margot nodded and they made their way to the back where Antonio met them with a large paper sack.

"Here is your dinner and I added a piece of my famous tiramisu. It will not match up to your confections, *mia bella,* but I hope it is a sweet ending to a not so sweet day." He looked worriedly at Taylor then back at Margot, who patted him on the shoulder.

"Thank you, Antonio. It's not your fault."

He nodded. "Thank you. But he is gone. I have fired him. Please, do come back soon."

Margot nodded and the women walked out into the fading evening light. She clicked her key fob and the car beeped back just as a shape emerged from the darkness of the alley behind the restaurant. Taylor gasped and latched on to Margot's sleeve as Marco's face became clear to them both.

"Dude, seriously. Leave me alone!" Taylor said.

"Hey, I just want the—" he began, but when he got too close, Taylor lunged forward and shoved him away with both hands.

"Stay. Away!" she screamed.

Margot was stunned by the action and her scream as much as Marco was, but he caught himself before falling over just as the back door opened. His eyes were wide as they darted to a young couple exiting with a to-go box in hand.

"Whoa," Marco said, holding up his hands.

"I swear, if you don't get out of here..." Taylor was seething in rage now and Margot placed her hand on the girl's arm.

"You need to leave," Margot said, stepping between her niece and the young man.

He opened his mouth as if he was going to say something then closed it and ran off behind the alley. Taylor was shaking again and Margot felt her own heart pounding. The couple stared at them wide-eyed, but Margot flashed a fake smile their way.

They looked between her and where Marco had run off, but Margot didn't wait for them to say anything. "Come on, honey, let's go."

Once she and Taylor were in the car, she locked it and looked over at the young woman. She was visibly shaken and Margot's heart broke.

"Are you all right?"

Taylor gave a short nod.

"I think we should call the police."

"No!" Taylor looked at Margot with fear and apprehension hiding behind her blue-eyed gaze. "Please. Let's just go home. I...I want to go to bed."

Margot looked at her for another moment before turning on the car. This was not how she'd envisioned her first night with Taylor going, but at least the boy had left them alone and Taylor was safe. But, despite her niece's protest about calling the police, Margot planned to put in a call the next day to a friend on the force. If nothing else, at least she could give him a heads up that there was a volatile young man on the loose in their small community.

CHAPTER 3

THREE O'CLOCK CAME EARLIER than normal—or at least it felt that way the next day as Margot unlocked the shop door and flipped on the lights. The scent of Lysol and lemons greeted her and she smiled. Every time Rosie worked, she cleaned as if *The Parisian Pâtisserie* was a hospital, not a bakery. Then again, clean was better than dirty.

Dumping her large purse on her desk and flipping the switch to start the coffee, she thought about Taylor, still asleep in her guest bedroom. After the night they'd had, she decided to give the girl a day to adjust to the new time zone as well as living in her small row home. It was a rude awakening to anyone when they started work at a bakery and needed to be ready to go as early as three.

Besides, the way Taylor had looked when they got back, she wasn't sure if the girl would be able to sleep at all. It was difficult, having someone in your care. Granted,

Taylor was nineteen and an adult, but Margot still felt responsible for her.

Pushing up her sleeves and turning on her classical music, she began several projects at once, making sure the dough that needed to rise was set to go ahead of schedule today. She worked diligently and by the time seven o'clock rolled around, she was ready to open her doors.

The morning crowd didn't usually show up until eight, thanks to the high percentage of senior citizens living in North Bank, but there was always the chance that someone on their way to work would stop in for breakfast or a cup of coffee or both.

One look out the front door and she knew she'd have a few minutes to spare. Remembering her promise to herself, she picked up her phone and scrolled through her contacts.

There, resting under the As, was the name she was looking for: Adam Eastwood.

With the name came a rush of memories. Adam, lead detective on the police force in North Bank, had known her husband Julian back when they'd been on the police force in New York. The connection had only been made after Julian's death and the new detective who had filled his shoes made a point to come introduce himself to Julian's widow.

Even still, it boggled her mind that they had known one another and that Adam was now doing Julian's previous job, but either way, she saw it as a blessing. They had fallen into an easy friendship and he was a connection— albeit small—to the friends she'd made when Julian was alive.

Biting her lip, she tapped his number and the phone buzzed to life.

"Margot?"

"Hi, Adam." She took in a breath. Was she really going to do this?

The memory of the anger and fear on Taylor's face resurfaced. The young man might be gone from *Pane Dolce,* but that didn't mean he still couldn't cause trouble in their small town.

"Wow. It's been a while. Uh, what's up?" Adam's easygoing tone did nothing to hide his curiosity.

"I had something I wanted to mention to you. Kind of under the radar." Was she going about this the right way? Or would Adam think she was taking advantage of their friendship?

"What's that? Everything all right?"

She relayed the incident from the night before ending with, "I didn't like the look in Marco's eyes. I just… I don't know. If Julian were alive, he would tell me to follow my gut." She laughed imagining him saying that to her now. "So I am."

Adam's silence spoke volumes. Did he think she was over stepping? Being a worrywart?

"Did you say Marco Rossario?" His tone was rock hard, all manner of friendliness gone. It was a tone she'd heard Julian take on before—when he was on a case.

"Yes," she said tentatively.

"Oh, Margot." His tone sent a shiver coursing down her spine. "Marco Rossario was found dead by the river this morning."

THE LATE SPRING sunlight shone through bright, puffy clouds as Margot rushed down the sidewalk toward the police station. She'd left Rosie in charge of the bakery and, after a phone call to make sure that Taylor was doing all right, she'd set off for the station and a meeting with Adam.

It had been his idea. A purely informational meeting and one that she'd convinced him to leave Taylor out of, for now, but she had a sneaking suspicion that her niece would need to have a conversation with the detective as well.

A uniformed officer opened the door for her as he was leaving and nodded. She thought she'd seen him before but he was focused and barely took notice of her. After she checked in at the front desk, she took a seat and waited for Adam.

The station held all types of memories for her. Of coming to work with Julian for a spouse luncheon. Helping him decide on the perfect photo to hang to the right of his door, one that would always remind him of his home in France. Bringing him lunch when he'd forgotten it on the counter —that had happened more times than she could remember.

Sighing, she re-crossed her legs and focused her attention out the bright front windows. During those days, she had stayed at home, writing for an online news outlet. It had been fun, mentally invigorating work, but her bakery now was the fulfillment of a lifetime of dreams. If only Julian could have seen *The Parisian Pâtisserie*.

"Margot."

She turned to see Adam in the doorway. He cut an impressive profile at 6'3" with broad shoulders pulling the sleeves of his suit coat tight. He looked good. She'd always thought him a handsome man.

"Adam Eastwood. It's good to see you."

He grinned and came forward, giving her a light hug. "You too. Come on back with me. You remember the way."

She did. All too well. It was a shame that Julian and Adam had never been able to work together in North Bank.

They walked down a dingy hall, the same ugly green color as it had been all those years ago, and he showed her into his office. Since they had rearranged things in the department, it wasn't the same office as Julian's but it was similar, flooding her with memories.

"Please, take a seat."

She did and folded her hands in her lap. "How are you, Adam?"

He seemed to allow the momentary distraction from the reason why she was there and shrugged. "Busy. Too busy."

"Oh?"

"Not with anything town-related, exactly. I don't know if you remember, but my brother is a detective up in D.C. They've had some interesting cases recently and, because of my unique background, I've been called in to consult on a few. It means making the trip up to the big city almost every weekend—if not more—but it's interesting work."

"I do remember you mentioning Anthony was in D.C. How exciting for you."

"Something like that," he said with a grin. "But it's taken me away from North Bank a lot and…friends."

His gaze held hers and she wondered briefly if he included her in that circle of friends. But the thought of young Marco Rossario dead grounded her again.

"About Marco," she said, leaning forward.

"Right." Adam shuffled some papers around and then considered her. "So you say your niece got into an argument with him last night at *Pane Dolce*?"

Margot recounted what had happened. "I asked her if I should call the police, I even considered it after she turned me down, but she was insistent. She just wanted to go home. I just didn't like the look in his eye when he came up to her in the parking lot."

She thought back. His behavior had been strange. Almost as if he were asking Taylor for something—but how could that be possible? Taylor had only just come to North Bank. It had to be something else.

"I've been down to see Antonio and he shed some light on who Marco is exactly."

"A friend of Lorenzo's, or so I heard," Margot said.

"Exactly. I guess Carmela is vising her parents in Italy from now until the end of summer and her son has been staying in her house with Marco. I couldn't find Lorenzo to question, though."

Margot shifted back in her seat, mind going over what she knew of the Bianchi family. "Did Antonio know anything about Marco? I mean, aside from his friendship with his nephew?"

Adam's eyes narrowed and he leaned forward, elbows on the desk. "Why the interest, Margot?"

She laughed, sending him a smile. "You should know by now that I love a puzzle. Though, the death of a young man is much more than a puzzle of course."

Adam nodded. "I remember Julian telling me you liked to poke your nose into his cases."

"He did?" Her eyebrows rose at this news. She hadn't known that her husband had been in contact with Adam after he had moved from New York.

"We stayed in touch. He had many things to tell me about you." Adam's grin made a dimple appear and she felt her stomach clench at what he could mean. "But no. To answer your question, Antonio said he knew next to nothing about the boy. He'd hired him for the main fact that his other busboy had gone home for the summer and he was short a pair of hands."

"How…" She grimaced. "How did he die?"

"We found him at the base of the Miller's Bridge."

Margot's mind filled in the details of the old bridge that ran across South Fork, an offshoot of the Potomac River. It was a deep, rocky, and treacherous portion of the river.

"Are you thinking it was a suicide?"

"It's…inconclusive." He hesitated.

"Was he…pushed then?" She swallowed, the idea making her feeling nauseous.

"You know that's confidential," Adam said, pulling out

another sheet of paper. He eyed her. "But I don't know that it would hurt to tell you. He was stabbed."

Her eyes widened.

"We don't have the murder weapon yet, but I'm fairly confident that was his cause of death, not the fall."

Margot paled. A murder in North Bank.

He shrugged and folded the report closed. "I only told you this to assuage your curiosity and because you're a friend. Don't you go telling anyone." He fixed a hard stare on her.

"I wouldn't." She raised her hands in defense.

"I know." He held her gaze for a moment longer.

Margot resisted the urge to press him for more details—why, she wasn't exactly sure. The poor boy's fate was sad indeed and Adam would do a fine job investigating it. Maybe it was just that old habits died hard. She missed having Julian to talk to about his cases. Mystery books aside, real life was much more unpredictable. Maybe she was more like her late husband than even she realized.

"Well, thank you, Adam. I won't take up any more of your time. Besides, I've got to get back to Rosie. Who knows what trouble she'll get herself in."

Adam gave her his signature, easy-going smile. "You tell Rosie Mae I said hello."

Standing, Margot considered him for a moment. "Come

to the bakery some time and you can tell her that yourself."

"I just might do that." She turned but paused at the door when he called out to her. "I'll need to speak with Taylor too."

The words sunk in with a zap of apprehension. "I thought you might."

"Can I come by tonight? Maybe she'll feel more comfortable if we talk at your place."

Margot considered this and knew that would be true. Despite the fact she wanted to shelter Taylor from all of this, she knew Adam was just doing his job.

"Yes. Come by around seven and we can have dessert."

"If we're talking about your baked goods, I'm there."

She merely smiled and left the office, showing herself out. The sun still shone brightly, but dark storm clouds gathered on the horizon and Margot couldn't help but think of it as a warning.

CHAPTER 4

TAYLOR PULLED dishes from the table, simultaneously checking messages on her phone every few seconds. By the amount of texts she was getting, she was certainly popular. She'd seemed to recover from the previous night well, though Margot wasn't sure how she would take the news about Marco.

Glancing at the clock for the third time in the same minute, Margot knew she should have told Taylor about the expected visitor. It was nine minutes until seven o'clock and her stomach was twisted in knots.

"Taylor, I probably should have mentioned this before," she said, waiting until the girl looked up from her phone, "but my friend Detective Adam Eastwood is going to be stopping by in a few minutes. He, uh, he has some questions for...us."

Taylor blinked. "A detective? Questions? What are you talking about, Aunt Margot?"

Here was the moment of truth. "I phoned him this morning to relay the incident from last night at Antonio's place—"

"I asked you not to call the police," Taylor interrupted.

"I know, but I thought it best to warn him there was a disruptive man in our community. We're very tightknit with a big population of senior citizens. I feel responsible to watch out for them."

"Okay. Whatever. But *why* is he coming here?"

"That's just it," she said, twisting a dishtowel in her hands. "Marco Rossario, the young man from last night, he was found dead this morning."

Taylor paled at the news, her hand reaching out to steady herself on the nearest chair. "Dead? Did he, like, have an accident or what?"

"No, sweetie." Margot tried to break the news as calmly as possible. "He was murdered."

"Whoa." Taylor put a hand to her stomach and Margot prayed she wouldn't be sick. "I—I can't believe that. How? What happened?"

"Well—" A light knock sounded at the door and she shrugged. "That'll be Adam. Why don't you have a seat in the living room?"

Taylor nodded, staring down as she walked like she was processing the information she'd just gotten. And why shouldn't she be? It wasn't every day that you were around someone one day and they were gone the next.

"Hi, Adam," she said, opening the door to let her friend in.

"You doing all right?" he asked, pulling a baseball cap from his head. He'd changed out of the gray suit he'd worn that morning and now wore jeans and a plain black t-shirt. It tugged at his shoulders, showing muscular arms and proving he was more than fit for his job.

"I suppose. I just told Taylor about what had happened. Maybe it wasn't the best timing, but I didn't want to spoil dinner."

He offered a sad smile. "It'll be all right. You're doing great."

"No, I actually think I'm the world's worst aunt." She wrapped her arms around herself and shook her head. "I mean, a murder? In our town? And my sister thought it was a good idea to send Taylor here?"

"Hey." Adam reached out and rested a hand on her arm, squeezing gently. "You're doing the best you can. Besides, you had no control over this. Let's go have dessert and I'll talk with her. Don't worry, I'll make it as painless for her as possible."

"Okay." Margot led the way into the living room where Taylor was curled up on the couch, staring out the window with her phone forgotten beside her. "Hey, sweetie, this is my friend Detective—"

"You can call me Adam," he interjected. "You must be Taylor. I saw pictures of you as a kid. You've definitely grown."

She offered a weak smile and Adam sat down on the chair across from her.

"I'm going to grab some macaroons."

Adam flashed her a smile then began talking to Taylor again. Margot couldn't hear the conversation from the kitchen, but she sent up a prayer that it wouldn't completely frighten Taylor and that they'd still be able to get past this and have an enjoyable summer. Somehow.

"Yes!" Adam said when she came back into the room. "These are my favorite. Taylor, have you had your aunts macaroons before?"

Taylor shook her head but reached out for a chocolate hazelnut macaroon just as Adam grabbed the lemon. Margot selected her favorite, lavender and vanilla, and they munched on the airy French cookies for a moment before Adam spoke again.

"So, after he slipped you the note—"

"What note?" Margot interrupted. At Taylor's guilty look, she turned to Adam for an explanation then back to Taylor when he looked at her.

"He slipped me a note," she said, looking down at her cookie. "I mean, do you really think he needed to refill our waters so many times?"

"What did the note say?" Margot's tone came out harsher than she'd intended.

"Chill, Aunt Margot. He just wanted to talk with me. You know, ask me for my number or something. I didn't think it would hurt to talk with him."

"So you went to talk with him?" Adam asked, a small notebook in his hand where he jotted down notes.

"Yeah. He wasn't interested in talking, though." She blushed and looked out the window.

"So that's when your aunt found you guys in the closet?"

Something passed over Taylor's face, but she nodded. "Yeah."

Adam looked to Margot then back at Taylor. "You didn't give him your number or anything, right?"

Taylor looked down at her macaroon. "No."

Adam made another note then leaned forward to snatch another cookie.

"Look, I'm tired. Can I go to bed? Aunt Margot's going to get me up before dawn and I really should get some sleep."

Margot fought for composure, shocked that the girl was thinking of bed at seven-twenty in the evening, but she looked to Adam to make sure he was done with his questions.

"Sure," he said, folding the notepad closed and stowing it in his jacket pocket.

She shuffled past them, bypassing the macaroon plate and disappearing down the hall until they heard her door close.

"Huh," he said, his eyes searching the empty space in front of him.

"What?"

He met her gaze and frowned. "What?"

"When Julian used to 'huh,' it always meant something wasn't lining up."

Adam offered her a half-smile. "Are you psychoanalyzing me?"

She leaned back, savoring the last bite of her macaroon before answering him. "I wouldn't dream of it, *Detective*. I'm just a baker after all."

He held her gaze for a moment before pushing to his feet. "I've got to get going. I may not have baker's hours, but I do have a lot of work ahead of me. Thanks for letting me come by tonight."

Margot stood as well, wondering just how far she should

push. She could tell he was keeping something from her, but she didn't know what—or if she even had the leverage to demand the information.

"Macaroon for the road?"

"Absolutely." He took another lemon and grinned, taking a bite. "Delicious."

"Come by the bakery any time, Adam. There's more where that came from."

He held her gaze for a moment longer than necessary then turned toward the door. "I may do just that."

∾

"No, a little thinner. Yes, there you go." Margot instructed Taylor on how to make her famous chocolate-filled croissants as the clock raced toward seven o'clock and their opening time. Taylor was already yawning, but she'd get her second wind soon—that or Margot would be giving her another cup of coffee with an extra shot of espresso.

The timer dinged and she reached for the oven door, pulling out more macaroons. Their sweet scent wafted through the kitchen and mingled with the classical music, which Taylor had complained about at first.

Now, though, she hummed along to an aria that had a

familiar and repetitive melody. Margot resisted the urge to tell her niece 'I told you so' and instead worked on whipping up the fillings for her macaroons.

By the time Bentley came in, the small bell chiming his presence, she felt well ahead of schedule. His caramel pecan cinnamon roll and cup of coffee delivered, she eyed the newspaper in his hand.

"Anything...interesting in there?"

"You betcha there is."

Margot's stomach clenched. "Oh?" Knowing ahead of time about a murder in town wasn't something she wanted to gloat about.

"Sure thing. There's some controversy about putting a halt to the construction on the new senior center lodge. I'm *irate, seething,* one could even say *apoplectic.*"

"You've been doing crosswords again—that or reading the thesaurus I gave you for Christmas."

Bentley grinned up at her, his bristly moustache tipping up at the corners. "A little bit of both. But it's true."

This wasn't the news she'd expected, but she decided to go along with it anyway. "Why would they do that?"

He sighed heavily, leaning back and slurping from his coffee cup. "Darn politics. That's why."

"Politics?"

"Forget I said anything. We're working on it."

She knew by 'we' he meant he and other patrons that frequented the senior center. They were a rowdy bunch.

"All I know is that I wouldn't be caught dead on the wrong side of you all." She laughed but noticed his expression had turned serious.

"Speaking of dead," he said, conspiratorially, "A body was found at the river near Miller's Bridge."

So the news *had* made the paper. "Oh?" she said, trying to look surprised.

His eyes narrowed. "What do *you* know about it?"

"Me?" she feigned surprise. "I—I don't know..." She wasn't willing to lie to her friend, though she didn't want Taylor to be caught up in the middle of a scandal like this. Somehow, mentioning what happened at Antonio's restaurant opened her up for questions as well.

"Come on, tell old Bentley. I'm an old man. Who would I tell?" He grinned at her, his eyebrows wagging.

"You'd tell the entire senior center, who would somehow tell the rest of the town." She crossed her arms, daring him to contradict her.

"All right, so you may have a point there. Speaking of, you're coming tonight, right?"

"Coming..." Margot searched her memory for what was going on that night.

"It's World Dinner Night. You promised to bring French pastries."

"Oh," she gasped, a hand flying to cover her mouth, "With Taylor coming and all of this—" His look said, *I knew you had something to tell.* "I completely forgot."

"Good thing I'm here every morning to remind you of your commitments. Besides, bring the kid. We like to see a little life in that place every now and again. You know, someone under the age of fifty."

"Hey," Margot said, nailing him with a look.

"Present company excluded." Bentley gave a rasping laugh and looked back to his newspaper. "Besides, then you can tell me—and everyone else—what you know about this murder."

Spinning on her heel, she walked back toward the kitchen to avoid having to say anything else about what she knew —or didn't know—about the murder.

"What was he saying about tonight?" Taylor asked. Flour dusted her cheek and her lopsided ponytail was sliding closer to her neck than the top of her head.

"World Dinner Night."

"What is that?" she turned back to the dough she was kneading and Margot had to bite back her criticism of her technique. They would be the toughest loaves of bread to ever come out of her shop.

"Every third Tuesday of the month they do World Dinner Night at the senior center. Different restaurants around the area usually provide entrées or side dishes from different cultural backgrounds. I'm often called upon to bring French pastries. They open the event up to the community. You pay a small fee and get to enjoy the meal with the seniors. They are a crafty bunch when it comes to raising money, especially for the new building they are putting up—well, hopefully." Margot thought of the article Bentley had mentioned. She had thought they were close to their funding goal, but Bentley made it sound like they weren't. If so, where had the money gone?

"Are we going to go?"

Drawn from her thoughts, Margot looked at her niece. "Do you want to go?"

"I don't know." Taylor shrugged. "It kind of sounds fun."

Feeling like she could have been knocked over by a feather, Margot feigned surprise. "All right. Yes. We'll go."

"Sweet."

Taylor went back to kneading the life out of the dough and Margot slipped into baker mode as she thought of the desserts she would need to make for that night. Familiar recipes, ingredient lists, and baking times filled her head, but soon they were sifted to the side as she thought again about the poor boy that had been killed. It was awful to think of anyone dying, but the fact that she'd seen him the night before stuck with her.

There had to be a logical explanation. She thought of Antonio and what he might know. Would he be at World Dinner Night tonight? He often brought some of his favorite Italian meals to share. If so, she would make a point to talk with him.

But, for now, she had to focus on baking or the seniors would likely rebel.

CHAPTER 5

"So, it's like a fundraiser?" Taylor took a moment to look up from her phone long enough to show Margot just how excited she *wasn't* about attending the dinner that night before her eyes sought out the next text message.

"Yes and no." Margot maneuvered the car onto a side street shaded by large trees and began looking for a parking spot. She had a feeling the lot would be full plus she liked to leave the closer spots for the elderly. Finding an empty spot, she pulled in. "They are raising money to put up a new senior center lodge, as they are calling it. The old one is falling apart and they want to tear it down and put up a new one. They see it as future income for them, renting it out for parties, weddings, and the like, plus they want it to be more handicap accessible. It's really a great thing they're doing."

"Sure." Taylor was distracted by her phone again.

Part of Margot wanted to snatch the device away and tell her niece that it was time to grow up and start having face-to-face conversations with those around her, but she bit her cheek and prayed for strength. Getting after Taylor only a few days after she'd arrived wasn't the best way to approach something that probably had deeper strings in Taylor's life.

"Hey," Margot said. The tone of her voice was serious enough to draw the young woman's gaze. "I know it's not easy being here and I'm sure spending the evening with a bunch of senior citizens isn't high on your list of things to do, but these are great people. I've gotten to know them and they hold a special place in my heart. I guess…" She fumbled for the words under the weight of the young woman's gaze. "I just hope you could, you know, try to get to know them."

"Yeah. Sure." She slipped the phone into her purse and reached for the handle. "Ready?"

Margot almost laughed. The better question was if Taylor was ready for what she was about to walk into. Instead, she nodded and opened her own door.

They walked down Front Street and took the walkway leading around the building to the front entrance. There was already a short line forming and she waved to Sally and another woman Margot hadn't talked to much as they accepted payment for the dinner. When they got to the front of the line, Sally winked up at her.

"Lynellen, this here is the mastermind behind those wonderful French pastries!"

The other woman's eyes grew round. "Mercy. You don't say! Well, honey, you should go in for free because I think half of the folks who are coming today have mentioned those pastries."

Margot shook her head. "Absolutely not. If we're going to get the lodge built, we'll need every penny." She handed over ten dollars and introduced Taylor to the women then walked around the table and entered the dated center.

Light fixtures circa the nineteen-sixties hung across the room, more than a few bulbs burned out. It created a mood-lighting affect, even though she wasn't sure that was what they were going for. The green carpet had seen better days and the walls that had once been white were now a dull grayish color.

"Wow. You weren't kidding when you said they needed a new place."

Margot sent her a look that said, *I told you.* "They should be close to their goal, but I haven't heard updates. Except..." She recalled the conversation she'd had with Bentley.

"Yeah?" Taylor's eyebrows were raised.

"Oh, it's probably nothing. One of my customers said that something was going on. Maybe— Oh look, there's Mayor Penberthy."

"Who?"

Margot drew her attention back to her niece, who looked pale. "The mayor. He's over there talking to— Tay, why do you look like you've seen a ghost?"

"I—uh, never mind."

The girl's reaction was strange, but just then Bentley came up, smile widening as he took both of them in with outstretched arms.

"And look who we have here. The famous pastry chef and her budding new assistant. Happy to have you ladies here."

Taylor still looked distracted, but Bentley immediately drew them toward a table and began asking questions about what they wanted to eat. He was thoroughly enjoying his role as a waiter.

"Aren't you quite the host," she observed. "I should hire you part time at the *Pâtisserie*, but I have a feeling you'd eat more than you'd sell, Bentley."

His smile widened. "I'd be delighted. You could just pay me in pastries."

"I somehow don't think it would be equal."

He shrugged and said he'd be right back with their meals. Nearly the moment he was gone the mayor stepped into the spot he had vacated. "Why if it isn't my favorite baker!" His grin made the extra skin under his jaw jiggle slightly and his bushy white eyebrows wagged as if waiting for her to deny his statement.

"Mayor Penberthy, good to see you."

"And who is this lovely lady? Surely not your sister?"

Taylor shifted nervously next to her, but Margot laughed off his comment. "You charmer. This is my niece Taylor."

"Pleased to meet you." He clasped his hands in front of him. "But, Margot, you must tell me the secret to what makes your croissants so amazing."

"Now, Mayor," she laughed, shaking her head. "If I told you that, then you'd have no reason to come by the shop as often as you do."

He placed a hand on his ample stomach and gave a hearty laugh. "You've got me dead to rights there."

"Excuse me," Taylor said, fumbling with her purse while pushing the chair back from the table. "Restroom."

Margot watched her go, concern flashing through her mind.

"You enjoy your dinner now, all right?" The mayor patted her arm and then moved to the next table. He was no doubt garnering votes for the upcoming election. She'd seen him at every community hosted event over the last several months. And when not there, he was often stopping by the *Pâtisserie* for one—or more—of her croissants.

"See you were chatting with Mayor Penberthy." Bentley set their plates of food down with a scowl.

"Have a seat, Bentley. I have a feeling there's a story behind that scowl."

"Where's the kid?"

Margot looked around again, her gaze traveling to the bathrooms on the other side of the room. "Restroom."

He nodded and took a seat next to her. "Remember I was talking about the lodge funds at the shop today?"

"Of course. You were saying it was something political. Surely you don't mean..."

"Before you go getting yourself up in arms, let me give it to you straight. We're missing money."

Margot blinked. "Missing...you mean for the lodge?"

"Yeah." He looked around, rubbing his jaw, the sound of scraping whiskers matching his irritation. "We've got a young whippersnapper handling the funds for us and he says I've lost my marbles—granted, he's not the first to say that—but I've kept track of the money we've gotten and I *know* what he's showing us for totals is not accurate."

"You're taking into account food costs and—"

"Most of it's donated."

He had a point there. Margot frowned, her mind racing to

catch up to the full extent of what he was telling her. "You think... Wait, what does this have to do with the mayor?"

Bentley looked at the mayor then back at her. He was quiet so long she almost wasn't sure he was going to answer. "Mayor Penberthy's campaign has exploded over the last few months. He's raised more support than I thought was possible, considering not a whole lot of folks like him in this town, and it just doesn't sit well with me."

"You think he's stealing money from the senior center."

"I don't have any proof, mind you." Bentley leaned closer. "They think I'm some old man off his rocker, but I aim to get to the bottom of this."

Margot's mind reeled at what Bentley had said. He rushed off to take care of another table, but her thoughts stuck on his words. If Mayor Penberthy *was* taking some of the senior center money, how was he doing that? Who was the young man in charge of the accounts? And how did the mayor think he could get away with it? Per campaign rules, he would have to divulge where his backing was coming from. He couldn't simply claim an extra twenty thousand dollars had just appeared in his account.

If it was possible, maybe she could get together with Bentley and they could comprise a list of what he remembered from their donations from the last several months. She'd been there at many of them and they could easily guess how many had attended, multiply it by what was charged per head, and come up with a tentative number.

Then again, no one kept good track at these events. Having Lynellen and Sally at the front desk was helpful, but they weren't the kind to keep track. Bentley seemed to be the only one who'd noticed the missing money. Though, how no one noticed a large sum of money missing boggled her mind. Then again, if it hadn't happened all at once, it could explain a gradual decrease that didn't alarm anyone.

She trailed her finger over her napkin, lost in thought, until she realized just how long Taylor had been gone.

Frowning, she stood and made her way toward the bathrooms. An image of the night before rushed into her mind. But no, Marco Rossario wouldn't be cornering her niece; he was dead.

A chill rushed through her at the same time as a wave of sadness. If he really had been stabbed, that meant a murder in North Bank and that meant there was a murderer on the loose. How would she explain this to Taylor—let alone her sister?

At the women's restroom door, she knocked and called out. "Taylor, honey, are you in there?"

There was no response.

Margot's heart began to beat more loudly and she called out to her niece again without response. She was just about to try the handle when a commotion at the front of the center drew her attention.

There, surrounded by several uniformed officers, stood Adam. His gaze was fixed on Margot and she felt the air leave her lungs as he paced toward her, the determination in his steps. The look on his face betrayed any hope she'd had of his visit bearing good news.

"Margot," he said, the strain in his words sending off red warning lights in her mind. "Where's Taylor?"

"T-Taylor?" Her mind suddenly felt sluggish and she blinked to clear it. "I—I don't know. She came to the bathroom, but I've called out to her and she hasn't answered. I was about to go in..."

"Please, stand back." She watched in horror as Adam instructed a female officer to come forward. She knocked once and then, trying the handle, found it locked.

"Sir?" she asked.

Adam nodded and she stepped back as one of the other officers strode forward and kicked at the door. After a few kicks, the frame cracked and the door swung inward to reveal an empty bathroom, curtains blowing in the wind through the open window.

Margot looked to Adam. "She's gone."

～

THE COOL NIGHT air rushed over Margot's skin as she raced outside behind Adam. Her heart thudded in her chest and she felt a sickening knot tighten in her stomach. Not only was Adam—a police detective—looking for her niece, but her niece wasn't where she said she was going to be.

What was going on?

"Harver, Jackson, you search that way. Collier and Smith, you go to the left." The officers nodded and broke off in unison.

"You should stay here, Margot." Adam's expression could have been carved in granite.

"No, I can help you find her."

He looked as if he were ready to argue with her, but then nodded instead. "Stay right behind me."

She nodded and followed as they went toward the parking lot. Where would Taylor go? Why had she run in the first place? Better yet, why was Adam looking for her?

Margot wanted to ask all of her questions at once, but she knew now was not the time. Adam was focused and she remembered when Julian had gotten that way. The last thing he wanted to do was talk. Just like her late husband, Adam was a man of action—it was what made them both such talented detectives. They thought things through, but then they acted on those thoughts.

She followed as he ran through the parking lot, then he skidded to a halt and she nearly ran into him.

"Where did you park?"

"Down the street—I never park in the lot if I can help it."

He nodded. "Show me."

Adrenaline coursing through her, she nodded and turned toward the street. They jogged down a block and she spotted her car ahead, at least one more block away. Another car was double parked next to it, facing away from them. What was going on?

"Margot—" Adam said, his tone warning. "Get behind me."

"That's my—"

"I see it." His words were as sharp as steel. "Get behind."

She did and he picked up his pace. They were still five car-lengths away when the person standing at the second car's window stood up.

Taylor.

Margot gasped just as the car's brake lights disappeared and the back tires squealed in protest at being forced into movement without warning.

"No!" Adam yelled before kicking up into a fast run.

Taylor flattened herself against Margot's car, looking frightened as Adam chased through the burning tire smoke after the car. He returned almost immediately, jaw clenched.

"They got away." Then his gaze nailed Taylor. "Who was that?"

"I—I don't know. Just s-someone asking for directions."

He leaned closer, as if daring her to lie to his face. But was she lying? Margot had the uneasy feeling she was, but she couldn't be sure. And wasn't she supposed to be on her niece's side?

Adam radioed in to the other officers to give them their location, then he pulled out handcuffs from his pocket.

Margot felt the blood drain from her face. "What is this about?"

"It's a precaution."

"She's not dangerous, Adam," Margot snapped.

His eyes shifted and he seemed suddenly uneasy. There was something he wasn't telling her. Something about Taylor.

"What is going on?" Margot demanded.

He met her gaze. "I'm sorry, Margot, but..." He ran a hand through his hair, glancing to Taylor with narrowed eyes. "We found the murder weapon."

Cold dread spread through Margot.

"Taylor's prints were on the knife."

"What? You've got to be kidding! You think I killed Marco? No way! I just *got* here. Why would I kill him?"

Margot shot Adam a look and wrapped her arm around Taylor's shoulders. "Quiet, honey. This has to be some mistake."

Three officers arrived on the scene and another drove a squad car up the next moment, the blue and red lights flashing and bringing Margot back to *that night.*

No. She closed her eyes. She would not allow this to take her back—not to that night. Besides, her niece was frightened and needed her to be strong.

"This is ridiculous. She's nineteen, Adam. She is *not* a killer."

His eyes reflected what she knew to be true. He and her husband had both seen terrible things in their line of work. Unfortunately, no one was too young to be capable of murder. But surely not Taylor.

She looked down at her niece and saw that she was trembling. Her fear was real enough, but she *had* lied about the man in the car. Margot had seen that much in her expression. And she'd escaped from the bathroom at the senior center. And she'd had that fight with Marco.

Margot clenched her eyes for a moment, trying to drown out all of the things that seemed to lead to Taylor's guilt. She was innocent until proven guilty—though that wouldn't happen because she *hadn't* done this awful thing.

"It's okay, honey. You go with them and do what they say. I'll call your mom and we'll figure this out."

"No!" Taylor's reply was so sharp that Adam turned to look at her from where he was briefing an officer. "I mean...can you please wait—just a day or something—to tell Renee. This will literally kill our relationship or... whatever it is. Please, Aunt Margot, don't call her. Not tonight at least."

It went against everything in Margot's makeup as a sister to agree. "I...I can't do that."

"I'm an adult," Taylor said, drilling her gaze into Margot. "Just...give me a day to figure this out."

Margot bit her lip and looked between the young girl and Adam, who now stood nearby. He was waiting to take Taylor.

"Please—promise me, Aunt Margot." Now Taylor was crying, real tears that burned trails down her cheeks. It was the first thing she'd actually gotten worked up about.

"All right," Margot heard the words come from her mouth but she hardly believed she'd said them.

"Th-thank you," Taylor said as Adam reached out toward her.

"You have the right to remain silent..."

Margot watched as if she were part of a bad dream while her niece was placed in the squad car and the door closed.

Her empty eyes stared back at Margot, Taylor's complexion as white as whipped cream. The car drove away and Margot promised herself that she would do whatever it took to clear Taylor's name because, if she knew one thing, it was the fact that Taylor had not killed Marco Rossario.

What she didn't know was why her niece's fingerprints were on the murder weapon. Or how the police knew the fingerprints were Taylor's.

CHAPTER 6

MARGOT TRIED her best to focus on the task at hand, but it was nearly impossible. Watching the squad car holding her niece drive away had felt like a band of iron slowly cinching around her heart. Tighter and tighter until she wasn't sure she could feel, let alone breathe, anymore.

She'd wobbled on her feet but Adam had been there, wrapping his arm securely around her shoulder and directing her onto the sidewalk next to her car so she could calm down. He wouldn't even let her get in the car, let alone think about driving, until he was sure she was somewhat settled.

Then she'd snatched the keys from his grasp and leveled her gaze at him. Even in the dim light she knew he saw every emotion written in her eyes. He was a lot like Julian in that way. She told him in no uncertain terms he *was* coming to see her and they were going to have a conversation.

But now, as she glanced at the clock and then the door for the millionth time in the span of an hour, she wasn't sure he'd agreed so much as said whatever it would take for her to let go of his arm in the vice like grip she'd had it in.

It was nearing seven o'clock—still early, but she knew Adam was on a case and that meant little sleep and lots to deal with.

Her heart sank at the thought of Taylor in a jail cell, cold and alone. She had wanted to see her immediately, but she knew she had to bake in the morning if Rosie was going to have anything to sell when she took over later that day.

Margot glanced up again, but this time her gaze collided with Adam's. He stood on the sidewalk in front of the glass-fronted door, hands lazily in his pockets. But she wasn't fooled. Inside, Adam was like a highly-strung dog ready to attack the next lead he got or any new information in the case.

She wiped the flour dust from her fingers and unlocked the front door. He held her gaze for a moment, his eyes whispering an apology for arresting her niece, but she turned her back on him. She wasn't mad at him exactly, but she knew he was wrong.

"Coffee?"

"Please."

She poured him a cup of strong Ethiopian coffee and refilled her half-empty mug as well. Handing it over, she pushed a plate of *Oopses* in front of him. They were what she called any baked goods that didn't meet her satisfaction of looking professional. She often boxed them up and either took them to the senior center or down the street to her friend Tamera's shop.

"This is the best mistake I've tasted," he said, savoring the end of a caramel pecan cinnamon roll.

She couldn't help the half-smile that slipped into place, but even that felt like a betrayal.

He's not your enemy, Marg, she reminded herself.

"Adam—" she began but he held up a hand, his eyes still closed as he popped in the last bite and then followed it up with a swig of coffee.

"Perfection." He let out a contented sigh then opened his eyes. "Okay, now we can get down to business."

She crossed her arms looking up at him. "My nineteen-year-old niece is in custody for a *murder*. One she didn't commit, by the way. I'd hardy call that business."

"I'm sorry, poor choice of words." He grimaced. "I just mean that you're full steam ahead and I haven't even finished my coffee yet," he said, holding up the cup as if it were the proof she needed.

"But Taylor—"

"Is innocent until proven guilty."

"Which is something *you* will be trying to do!" She felt her cheeks heat.

"Hold on there." A deep V appeared in the middle of his forehead. "I don't *want* Taylor to be the murderer. Don't make it sound as if I'll be finding ways to pin this on her." He huffed out a breath. "I will do everything in my power to prove her innocent if that's true. But I won't ignore facts. You know me better than that."

The look of hurt in Adam's hazel eyes pierced her conscience and she dropped her arms. "I'm sorry. You're right. I do know you better than that." It was the truth and she felt foolish for doubting him in first place. Of course he would want to see Taylor proved innocent—if she were. Margot shivered, not able to believe her niece was capable of murder.

"What do you know?" she asked tentatively.

He sighed and took another sip of coffee first. "There isn't much yet. Forensics only linked the fingerprint to Taylor, but—" He paused as if considering how much he could tell her. In all reality, he had probably told her too much already—maybe even being here was too much—but she was thankful he had come anyway. "We haven't found any other evidence linking her to the crime scene."

Margo frowned, picking at a piece of deformed macaroon. "Why, Adam?" She met his gaze and knew he understood she wasn't asking about the evidence at the crime scene.

"We've tossed out ideas like crime of passion, something stemming from the moment of their altercation at Antonio's, but there's nothing solid yet."

"Not to mention the fact she was in *my house* when this crime was supposed to have been committed."

"Right," he said, sounding unconvinced.

"But...what? What aren't you saying?"

"Obviously, from her stunt last night, she is adept at climbing out of windows. I—" He hesitated, looking down. "—checked out the window from her room. Since your house is up against the hillside, it wouldn't have been hard for her to slip out unnoticed while you slept."

The sickening feeling in her stomach was back. She knew that what he said was true. But still...

"Why? Everything you've told me seems extremely weak when we're talking about *murder*. What motive did anyone have for killing Marco Rossario?"

"We don't know enough about him yet, but believe me, we're working on it." He shifted his position slightly closer to her, looking down with intensity. "Look, I'm doing everything I can—my whole team is. You know it better than most—it takes time and hard work. I'll give it my all, I promise you that."

Warmth spread through her at his words, but it wasn't enough to chase away the chill that was slowly taking over her heart. It was going to be a long process and a messy one for Taylor, and Margot had a feeling that more skeletons would come to light before this whole thing was over.

~

ROSIE BURST INTO THE KITCHEN, her robin's egg blue apron tied snugly around her large hips. "Honey, you best be headed out if you're going to make it in to see Taylor."

Margot knew the woman was right and she wanted to go, but her mind was lost in thoughts of their own. She couldn't stop thinking about her conversation with Adam last night.

No evidence of Taylor's presence was found at the crime scene—Miller's Bridge—but her fingerprints were on the murder weapon. That seemed like a very thin case, then again, fingerprints were a rock solid piece of evidence, weren't they? Where had the knife come from? What type was it? If Margot knew, it could help her discover some way the girl's prints had gotten on the knife other than during the murder of that poor, albeit misguided, boy.

"Hello to Mrs. Durand," Rosie said, waiving a hand in front of her face.

Margot blinked back to the present to see Rosie's smile, her white teeth shimmering against her creamy chocolate skin.

"Well, *there* you are. Happy to have you back. Now go."

She put her hands on her hips and gave a look that would have halted the Terminator.

"All right, okay, I'm going," Margot said. "Just let me finish this."

Rosie eyed the counter and nodded once. "I'm only letting you finish those because I intend to eat one—maybe more —and it would be a shame for them to sit there unfinished. But then you go." The woman bustled back to the front and she heard her loud greeting, "Welcome to the *bakery*, folks! Ready to taste the best French pastries this side of the Atlantic?"

Margot chuckled to herself, unsure where Rosie came up with half the things she said, but loving her all the more for them.

She turned her attention back to the task at hand as she whipped up the pastry cream to fill the last batch of éclair's. Her mind snagged on the evidence again. Miller's Bridge wasn't far from her shop. It was a short walk down the river walk pathway. Maybe...

She could envision the bridge, but for some reason she felt the need to *see* it in person. Maybe it would help her clear thoughts from her head. Maybe it would put more in. She wasn't sure. Either way, she felt the need to go.

Finishing off the pastries, she said good-bye to Rosie and pulled the small handmade satchel her friend Tamera had crafted onto her shoulder. She let herself out of the back door and walked down the stone pathway toward the bridge. If she timed it right, she could walk past there, get to her car, and make it to the courthouse in time for Taylor's bail hearing.

The back of her bakery looked out over the Potomac River, as did all of the shops along this stretch of riverfront property. They were situated high up on an old stonework wall lined with wrought iron fencing that added to the charm. She passed the small café situated next to her shop. The bright yellow umbrellas that covered the outdoor seating in the back mimicked the sun even if wasn't quite warm enough to be outside yet.

Then she passed the antique store that housed more than its fair share of Civil War history and paraphernalia. Then the pet shop, shoe store, and paper goods shop where she often bought her packaging materials for the bakery. At the end of the row was Tamera's craft boutique. Margot smiled, thinking of her friend on her honeymoon right now in Hawaii. She had met and married the man of her dreams at age fifty-two, giving all women hope that maybe good things did come to those who waited.

Once Margot was past the last shop, she took the pathway that diverged to the right and stayed level with the river. The breeze was stiff and the river looked more choppy than normal, but the sun helped balance out the cold.

A few more minutes of walking and she turned the bend to see Miller's Bridge above her. It stretched out across the river and was tinged with a green patina and looked more industrial than anything else. It was functional, but not for cars—not anymore. Now only foot traffic, bikes, and the occasional mother with a stroller used it to cross over to the small island in the middle of the Potomac. The bridge had once continued across the river to another peninsula that looped back up into northern Virginia, but that bridge had long since been taken down and now only this small portion of it remained.

Yellow police tape snapped in the wind, closing off the path for everyone and screaming that something bad had happened here. From her low vantage point she could see that no one was at the scene, then again, she hadn't really expected the police to *still* be there, had she?

She looked across the railing sections, but nothing appeared out of the ordinary. Looking down and out across the river, some of the rocks were visible above the waterline. She knew many more lay just beneath the surface as well. To someone living, they would have been perilous.

Margot shivered at the thought, reaching up to wrap her arms around herself to ward off the chill, but it went deeper.

Seeing all that she could from the path, she took the steps that led up to the bridge's entrance from street level. The bright yellow tape warned her to stay off of the bridge and she obeyed it, but she could still see well enough to the middle of the bridge from her vantage point.

The railing was tall, at least waist-height if not slightly

taller, depending on a person's height. She envisioned Marco from the night before, trying her best to distance herself from what had happened. She assumed the railing would have hit him in the middle of the back.

She used her phone to snap pictures of the bridge from several angles for later observation and checked her watch. It was time to get to the courthouse.

Reaching the tall building, she ran up the steps and made it through the meager security with plenty of time to spare. As she sat in the courtroom and her clock ticked five minutes past the hearing time, she frowned. She was in the right room, wasn't she?

Then a thin clerk with mousey brown hair and a low and tight bun stepped onto the floor. "The bail hearing of Miss Taylor Garvey will be postponed until tomorrow afternoon."

Margot felt her pulse spike. Postponed? Why? What was going on?

She picked up her satchel and rushed out of the large double doors and straight into Adam's solid chest. He reached out and steadied her. "There you are."

"Why is it postponed?"

He blinked, catching up quickly. "Judge Castor is sick and Judge Pellenworth couldn't spare time for another case. It's been a madhouse."

"So my niece has to stay another day in *jail* because

someone is sick? This is ridiculous." Margot heard the desperation and anger in her tone, even felt the gazes from many in the echoing atrium where they stood, but she didn't care. This was Taylor they were talking about. What happened to 'innocent until proven guilty'?

"Come on," he said, as if sensing her meltdown. "I'll get you in to see her."

CHAPTER 7

MARGOT FELT the chill enter her the minute she stepped into the jailhouse. She hated knowing that her niece was staying there and she hated the fact that she hadn't told her sister yet.

Adam helped her sign in and then she walked down the hallway toward the holding cell. Taylor looked small, dwarfed by the orange coveralls she wore. She sat on the bed, knees to her chest and looking forlorn. It tugged at Margot's heart and she felt like a failure.

How had she allowed her niece to be arrested for murder? Julian would have done something—could have...what? Foreseen that this would happen? No. As good of a detective as Julian was, there was no way he could have prevented this. Maybe she shouldn't have agreed for the girl to come out to visit. Then again, did Marco's death have something to do with her niece or was it a case of mistaken identity or being in the wrong place at the wrong time?

Those excuses both felt flimsy even as she thought them. Fingerprints on a murder weapon didn't just happen. They were either left by the killer or planted there.

That thought churned her stomach even more. Was her niece being framed for the murder of some part-time waiter? Or had she really been involved?

"Aunt Marg," Taylor said, standing up so fast she nearly fell over.

She rushed to the bars and Margot could see tears in her eyes, which made her appear even younger. No, this little girl didn't have any hand in murder. She may be nineteen, but she was innocent. Margot felt it in her gut— something her husband had said was a good indicator.

Adam had remained at the entrance, promising to wait for her while she spoke with Taylor, but now she wanted to simply sit on the floor and wait with her niece. It wasn't possible, of course, but it felt so wrong knowing that she would have to leave the girl behind.

"They canceled your bail hearing for today," she found herself saying.

"I know." She dropped her gaze, her slim fingers gripping the bars. "Someone came in and told me. I—I guess I have to wait until tomorrow."

"I'm sorry, sweetie," she said, wishing she could wrap her

up in a hug. "I'll be there at the hearing tomorrow. I'll post bail and we'll get you out of there, all right?"

She nodded, tears filling her eyes again. "No matter what they said—" Her voice broke. "I didn't do it."

"I know, Tay. I know you wouldn't do anything like that."

She dropped her gaze, her knuckles turning white on the bars. "I wouldn't kill anyone."

"I need to call your mother—"

"Please," she interrupted. "Please don't call her. Not yet. I...I want to be the one to tell her. I'll be out on bail tomorrow, right? I can call her then."

Margot felt like she was betraying her sister, but Taylor was also an adult and she couldn't force her. Then again...

"If you don't call her tomorrow, I will."

Taylor met her gaze for a moment then finally nodded. "Okay."

"Ma'am," an officer said, coming down the hall, "I'm afraid that's all the time you have."

She nodded then looked back at Taylor. "Stay strong, sweetie. I'm going to find out who did this."

Taylor looked shocked by her words, but Margot didn't take them back or provide any explanation. She just knew that she would do anything to help this wide-eyed young girl whom her husband had written letters to. This young woman who had her life ahead of her.

Forcing her own tears back, Margot squeezed Taylor's fingers through the bars then turned to be escorted out. Her heart ached at leaving her niece there, but she knew she could do far more good tracking down who had framed her niece for Marco's murder, because at this point, that was the only plausible reality.

~

"CAN I TAKE YOU TO LUNCH?" Adam asked when they were back outside and she could feel the freedom to breathe again. The air of the jail had been stifling.

She considered the fact that she was hungry, but also the reality that she needed time—and distance—to think about her next move.

"Not today. I'm sorry, Adam," she said, shrugging. "Another time?"

"Of course. Sorry—bad timing."

"I'll see you later."

He looked at her through narrowed lashes, the dark fringe making his hazel eyes appear mysterious. "You're not going to do anything...foolish, are you?"

"What do you mean?" Her eyebrows rose in surprise.

He considered her, his hands casually resting in the

pockets of his light gray slacks. "I know you, Margot. Julian talked to me about you and he said that, on more than one occasion, you got in over your head in following along with his cases."

She feigned ignorance. "I don't know what you're talking about."

"Ah, but you do," he said, pointing a finger at her. "See— that look right there. It tells me that you know *exactly* what I'm talking about."

She stared him down. If he wanted her to say she wouldn't try and clear her niece's name, then *he* was the foolish one. But she wouldn't give him the satisfaction of thinking he'd pegged her.

"Just...be careful." The pleading in his tone surprised her, but she tried not to let it show.

"I'm a baker, Adam. How dangerous can that be?"

He shook his head, a small smile slipping onto his handsome features. "Right."

She headed for her car, her mind scattering to a million different things. Where she should go next. Adam's warning. The look on Taylor's face. Adam's invitation to lunch—

Her stomach grumbled. Lunch wasn't a bad idea. Turning the car on, she contemplated where she should go to grab a quiet bite. Her gaze trailed the distance then dropped in front of her. The receipt in the middle console caught her attention.

Antonio's.

"Of course!" she said to the empty car.

It was a short and familiar drive to *Pane Dolce* and, before she could think past what she would say to her favorite Italian restaurant owner on the death of one of his employees, she was asking for the secluded corner booth and to see Antonio when he had a spare moment.

The large, usually jovial man joined her at the table, sliding in across from her with a heavy sigh.

"*Mia bella,* what is this world coming to? Eh?"

She offered him a sad smile. "I'm sorry about Marco."

"*Pfft,*" he said, waving a hand at her. "I am as shocked as you are—and dare I say, as unaffected." He looked apologetic. "I mean, I feel bad for the boy...to go in such a way." He made a face of disgust. "But some would say he had it coming to him."

"What do you mean?" she said, trying not to sound too interested.

"He was a—how do they say? *Playboy.* I hired him, as I told you, because of Lorenzo, but if I hadn't let him go that night you were here, I would have let him go soon. He wasn't a good worker. Flirting with all the women. And he was late. *Whew,* late all the time because of his 'errands'." He made a motion of air quotes and gave her a knowing look.

"Errands?" she repeated. "What do you mean?"

The man shrugged, motioning a waiter over. "Margot Durand, meet my nephew Lorenzo."

She looked up at the dark-haired boy with tan skin and striking blue eyes. He was handsome in a model-looking type way, but he looked less sure of himself. Unlike Marco, he barely made eye contact with her, only muttering an obligatory greeting.

Antonio ordered for her without even asking, telling his nephew to put a rush on it, then turned to look back at her.

"I am not sure of these errands…" He arched his eyebrows at her. "But the car he drove and the clothes he wore on his days off—you know, when he'd come in to pick up his check—they were fancy. Too fancy for what I was giving him."

Margot nodded, trying to piece things together in her head. A rich, playboy-type who ran suspicious errands on the side.

"Drugs?" she asked.

"No!" Antonio shook his head violently. "None of my employees use drugs. I do the tests and make it all legal."

She smiled to assuage him, but in the back of her mind

she was thinking of all of the ways Marco could have passed the test without actually being drug-free. Then again, Antonio would have noticed in his behavior if he'd been a user. Maybe a dealer then? But why have the job at Antonio's?

"There you are," came a syrupy voice attached to a lithe figure clad in impossibly tight workout clothes. "Antonio, you simply *must* agree to cater my party. I won't take no for an answer. Oh, hello, Margot."

Margot looked up to see Mrs. Penberthy. Her fake smile matched her clothing choices—plastered on.

"Oh, Kim, nice to see you," Margot said through a forced smile of her own.

"But really, Antonio..." She paused to type something out on the cell phone that was permanently attached to her hand. "I need to hear a yes out of you. Just one simple word. Come on now. You know I get what I want." She leaned forward and placed a finger on the side of Antonio's round face, tapping to accentuate each word. "Just. One. Word."

Margot resisted the urge to roll her eyes. Kim Penberthy was over-the-top in every sense of the phrase. Maybe it was something that worked well for her station as wife to the mayor, but in small company—or really *any* company —it was too much in Margot's opinion.

"Ah, my dear Mrs. Penberthy. You flatter me," Antonio said, eating up the attention. "You have persuaded me. I shall be happy to cater your party. My assistant will set everything up for you. I shall do my famous lasagna, no?"

"Uh, no," she said, wrinkling her nose. "I love it, don't get me wrong, Tony, but this needs to be...stunning."

"Stunning?" he repeated, looking confused.

"I'll do some research and get back to you. It'll be a party like no one has seen before. Ta ta," she said, tossing a hand over her shoulder as her long blonde ponytail swished about her shoulders.

"Stunning?" Antonio said, looking back at Margot. "Is my lasagna not stunning?"

Fighting back a smile, Margot reassured him with a pat on the hand. "It is."

Her lunch arrived and Antonio stood, wishing her a good day and a happy lunch—on him. She shook her head but he insisted before chasing after a waiter who was apparently taking a plate to a table without the proper garnish.

Margot ate the pasta dish while her thoughts centered on Marco. He had money. He was often late. He ran errands. It didn't mean anything other than the fact that there was much more to Marco Rossario than she had first expected. And that information could hold the key to his murder.

CHAPTER 8

MARGOT CHECKED her text messages as she walked back to her car, the memory of the brief encounter with Marco and Taylor that night coming back to her and momentarily distracting her. Something about it felt off— why had he risked coming outside to see Taylor? Obviously, he was either very much besotted with her niece or...there was something else behind it. What had he said? Something about wanting something?

Slipping into the sun-warmed car, Margot felt the affects of her less than restful night's sleep. Her brain felt foggy, her memory compromised. How was she supposed to rest comfortably knowing that Taylor was in a jail cell?

She stifled a yawn and looked down when her phone vibrated in her hand. It was a message from Bentley asking her to come to the senior center. After a quick call to Rosie to make sure everything was running smoothly at the bakery, she put the car in gear and drove to the dilapidated building.

She found a parking spot near the lot and jogged up the steps to the center's entrance. Gone were the few decorations that had been put up for the World Dinner Night. The main area of the center looked as drab and worn down as she felt from lack of sleep, but she pushed past it and headed for the perpetually filled coffee pot.

Fortified with liquid energy, she headed to Bentley's favorite spot. There was a small reading nook located at the back of the building. Since the center was situated on the side of a hill—like most of the town—the view was spectacular. It looked out over the town and to the river. On clear days like today, you could see boats and all manner of seagulls dotting the horizon.

"There you are," he said, putting down the large novel he was reading. Probably something by Grisham, she thought. Bentley seemed to worship the guy.

"Hey, Bentley," she said, leaning to kiss his cheek. "Got your text. What's going on?"

He shifted over and she joined him on the window seat. "I've got a bad feeling."

"Is this about what you were telling me last night? I really don't think—"

"Oh, you poor dear." Margot and Bentley turned to see Lynellen standing there, hands clasped together in front of her bosom, eyes almost teary. "I heard what happened. You must be beside yourself, you poor dear."

Without warning, Lynellen came toward Margot with outstretched arms and suddenly Margot was encased by the scent of baby powder and a cheap knock off of Chanel No. 5.

"I—I'm," Margot coughed. "Wait, what are you talking about?"

Lynellen shook her head, the sheen of tears unmistakable at this close distance. "That poor, sweet, innocent—or not —" She glanced to the side with a worried look. "—niece of yours. Struck down in her youth."

"She's not dead, Lynellen," Bentley was quick to correct her.

"No, but she might as well be for the world of trouble she's in." Lynellen shook her head. "I'm so sorry to hear about all of the problems our youth get in these days. Just the other day, I was telling my grandson that—"

"Lynellen," Bentley interrupted, "I know it's tragic and all, but I'm having a chat with Margot here."

"Oh. Yes." Lynellen nodded emphatically, "Smart, consulting a lawyer and all. Though don't you think you should get one who still practices?"

Margot shot Bentley a surprised look but he was too busy convincing Lynellen to leave them alone. When she'd finally wandered off Margot folded her arms and met Bentley's gaze.

"You were a lawyer?"

He shrugged. "I did my time as a defense attorney back in the old days. But that's not why I have you here. Though it is a shame to hear about Taylor. I don't believe it for a second. And know that I wouldn't be bothering you at such a time, but…I've just got this feeling."

Margot took a moment to take in an image of Bentley in a suit arguing at trials—it explained the Grisham obsession. She blinked. Right. She needed to finish up this conversation and then move on to her next step in helping Taylor, even though she wasn't sure what that step should be.

"What is it?"

His furrowed brow deepened. "It's about what I told you last night. Someone is stealing money from our fundraisers. I've thought about going to the police, but all of the papers we have *show* that my gut is wrong…but I feel it, here." He tapped the middle of his chest. "Something is off."

Margot blinked. Could this in some way be connected with Marco's murder? It was a stretch—no, it wasn't even that. It was pure conjecture and guesswork, something Julian had told her never to do, but she couldn't ignore the timing of it all. Could she?

"Margot?"

"Sorry. I was lost in the land of *what if*."

"Well, come back to the present," he said gruffly. Bentley was more ornery than usual. "I'm sorry," he said, shaking his head, "I just can't believe that anyone would have the gall to pull a stunt like this. We just want our lodge— what's so bad about that? But everyone else on the committee swears things are in order." He tossed up his hands. "It's like I'm talking to a bunch of sheep, I tell you. You'd have to be a heartless fool to target senior citizens, wouldn't you?"

It was a valid question. Was someone stealing money to benefit themselves or was it actually a roadblock to the lodge's construction?

"I don't know, Bentley. It does seem like a cowardly thing to do." *If it's happening.* She hated the hint of suspicion in her thoughts.

"I need you to do something for me."

Margot felt wariness creep up on her. She was someone who often had trouble saying no—to anything—and the look in Bentley's eyes told her she wouldn't be able to turn him down either.

"What?" she said, letting out a sigh.

"I need you to go to the mayor's office tomorrow to see if you can talk to Eve, the mayor's assistant. I can't be sure, but I think she knows something about all this."

"What do you expect me to do?" Margot said, laughing. "Barge in there and give her the inquisition?"

"I've got a theory." Bentley leaned in closer, whispering conspiratorially, "I want you to tell her that you're interested in doing a fundraiser to, I don't know, add on to your bakery or something, and see how she responds."

Margot was already shaking her head. "Bentley, that is ridiculous. One, I have no space to expand and everyone knows that, and two, what do you think she'll do? Open up and tell me she's got a great way to make money—stealing from senior citizens?"

"No. Not at all. See, that's the beauty of it. She'll just *know* about the scheme and we'll see what goes on from there. Word has it *she* was the one who recommended the kid who does our finances."

Margot fought to keep up. "Wait, you think Eve is in on this?"

Bentley leaned back, his frown deepening. "I think she might be."

Margot nearly laughed. "Eve is one of the sweetest people I know."

"Margot," Bentley said admonishingly. "Julian taught you better than that. She may *look* innocent, but that doesn't mean she is."

Margot had a hard time seeing the former school teacher turned stay-at-home-mom turned assistant to the mayor as anything but sweet. Still, it was odd that she had recommended someone who had turned out not to be 'above board.' *If Bentley's right.* There it was again—that hint of doubt.

"I still don't see it, but I'll reserve judgment."

"Good girl."

"Okay, one more question." She stared Bentley down. "Who is this mysterious accountant?"

"I don't know really, had good credentials—or so I thought. Name's Lorenzo something."

Margot sucked in a breath. *Lorenzo?!*

"Lorenzo Bianchi?"

"Yeah, that's the kid. Wait—he's not doing any accounting for you, is he?"

"No," she said, her gaze trailing out over the window and to the water beyond. He wasn't, but he was definitely now on her radar.

MARGOT HAD STAYED up too late. It was nearly impossible for her to fall asleep at eight like she usually did. Her mind had whirred a hundred miles a minute with worry about Taylor, thoughts about Marco chased by the image of Lorenzo Bianchi, and the curiosity of how this all fit together—if it did. Somehow.

Again, Julian's voice came back to her

Sometimes, ma chérie, it is not the obvious that draws two things together but the lack of an obvious connection that does it.

An ache had filled her chest with a longing to talk all of this over with Julian. She'd almost called Adam, but it wasn't a good idea. Knowing him and knowing that he was part of this case—a vital part—she couldn't risk him knowing of her involvement in anything until she had solid evidence. If then.

When sleep had finally found her, it had been restless and lacking.

Now, she was in the midst of her morning routine with an added batch of croissants for her trip to the mayor's office later that day. It felt dishonest to be planning this trip with the express intent of gaining information on a woman she respected, let alone liked and went to church with, but how could she dismiss the fact that Eve had recommended Lorenzo?

Still, the facts weren't lining up. If Eve was somehow part of this scheme—something Margot wasn't convinced of— then why had she asked for help with a car bill from their women's group?

Unless...Margot stiffened, standing up and forcing her shoulders to relax. No, Eve couldn't have slipped into something illegal because of money problems. Then again, money was the root of most evils in this world—not to mention a great motive.

Margot thought of what motive there had been for Marco's death. Maybe she would talk to Adam again, but only to find out if he had any leads on that aspect...if he'd tell her. That still remained to be seen.

The pastries in the oven to bake, she cleaned up around the shop, took note of what items she needed to restock, and then made a quick reminder to contact Adam after the bail hearing. Just the thought of it made her sick to her stomach. She needed to contact her sister and—

A thought struck Margot. Taylor was usually texting on her phone twenty-four/seven. She assumed that she texted her mother some of that time. Then again, did nineteen-year olds still text their parents? Would Renee worry?

But Margot pushed the thought from her mind. Her sister had *her* number. She could always call her, couldn't she?

Feeling flustered and over-tired, Margot sunk down into her desk chair and, setting an alarm for seven, rested her head back against the cushioned headrest.

BEEPING and pounding wove together to create a strange sort of dream for Margot. She was in a burning building about to jump from the third story into the arms of a waiting fireman, though how she would make it she had no idea. The beeping of the fire truck backing up reminded her if she waited, she could just climb down the ladder but the pounding of the fire behind her was too fast, too loud, she would have to jump and—

She gasped and sat upright, the alarm on her phone sounding and the pounding from her dream a reality. She rushed to the front door, relieved to see Bentley there, morning paper under his arm.

He grinned, nodding in the direction of her hair. "Sleeping on the job, I see."

"I didn't sleep well last night." She reached up and felt the bump of her hair. "The usual."

"Yep. And tell me you're planning on making a trip—"

"To the mayor's office, yes," she said, grinning. "Give me one minute to get your order."

The rest of the morning went by quickly and when Rosie came to take over for the afternoon, she had her box of croissants—some even chocolate-filled, the mayor's favorite—ready to go. With a wave goodbye, she headed out the door.

She pulled into a space across the street from the office and took a deep breath, staying in the car. She wasn't exactly sure how to play this. She remembered Julian's comments about his undercover work in his younger years, but that had mostly been gang related. She shivered just thinking about her late husband keeping company with gang members.

Movement across the street drew her attention. The mayor, potbelly stomach leading the way, stepped from the office and donned his fedora. His gaze trailed around, a look of pride settling over his features. She smiled. Though she didn't agree with him on all of his political platforms, he was a nice man. She was about to race out to catch him when a thought brought an invisible hand down on her shoulder.

She was really here to see Eve. Wasn't this better?

She let the mayor get into his car and drive away before she stepped out into the warm sunshine and darted across the street. The small electronic beep indicated her entrance into the office and she went down the hallway to where Eve's desk sat.

The woman looked up, a smile creasing her face. She pulled her glasses off and rested her elbows on the desk in front of her.

"Margot Durand, this is a surprise. Are those for me?" she said with a conspiratorial laugh.

"Afraid not. I thought I'd drop these off for the mayor. Croissants, his favorite."

"He's going to love that—though Kim would have a fit if she knew." Eve's eyes drew wide. "You can leave them with me. I won't eat more than one, I promise." She winked.

"Oh sure—and you really should have one! There are more than enough for the mayor."

Eve accepted the yellow box and placed it under the high counter of her desk. Then she looked back up at Margot, probably wondering what she was still doing there.

"I, uh..." This was the part Margot wasn't good with. Fabrication. "I'm considering doing a fundraiser. You know, new bakery equipment isn't cheap. I'd heard someone mention you knew a good accountant?" She held her breath. Everything she'd said wasn't a complete lie. She *had* considered doing a fundraiser and bakery equipment *was* expensive.

"Actually, I do." Eve leaned forward. "But I have to preface this with the fact that he's not a real accountant—well, yet."

This wasn't what Margot had expected. "Um, what do you mean?"

"I'm doing night school—remember I mentioned it at our women's Bible study at the beginning of the year. Anyway, I've met some amazing people there—all trying to get their lives on track or start a new business. Things like that. And this young man is exceptional. I overheard our teacher talking about him and said he was his best student. I've referred him to a few people."

So that was why Eve had recommended Lorenzo to the senior center. "Wow. Sounds great. Can I get his contact information?"

"Sure!" She beamed as she wrote it out on a sticky note. "Here you go."

"Thanks. I really appreciate this." Then, turning to go, she said, "Enjoy that croissant."

"Oh, you know I will."

CHAPTER 9

THE BAIL HEARING went faster than Margot had expected and soon she was in the hallway waiting for Taylor to get changed. She saw Adam from across the room, but officers surrounded him and it looked like he was in a heated conversation. No matter, she had nothing to talk with him about anyway. Not yet at least.

Though she did have a call to make to the night school teacher. The thought of Lorenzo being a bright, shining star in accounting would surely explain a lot for his skills with hiding money from the senior center—if that was what was happening.

She pulled out her phone and ran a quick search for the local night school. It wasn't difficult to find the teacher who dealt with most of the math classes. Thankfully, his phone number was listed and, with a glance around to make sure Taylor wasn't coming yet, she made the call.

It rang four times then slipped to voicemail. Uncertain of what to say, she merely said she was looking for information regarding one of his classes. Leaving her information, she pressed end and turned to see Taylor walking down the hall in the clothes Margot had brought for her.

"Hey, sweetie," she said, wrapping her arms around the girl. "How you doing?"

"Can we just go home?"

"Of course." She maneuvered them out of the courthouse and soon they were on the way home. Taylor nearly raced up the steps, but she didn't blame the girl.

Once they were inside, she turned to look at Taylor, arms crossed. "We need to call your mom."

"I know." Her shoulders slumped.

"Why don't I make us coffee and you can call her." Handing Taylor her phone, Margot turned to the coffeemaker and began to prepare a pot with fresh, dark grounds.

She tried not to overhear what her niece was saying, but it was nearly impossible. Things weren't going well. Then, with stomping feet and an explosion of air from clenched teeth, Taylor came back into the kitchen and thrust the phone at her.

"She wants to talk to you."

An uneasy feeling twisting in the pit of her stomach, she accepted the phone. "Hey, Rae."

"My daughter was charged with murder and you didn't even think to call me! And I trusted you to take care of her and keep her out of trouble! I'm getting on the next flight! I'll be there as soon as I can."

Margot took a deep breath and nodded for Taylor to help herself to the coffee while she walked into the living room, sinking onto the bright white couch that nestled in golden light coming in from the windows.

As she explained what had happened, her sister attempted to interrupt almost every sentence but she finally got to the end. "I know we should have called, but it was Taylor's choice and I honored that."

The silence on the other end of the line was telling. "What will Dillon think?" Her sister's voice was small, almost too quiet to hear.

"It's going to be okay. She didn't do this and the police will find that out."

"She's got a record." Renee almost whimpered. "It's sealed, but with a murder case, they'll dig. I just know it."

Margot cringed, but didn't let that enter her voice. At least that explained how the police had Taylor's fingerprints on file. "She didn't do this, Rae. She's innocent and the law will prove that." *I'll prove that.*

Finally, after half an hour, Renee finally agreed not to fly out. She only relented after Margot reminded her that there was nothing she could do—yet. They would wait it out and see what was going on. When they knew more, then she'd come.

"That was pretty bad," Taylor said, slumping onto the couch.

Margot shook her head. "Do you know Lorenzo Bianchi?"

Was it her imagination or did Taylor pale?

"No. Who's that?"

Was her niece lying to her?

"He's—" A knock on the door interrupted her explanation and she opened it to find Adam, Chinese carryout in both hands and a smile on his face.

"Thought you ladies might like some lunch."

She smiled, glancing back to Taylor. Her niece looked at Adam warily, no doubt wondering at first if he'd been there to take her back to captivity.

"Come on in."

He did and, as soon as the food was opened, Taylor took her plate to her room and shut the door.

"How are you doing?" Adam asked, using chopsticks to pick out a piece of broccoli.

Margot massaged her temples. "I've been better."

"And Taylor?"

"I don't know." She looked up at Adam. "Have you learned anything more?"

His gaze narrowed. "You're not asking me to share information of an active case are you?"

She allowed a weary smile to answer him.

"The only thing I can say at this point is that I'm struggling to find a connection between Taylor and Marco. No texts, calls, nothing. It's... It doesn't make any sense. As much as I'd initially thought the crime was one of passion, the facts aren't adding up."

So it was premeditated?

"Why would my niece—who knows no one here in town —murder some random man in a premeditated manner? Come on, Adam. This doesn't make any sense"

"And yet her fingerprints were on the knife from Ant—" He slammed his mouth shut.

Antonio's. Of course!

"Look, forget I said anything. Just keep her out of trouble and if you hear anything, you come to me. You hear me, Margot?"

"Sure, if I—" Her phone rang and she checked the caller

ID. She recognized the number of the night school professor. "Sorry, I've got to take his."

He nodded and she slipped into the kitchen.

"Hello, this is Margot Durand."

"Hello, Ms. Durand, this is Frank Crestwood. I had a call from you."

"Yes, I just had a quick question regarding your accounting class." She cringed, hoping that Adam wasn't listening in. She pushed further into the kitchen.

"Oh, are you interested in a class? We have one scheduled for the summer, but it doesn't start for a few more weeks."

"Um, no, actually. I was interested in knowing who your best student is."

He hesitated. "My best...student?"

"Yes, my friend Eve is in that class and she'd mentioned the name of your best student. I have a project I need a little accounting help on, nothing major of course, and I thought it would be nice to give someone a chance while they're still in school. I own the *Parisian Pâtisserie*."

"Oh, I see. Well, in that case hands down it's Victor Karvo. Great guy. Very promising."

"Not Lorenzo Bianchi?"

"Lorenzo—" The man broke into a fit of laugher. "I'm sorry. That was unprofessional." Margot rolled her eyes.

"He's...trying his best. But I wouldn't lump him in with the best. Would you like me to give you Victor's contact information?"

Rather than raise suspicion, she accepted the information and hung up. So either Eve was in on the scheme and recommending Lorenzo had been part of the whole conspiracy...or, what was more likely, is that she over heard Frank talking about his best student and gotten the wrong name.

If Lorenzo wasn't doing well in class then why had he agreed to—

"Did I hear you say Lorenzo Bianchi?"

Margo froze, her stomach clenching.

"Eavesdropping?" she said, spinning around. "Would you like some coffee?"

"Don't change the subject, Margot. What was that call about?"

She merely smiled. "Coffee?"

He crossed his arms over his chest, the taut fabric of his light blue button-down stretching. "Don't do this, Margot."

"I'm not *doing* anything other than offering you coffee." She smiled sweetly but saw the distrust behind Adam's eyes.

She knew the risks involved, but weren't they worth it if

that meant she would free her niece? No matter what she uncovered, she would turn it all over to Adam anyway— she just had to have enough *to* give him. Not hints of conjecture and speculation.

No. She would need hard facts, which meant she needed to start rocking the boat.

CHAPTER 10

THE NEXT MORNING found Margot delivering a stack of cookie boxes to the senior center. It was still early and she'd negotiated for Rosie and Taylor to run the shop that morning with a promise that she would be back that afternoon to take over.

Bentley made a bee-line for her the minute she stepped inside, but the rest of the senior residents who'd been caught in the midst of a ping pong tournament also swarmed her but for a different reason.

When the boxes were taken and she was left alone, Bentley all but carried her to a corner.

"Well," he said, leaning in toward her. "How did it go? What did she say? Do you think she's in on it?" His inquisitive nature made her laugh, but she could also see traces of the former prosecutor in him. How had she not known he was a lawyer before?

"I went to the mayor's office," she said, glancing around as if this were a top secret meeting in the senior center of all places. "Eve definitely has nothing to do with it."

She explained what she'd found out from her friend and the subsequent call with the professor.

"See? She recommended him for the simple fact that she'd heard—mistakenly—he was the best in the class."

"Hearsay," Bentley murmured.

"Don't you dare lawyer me." She squared her shoulders at the older man. "I know and trust Eve. You're not the only one with gut feelings."

He raised a hand as if to wave off her comment. "It's too coincidental."

"I'd go to the beginning of all of this. Who said it was a good idea to hire a kid who was in night classes anyway?"

"Kim Penberthy."

"Kim," Margot repeated, frowning. "What in the world is Kim doing with her hand in senior center politics?"

"Kim's got her hands in a lot of things." Bentley shrugged. "Speak of the devil."

Margot followed his gaze to the door where Kim Penberthy had just walked in. She gave a once-over of the room then waved to someone on the other side. When she walked past, she halted when she saw Margot.

"Fancy seeing you here." She looked between Margot and Bentley. "What's that, three times in one week?" She let out a fake laugh.

"It is a small town," Margot pointed out.

"Why are you here?" she said, narrowing her gaze and looking between them.

"Dropped off some cookies."

"Here to see me." They spoke at the same time and Kim raised her eyebrows.

"Dropped off cookies," Margot said, pointing to the nearly empty boxes on the table near the ping-pong tournament group. "Then came to talk to Bentley."

"I see." Kim's tone turned cool. Then with another fake smile, she strutted away, her four-inch heels cutting a leather-clad path through the room toward a group of the more stylish senior center visitors.

"Women's group," Bentley explained.

"Strange. I had no idea she was connected here."

"I think she golfs with Sharon at the Passaeo Club once a month. Wives of past mayors or something." Bentley turned his attention back to Margot and away from the group of women who kept shooting them strange glances. "Probably heard we were getting a committee together and wanted her hand in yet another thing in this town. As if her husband didn't try and run enough of it."

"Bentley," Margot reprimanded.

"Eh, I've never liked politics." He rolled his eyes. "But back to this Lorenzo kid—"

"I'll look into it, okay?"

Bentley's pale blue eyes met hers. "Hey, you take care of that niece of yours, all right? I'll see what I can find out about him."

She was about to disagree but with the look on his face and the reality that there wasn't enough time in the day, she nodded in agreement.

"Keep me posted."

"You betcha." He grinned, wagging his eyebrows.

Margot headed back to the bakery, mind on the cases. She snorted into the quiet interior of the car. Cases? Since when had she labeled herself a detective? Then again, that was what they were. One, a case of murder involving her niece. Two, a case of missing money supposedly stolen from the senior center building fund. Three, the case of whether or not Lorenzo was a good kid or a calculated thief. Then again, was her overly suspicious, retired lawyer friend to blame for the second and third cases? Was there even an issue there? Without seeing their books, she wasn't sure what she could do.

Walking into the shop, she heard a little yelp and, thankful that they had no customers, dashed to the back of the shop where her niece was nearly on the floor, a huge sack of flour toppled on its side. Mercifully, it was unopened, but still her heart did a little leap at the sight.

"Thank *goodness* you're back. Rosie here is no help and I'm just weak apparently."

Rosie grinned at this. "I told that youngster I ain't getting down there, risking my back going out again. Uh uh. No way, no how."

"Of course not, Rosie." Margot shook her head and donned an apron. "You really can't get this up on the counter?" She looked at Taylor skeptically.

"What?" Taylor said, shrugging. "I don't lift weights or anything."

Bending down, she helped the girl lift the flour up onto the counter. It landed with a thud and a poof of white dust.

"Whew. I'm out." Taylor dusted off her hands and removed her apron.

Margot had promised that Taylor could go home when she came back, but now worry seeped into that decision.

"Wait, you're not having second thoughts, are you?" Taylor leaned forward. "You are! I can see it in your eyes. Come on, Aunt Marg, I'm exhausted. We were here at three-thirty!"

"Late mornin' for you, eh, girl?" Rosie observed.

Margot grinned at her friend and fellow worker. She knew when Margot usually showed up.

"I'll take her home," Rosie said.

"You drive?" Taylor asked.

"Taylor!" Margot reprimanded but Rosie was already laughing.

"Better than you, girl. Come on." As she walked past, Rosie put her hand on Margot's arm. "Don't worry. The Lord's in charge. I'll see that she gets home, but He'll see that she's safe."

With her friend's reassurance, she nodded and grabbed Taylor in a hug. "Stay at my place, okay?"

"I will," she said, meeting Margot's gaze. Hopefully it was the truth.

MARGOT HAD JUST FINISHED PREPPING everything for the morning, affording her and Taylor an extra hour of sleep, when her gaze snagged on the oversized bag of flour. It had taken her *and* Taylor to lift the fifty-pound bag up onto the counter. Only fifty-pounds but that was a lot to the nineteen-year old. It would be a lot to most women.

Her mind started whirring. If she remembered what Adam had said correctly, then Marco had been stabbed at the bridge and *then* gone over the railing. The tall railing.

Was it even physically possible for Taylor to hoist a grown man, let alone one who looked like working out was more than a hobby, over the railing? It didn't seem possible.

She finished her preparations and closed the shop, exiting out the back door instead of the front this time. The day had turned from warm to chilly, clouds coming in from over the ocean just beyond the peninsula across the river. She wrapped her arms around herself as she walked down the path that led to Miller's Bridge again.

Even from the distance, when the bridge came into view, her doubts were rooted more firmly. There was no way her niece could have gotten a grown man over the railing —which would be at least chest-height to her—after stabbing him. She'd said it herself, she didn't lift weights and she couldn't have lifted him.

Then again, could adrenaline account for that extra strength? But then, wouldn't there have been blood all over Taylor? Where would she have washed it off? Where had those clothes gone? Wouldn't she have incurred bruises from her encounter with Marco on the bridge? It was unlikely she—or anyone—could have stabbed him without a fight.

She stepped over a crack in the cobble stone path, pausing to look out to the river over the low stonewall. This was a place of history but now all it reminded her of was murder. And now fear that she might not be able to prove Taylor's innocence.

Then again, it wasn't up to her, was it?

A gust of wind brushed past her just as the bushes at the side of the pathway rustled. Likely a squirrel looking for—

A dark figure rushed from the bushes toward her, covered from head to foot in dark clothing. It barreled straight into her, sending her stumbling backwards with the force. When her calves hit the low rock wall, she tipped back with a scream escaping her lungs.

Then she fell over the side.

CHAPTER 11

"ARE you sure you're all right?" Adam said. His deep hazel eyes held such compassion, but she was angry more than anything else.

"I'm fine. Just mad at myself." Margot pushed a wet strand of hair out of her eyes.

He frowned. "What? Why?"

"How did I not see them coming? And my favorite pair of Ralph Lauren flats are gone."

Adam actually laughed at that, but sobered quickly. "I'll buy you another pair. I promise. But do you feel up to telling me what happened?"

Margot shuddered, pulling the blanket more tightly around her wet shoulders and thinking back to the terrifying moment when she'd fallen over the side of the cliff down toward the water. Thankfully, her brain jumped into action and she'd righted herself in the fall in time for the water to accept her pointed feet with a minimal splash and thankfully no rocks.

She'd been lucky, so said the man who'd heard her scream and found the river access ladder. He'd helped her up when she'd surfaced, no worse for wear aside from being cold and missing her favorite shoes.

She explained she was taking a walk—for the moment leaving out her assumptions that had led to the walk—and had suddenly been shoved over the side of the low rock wall by a fast-moving mass in black. She recounted what she could remember. Black hoody. Black knit facemask. Black track pants.

"Anything stand out to you? Logos? Skin color? Height? Build?"

She closed her eyes to walk herself through what she'd seen. "At first I'd assumed they were large, but I think the clothing was actually baggy. When they hit me, it felt more like...I don't know, something bony wrapped in softness."

She opened her eyes at Adam's chuckle. "Want to explain that one?"

"I can't. I mean... Whoever it was came at me like a freight train and carried enough steam to push me over the ledge, but they weren't exactly bulky. Just strong."

Adam took notes in his small notebook. "See anything defining?"

"No," she said with a sigh. "There was no skin showing. They even had gloves on. And everything was black."

"Right." He capped his pen and looked up at her. "Now want to tell me why in the world you were out here by yourself?"

She saw the concern in his gaze and it snagged at something in her heart. Something untouched in a long time. The feeling that came from someone caring—really caring—about you. It was a good feeling, but also a confusing one coming from Adam.

"I…" She swallowed, knowing that it was best to get it all out in the open. "Today in the shop, one of my fifty-pound bags of flour needed to be hoisted up onto the counter. I came in to find Rosie giving Taylor a hard time about not being able to lift it. I had to help her. It was only fifty pounds, Adam. How in the world would a nineteen year old girl who can't lift a fifty-pound bag of flour get a muscled twenty-something man over that railing?" Margot pointed to the bridge for affect.

Adam's eyebrows rose. "Adrenaline—"

"You're really going to blame this all on adrenaline? And then what about the blood? Where is it? And where are her bloody clothes? It just doesn't add up. Can't you see that?"

Adam took in a sharp breath then placed his hand on her arm, guiding her a few feet away from where techs were going over the area combing for any clues as to who could have pushed Margot.

"Don't you think I've thought of all of these things, Marg?" His expression was so serious, she faltered for a reply. "And don't you think I'm working my hardest to get to the bottom of this to clear your niece?" Even as he said it, he looked around to make sure no one was listening.

"I—"

"No." He placed a finger on her lips to silence her. "I believe she's innocent, but I am searching for justice above all. But you've got to let me do my job and I can't do that if I'm worried that you're out there tracing down leads and placing yourself in danger."

"I'm not in dang—"

"What do you call being shoved into the Potomac?"

She opened her mouth then closed it.

"Please, Margot." Adam's eyes bored into hers. "Be careful."

Part of her snatched at the reality that he wasn't telling her to butt out, only to be careful, but the other part saw the haunted look in his eyes. It was probably the same look she'd given Julian when he left for cases. The one that said *I care too much to have you get hurt.*

"I will," was all she could manage.

He held her gaze longer than necessary then stepped back. "You're free to go, Mrs. Durand."

≈

MARGOT GOT home in time to find Taylor raiding the kitchen for a snack. Her eyes grew wide when she took in her disheveled, wet appearance and borrowed muck boots.

"Take a swim, Aunt Margot?"

"Not exactly." She relayed what had happened, again leaving out the reason for her walk, as Taylor's eyes grew to the size of Danishes.

"No way! They went after you? But...but doesn't that like, clear me or something?"

Margot gave her niece a rueful smile. "There's no connection to the case and me being shoved over a wall. What makes you think there is?"

She could tell her question threw her niece for a loop. "I—uh, oh, I don't know. You were...by the bridge, right? The one they found the body below. Made sense that it was about the murder then."

Taylor had recovered, but barely.

"Mind if I watch some TV?"

Margot shook her head. "No. Go ahead. I'm going to work on a new recipe in the kitchen."

"Cool." Taylor grabbed the bowl of popcorn and a diet soda and went to the living room. The sounds of a television sitcom soon floated into the kitchen as Margot leaned up against the counter. After a day in jail and being out on bail, Taylor seemed awfully relaxed about everything. Was her cavalier nature due to the fact that she knew she hadn't done anything wrong, or was it something more...dangerous? A mental disability perhaps?

Margot rubbed her temples. She was jumping to conclusions—ones that involved the thought of her niece being guilty—and that wasn't acceptable. She *knew* the girl. Not well, but she did know her enough to be assured of the fact that she wasn't a psychopathic killer.

She turned her attention to the stack of papers on the counter that contained her notes for a few new recipes she wanted to introduce into the bakery. She moved some aside and noticed that Taylor had left her phone on the counter. She went to pick it up but hesitated. This wasn't the same phone she'd been using before she was arrested...or was it?

Margot turned it over in her hands and frowned. Taylor's other phone had been black but this one was dark blue. With a glance to the entrance of the kitchen, she pressed the home button and the phone flashed to light. One swipe opened the phone and she could see that it looked like any young person's phone. Full of apps and a background photo of the beach.

Another glance to make sure she was alone and Margot pressed the application button for the text messages. She remembered Adam's conversation about not having a connection between Taylor and Marco. Margot had believed it was because there wasn't one, but what if they just couldn't find a trail due to not having all the right information—or the right phone.

Margot was sure they had traced this phone number and all of Taylor's contacts, but she needed to see for herself.

She typed in *Marco* into the messages search bar. Nothing came up.

Then she typed in Lorenzo.

Holding her breath, she pressed enter and waited.

Nothing.

Releasing her breath, she closed the app and put the phone back on the counter. Then, thinking better of it, she walked toward the living room only to stop in the doorway. Taylor was asleep, bowl of popcorn forgotten by her side and the TV blaring.

Margot knew the instant the idea came into her mind that she was going to regret this one way or the other. Either it would work to help prove Taylor's innocence or it could bring up evidence of a connection between Taylor and the crime. Either way, when she slipped noiselessly down the hall to Taylor's room, her motive was justice, not snooping. At least that was what she told herself.

She placed the blue phone on the small bookshelf and turned toward the bed. First she checked under the pillows, then in the drawer, then under the mattress until her hand slid onto something cold, solid, and the shape of a phone.

Heart pounding, Margot looked at the door then pulled the phone out. It slid easily into the palm of her hand and looked identical to the blue phone, differing only in color. No wonder she'd thought it was the same phone.

But why did Taylor have two phones?

Stepping to the door, Margot stuck her head outside and then rushed across the hall to her room. She'd rather be caught in there than in Taylor's room, as long as she had time enough to replace the phone under the mattress.

Then, sitting in her bathroom with the door locked, she pressed the power button. The phone came on. The lock screen picture was of Dillon and Renee. Margot's smile was immediate at seeing the happy, in-love look on her sister's face. How sweet of Taylor to have that on her phone. Scratch that—her second phone.

She swiped right to unlock it, breathing out a sigh of relief when it didn't require a password. This phone was much different than Taylor's other one. It had almost no apps except for one about the stock exchange, a news outlet app, and then a twitter account. The thing that threw Margot off was the lock screen picture. It was of an oilrig in the middle of the ocean. Was this for Taylor to remember her father?

She found the messages icon and tapped it. Many came up, but the names drew Margo's suspicion. Especially the one named, *Honey Bear*.

Tapping on it, she could tell right away that Taylor hadn't written these messages. There was no abbreviated text like Taylor used, and...something caught her attention. The phrase "like a kite caught in a rainstorm" made her catch her breath. That was something Margot had only heard Renee say.

Then the pieces began to slip into place. This was Dillon's phone. She remembered Renee explaining that, when he was on the oilrig, phone service was non-existent most of the time so he often relied on his computer and Wi-Fi to communicate with her. The only explanation was that he'd left his phone at home and Taylor had been using it to text... Who? Who would she text?

Margot scrolled through the contacts but nothing stood out. Then, as she was about to go back to the messages to see what she could find, a text popped up. It only registered a phone number with a local area code for North Bank. Interesting. She memorized the number then pulled down the notifications tab at the top, reading the short message:

MEET ME TONIGHT? <3

MARGOT'S PULSE RACED. She wouldn't risk tipping Taylor off to the fact she'd found the phone by opening—or deleting—the message. As badly as she wanted to, she knew what she had to do.

CHAPTER 12

THE NIGHT WAS quiet though windy as Margot pulled on a black sweatshirt while keeping an ear out for any sound that Taylor was still awake. Or worse yet...sneaking out. Margot hated the thought that she'd have to sneak out to follow her niece, but she'd thought of all of the alternatives and this was the best option.

Adam would have a fit if he knew her plans, but in all reality, a teen—even one over the legal age—entrusted to her care was *her* responsibility. If there had been any indication it had something to do with the case, she would have told him, but it didn't. The heart at the end of the message ensured that.

Just then the faint squeak of a window hinge drew her attention to her own open window. They were almost on opposite sides of the house, but she could still hear the window scraping open and the residual crunch of leaves on the trellis that led up to the window.

Pulse racing, Margot slipped from her room, careful to close her door again, and ran to the door. Slipping outside, she hid in the shadows, thankful for her full black wardrobe, and waited to see where Taylor would go once she was clear of the house.

The girl landed with a light thump and paused, taking in the surrounding area. She looked back up at her window then turned toward the steps that led to the street. Margot followed at a careful distance, watching where she stepped and staying in the shadows where possible.

North Bank wasn't a large town, nor had it ever been scary—even at night. It was filled with small town charm and nice people. This close to Washington, D.C., it was a little bit of an anomaly, but she liked that fact. She could get into the city and see the museums when she wanted without the hectic nature of the city *or* the exorbitant price tag that row houses came with. North Bank suited her just fine.

On a night like tonight though, she wasn't so sure it felt as safe as she'd initially thought. Around every corner lurked the possibility of a murderer. Every car driving past could contain a threat. Even a cat running across her path made her cover her mouth so a scream wouldn't escape.

She felt foolish, but her nerves were on edge following her niece to who knew where to meet some person— presumably a young man—with who knew *what* intent.

Taylor turned up a street Margot recognized. Were they

going to the senior center? Frowning, she followed but kept her distance. When her niece got to the center, she checked her phone—presumably the black one that was actually her father's—and slipped around the side of the building. The back side met the sloping hill of a cliff and Margot elected to take the upper ground where bushes would cover her presence. Though that meant she needed to be even more careful to not make noise that would attract Taylor's attention.

Her focus was so intent that, by the time she got close enough to Taylor, another person had arrived.

Lorenzo!

Margot pressed her lips together to keep in her gasp of surprise, but then again, was it really that surprising? She had known Lorenzo was mixed up in this some how, but *how* in the world had he gotten involved with Taylor, let alone gotten her phone number? Margot had been with her ever since she arrived—well, almost.

"What's going on?" Taylor said, stepping closer to the boy than Margot approved of.

"You texted me. Said you wanted to meet." His voice was low, the hint of an accent still lingering there. If Margot remembered correctly, he had come over from Italy with his mother, who was back there now for the summer.

"Um, no," Taylor said, her hands now clasping his, "*You* texted me, you dork." She giggled and went up on tiptoes to give him a quick kiss.

Margot felt her blood boil. This girl was never leaving the house again.

"No," he said, pulling back. In the dim light from the streetlight in the parking lot, Margot could see the frown on his face. "*You* texted me."

"No—" Taylor was frowning now, looking confused.

"Whatever..." He shrugged, wrapping his arms around her and pulling her close. "I guess whoever texted who, this was a good idea."

Margot rolled her eyes. She was about to bust this little meeting up, when something in their conversation drew out her suspicion. Neither one of them admitted to having texted the other. Why would either of them lie? And, from what she'd seen on Taylor's second phone, she *hadn't* texted him. Why would Lorenzo lie about texting her? He obviously was happy to see her. It made no sense.

A chill raced up her spine. Something wasn't right about this meeting.

Her gaze shot back to the couple then to the surrounding area shadowed in darkness. The back wall of the center was blank, no windows or doors, then she looked the way they'd come in. Nothing but the faint light filtering in from the parking lot's street light. Then, with a shallow breath, she looked to the other side of the building. It was much darker there, covered by a tall oak tree and mostly hidden from light by the bulk of the building.

Movement caught her eye. There was definitely something—or someone—there. Heart hammering in her chest, Margot sneaked around the bush, closer to the couple but also to get a better view. It was so dark she couldn't be certain, but it looked like an arm holding a gun had snaked around the corner.

Now her palms were sweating and she was positive she was hyperventilating. The couple was too distracted to notice, but Margot was positive they were the killer's targets.

Margot felt the press of an invisible hand on her back pushing her forward to do something. She had to time it just right, but she would have no indication when the killer would strike. Then again, if she didn't act soon, it could be too late.

In a rush of adrenaline, Margot jumped forward, off the higher ground and toward the couple, yelling, "Get down!"

The minute she connected with both Lorenzo and Taylor, sending them toppling down, a gunshot rang out through the night.

"What—" Lorenzo cried out.

"Ahhh," Taylor screamed.

Shaking, Margot grabbed Taylor. "It's me, Tay. It's Margot."

Her niece stopped fighting but Lorenzo jumped up,

looking down at Taylor and then, before any of them could say anything, he ran off and disappeared into the night.

∾

Margot placed a hot cup of tea on the coffee table in front of her niece and then handed the other to Adam.

"Thanks." He looked between the women, his frustration evident. "My officers didn't find the shooter—only one bullet casing and an unfortunate tree that seemed to be the recipient of the kill shot."

Taylor flinched at the word kill.

"Adam—"

"I should have taken you both back to the station for questioning," he cut in, the tension in his shoulders easing only slightly, "but the chief said you'd been through enough for one night."

Margot turned her gaze to her niece. Tears streaked her face and a light bruise marred her pretty features, but thankfully, that was the worst of it.

"It could have been much worse," Margot said.

Adam nodded and turned to look at the girl as well.

"I'm sorry," Taylor whispered, staring down into the cup.

"Taylor," Margot cut in, cradling her own cup of tea to eat

away the coldness that seemed to sink to her core. "You've got to tell us what's going on. No more of this bottling things up and keeping secrets. You were almost killed tonight." The words sent more icy shivers down her spine.

Another tear streaked down Taylor's cheek and she sniffed, wiping it away with the back of her hand.

"I care about you. I just… I guess I don't know what to do. Maybe I should just have your mom come out and—"

"No." Taylor looked up, first at Margot then to Adam. "I'll tell you everything."

Margot met her gaze.

"Please—just don't call Renee. Not yet."

Margot felt somehow dishonest for threatening to call Taylor's mother, but the suggestion had gotten her the results she'd hoped for.

"Level with me, Taylor." Adam's tone left no room for argument and she saw the girl deflate a little. "How do you know Lorenzo?"

"Okay." She wiped her eyes again, then steeled herself with a deep breath, "When Dad told me that I was coming out to North Bank for the summer, I wasn't happy. I mean, you can guess why, right?"

"Yes," Margot agreed.

"Getting up at three in the morning every day is such a bummer. Anyway, I wasn't really into it all, but I thought, you know, that I could make the best of it. So...I kind of borrowed my dad's phone and got on a dating app. I put in the North Bank area and ended up meeting someone on the app."

"Lorenzo," Margot guessed, feeling Adam's gaze on her.

"Yeah. And, Aunt Margot, no matter what you think, you're wrong. He's a nice guy. We hit it off and started chatting via text. It actually made me excited to come out here, you know?"

Margot bit her cheek to keep from saying anything. They needed to hear the whole truth before she gave her two cents.

"Go on," Margot said.

"I honestly don't know what happened, though. When we went to that Italian restaurant that first night, the waiter —Marco—slipped me a note. He said he knew Lorenzo and wanted to meet with me about him. I thought... I don't know, I thought he knew where I could meet up with Lorenzo because I hadn't heard back from him since I'd landed. So I went to talk with him..."

Margot leaned forward, her stomach clenching. "Why did he attack you?"

"That's just it. When I went back there, he was all flirty. I mean, yeah, he's handsome and I flirted a little too, but I didn't get why he'd do that if he was friends with Lorenzo and knew we were texting. But then he asked me where 'it' was. I had *no* idea what he was talking about. I told him that, but he didn't believe me. He said Lorenzo said I would give it to him."

"He didn't say what it was he was looking for?" Adam interjected.

"No!" Taylor blew out a stream of air and shook her head. "Sorry, he just made me really mad. I told him I had no idea what he was talking about and that's when he grabbed me and shook me as if I'd drop it loose or something." She rolled her eyes. "That's when you came in Aunt Margot—thankfully."

"Then he came back outside to what? Convince you again?" Adam's hazel eyes focused intently on the girl.

"I guess." Taylor took a sip of her tea.

Margot considered the facts. Replaying the scene in her mind, she tried to remember the exact situation when she burst into the janitor's closet. She had assumed they were locked in an amorous embrace, but it could have been like Taylor explained.

But that didn't explain how Taylor's prints had gotten on the knife.

"Did you use a knife at the restaurant?" Even as she asked the question, she met Adam's gaze.

"Margot..." he cautioned.

"A knife? No, I don't think—" Taylor frowned, her eyes

129

searching the ceiling to remember. "Wait. I didn't use one, but I did unroll the silverware from the napkin and I'm sure I touched it—" She stopped, her eyes widening. "I *did* touch it. Oh my goodness, do you think…" She looked at Adam and Margot felt her gaze trail to him as well.

He let out a sigh and nodded. "It was confirmed that the knife was from Antonio's."

Taylor's eyes grew large, but Margot cut her off before she could say anything. "Tay, honey, I know that you didn't kill that man, but you kept so much from me—from the police. A whole different phone and a connection to North Bank. Why didn't you say something?"

Taylor cringed, cupping her tea between both hands. "I was just afraid I'd get Lorenzo in trouble. He's working so hard to get his accounting degree and…" She shrugged. "I like him."

"So that was him you were meeting with at the senior center?"

Taylor nodded and Margot let out a breath. Adam nodded in her peripheral vision.

"All right," he said, running his hand along his pants. "That's enough for tonight. Why don't you two ladies get some rest?" He met Margot's gaze. "I've stationed an officer outside the house for tonight, just in case."

Taylor put her tea down and rubbed her arms.

"Thank you," Margot said, standing. "Why don't you go on to bed, honey?"

Taylor nodded and left for her room as Adam stood as well.

"What did I tell you about being careful?" His gaze was hard and unblinking.

"I know," Margot clutched her arms, feeling cold as well. "It was foolish but I didn't think the text had anything to do with the case."

"Right." Adam didn't sound convinced. The silence stretched out until he spoke up again. "Look, I shouldn't do this, but...I'll be going by Antonio's again tomorrow to review his security tapes. Maybe something will jog your memory. Want to join me?"

She'd been prepared for a scolding but instead she'd been invited to join him on case business?

She smiled up at him, feeling hopeful. She would find something on those tapes—she had to.

"Well, Detective Eastwood, it looks like the bakery is going to be closed tomorrow."

CHAPTER 13

EVEN THOUGH SHE had the luxury of sleeping in, Margot's body didn't think too highly of that. She hadn't woken up at three, but five o'clock rolled around and, despite her exhaustion, she couldn't convince herself to go back to sleep.

Rising, she dressed and did her morning exercises, riding her stationary bike and going through the motions for her next Krav Maga class. Then she showered and decided it was a good morning to make crêpes.

Soon, the smells of Nutella, strawberries and cream, and apple cinnamon-filled crêpes scented the air.

"It smells so good in here," Taylor said, coming into the kitchen with her hair in a messy ponytail and still in her PJs.

"Thought you might enjoy some crêpes."

"You're seriously the best, Aunt Marg!"

Margot handed her niece a cup of coffee and a plate, and soon they were both enjoying the sweet crêpes.

"What's going on today?" Taylor asked, looking a little wary. Was she wondering if she had to go back to the police station?

During her early morning, Margot had thought long and hard about what she would do with Taylor while she and Adam were at Antonio's. It felt foolish thinking of her niece like she was a child needing babysitting, but it was more than that. So far, despite her honesty the night before, she still had kept things from them. In order to keep her safe, and above suspicion, Margot had decided something.

"I'm taking you to hang out with Bentley today."

"Bentley—wait, that old guy who always orders the caramel pecan cinnamon roll and a cup of coffee?"

Margot frowned at her use of 'old guy,' but nodded. "Yes. He's a very nice *elderly* gentleman and I'm sure he can put you to good use at the senior center."

The young girl frowned. Was she thinking about the night before?

"Don't worry," Margot was quick to add. "I talked with Adam and he's going to have an officer accompany you for the day."

"Am I in trouble?"

Margot almost laughed. Did she mean aside from the murder charge? Then again, it was good that she was so confident in her own innocence. Margot was too, increasingly so as more of the facts began to line up.

"Just trust me on this. It'll be good for you to spend some time with Bentley and you'll be protected."

She nodded, taking a bite of a Nutella-filled crêpe. "Hey, Aunt Margot?"

Margot stopped collecting the dirty dishes from the table to look down at her niece. "Yes?"

"Thanks." Her cheeks colored. "For, you know, believing in me. Renee thinks the worst of me all the time. I think she would have freaked out if she were here, but you've been really cool about all of this."

Margot wasn't sure 'cool' was the term to describe how she'd felt, but she nodded and accepted the girl's thanks. "You're welcome. But, Taylor, can I tell you something?" Taylor nodded and Margot sat back down, leaning against the table.

"Despite what you may think, your mom loves you. A lot. And I'm not just saying that because she's my sister. When we have our calls, she always spends at least half of them talking about you and Dillon. She cares so much for you both. And I think you and I both know she would never try to replace your mother."

"Yeah…" Taylor looked down at her plate. "I know she cares. I guess…I don't know. It's easier pushing her away, just in case…"

Margot leaned forward. "In case you lose her too?"

When Taylor looked up, she was shocked to see tears in her niece's eyes. "Yeah. It hurt bad enough losing one mom, I just don't want to lose another."

Margot reached out and placed her hand over the girl's. "I know, sweetie, but don't you think by holding back you're missing out on something? Like a second chance at having a mom again?"

Taylor sniffed and wiped under her eyes. "Maybe you're right."

Words bubbled up to the surface, but Margot held them back. Taylor didn't need someone telling her what to do, she needed to decide it for herself.

"We leave in half an hour. Think you'll be ready?"

As if grateful to have a chance to slip away, Taylor nodded and padded down the hall to her room while Margot cleaned up the dishes.

They left, Margot noting the plainclothes officer who followed them, and arrived at the senior center right on time. As if he'd been waiting for them, Bentley came out side. "Hiya, Taylor," he said, nodding to her niece.

"Hi," she said, looking oddly shy.

"Listen," he said to Taylor as she got out of the car, "we're going to get along just fine. I promise I won't bore you with old stories...that is, unless you'd be interested in hearing about some of the cases I tried."

"Cases?" Taylor's interest was piqued.

"I was a lawyer," Bentley said with a grin.

"That'd be cool."

"Good. Talking with you will get me out of the next fundraiser Kim Penberthy has planned."

Margot leaned forward. "*Another* fundraiser?"

Bentley shook his head. "Yeah. Figures. But this time, I'm keeping track." He patted his pocket where she could see the top of a notebook sticking out. "No one's going to pull the wool over old Bentley's eyes. Come on, kid, let's go."

"I'll be back in an hour, two tops," Margot said, then rolled up the window.

Bentley waved a hand at her in farewell and she pulled out of the parking lot, glad to see the officer's car parked there. She breathed out a sigh and thought of her conversation with Bentley that morning. He'd drilled her on what she'd found out about the missing money, but the pieces still weren't there. She needed to talk to Lorenzo, but after last night, she had a feeling he was laying low if the police hadn't already caught up with him. Then again, what could they hold him on? What was his part in all of this? Aside from his connection to Taylor, of course.

Then again... Her eyes narrowed as she pulled up in front of the police station. Neither Taylor or Lorenzo had admitted to texting one another. Was it possible the texts were fake? But who were they from?

A tap on her window nearly made her scream until she saw Adam's smiling face.

"A bit jumpy this morning, huh?" he said when she rolled down the window.

"If your niece had been the one shot at last night, you'd be jumpy too."

His expression sobered and he circled around to get in the passenger seat.

"What are you doing?"

"Mind if we take your car?" His grin returned and he held up the two coffees. "Had a feeling you'd need another one of these."

She let his easygoing demeanor sooth her and she accepted the coffee from him.

"To Antonio's," Adam said, holding up his coffee as if pointing the way. She rolled her eyes at his obvious good mood.

"How are you so awake?"

"It's all an illusion," he said, a smile in his voice. "That and caffeine. Does wonders on the mood."

As if to prove his theory she took a long sip of her coffee. "Black. Just the way I like it."

"I know."

The familiar statement caused something to stir in her, but she pushed it aside. They were hopefully going to get some answers today while at Antonio's. They had to, because the case against Taylor, while not error-proof, didn't offer many alternatives.

"Answer me this," she said, hoping he would be able to. "Have you talked to Lorenzo?"

"Business as usual, huh, Marge?" She smiled at the nickname only Adam used for her. It had annoyed her to no end at first, but now—though she'd never admit it to him—it had grown on her. "Can't a man have a moment's peace in a car ride?"

"No. Now spill it."

Sighing as if giving up, Adam straightened in his seat. "We can't find him. We've checked the apartment rented out in his name, I talked with Antonio on the phone last night— poor guy, definitely woke him up—and canvassed his neighborhood. No one knows where he is."

"Do you suspect him?"

"I'm requisitioning his phone records, should have something this morning. I also put in an order for your niece's *other* phone. I'm not sure what to think of our boy

Lorenzo. He's involved—if only by association with Taylor—but beyond that I don't know."

"He was doing accounting for the senior center."

"What?"

She filled Adam in on her conversation with Bentley and then Eve, explaining the phone call she'd made to the professor.

"So, not the brightest candle in the class but is he smart enough to 'cook the books,' if I can use that term?"

"It doesn't feel right," Margot said, drumming her fingers on the steering wheel as they pulled into Antonio's nearly empty parking lot. She turned to look at Adam when they'd come to a stop. "I don't know him, so I could be wrong, but from what I've heard people say about him, he's a good kid, going to night school to become an accountant and working part time for his uncle. Aside from being friends with the murder victim and dating the suspected murderer, I'm not sure how he fits into all of this."

Adam nodded slowly then put his hand on the door handle. "Let me think about it."

She climbed out and followed him into the empty restaurant. The only person she saw was Antonio sitting in one of the booths with sun streaming in through the window. He rose when they entered and came toward them, his smile lacking the brightness it usually did.

"Hello, *mia bella*." He kissed her on the cheek. "Detective."

"We'd like to take another look at those security tapes."

"*Si*. Right. Of course. This way."

Margot sent Adam a worried look, but he didn't seem to notice, or he ignored her. Poor Antonio.

"I am saddened by the absence of my nephew. It is not like him. He is a good boy," Antonio said as they walked down the hall to his office. He was a man who wore his heart on his sleeve, but still, it hurt to see him so upset.

"I'm so sorry, Antonio."

He waved a hand and ushered them into the room. "Here are the cameras. They face the parking lot, the door, and one view of the cash register. I had them installed after a robbery several years ago."

"Thanks, Antonio. I can run this if you have things to do."

The man nodded and shuffled out of the office, shoulders drooping.

"Poor man," Margot said.

"Yes, but I'm not so sure *he* isn't involved."

"What?" Margot was shocked Adam could even think Antonio was somehow involved in all of this.

"Margot…" Adam's tone held a warning. "You can't look at anyone in a case as a friend. They're all suspects."

"Am I a suspect?" she challenged, meeting his gaze and sure her cheeks were flushed at the heat of passion she felt for the fact that Antonio was innocent.

"No." He held her gaze for a long time and looked like he wanted to say more, but the screen flickered and drew their attention back to the monitor.

"That's the table we sat at that night," Margot observed. "The one Antonio's in now."

Adam sat down and began pressing buttons and turning dials. "Interesting," he said to himself.

"What?"

"When we were here last, we focused on the parking lot. We saw Marco come toward Taylor, saw her push him away, and that was that. I didn't even *think* to watch you *in* the restaurant. I'm sure a tech did, but do you mind watching through it?"

Her confidence boosted at his belief she might see something they missed, she nodded and leaned over to watch. He slowed the tape down when one camera picked up her car pulling in. They ran through them being seated at their table and then he let it play through.

Margot watched intently, seeing Marco come up to the table several times, even catching when he slipped the note to Taylor, and then she saw Taylor bolt from the table after slipping a note into her pocket. Next, she walked past two tables and—

"Wait," she said, peering closer at the screen.

"What? What do you see?"

Realization washed through Margot as the pieces began to fit together like a perfect puzzle. She knew who had murdered Marco—but could she prove it?

CHAPTER 14

MARGOT'S HEART raced as Adam, driving her car, sped from Antonio's restaurant toward the senior center. She couldn't exactly explain the feeling of needing to rush to Taylor, but something told her that the killer wasn't about to sit by and wait for them to discover their identity.

"Are you sure about this, Marge?" Adam said, his hands clutching the steering wheel as if his racing through the streets was the most natural thing in the world.

"I'm positive."

They careened around a corner. They were almost to the center now.

"We don't exactly have proof."

She tapped her foot on the carpeted floor. It was true. Though the surveillance tape didn't show the killer's face, it had shown enough for Margot to recognize who had taken the knife from their table and then slipped out the front door.

Adam shot into the parking lot and skidded to a stop out front. This was it. The moment of truth.

"I want you to wait in the car while I—"

"Absolutely not."

He looked at her as if she'd lost her mind. "You're not going in there, Margot."

"Yes. I am." Her gaze left no room for argument. "I've got to get to my niece. I'll be fine."

His shoulders slumped. "Let me radio my officer first."

Hand on the door, she waited.

"Yes, sir?" came a crackly reply.

Adam nodded toward her and she slipped from the car. She knew Adam wouldn't be far behind, but she was more concerned with finding Taylor. They needed to get her to safety before the killer made her their next target.

The recreational space at the front was almost empty, only a few seniors occupying the chairs around the perimeter, and she raced toward Bentley's favorite spot. Sliding on the slick floor, she rushed around the corner and came to a halt. It was empty.

Where were they?

She ran through the logical areas they could be. They

weren't in the rec space, and they weren't in the reading room she'd passed on the way to this spot...then she heard voices at the end of the hallway where the office was. She couldn't make out the words, but the tone was harsh. It sent a thrill of fear through Margot.

Sliding out her phone, she shot a text to Adam and then followed the sound.

"I—I don't get it. What's going on?"

Margot's heart shot to her throat. It was Taylor's voice, thin and high.

"Come on, Taylor," Bentley said. "Just stand next to me."

"That's right," a woman's voice said. "Stand right there."

Margot's stomach clenched. Just as she'd expected. It was Kim Penberthy.

"Now if you'll just—"

"I don't think so, Kim," Margot said, coming around the corner into a possibly hostile scene.

Kim stood next to a desk, a silver revolver in her hand aimed at Bentley and Taylor.

Oh, God! Keep them safe!

"Isn't that just like you, Margot. Sticking your nose into everyone's business."

Margot fought the urge to lunge to get the gun away from

the crazy woman. It would do no good to startle her, since her finger rested lightly on the trigger.

"Just hold on there, Kim," she said, raising her hands in a defensive position. "No one's going to stop you. Just do what you need to do."

"What I *need* to do? I *need* for this to all be over." She blew out a frustrated breath. "I needed it to be over with Marco's death. That was the plan—and the plan is *always right*."

Margot started to feel sick. Kim was obviously at a tipping point; if she wasn't already over the edge, she'd be there soon. It wasn't good that she was talking so openly about the situation. Then again, if she could get her to confess... But that would only work if they weren't killed. Where was Adam?

"*You* killed that guy?" Taylor said. Margot shot her a look, but she ignored it. "Why did you blame me?"

Kim shook her head and looked down at the papers spread out before her. In the shuffling, Margot picked up a noise behind her in the hall. Her heart hammered in her chest as she caught a glimpse of something—more like someone—in the reflection of the picture hanging up behind Kim.

It had to be Adam. That or her eyes were playing tricks on her. This was it—her chance.

"She did kill that poor young man," Margot said with

more boldness than she felt. "Because she was being blackmailed."

Kim's head snapped up. The gun lowered and Kim turned it toward Margot. The feeling of its deadly weight pressed against Margot's chest, but she pushed her fear down. She had to focus.

"What do you know about it?"

"I didn't, until I saw the tapes at Antonio's—the ones that show you stealing the knife from Taylor's place setting. Then it all just fell together."

"Oh? Why don't you enlighten me, if you're so smart, Margot Durand."

Hoping it would buy them some time, she pressed forward with what she'd put together. "It started when Eve suggested Lorenzo to you as an accountant for the senior center fundraisers. You're too smart of a woman to just take someone's suggestion, so I have a feeling you followed up on Lorenzo and found out what I did—he wasn't the best in the class by a long shot. I don't know exactly, but I have a feeling you convinced him to let you help him. He probably needed the money and you were all too eager to get your hands on the accounting sheets."

Kim's expression hardened. "Go on, if you're so smart to think you know it all."

"It gets a little murky for me here, but I have a feeling Marco—being the helpful friend that he was—started looking into the discrepancies Lorenzo thought he was seeing. Marco saw an opportunity to blackmail you. I think he wanted to talk to Taylor that night at Antonio's because he was convinced Lorenzo had given her proof of the embezzling. If he got it from Taylor, then he could use it against you." Margot shifted, sneaking a glance at Taylor to see that she was as baffled by all of this as Bentley was. "I'm sure the phone records—and someone tech savvy— will find that the texts Marco got weren't from Lorenzo at all, but from you."

Kim leveled her gaze at Margot, but didn't interrupt. But Margot needed Kim to admit to it or else it was all just conjecture.

"If I remember correctly, you used to work at a phone tech company before you married our illustrious mayor. Maybe you learned a few tricks there. Anyway, I think after that, it's pretty clear. You lured Marco to the bridge —probably with another false text—and used the knife you'd stolen from Taylor's place setting to kill him."

Kim laughed derisively. "Sounds a little too perfect, doesn't it, Marg? Besides, you can't prove I was at Antonio's."

The hard look in the woman's eyes told Margot she somehow knew they couldn't identify her. "But you made a mistake, Kim." The woman shifted, her eyes narrowing. "When you saw me at the senior center the other day, you said you'd seen me *three* times in a week. I didn't think anything of it, but then I realized you had seen me at Antonio's restaurant—that was the third time."

"You're too smart for your own good."

"I'm right, aren't I?" Margot pressed.

"You're right," Kim said, nodding. "But no one will ever hear the truth—from any of you."

Suddenly, Kim shifted, taking a step around the desk and coming toward Margot. "We're going to take a little walk—"

"Stop right there, Kim Penberthy."

Margot gasped as Adam came into the room, his gun trained on the woman. Noise outside the window drew a quick glance and she saw more officers, guns out and trained on Kim.

"You," she said to Margot through clenched teeth. "It would have worked except you couldn't keep your nose out of it." With a huff, she dropped her hand. Adam moved forward in an instant, taking the gun from her and calling in another officer to cuff Kim and read the rights.

Margot turned toward Taylor and Bentley, grasping her niece in a tight hug. "I'm so glad you guys are all right."

"Dang, Aunt Marg, you just faced down a killer."

Despite the scare, Bentley had a small smile on his face. "I knew you'd solve all of this. I just knew it."

CHAPTER 15

BRILLIANT SUNLIGHT SHONE on the small round tables Margot had forced Adam to drag out from her storage shed. They now sat behind the shop, waiting to invite patrons brave enough to tackle the brisk wind.

Bentley, Taylor, Lorenzo, Adam, and Margot all sat around one such table, sipping coffee, eating pastries, and tugging their coats a little closer.

"You said summer was coming, didn't you, Aunt Marg?"

Margot shook her head, smiling at her niece with her hand wrapped around Lorenzo's. "Eventually."

"She's right, you know," Bentley said. "The sun always comes out. Just takes a little time."

They sat in amiable silence for a few minutes before Taylor stood, Lorenzo following her lead. "We're going for a walk along the byway. That okay?"

Margot looked between the two. So much had transpired in the last few days, but she knew she couldn't keep Taylor under lock and key every hour of every day.

"Sure, just be back by three. We're leaving then to pick Renee up from the airport."

"I remember," Taylor said. "It'll be nice to see Mom."

At the word 'mom,' Margot felt tears in her eyes but she held them back, pressing her lips closed.

"Thank you, Mrs. Durand," Lorenzo said. "I'll watch out for her."

"And you'll be on your best behavior," Adam added with a stern look. The young man paled and nodded. Margot watched as they took off down the walkway toward Miller's Bridge hand in hand, a smile on her lips.

"Can you believe it?" Bentley said.

Margot laughed and looked at him. "What?"

"Just...all of this. And there they go, happy as two lovers can be."

"It was a bit of a whirlwind, but I'm glad it's over now," Margot agreed.

"Speaking of over," Bentley stood, taking his coffee cup with him. "I'm going to go harass Rosie for some more coffee."

He shuffled inside and Margot turned to look at Adam. "You're quiet."

His hand rested around his nearly empty cup, but he didn't meet her gaze for a long time. When he did, there was an unreadable expression in his eyes.

"Margot, you gave me the scare of a lifetime."

She swallowed, remembering the face-off with Kim only a few days previous.

"She's behind bars now. I'm safe."

He shrugged. "True. Once we found the text messages she'd sent to Marco, Lorenzo, and Taylor, her case fell into place. We've got several witnesses placing her at Antonio's as well. I still can't believe she was funneling money from the senior center fundraisers into her husband's campaign. But she could have killed you."

Margot felt ice flood her veins. "But she didn't."

"True, but still…"

"She had many chances to do that—like when she was going to murder Lorenzo and blame Taylor that night behind the senior center, but God didn't allow it."

"I know," he said, leaning forward and dropping his hand on top of hers on the metal table. "I just worry about you. Julian would come back and haunt me if I let anything happen to you."

She smiled, shaking her head. "He would be thankful that I have a good friend like you to solve mysteries with."

Adam grinned, leaning back in his chair. "Speaking of mysteries—how did you know about the connection between Kim and Lorenzo? That the boy wasn't involved."

Margot swallowed and looked away.

"You totally guessed," Adam said, incredulous.

"Can I blame my gut?" She laughed. "When I realized it was Kim in that tape from Antonio's, I started to work back in my mind. She fit into every scenario. She works out a lot so she's strong—strong enough to haul a dead body over Miller's Bridge and strong enough to barrel into me and push me over into the river. Plus, she's always had her hand in the mayor's campaigns and when I saw her at Antonio's asking him to cater a big party, like one for a mayoral election win, I got suspicious."

"But still…that was a leap."

She shrugged. "I knew Taylor was innocent. So once I heard Bentley talking about how Kim was part of the fundraising committee—and her mess-up about how many times she'd seen me that week—I knew that she was the one behind it all. Her husband stood to gain a lot, but she stood to gain more as his wife. Besides, with Marco running "all those errands" and obviously having money like Antonio had said, it made me think he had more going on the side than just a busboy job."

"Still, you took a risk."

"I did." She nodded in agreement. "But, Adam, just like you won't sit on the sidelines when you know that there's a bad guy out there, I couldn't sit by and do nothing when I knew Taylor was innocent."

He opened his mouth to speak but then closed it, his frown deepening.

"What, Detective Eastwood?"

The corner of his mouth quirked. "I just don't like the thought of you being in danger."

His words reminded her of Julian. He'd always been so protective. But there was a truth that she'd always held on to when she thought about her husband being in harm's way and she felt the urge to share that with Adam now.

"Adam, we can't live our lives afraid. You don't do that when you charge into a heated situation and I couldn't let fear rule me from stepping in to help my niece and Bentley. I have to trust that God will protect me and give me the strength to stand up and speak when the time is right."

"I just wish that guns weren't involved when the time was right."

She couldn't help her smile. "I'd prefer they be left out of the situation as well."

He held her gaze for a moment longer, then nodded once. "I understand. Just promise me you'll always be careful."

"I wouldn't be anything else."

"Who want's more coffee?" Bentley said, coming back out to the patio with a carafe in one hand and an éclair in the other.

"You're going to eat me out of house and bakery," Margot said, holding up her cup.

The older man smiled and wagged his eyebrows. "Probably, but what a way to go."

They all shared in a laugh and Margot sat back, enjoying the warmth of the sun on her back and the warmth of the company that surrounded her. Just like Bentley had said, the sun always did come out—just like the truth. Sometimes it just took a little time and a little investigating.

~

DESSERTS AND DECEPTION

CHAPTER 1

MARGOT DURAND DRUMMED her fingers on the steering wheel as she maneuvered her car into position in the airport pickup zone. It was growing dark and she hoped that Tamera's flight hadn't been delayed. Margot hadn't thought to check it before she left North Bank for Ronald Reagan Airport near Washington, D.C.

The sound of classical music wound through her scattered thoughts. She was tired. It had been an early morning—a baker's morning, as she liked to call them—and she was considering, once again, hiring an assistant. She had the overhead and the fact was, if she *did* hire someone competent enough, her mornings wouldn't have to be quite so early. But the fact of the matter was that she was a tough boss to work for. She demanded perfection of herself and any assistant would have to be strong enough to put up with that.

Spotting Tamera, she pulled her car to the curb and

hopped out, thoughts of hiring an assistant pushed to the back of her mind as she embraced her best friend.

"You're back!"

Tamera laughed and pulled back to look at Margot. "You look tired."

"And you look tan."

Tamera positively glowed, her smile widening as her blush deepened. "We spent quite a bit of time on the beach."

"Good for you," Margot said. She leaned down and picked up her friend's suitcase.

"I can get that."

"Nonsense," Margot said, popping the trunk of the car. "Hop on in. It's way too hot out here."

Tamera agreed and slipped into the passenger's seat as Margot made her way back behind the wheel. She pulled into traffic and soon they were heading down 395 toward North Bank, Virginia, and their small, historical hometown.

"Gosh, it's good to be back."

"You know, some people actually prefer vacations to real life." Margot laughed at the look her friend gave her.

"I love my store and being away from the Craft Boutique

for two weeks just about killed me." Tamera sighed. "Speaking of, can we stop by?"

Margot snuck a glance at her friend. "You're not serious."

"I am."

"You just got back!"

"And my store has been closed for two weeks. *Two* whole weeks, Marg. That's a long time. I...I miss it."

Margot couldn't help her grin. "I suppose I understand. I don't remember the last time I left the *Pâtisserie* for that long." *Or at all.* She added the need for a vacation to her mental to-do list.

An image of the *The Parisian Pâtisserie* filled Margot's mind. Her little shop sat along a row of others like it, their back doors looking out over the Potomac River and their entrances facing the main, cobbled street of North Bank.

Margot's bakery boasted all the goodness of a French bakery mixed with traditional American baked goods to please everyone. The shop's pale yellow exterior fit in with the bright colors of the other shops, but inside, she'd decorated with an eye toward a true French bakery as best she could.

It would be difficult to leave her shop for that long, just as it would be difficult to hire someone else.

"What's on your mind, friend?" Tamera's softly asked question broke into Margot's thoughts.

"Sorry. I just…I had lunch with Adam the other day and—"

"You *did,* did you?"

Margot sent her friend a look. "It was just lunch. We do that all the time."

"Ever since you and he became reacquainted at the end of spring, you've been seeing much more of one another. I've noticed. That's all."

Margot thought of the case her friend was talking of. Her niece, Taylor, had been accused of murdering a young man who'd been new to town. She shivered just at the memories.

"We're *friends,*" she said, emphasizing the word, "and friends have lunch together now and again."

"All I'm saying is don't close yourself off to…more."

Margot wasn't even going to give Tamera the courtesy of answering that. "Anyway, he said that I should consider hiring someone to help me at the bakery."

"What happened to Rosie?"

"Oh, no, I've still got Rosie." Margot smiled. "I'll never let her go."

"She's like a rare jewel, that's for sure," Tamera agreed.

"He was saying for the baking part."

"Oh." Margot caught Tamera's nod out of the corner of

her eye. "But that's a pretty personal thing. Right? I mean…it means sharing your recipes and stuff like that."

"Yes." Margot had thought through all of these things multiple times. "I can't get away from the fact that it would be great to have someone to fall back on. A way that I could keep from closing the shop every time I get sick or want to take a day off."

"I can't believe you've made it this long without help."

"You have."

"Yes." Tamera nodded. "But I have a different clientele. And my stock keeps."

"True. But I did have help at one point. You remember Casey, right? But then she went off to grad school and I slipped back into old habits. Thankfully, my ability to pay the bills doesn't revolve around the bakery, but still…" The money she'd received when her husband had been killed in the line of duty, or so the reports said, was well invested. She would be fine to retire any moment she wanted to, but the bakery was something special to her. More than a paycheck, it was a passion.

"I understand. But I'm inclined to agree with Secret Agent Man."

"Don't call him that," Margot said with a smile.

"He's got a point. And think of it this way, you're not just helping yourself, you're helping someone else."

Margot let go of the breath she'd been holding and exited the freeway. Turning toward town, she thought through what her friend had said. It was a good point. There were plenty of people out there who needed jobs. Maybe she was being selfish by not hiring someone.

"Good point, Tam. Maybe it's time to start looking for the right person to hire." She turned onto a side street.

"Hey, where are we going? You promised to take me to my shop!"

"And I will," Margot said, flashing her a devious smile, "but first we're stopping by Claytons."

Tamera let out a girlish giggle. "I have *missed* Claytons. Let's go!"

Margot relaxed back into her seat, finally feeling some peace in her heart. Two of her good friends thought hiring someone was a good idea, and she couldn't ignore that. But now it was time to put thoughts of work aside and focus on what was truly important in this moment.

Ice cream.

$\sim$

"THAT WAS SO GOOD," Tamera said, clutching at her flat stomach. "I'm going to have to take an extra-long run in the morning."

"Does that mean I get to take you *home* now? To that handsome husband of yours?"

Tamera laughed. "Not a chance. To my shop we go."

Margot shook her head but put the car in gear, turning down the street that would take them toward the Craft Boutique.

"Did you tell Hubby you wouldn't be home right away?"

"Yep," Tamera said, the smile evident even in one word. "He actually came back two days ago and will be working late. I assume he'll be getting home about the time I do."

"He's been working a lot, huh?"

"He's a trial lawyer in D.C. What do you expect?"

Her friend's words were laced with something Margot couldn't put her finger on. "How was the vacation?"

"Perfect. No, better than perfect. It was so relaxing. Marg, it's what I always imagined a honeymoon could be."

"So it was worth the wait?"

Tamera laughed, the sound low and booming in the small car. "In more ways than one. Part of me wishes I could have taken the time off when we first got married. I mean, the three days in Nantucket were great right after the wedding, but *this* was the honeymoon I had wanted. George seemed to love it too."

Margot remembered her friend's absence at the end of

spring that year. She'd missed almost all of the controversy surrounding Taylor's visit, but thankfully, she'd come back in time to meet Margot's sister Renee.

Margot pulled her car into a parking space in front of the boutique, thankful for the later hour, which meant almost no traffic on Front Street.

"You're finally back, eh?"

Margot nearly jumped out of her skin. "Mrs. Henderson. I didn't see you there."

The older woman stood with one hand shoved into the pocket of her jeans and the other wrapped tightly around a leash, at the end of which was a portly corgi. Its tail wagged even as the woman frowned at Tamera and Margot.

"Hello, Phyllis," Tamera said, smiling as if Phyllis Henderson's frown was anything but. "Nice night for a walk, eh?"

The woman grunted and kept walking. Margot watched her go, shaking her head. "I swear she does nothing but spy on people."

"She runs The Pet Depot, silly," Tamera said with a grin.

"You I know what I mean."

"I do. But give her a break. She lives above the shop and has nothing else to do."

Margot nodded in agreement and followed Tamera to the door.

"Hello, beautiful," Tamera whispered to the door.

"You've officially lost it."

"For the longest time, I didn't have anything else, Marg."

"But now you've got George. Does he know of this love affair you have going with your boutique?"

Tamera shot her a look, barely indiscernible in the darkness. "He knows. And he's slowly helping me let go."

Margot followed her friend's laughter into the shop, the scents of paper, scented candles, and an odd scent she couldn't place greeting them.

"Does it...smell strange to you?"

Tamera sniffed. "Maybe a little. It has been closed for two weeks. That's a long time."

"True."

"I've got to get to the back of the shop to get the lights. Give me a second."

Margot watched her friend pick her way through the darkened shop, the only light coming from a streetlight almost a block down. She was about to pull out her phone to turn on the flashlight when Tamera shrieked.

"Tamera!" Margot called out. She rushed toward the

sound but her foot caught on a table, almost sending it toppling over. "*Oof.* Tamera, what is it?"

"Oh my gosh, Marg. I think...I...I..."

"What's wrong?" Margot was almost to the back of the shop now.

"I think it's a body."

Margot's blood ran cold. "What?"

Just as she reached the back of the shop, the lights came on to show Tamera standing over a body, face down on the floor. It was a man dressed in khaki shorts and wearing a Hawaiian print shirt. A dark brown fedora was off to the side of his head, turned upside-down. Margot noted smudges of what looked like—was it makeup?—on the inside rim.

Without thought, Margot knelt next to the man and felt for a pulse, pressing down nausea as she did. His skin was cold and firm to the touch.

"Tam, you need to call the police. Now!" Margot stood back up, wrapping her arms around herself.

There was no doubt. The man was dead.

CHAPTER 2

"MARGOT DURAND," a deep voice said behind her. "Fancy meeting you here."

She turned to see Detective Adam Eastwood. He wore running shorts and a t-shirt that fit him much too well. She swallowed and forced her eyes from his muscled chest to meet his intent stare.

"Adam," she gasped.

"I hear you found a body?" There was sweat on his shirt and dotting his brow. Had he been on a run? "Margot?"

She blinked. Her thoughts were scattered and she couldn't get the picture of the man lying dead on the floor out of her mind.

"Y-yes."

"Hey," Adam said, stepping closer, "it's going to be all right. I'm here now."

His words were comforting—almost too much so—and she suddenly felt self-conscious, looking to where Tamera stood talking to another officer.

"Want to tell me what happened?"

She was surprised to see he had a notepad in his hand and was ready to get down to business. As the town's resident detective, she knew he had a job to do and she was part of that job. Nodding, she explained exactly what had happened, ending with the fact that she'd felt for a pulse but, finding none, had Tamera call the police.

"Good, good." He scribbled some notes and then looked up at her. "Did you recognize the man at all?"

"No." She shook her head. "But I didn't get a good look. I almost turned him over but when I didn't feel a pulse, I figured I shouldn't disturb the crime scene."

"Good thinking." He wrote some more. "And Tamera, you said you'd just picked her up?"

"Yes. Well, we got ice cream first."

"Claytons?" His easy grin told her he was trying to calm her down.

"It's the only place to go for ice cream, really."

"Agreed. And then you came here? Did you see anyone?"

"No— Oh, well, we saw Mrs. Henderson walking a dog."

"Phyllis?"

"Yeah."

"Noted." He looked up just as Margot heard a familiar voice. "Looks like George is here."

Margot turned to see George with his arms around Tamera. She was crying into his chest and, for a moment, Margot envied her—if only just a little. There had been a time when Margot had cried like that into Julian's chest, but that had been in the past.

"Why don't we go over there?" Adam suggested, as if sensing her mood.

They walked over just as the EMTs were bringing out the body. It looked as if one of them hadn't zipped up the body bag all the way and the stiff wind from the Potomac yanked the flap back and forth.

George's gasp drew everyone's attention.

"That's Mark!"

Adam rounded on George with wide eyes. "You *know* the victim?"

George stammered, unable to take his eyes from the body.

"Hold on, guys," Adam instructed. Then, turning to Margot and Tamera, he said, "You may want to look away. George, can you take a quick look? To verify you know the victim?"

Looking grim, George took a step toward the body. Before Margot could turn her head, one of the EMTs pulled back the flap and exposed the man's face. It seared into her memory and she gasped, pulling her gaze away.

"Tell me this isn't happening," Tamera said, Margot coming to her side. "Tell me I didn't just find a dead body in my craft shop."

Margot wanted to be able to tell her friend that, but the truth was it *had* happened. She wrapped her arm around Tamera and pulled her close, risking a glance back toward where George stood. From her perspective, she could just see the lines on his forehead deepen. His nod to Adam told her all she needed to know. George *did* know the victim. But how?

"Marg, can we go? I just...I don't want to be here."

Margot swallowed down her curiosity. It wasn't so much that she wanted to butt into Adam's investigation, but why had this man—whom George apparently knew— been found in Tamera's boutique? Margot almost felt responsible, though she knew that was foolish. She'd only been in charge of keeping a set of Tamera's keys and checking on the place every once in a while.

She'd just been in there...when was that? She thought back. Three days ago. Everything had seemed fine and there had *definitely not* been a body in there when she checked on the place in preparation for Tamera's homecoming.

"Marg?"

Margot blinked. Tamera had asked her a question. Right. "I'm sorry. I was…distracted. Um, let me ask Adam if we can go." Tamera gave a vague nod and wrapped her arms around herself.

Margot waited until the EMTs had gotten back in the ambulance before she approached Adam. He and George were in the middle of a conversation and she hated to interrupt, but she wasn't sure what else to do. She came up quietly, waiting.

"I don't know *how* he got in there—" George pointed to the boutique. "—or how he was killed. I mean…I don't even know how he would have gotten down to North Bank."

"Because you know he doesn't have a car?"

George shook his head and raked a hand through his greying hair. "The last I knew, he was staying in protective custody in D.C. awaiting the trial."

"Protective—" Adam sighed and now he ran a hand through his dark, short-cropped hair, mirroring George. "What can you tell me about his protection?"

"Not much. I'm part of a team of lawyers, Adam. I know what I'm focused on and that's about it." George shrugged. "More or less."

Margot saw Adam's eyes narrow and she had a feeling he didn't believe George—or had some doubts about what he was saying. Why? George wouldn't lie. And what was this about being on a team of lawyers? Margot's thoughts raced to catch up.

She knew George was a lawyer in D.C. and that he commuted from North Bank. It had to be a nasty commute, but Tamera insisted that he enjoyed the time on the metro and that it was a small sacrifice he was willing to pay in order to live in the less-hectic area of North Bank. But if George knew the victim *and* the victim had been under protective custody...that meant he was likely a witness in a case. Didn't it? But what case?

"Margot?" Adam's gentle voice accompanied his light touch to her arm and she jerked her mind to the present.

"Uh, Tamera—and I—were wondering if we can go. It's late and she's tired, understandably."

"Right." Adam looked at George then back at Margot. "George, why don't you go ahead and take your wife home. I'll have more questions but they can wait until tomorrow."

George nodded and Margot could see him swallow. Was he nervous? Or just shaken by the night's events?

"Thanks," George said to Adam. "And thanks for picking up Tamera tonight," he said to Margot.

She offered him a tired smile as he turned and went to his wife. Her friend dissolved into her husband's arms and, for a brief moment, Margot felt the slight stab of jealousy again.

Pull yourself together, Margot. There's been a murder!

She blinked and the feelings were gone, replaced by the reality of what had happened that night.

"Hey," Adam said, coming to stand next to her and wrapping an arm around her shoulders. "You look tired yourself. Doing okay?"

She wasn't sure how to answer that. The image of the man's pale face still haunted her. But, more than that, she wanted to know who he was. What case had he been a witness for? His death was surely linked to that. Though Adam would know all of those things.

"I'll be all right. Just shaken."

"Understandable." He turned her to face him, letting his hands rest lightly on her arms just above her elbows. "Now why don't you go on home? Get some rest? I may have more questions tomorrow, but I can come by after the shop is open or...later. I could bring dinner."

His words didn't register at first, but then she lifted her gaze to his. He was giving her a look she couldn't quite decipher. But, the moment she thought she saw it, it was gone.

"Uh, sure. Tomorrow," she said, noncommittally.

"You're still considering hiring someone, right?"

She laughed. He was so insistent about it. "I'm considering it."

175

"Good. Now go home and sleep. Okay?"

She nodded.

"Do you want me to drop you? I could drive your car and finish my run on the way back to my place," he said with a laugh.

She shook her head. "You probably need to finish up here, I'm assuming. I'll be fine."

He nodded, holding her gaze again. She almost thought he would say something else, but instead, he dropped his hands, releasing her from their warmth and the connection to him.

He was right. She needed to get home and sleep.

Or see if she could find what case the man had been a witness for.

No! She reasoned with herself as she walked toward her car. She was *not* getting in the middle of this.

MARGOT LAY IN BED, staring up to the darkened ceiling that held shadows cast from the trees in front of the streetlight outside of her window. She should be sleeping, it was way past the time that she should have been in bed, but she couldn't fall asleep. Every time her eyes closed, the man's face floated before her.

At first it had been frightening, but the more she tried to

push the face away and find sleep the more she began to reason through what she'd seen at the crime scene that night.

They hadn't been in the boutique long but she knew a few things for certain. The front door hadn't been broken into so the killer and victim had either broken in the back or had a key for either door. As far as she knew, only she, Tamera, and probably George had keys. It was possible the old landlord still had a pair too, but Tamera had bought the building outright with inheritance money after her father died. Had she changed the locks?

After mulling over that for far too long, Margot rolled onto her side and thought about what she could remember seeing.

They had walked through the darkened part of the shop. Tamera had gone ahead because she knew the way in the dark better than Margot. She had turned on the lights in the back and screamed—of course, because she'd seen the body. A natural reaction. Then…Margot had rushed to the back, nearly falling over a table leg, and seen the man.

Nothing was out of the ordinary in her memory. Now she considered how they'd found the man. He'd been face down when she went to search for a pulse and she suppressed a shudder at the memory of his cold skin. No pulse. No blood.

Odd. She wondered what the cause of death would be. From what she'd seen of his back and then the brief—but still too long—look at his face, there hadn't been any trauma to report. Drugs? Poison?

Then there was the fedora. The temperature had been pushing ninety degrees even in the evenings most nights for the last week. There was no cause for a man to be wearing a fedora whatsoever, at least not at night. Then again, some men liked to wear hats all the time. Maybe he was like that?

Sighing, she rolled onto her other side. This was ridiculous. What was she going to do? Solve the murder from her bed at midnight? Unlikely. But there was something about the scene that had been off to her and she couldn't put her finger on it. Even now, as sleep began to take hold, she felt unsettled. She'd seen something—she knew it—but she had no way of knowing what it was.

Maybe she would remember in the morning. Maybe...

CHAPTER 3

THE SMELL of heavy sweetness laced the air as Margot pulled the last batch of walnut, chocolate chip cookies from the oven. She'd worked past her allotted morning time, feeling the strain of only a few hours of sleep, but she was finally done and she'd only had a few customers drawing her from the back. For once she was thankful for a quiet morning.

"Hello?" a rough voice called from the front.

Her smile slipped into place easily and she called out, "Be right there, Bentley!"

His lack of response was typical and she rushed to slide the cookies off the baking sheet so they wouldn't over bake. Then she cut an extra corner out of an *Oopsie*—what she called any baked good that didn't meet up to her standards for the shop—and added it to Bentley's usual order.

"Thought I'd fall asleep before you made it out here," he teased good-naturedly.

"How about an extra slice of a caramel pecan cinnamon roll and a cup of coffee on the house to make up for it?"

"You barely make me pay as it is. But I accept."

She grinned and slid the baked goods in front of him. "When am I going to get you to try something else?"

He took a bite, his eyes closing and some of the wrinkles smoothing out. "Never," he whispered.

She laughed, shaking her head. "You're set in your ways, aren't you, Mr. Lawyer?" Ever since she'd found out he used to be a trial lawyer in D.C., she hadn't let him forget she knew his past.

"Quite right, Detective."

She shook her head, taking his nickname in stride. Around the same time she'd found out about his past profession, she'd also helped solve a murder case and he'd taken to calling her Detective. Thankfully not around Adam—yet— but she had a feeling it was only a matter of time.

Her thoughts slipped to the night before. All of this talk about lawyers and detectives caused her curiosity to run wild, but she couldn't go there. That was Adam's job, not hers.

"Heard about the hubbub last night," Bentley said casually.

She stopped scrubbing the already-clean countertop and turned to look at him. "You did?"

"News travels fast in this town. Besides, Phyllis Henderson is best friends with Anita Mallord who lives two doors down from me in the senior living apartments. Of course Phyllis had to come and see her last night and then *she* nearly knocked down my door to tell me about it. Police cars and a body wheeled out on a stretcher." He tossed his hands up and shook his head. "What is this town coming to?"

Margot wasn't sure what she could—or should—share about it all. Just as she was about to make a non-specific comment, the front door opened and Adam walked in. His hair still looked damp from his morning shower and she caught a whiff of his aftershave moments after his entrance. It smelled sweet and spicy.

"Adam," she said, surprised. For some reason, talking about last night with Bentley when he walked in somehow felt wrong. "What are you doing here?"

"I told you I was going to stop by," he said with an easy grin. "Hey, Bentley, how are the crosswords going?"

Bentley tossed up a hand. "Terrible. Atrocious. Abhorrent."

Adam grinned. "But you're still working on them, eh?"

"You betcha, boy. It improves my vocabulary."

"I'm sure it does. Hey, Margot," Adam said, turning toward her, "can we chat in the back?"

She nodded and led the way to the kitchen. The warmth of the oven filled the space, as did the scent of cookies and pastries, but Adam didn't seem to mind. He zeroed in on the *Oopsies* and helped himself after a glance for permission. She poured him a cup of coffee and then crossed her arms, leaning back against the counter.

"I thought you were coming around lunchtime? Or later?"

"Is now a bad time?" he asked around a mouthful of pastry.

"No, I just..." What? Was caught off guard thinking about the murder like a detective—again? "No. It's not a bad time."

"Good." He wiped his mouth with the napkin she handed him and then took a sip of the hot coffee, letting it wash away the sugar that no doubt coated his throat. "So, I've got to ask you some additional questions. That okay?"

"Of course." She wasn't sure why he looked so hesitant. This was part of his job, she knew that better than anyone. Last night would set the course of Adam's days from now until the culprit was arrested. Of anyone, she knew this better than most. Her late husband Julian had been a detective with the same precinct as Adam. She knew how it worked. Knew what his life would look like from here on out.

She was about to tell him as much when her cellphone rang. Sending him an apologetic look, she rushed to her small office and snatched her phone from the desk. She was about to silence it when she noticed it was Tamera. Considering the previous night, she decided to answer despite the fact she was making Adam wait.

Tamera was her friend and a fellow businesswoman in a small town. Adam would understand waiting for a few extra minutes.

"Hello?"

"Oh, thank God you answered!"

Tamera sounded frantic. Had she found another body? The thought, as strange as it was, crossed Margot's mind but she pushed it away.

"Calm down, Tam. What's wrong?"

Tamera panted as if she'd run from somewhere. "I was," gasp, "just out on," gasp, "a run and I came back," she took a moment to swallow, "to find a message on my phone from George."

Though Margot had no idea what the message was about, she knew by Tamera's frantic gasping that it wasn't anything good.

"What is it? What did he say?"

"He's—" She gasped again, but this time it sounded more like a sob. "He's been arrested."

"What?!" Margot forgot the fact that that she was in her shop or that anyone else could hear her. Her shouted reply came from pure shock.

"I know." Tamera was crying now, the tears heavily lacing her voice. "I can't believe it. He couldn't tell me much, but I knew I had to call you."

"Arrested, not brought in for questioning?" she clarified.

"Arrested," Tamera all but wailed back.

Margot reasoned through all of the things that could have caused George to be arrested. She could only assume that it was in response to the murder, but he had helped identify the victim. That was hardly cause for being arrested, was it? It had to be something much worse.

"Please, help him Marg! You know Adam and—"

"Adam," Margot said out loud and heard the scrape of a ceramic mug on her metal countertops. He was out there right now in her kitchen. Had he come by because he already knew George was arrested? Was that the reason for his hesitance?

"Tam, I've got to go." She straightened and mentally prepared for a battle of wills with Adam. "But don't worry. I'll talk to Adam and call you back as soon as I hear anything. Okay?"

"Promise?"

"Promise. Now go take a shower, eat something, and try to calm down. It'll be all right."

It had to be, because Margot knew there was no way George Wells had killed anyone.

MARGOT WALKED BACK into the kitchen and stood at the counter, arms crossed and hip pressed against the cold metal side. Adam looked appropriately contrite but she waited, wanting to hear it from him.

"That was Tamera?"

She merely nodded.

"And she told you we arrested George this morning."

She nodded again.

"Okay, so maybe I should have led with that today. And don't keep nodding. Your silence throws me off."

She dropped her arms. "Why didn't you tell me? You know Tamera is my best friend."

"I was going to get there...eventually."

"Sure, after you ate all my pastries, drank all of my coffee, and I answered your questions. What was it going to be, 'Oh, by the way, Margot, we arrested George, bye'?" She raised an eyebrow and the corner of his lip inched upward.

"Actually, I was going to call you once I was in the safety of my car." He cracked a smile and she shook her head. "No, really, Margie, I was going to tell you."

He used his nickname for her and, though she'd once hated it, she had to admit she was used to it now and it had a softening effect on her.

"Then tell me what's going on. Why did you arrest George?"

He scrunched up his face like he did when he wanted to tell her something but couldn't because of protocol. She understood it, even if she disliked the fact that she couldn't get all of the information she needed from him. It sounded so awful, like she was using him merely for his role as detective, but that wasn't the case.

"All I can say is that there is a witness that places George at the craft boutique during or around the time of the victim's death and we couldn't verify his alibi."

"What?" Margot felt like the air in the shop had just disappeared. George had been seen at the boutique? Normally that wouldn't bet too strange, but Tamera hadn't even been back yet and he was there? But why?

"Wait, when was time of death?"

"We're still waiting on the final results from the medical examiner, but his initial assessment puts it at or around five last night."

"What? That seems unlikely."

"Why do you say that?"

Margot paced to the sink and poured herself a glass of water before answering. "It would still be light out at five. How would someone kill a person in broad daylight?"

"They were in the shop—"

"You don't really believe that, do you?"

He frowned, eyes narrowing. "What makes you think otherwise?"

"Last night when we came in, it was dark—really dark. I had just reached for my cell phone to turn on the flashlight app when Tamera walked through to the back to get the lights. Nothing was out of place. Nothing moved—at least I don't think so, or else she would have been tripped up. She knows that store like the back of her hand. So, no struggle. Besides, where was the blood? Then again, we don't know how he died..." She trailed off. Her gaze had gone to the window while she thought and only when Adam lightly touched her shoulder did she jolt back to the present.

"Hey, nice to have you back among the living."

She made a face at him. "I was thinking."

"And that's what worries me."

"What's that supposed to mean?"

His head tilted to the side. "Margot, you know how I feel

187

about you putting yourself in the middle of dangerous situations and—"

"If George is the murderer, then you have him in custody." She folded her arms again and waited.

He rolled his eyes. "All right, so I don't think George did it either."

"I knew it! Then why did you arrest him?"

"Because my chief doesn't listen to gut feelings or the fact that George is a friend of a friend. He goes by facts—like George being at the scene of the crime apparently both times. When it allegedly happened and when the body was found."

"But he was coming to pick up his *wife!*"

Adam held up a hand as if to say, *I know, I know.* The facts didn't look good for George, but it was encouraging to hear that Adam was on her side. Not that she could really have a side at this point—merely the side of her friend.

"I do still have a few questions I need to ask you, if you'll cooperate?"

She cracked a smile. "For you, Detective Eastwood? Absolutely."

He seemed pleased by her reply and pulled out his notebook. "What can you tell me about George?"

The question, seemingly innocuous, meant so much more now that Margot knew he was in custody, but she tried to separate that from her thoughts and focus merely on the questions.

"I've been best friends with Tamera for over fifteen years. About a year ago, she signed up for one of my baking classes."

"I saw you offered those. I've wanted to join—I've always wanted to be able to bake." The genuine interest in Adam's eyes caught her off guard.

"Really?"

"Yeah." He shifted nervously and looked down at his notepad. "Sorry, where were we?"

A new image of Adam Eastwood formed in Margot's mind, but she refocused on the task at hand. "I often get clients from the D.C. area, being so close and all, and since I supplied pastries to a few well known parties, I would often get higher profile guests." She thought back to the night class she'd offered. There had been six students, all of differing ages, genders, and interests. It had been a fun class. With the hint of a smile still on her lips, she continued. "George was part of that class. When we did introductions and he said he was a lawyer in D.C., I wondered how in the world he'd heard of my class, let alone *why* he'd want to come down to North Bank for a night baking class, but it turns out his firm had purchased pastries from me and he'd liked them so much he looked me up, and that was that."

"So he and Tamera hit it off?"

"You wouldn't believe how terrible of a baker George turned out to be." She laughed just thinking of it. "But, though Tamera has never really baked, she's been around me for years so she stepped in to help. And the rest, they say, is history."

"All right." Adam nodded. "Did he ever mention cases or anything when you were around?"

"You mean did he ever talk about plotting to kill off a star witness? No."

Adam's head jerked up. "How did you know he was a star witness?"

"Simple deduction. But I'm right, aren't I?"

Adam nodded, though he looked like he'd rather be doing anything but. "Last question—for now." He folded his notebook and looked up to meet her gaze. "What do you think about George?"

"Is this off the record?" she asked, indicating his notebook.

"It's more 'next to' the record. I'm asking you for a personal feeling, not fact-based judgment, based on the time you've spent around him."

"I think he's a good guy. I mean, I don't know him as well as Tamera, but I *do* know Tamera. If she trusts him, which she does, then I do too."

Adam nodded and reached for his pocket where he pulled

out a buzzing phone. "Sorry. I've got to take this. I'll let you get back to your shop." He hesitated as if he wanted to say something else, but then nodded and went toward the door, pressing the button as he went. "Eastwood here."

She watched him go, wondering about what he'd said. She *did* think George was a good guy, it was obvious he loved her friend, but she didn't know much about him. Maybe it was time to change that.

CHAPTER 4

"SHAME 'BOUT that man who was killed last night. You seen Tamera at all, sweetie?"

Margot shook her head, pushing up her reading glasses. "Sorry, Gladys, I'm just trying to finish this article here."

"Oh sure, sure." The older woman, a regular at the senior center, nodded and placed her other hand on top of her cane that rested upright in front of her. "But really, in *our* little town? What's North Bank comin' to? Turning into the big city. A den of evil, if you ask me."

And that was why Margot *didn't* ask. She kept her attention focused on the screen. Her home computer had ended up in the shop the week before when her power had surged and it suddenly wouldn't turn on. Left with her phone, she decided to use the computers at the local library. Unfortunately, Gladys had found her and wanted to chat, disrupting Margot's research into George Wells' online presence and life.

"And to think Phyllis saw him." The older woman shuddered. "Terrifying."

This drew Margot's attention. "What did you say?"

"I said it's terrifying! I wouldn't want to see a murderer, you know."

"No," Margot felt her heart pounding in her chest. "What did you say before that? Who saw him?"

"Why, Phyllis Henderson of course."

Of course! Margot leaned back, her mind whirring with the new information. "Let me guess, you heard it from Anita?"

"Say, you're really turning into some kind of detective." Gladys practically beamed. "I did. She came down to my room to tea yesterday and told me all about it. Poor Phyllis."

Sure, poor Phyllis. Margot had a feeling she had embellished on what she'd seen. Then again, Margot couldn't be sure until she knew what she'd said.

"Can you tell me what Anita said?"

"Sure, dear, though I thought you were looking in that computer of yours?"

Margot ignored the slight and urged the woman on.

"The way Anita tells it, Phyllis was walking Mr. Golden and—"

"Who?"

"Oh." Gladys gave a throaty laugh that would surely get them kicked out. "Mr. Golden, her corgi. He's very sensitive to heat and must go out at night." Margot nodded so the woman would continue. "Anyway, Anita says that Phyllis says that she was walking down Front Street when a man in a fedora—of all things—walked past her. That's when she looked up and saw George going into the shop. Can you believe it? She saw him *right* before he committed a murder." The woman gave a look of pure disgust.

Margot wanted to remind her that George was innocent until proven guilty, but she had a feeling it wouldn't do any good.

"Did she say anything else?"

"Not that I can recall. You could talk to Phyllis though, I'm sure she'd tell you." She would, and everyone else who even breathed next to her.

"Thanks so much, Gladys. You've been very helpful."

"Sure thing, sweetie," she said, patting her hand. "Oh! There's the bus—my ride—I'll see you around. Don't forget those nice pastries the next time you stop by the senior center."

Margot agreed and watched her leave before turning back

to the recent search she'd put in to the database. So Phyllis was the witness *and* she'd seen a man in a fedora? It was all too bizarre to piece together now.

Margot drew her attention back to the screen. She'd done the usual Google search and come up with nothing more than a little-used Twitter account, a Facebook page, and a few articles where George's name was mentioned in conjunction with his firm.

On a whim, she clicked the second page of results. An article at the top caught her attention.

Victor Carow: Is his fate sealed?

She clicked on it. It was just a basic article written in the *Washington D.C. Post* that talked about Victor Carow's "reign of terror," as they dubbed it. Apparently, he was a well-known drug lord coming out of Baltimore. What seemed to make him special, though, was the fact that he catered to the elite as well as the average street druggie. That, and the fact that there has been no solid evidence about him specifically.

"How is that possible?" she breathed the question to herself.

She was about to click back to try one more search when a soft voice spoke up behind her. "You're interested in this too, eh?"

Margot looked up to see Wilhelmina leaning down. She blushed and stood up. "I'm sorry, Margot, that was rude."

She pushed up her wire-rimmed glasses and tugged at the hem of her royal blue sweater.

"It's all right. What do you mean by 'too'?" Margot leaned forward, wondering what the young librarian could know about Victor Carow.

"Oh, just that Barbara and I were talking about it all this morning." She rubbed her hands up and down her arms as if caught by a chill. "We saw the news this morning that said the star witness in this case had been killed." She indicated the article still up on the screen. "Frightening thinking of *another* murder taking place here in North Bank."

"Yes, very, but what do you mean by 'too'?" Margot felt like a broken record, but she had a vested interest in this. She had promised Tamera she would help George and this information could be valuable. It could also lead nowhere.

"A few weeks back, maybe a month or more, someone came in and was researching that very same thing. I wouldn't have remembered it at all, I actually didn't see the man, but Barbara helped him with the computer—some kind of error code had come up—and she saw that he'd been reading about Victor Carow. I guess Barbara knows someone living in D.C. who's talked about this man and—"

"Sorry, but you don't know who it was?"

"No, dear, Barbara helped him."

"Is Barbara here? I'd like to talk with her."

"Oh, I'm sorry to say she left for her vacation after her shift was over at two."

Margot's hopes fell. "Do you have her phone number?"

"I do," Wilhelmina said but bit her lip, cuing Margot to the fact that she was either nervous about giving it over or something else was wrong.

"I understand you may not want to give it to me, but—" But what? She was trying to get her friend's husband out of jail? That sounded a little too drastic. No need to frighten the poor woman any more than she already was.

"Oh, it's not that," Wilhelmina said with a short laugh. "I just don't think it'll do you any good."

"It won't?"

"Nope. She's gone hiking in the Blue Mountains. She told me she'd be out of service for several days."

Margot contained her groan for the most part. "Can I get it anyway? Maybe I'll try her now and see if I've caught her before she's out of range."

"Sure thing. I'll be right back," Wilhelmina said, spinning on her ballet flats.

Once Margot had the number, she pressed dial the minute she stepped out of the library but it immediately went to voicemail. Terrific. The first lead she had and there was no way to verify it.

≈

MARGOT BIT her lip as she maneuvered her car down the narrow streets in the older part of town. She had a feeling that Tamera could use some companionship right now and, if she *was* home and not at the police station, Margot was going to console her in any way she could.

Turning down the cobblestone street, she spotted Tamera's light blue car parked in front of her stone row home. George's larger SUV was also parked in front, letting Margot know that Tamera was indeed home, unless she'd gotten a ride to the station.

Taking a chance, Margot parked down the street where a spot was available and walked the block back to Tamera's bright red door. She knocked, but there was no reply. Knocking again, she heard nails on the floor and one bark. So Mr. Puggles was in the house—that probably meant Tamera was too.

"Tam, it's me," she said through the door.

Finally, the door swung open and a furry ball of energy butted up against her legs. "Hello, Mr. Puggles," she said, leaning down to scratch the pug behind the ears. When she stood, she met her friend's gaze. "I couldn't stay away...from Mr. Puggles."

Tamera cracked what almost could have passed for a smile and stepped inside. "You might as well come in. Tea?"

"I'd love some."

They walked into the French country-inspired kitchen painted in bright yellows with deep red accents, figures and pictures of chickens scattered throughout.

"How are you, Tam?" she asked as she slid into a chair at the bar.

"How do you think?" Tamera's back was to Margot, but her inflection was clear. She was on the verge of tears.

"Not good, I'm sure. Do you want me to take you down to the station?"

Setting the kettle on the stove, she turned to face Margot. "Not yet. George said it would take them a while to p-process him." She covered her trembling lips with a hand.

"He's right. But you should go down in a little while. I'll go with you. We can see if Adam will let you talk with George."

Tamera nodded, not trusting herself to speak.

"I know it seems impossible, but think of it this way—the police are only doing their job following up on a lead. They have to take all tips seriously until they find out who did this."

"I know. It's just..." She took a deep breath. "What *was* he doing back so early?"

"What do you mean?" Margot leaned forward, trying to understand what her friend was talking about.

"When they took George into custody, I called his boss—I didn't know what else to do. He assured me that, should he need it, they'll send someone to represent him. He said he'd never seen a harder worker than George. I agreed and said only a man like George would cut his honeymoon short for work."

Margot swallowed. She didn't like where this was going. "It wasn't for work?"

"No." Tears swelled into Tamera's eyes. "He said that he hadn't been called back."

Though Margot was not willing to entertain the idea that her best friend's husband had in fact had anything to do with the murder, the circumstances were starting to become rather suspicious.

Just then the teakettle sang, drawing Tamera away for a moment as Margot considered this new information. If George hadn't come back for work, then why had he come back? There were a million reasons, but it had to be something very strong in order to draw him away from his honeymoon.

Tamera set down a cup of tea in front of Margot and the minty aroma swirled up to greet her. She breathed in and allowed it to calm and refresh her. They would figure this out.

"Marg, do you think—" Tamera couldn't even get the words out.

"No. He didn't do this."

"But—"

"I know it looks...concerning, but we'll get to the bottom of this. The police may have already figured out why he came back."

"I just don't even want to think about the fact that he lied to me, Marg. Lied to my face about having to come back for work. Why would he do that unless...?"

"Tamera," Margot said, waiting until her friend's eyes met hers. "Do you love George?"

"Absolutely."

"Does he love you?"

Tamera took a deep breath and, meeting Margot's gaze, she nodded. "I have no doubt that he does."

"Then that settles it. There's an explanation for everything and we *will* come to the bottom of it. Now let's finish our tea and go to the police station."

CHAPTER 5

MARGOT WALKED next to Tamera as they ascended the steps of the small police station. North Bank, not a large town, wasn't known for its crime, though recent history would tend to disagree with that reality. They stepped into the station, which smelled like stale coffee and sandwiches.

After checking in, they waited only a moment until Adam came into the front room.

"Hello, ladies," he said, looking appropriately grim. The greying hair at his temples gave him a sage look, but Margot could already see that a late night had affected him. His shoulders drooped with the weight of tiredness. "I suppose you're here to see George?"

His question was directed at Tamera and, after looking to Margot, she agreed. "Yes. If I may?"

"I think we can arrange that. Harver," he called into the

room, "a moment."

A younger deputy came toward them, his belt cinched up tight to accommodate his lithe frame. "Yes, Detective?"

"Will you escort Mrs. Wells to the holding cell area? Give her some time with her husband, all right?"

"Sure thing, sir." The young man turned to Tamera. "This way, ma'am."

She looked to Margot as if she couldn't bear to go alone, but Margot encouraged her with a slight nod. The pair disappeared into the depths of the building and Margot turned to look at Adam. "Can we talk?"

"Of course." He led the way back to his office and Margot sank into a chair facing his desk.

"Adam, this is ridiculous."

"I assume you're not talking about the fact that I still have my cup of coffee from five a.m. half-full on my desk?"

His attempt at humor warmed her, though it didn't distract from the reality of the station or the fact that she was, once again, back in Detective Adam Eastwood's office. And not to drop off a box of cookies.

"Not exactly."

He propped his elbows on the desk, resting his head in his hands as if it was too tiresome to keep his head upright by itself. "Then you must be talking about George."

She gave him a look that said, *Of course that's what I'm talking about.*

"Look, I know you're friends with Tamera and all, but—"

"It's not just about that. I mean, it is in a way, but—" She huffed out a breath. "George is no murderer."

"There are a lot of things unknown about the case at this present moment."

"You sound like a press release," she said, leaning back and crossing her arms.

"What can I tell you? We still don't have cause of death from the M.E. yet, we don't know how in the world Mark Jennings got to North Bank *or* how he got *inside* of Tamera's shop. Neither do we know the status of George Wells. It's just…" Adam sighed and roughed a hand over his face. "Never mind."

"It's just *what* exactly?" She leaned forward.

"How well do you know George Wells?"

Margot felt—as much as saw—the switch in Adam. He went from tired friend to alert investigator.

"What do you mean? I told you everything this morning."

"I mean, you are close friends with Tamera. You introduced her to George, in a manner of speaking."

"I'd hardly say placing them as partners in a cooking class

constitutes introduced. I didn't know much about him before the start of the class anyway. But I suppose I did facilitate their relationship in a way."

"Exactly. So tell me more about George? What was he like in class? What did you know from him before, during, and after?"

"Why does it feel like I'm being interrogated? Didn't we go over this earlier?"

"Margot…" He gave her a stern look.

She tossed up her hands. "I knew next to nothing before the class, just that he was going to be coming from Washington, D.C. and said he was happy the class was later so he could avoid traffic."

"Then during the class?"

"It was more than a year ago."

"Think back. You have an exceptional memory."

She leaned back, staring up at the ceiling in thought. "I always have us do introductions. Just fun things. If I remember correctly, he said he was from D.C., a lawyer, and widowed."

"Interesting."

"What? Why is that interesting?"

"It's not much. Most people share something else, right?"

"Not exactly." She thought back to the class. "Tamera shared even less."

"What was your take on him? In the class specifically."

Margot didn't like the way Adam was all but interrogating her, but she reminded herself he was merely doing his job.

"Honestly? I thought he was a good guy. A guy I would be happy to see my friend date—should he ask."

"And what made you think that would be a possibility."

"Chemistry," she said, smirking, "and not just with regards to the baking."

He rolled his eyes and dropped his hands, leaning back in the chair. Inquisitive Adam was gone for the moment.

"I trust him, Adam. You've got the wrong man for this."

"That's just it. I don't trust him. He's hiding—" Adam cut off, his eyes flicking to her.

He swallowed and shook his head, returning his gaze to the ceiling even as his pointer finger tapped lightly on a file on his desk. "Just trust me when I say there are *things* you may not know about the man." His finger pounded the folder one more time.

Margot's thoughts flew to what Tamera had admitted. Was she bound to tell Adam that George hadn't come back for work? Opening her mouth to say something, she was interrupted by Adam's phone.

"Sorry," he said, standing. "I'll only be a minute."

He stepped from the room, closing the door behind him, and she slumped back into her chair. She should tell Adam, he needed to know everything, but they hadn't even proven that George hadn't come back for a good reason. Maybe to surprise Tamera? Though it seemed counterintuitive to leave one's honeymoon to surprise the one you left.

Something about Adam's tapping drew her focus to the file folder on his desk. It had a label from the computer forensics team across the top. Standing, she extended one finger and popped the top of the folder over.

Her heart beat more soundly in her chest as she read upside down. It looked like a printout of an email. Frowning, she scanned the address. It had George's name at the top but the "sent to" line seemed like a made up email address: beaky123@smail.com.

She skipped down to the body of the email. The first line simply read: It's time.

She was about to walk around the desk to more easily read the rest of the email when she heard footsteps coming back down the hall. Flicking the file closed, she resumed her seat and tried to act interested in her phone as Adam stepped back inside.

"Sorry about that."

"It's all right," she said, slipping the phone into her bag. "I really should be going. I assume Tamera is about out of time anyway."

He nodded, his shoulders drooping again. "I'm really sorry about this, Margie. You know that I'll do my very best to figure out what's going on here, no matter what, right?"

She stood, nodding and reminding herself to keep her gaze from slipping to the file folder. "I know that, Adam. You're just doing your job." *And I'm doing mine—helping a friend.*

Her thoughts buzzed with the email as she walked down the hall. It was only when she and Tamera were back in the car and heading back to Tamera's house that she realized she hadn't told Adam about George coming back early.

"HOW WAS YOUR CONVERSATION WITH GEORGE?"

They were almost back to Tamera's house and her friend had been quiet for so long, she'd wondered if she'd fallen asleep after the rush of adrenaline had left her.

Tamera let out a huge sigh just as Margot pulled into a parking space.

"That man," she said, though her tone wasn't angry or as devastated anymore.

"What? What did he say? What happened?"

She hefted another sigh and turned to look at Margot. "He says that he went to the shop to get glue."

Margot frowned. "Glue? What?"

"I know." Tamera shook her head. "He said he was making me something, trying to be 'crafty' like me, and that the one thing he was missing was a glue stick. He says he knew I had a whole stack at the shop so he went there, opened the door, took a glue stick, and left. That's it."

Margot leaned back in her seat, contemplating this. Walmart was closer to Tamera's house, so why would George make the trek down to the shop? Unless he either needed to be there for something else or was in the area.

It would make sense why he hadn't found the body—assuming he was there during the time that Mark was killed or after the fact. But did that mean he'd been close to the killer? Interrupted them perhaps? But no, George would have seen something—unless he hadn't relayed that part to the police or his wife. Margot felt sick to her stomach.

"Did he turn on the lights?"

Tamera pulled her attention from the window. "What?"

"The lights. Did he turn them on when he went in there?"

"I don't know—wait, no. He said he used the flashlight on his phone. He went in the front instead of the back."

"Like we did."

"Yes."

She sat back in her seat, forcing herself not to jump to conclusions. "Where's the glue now?"

"That's just it." Tamera turned weighted eyes toward Margot. "He told the police this—of course, because he wanted to exonerate himself—but they can't confirm that he actually took the glue *and* they can't find it."

Margot frowned. "Where did he say it was?"

"That's just it. He can't remember either."

"I'm confused..." Margot was beginning to doubt this whole story. He was a trial lawyer, he wouldn't just misplace a glue stick. Had George fabricated all of this to get out of telling the truth? Then again, wouldn't he come up with a better story?

But no, she couldn't think like that. He was innocent until proven guilty—which, hopefully, he wouldn't be.

"What he says happened is that he went in, got the glue, then came back to the house. He'd left Mr. Puggles inside and apparently that silly dog had chewed up one of his favorite pairs of slippers while he was out. I think he was mad that we left him with Abby for the two weeks we were gone." Tamera shrugged but continued. "So he had to clean up that whole mess and by the time he was done, I called him and he went right back down to the shop where the rest of this all takes place."

Margot began to nod. "And the slipper?"

"The—what?"

"Is it in the back trash?"

"Yes, I saw it there yesterday."

So one part of his story could be verified. "So then we have to find the missing glue stick—a brand new one—to corroborate his story."

"Yes. As soon as I get home I'm going to tear the house apart looking for it."

"But...why a glue stick? What was he doing?"

She blushed and looked down. "He made me a card. Said he'd looked up tutorials online and wanted to have it done by the time I got back."

Again, it seemed to fit. "Do you have the card?"

"He told me not to look at it yet—even in jail, he's still playing the romantic—but he told me where it is."

"I'll need to look at it."

Tamera nodded. "Margot, I know it sounds farfetched. But with Mrs. Henderson seeing him go into the shop and then the body being found...it just looks bad. But it's all circumstantial—so George says."

It was, but the email Adam had apparently found made it more than that...but she couldn't divulge that information to her friend. At least not yet.

"Well, let's go look."

"What?"

She reached over and grabbed her friend's hand, squeezing lightly. "We'll look for the glue stick and maybe come across something else that will help too."

"I won't give up," Tamera said. "You remember all those years that I complained to you about being single. All those terrible first dates I went on. All the tears I cried." She rested her head back against the headrest. "It all faded when I met George. He's not perfect and sometimes he drives me nuts—as I'm sure I do to him too—but he's the one, Marg. He's the one meant for me. The one that completes me. I just can't— I can't imagine him doing anything like this. Besides, it makes no sense."

"I know. None of it makes sense."

"No, I mean, why in the world would George kill Mark? *That* makes no sense."

"Because he was a witness?"

"No, because he was *the* witness. I remember the day George came home saying they had finally found someone to testify. It was nothing short of a miracle. George believes in ending what Victor Carow does. He wouldn't jeopardize the trial like that."

Margot nodded and they went into Tamera's house to look for the elusive glue stick, but her thoughts stayed with Victor Carow and the now-dead star witness in the case against him. Was it possible that the emails George had gotten were from him—or someone associated with him?

Had George's loyalty been bought?

CHAPTER 6

THE FEELING of stiff dough beneath her hands made Margot pull back, blinking. She'd gotten lost in thought again and had almost overworked her dough. That was happening more and more. The puzzle of the murder of Mark Jennings was too mind-bending for her to let go. Though, calling it merely a puzzle seemed to lessen what it really was. A murder of a man who had just stepped up to do the right thing.

The front door opened and, looking through her view window, she saw a young man step into the light streaming in from the front window. He had short-cropped blonde hair and a medium build that reminded her of a runner. He looked athletic, but not a gym junkie.

She took all of this in in the moment it took for him to come to the counter and lean down to look through the pass-through.

"Hello." His voice was smooth, probably a tenor if he sang, and he offered her a kind smile. Not over the top or egotistical, but decidedly confident.

Dusting off her hands, she came through the door and stood behind the counter. "How can I help you?" She didn't ask if he wanted a pastry because she had a sense he wasn't here for that.

"I heard that you had an opening for an assistant. I wanted to apply for the job."

"An—an assistant?" Margot wracked her brain. How had this young man heard that? She hadn't fully admitted to herself that she was interested in hiring, let alone placed an ad anywhere.

"I have a certificate from The Art of Pastry program associated with Kingston College in Vermont. I am a hard worker, and my specialty was in French pastry making. I think I would be a valuable asset to your business."

She blinked. For being so young, she'd guess somewhere in his early twenties, he carried himself well and put forth a compelling argument for hiring him. But there was the matter of him having information she hadn't given to anyone. Well, almost anyone…

"Adam," she said, shaking her head.

The young man tried to hide his grin. "My name is Dexter. Dexter Ross."

"But you know Adam Eastwood, don't you?"

He looked back at her, good-natured guilt written on his features. "I'm originally from New York and knew Adam when I was younger."

"And now you're in North Bank, Virginia. Why is that?"

"I needed a change of scenery."

"And you know French pastry making?"

He nodded vigorously.

"And you have references to go along with this resume I'm assuming you have ready for me?"

He gave her a wicked grin. "Does that mean I can interview for the job?"

She dropped her arms to her side just as Bentley walked in. "Morning, Mar— Who are you?"

The older man eyed Dexter as if he might be able to gain the answer to his question without the boy saying anything.

"I'm Dexter, Mrs. Durand's new assistant." He turned back and winked at her.

He was shameless.

"Meet Dexter," Margot said, trying to hold in her smile, "he's hoping he's lucky enough to prove to me he's up to par to be my assistant."

Bentley eyed him again, giving him a once-over, then he nodded. "One misstep, boy, and she'll take you out."

Dexter's eyes widened. "She doesn't take those Krav Maga classes for nothing." Then Bentley turned to Margot. "The usual, dear, if you will."

She smiled at the older man, loving his protective nature. "I'll get that for you in just a moment. Dexter, this way please."

The young man followed her back to the kitchen. "Nice setup you have here."

"Nice setup is exactly what I'd call this." She faced him, arms over her chest.

"Hey," he said, raising his hands up in a defensive position, "Adam only mentioned that there might be a position open here. He said the rest was up to me."

"To charm your way in, huh?" She cracked a smile.

"Does that mean I'm charming?" He grinned again. It was infectious. "He may have mentioned that you don't have much help and are looking for someone who can take some of the burden of baking, not just running the shop. I have expertise in both." Then he reached into the leather satchel that was slung over his shoulder and pulled out a manila folder. "My credentials, references, and competition stats."

She scanned through the work list and had to admit it was impressive. "Chef Corbett? Really?"

He nodded.

"I'll need to follow up on some of this—"

"I expected as much," he said with a congenial smile.

"Why don't I give you a call once I've made my decision."

He inclined his head. "My number is listed at the top. I look forward to hearing from you."

"All right. Thank you, Dexter."

He flashed another confident smile then disappeared through the kitchen door. She heard him say good-bye to Bentley and then was gone. Her hands worked to cut the caramel pecan cinnamon roll for Bentley, but her mind was on the young man. If what she'd read was accurate and not a fabrication, he was more than qualified to work for her. But could she trust him?

Once the order was delivered, she went back into the kitchen and pulled out her phone.

Adam answered on the second ring. "What's up, Margie?"

He sounded distracted but she pressed on. "Do you know a Dexter—" She looked down at the sheet in front of her. "—Ross?"

"Oh Dex," Adam chuckled and then said something muffled before coming back to their conversation. "He's a good kid. You really ought to give him a chance."

"So then his credentials are legitimate."

"Yep." Someone spoke on the other side of the phone. "Are you sure about that?"

"What?" Margot asked.

"Right, we'll get it up here however you need to. I need a look inside ASAP."

"Adam?" she tried again, knowing that he wasn't speaking to her now.

"Sorry," he said, coming back to their conversation. "We think we just found the car that Mark drove down to North Bank."

MARGOT PICKED up her pace as she walked from where she'd parked at the small turn out down Route 1. Adam stood with his back to the sun, squinting as a large tow truck with a winch attached to the back worked at pulling up the car over the side of the ridge.

"Margot, what are you doing here?"

She skirted a few officers who were taking pictures and writing notes. "You said you found the car."

He frowned at her. "Did you think that was an invitation to come down here?"

"Wasn't it?"

He laughed. "No, but since you're here." He indicated the

cliff face. "Take a look."

She walked with him to the side and they looked over the edge. The sheer rock wall dove to the river at an impressive angle that only began to lesson twenty feet from the water. It was there that the car had landed, front end down. She also saw a worker rapelling down the cliff face toward the car. Even from this height they could see that the back license plate had been marred by something —was that paint?

"Do you think the murderer took pains to paint the license plate?"

"It would seem that way."

"But George—"

"I know. We're following up on all of this." She pressed her lips together and he looked down at her. "Hey, I don't want it to be George just as much as you do, but unfortunately there is still time in the timeline for him to, conceivably, have done this."

"How is that even possible?" she asked, looking around. "The killer had to have come here, set the car to drive off the cliff, and then *somehow* made it back to civilization on foot."

"Margie," he said, a pained look coming onto his handsome features. "We're not that far from where Tam and George live."

She blinked, looking around again. What Adam said was

true. Though this area of the road was faced by sheer cliffs, there was a popular beach not more than a mile or so down the road from there. Because of that, there were many paths that led from the small communities to the river access. She could pick out the exact path that would lead to Tamera and George's street from where she stood.

This was not good.

"Still—"

"I'm not ruling anything out."

"Hey, Detective Eastwood," a man called out to him.

"Yeah, Hal, what is it?"

Margot walked over with him, not interfering but still wanting to know what the man had to say.

"Looks like my guy has a solid lock on the car."

Margot swallowed. Hopefully the worker would return to the safety of this side of the cliff soon.

"Great. Can you start pulling it up?"

The man nodded. "Yep. Wanted to get your OK first."

"You have it."

The man nodded and turned back toward his team. "Haul her up!"

A terrible scraping sound ensued as the winch worked overtime to pull the heavy car up from the cliff. Margot kept her arms wrapped around her, the wind coming from the river chillier than normal despite the warm, humid day.

"You really should hire him," Adam said out of the blue. They had been standing, mesmerized by the slow process to bring the car up, when he broke into her thoughts.

"What?"

"Dex. He's a good kid. A little too creative at times," he said, smirking to himself, "but a good kid. I'll vouch for him."

"So he's as talented as his resume says he is."

"More than," Adam said. Something in the way he said it caused her to file that piece of information away for later.

"I have to admit that it's tempting. He's got a good resume and, once I see how he does in the kitchen, I could use a break every now and again. It'll be slow going though—to make sure he's up for it."

"He will be."

She shook her head and her silence drew his attention.

"What?"

"You're impossible."

"Hey," he said, turning to face her, his hands sliding onto his hips, "I see how hard you work. I know you're there every morning before the sun is even up. You barely have any time for yourself. In fact, I actually saw you more when Taylor was here than I have in the past few years—and that was just for a few months."

She smiled at the memory of her niece and the great help she'd turned out to be. But her smile faded at the look in Adam's eyes. Why was this so important to him?

"It's just the life of a baker—"

"No, it's not. You work harder than anyone I know and I think you deserve to take a break every now and again." He shrugged. "Maybe go out to dinner. With me."

Suddenly the shift in the wind wasn't the only thing that had changed. This conversation had gone from banter to seriousness within the span of a moment.

"We've had dinner lots of times," she said, trying to defend her tendency to overwork.

"I'm not talking about me bringing you Chinese at the bakery because I know you haven't eaten. I'm talking about…dinner." He cleared his throat and his eyes skipped to the men still working to bring up the car. "Like, a dinner date."

Margot felt everything slow down for a moment. Was Detective Adam Eastwood asking her on a date? She opened her mouth then closed it, unsure if she knew what to say or not. The look in his eye pleaded with her to say something, and she knew he deserved that much, but she was struck utterly speechless.

"Margot, I—" he began but a shout from the crew drew their attention.

"The car is up," she said, too much relief sinking into her words.

They rushed to the car and the first thing Adam did was check the front license plate.

"Collier, take down this plate number. I want you to run it ASAP."

"Yes, sir," the young deputy said, rushing to his side. Once he had it, he ran off to his squad car with the plate number and Adam stood by as one of the workers pried open the passenger side door. When it stood wide open, though leaning toward the ground unnaturally, Adam ducked inside to the glove box.

Margot couldn't help her curiosity and slipped up next to him to peer over his shoulder. She may have been somewhat blindsided by his request but her attention was back on the case as she knew his was.

"Is that the registration card?"

"Yes, and it looks like the car is registered to…" He squinted. "A Christina Jordan. It's a D.C. address."

"But, Adam, who is Christina Jordan?"

He looked down at her, tapping the paper against the mangled roof of the car. "I don't know, but I aim to find out."

CHAPTER 7

IT HAD TAKEN all of her convincing and a sheer bit of luck, she was sure, but Margot had convinced Adam to let her come along to D.C. while they questioned Christina. Thankfully, he hadn't brought up his mention of dinner again.

Part of Margot knew she wanted to say yes to him. What she'd said was true, they had had dinner on multiple occasions, but what he was asking was *more* than dinner and she still wasn't sure she was ready for that. Besides, if the current situation was any indication, they would be busy for quite some time solving this case.

Correction. Adam would be busy solving the case. She would merely be busy keeping George out of jail.

They took the 4th Street exit into Washington, D.C. and Adam maneuvered them through the light day traffic. She was surprised, expecting it to be more congested, but it was still early. They turned up Independence Avenue and Margot saw the Capitol building, the dome shining and bright after its recent construction. The tall House and Senate buildings gave way to the Library of Congress and the Jefferson Building.

Paused at a stoplight, Adam turned to look at her. "I shouldn't have let you come with me."

"Oh, Adam," she said, giving him a look that said he was being foolish. "You called and talked with this woman. She's a librarian at Georgetown. How dangerous can this be?"

He smirked and shook his head. "You do have a point there. Though something's been bothering me."

"What's that?"

"According to his file, Mark lives down the street from Christina."

"And?"

"Well, the dates are funny to me. As is the fact that she—a librarian at Georgetown as you've so nicely pointed out—lives in Capital Hill."

Margot followed his logic. "When did she move in?"

"January."

"And Mark—"

"Moved in last June, right before the trial."

"You think she could be involved in all of this? Really? A librarian?"

He smirked. "I'm not in the business of making guesses. Librarian or not, she could be dangerous. She could be a plant from Victor's gang. I should have done more research before coming." He said the last part to himself, but Margot reached over and rested her hand on his arm.

"I know how to take care of myself."

"But you shouldn't have to—not if I've done my job well."

They were maneuvering through the one-way streets, Adam checking each street sign until he saw 7th Street. Taking a left, he went two and a half blocks then he pulled into a spot in front of a white and green row house. Turning off the car, he paused and looked toward Margot.

"I want you to pay attention and stay behind me."

"What's she going to do? Come at us with the Dewey Decimal System?" He didn't seem to appreciate her humor. "I will. I promise."

Apparently satisfied with her answer, he got out of the car. She followed as they took the steep steps up to the black front door, a cheery 4th of July-inspired wreath still hanging from a hook. Adam pressed the doorbell and they waited.

When the door opened, the woman in front of them looked so unlike any librarian Margot had ever seen. She wore black skinny jeans, a long black t-shirt that read

"Cats & Coffee" in bold white lettering, and had dyed black hair cropped at her jawline.

"Uh, Miss Jordan?"

"Nah, that's my roommate. Chrissy!" the girl yelled into the house. "You've got company." She stepped back, an expression of sheer indifference on her face. "You can come in."

"Thank you," Adam said.

They stepped inside into a wide-open space that held an eclectic mix of styles. From a winged back chair by the faux fireplace to a Papasan chair pushed into a corner near a toppling pile of books. The artwork was equally as mismatched. As if the classical style had met impressionism but, like water and oil, didn't mix.

The sound of someone in heels descending the stairs drew their attention toward the narrow staircase. First appeared kitten heels on tiny feet, then a narrow, black pencil skirt, followed by a floral print blouse, necklace of pearls, and then a softly smiling face. The tiny, dark rimmed glasses perching on the nose of the woman before them completed the look. It was classic librarian, except...

Margot jerked her eyes up when she realized she was staring, but the woman in front of her had all manner of tattoos on both arms peeking out just below the forearm-length blouse she wore. Was that indication of a gang affiliation? Or just an affinity for decorative skin ink?

"Hello, can I help you?"

"Miss Jordan, I'm detective Adam Eastwood. We spoke on the phone earlier."

"Oh yes, please, have a seat." She indicated the winged back chair and small love seat. Margot took the chair, Adam the love seat, and Christina pulled over the footstool to the Papasan chair.

"I assume you've heard in the news..." Adam hesitated.

"About Mark? Yeah, I've heard."

Margot watched as she tugged at the edge of her skirt even though it was already over her knee. Was she nervous? But as Margot watched her expression, she saw something else. Sadness.

"You were close with Mark?" Margot asked.

Christina nodded, her lower lip trembling.

"May I ask what the nature of your relationship was?"

Christina met Adam's gaze. "Why?"

"Miss Jordan..." He softened his tone. "Christina. We found your car at the bottom of a cliff. With Mark dead and the car the one connection to how Mark came from D.C. to North Bank, it's imperative we have your full cooperation."

"Look, if I'd known—" Her voice broke, but she

swallowed and tried again. "I never would have lent him my car. Never."

"So, you were in a relationship with him?" Margot asked, hoping that gentle reminder would encourage the woman to share more.

"Yeah. No. I mean, I thought we were moving that direction."

She sniffed and Margot handed her the box of tissues from the marble top, claw-footed table next to her chair. One of the tattoos poked out when Christina's sleeve pulled up and Margot caught a glimpse of the shape of a book. Probably *not* gang tattoos then.

"I met Mark at a coffee shop down the street a few years ago. We talked, he liked books, and we hit it off. At the time I was still living in Georgetown, but I liked to take the weekends to explore new parts of D.C. You know, see the sights in my own city."

Margot nodded, encouraging her with a smile.

"Then this whole trial thing happened. We had to stop seeing each other for a while and I really missed him. Like *really* missed him. My lease was up and I'd found out from Mark where they had relocated him so I...moved." She blushed and looked down. "Sounds desperate, right? I really cared for him and hoped we could, you know, make a go of it. Try out a relationship."

"So explain to me why he had your car?"

"My car and my favorite hat," she said with a humorless laugh.

Margot and Adam exchanged glances.

"He said he needed to run a few errands. I let him use my car all the time but he usually was going to the store so he wouldn't need to lug things around. And there was usually someone with him—protection, you know? He kept my keys and when I looked outside the other night, the car was gone. I figured he had to run an errand but got really worried when he didn't show back up. Then I saw the news—" She clutched the tissue to her nose.

"What do you mean he borrowed your hat?"

Christina sniffed loudly. "He said he needed to borrow a fedora. I didn't question it." She let out a long sigh. "I don't know what else I can tell you."

A fedora. The pieces began to fit. The makeup on the inside of the hat now made perfect sense.

Thanking Christina and making sure she had his card in case she thought of anything else, Adam thanked her for her time. Then they left, the sounds of the busy city greeting them and Christiana's words circulating in the air around them.

ADAM PULLED BACK on to 395 and turned the radio down. Margot glanced to the side, trying to read him. She'd been around him enough to know that he needed time to process things. She would be surprised if he brought up the case now, because she had a feeling he needed to mull over what they had heard.

"So, Dex," he began.

She huffed out a breath. "You've got to be kidding."

He grinned at her, his eyes staying on the road. Part of her wondered if he'd bring up going to dinner again, but another part of her hoped he wouldn't. Now *she* was the one who needed processing time.

"He's a good kid," Adam said in a singsong voice.

"I know. I just...I haven't had time to go over his credentials and—"

"What? A recommendation from me isn't good enough? What if I told you I've already run a background check on him?"

"You did?"

"Would that change you hiring him?" He looked hopeful.

"Adam, why are you insistent on me hiring Dexter?"

Adam let out a deep breath. "He told you he knew me, right?"

"Yes, he mentioned he knew you when he was younger."

"Well..." Adam swallowed. Was he uncomfortable? "I

actually took care of him for a while. While his mom was...unavailable."

"Unavailable?"

Adam cringed again. "Drugs. She was in rehab."

Margot's whole notion of Adam shifted in that moment. He had long since been her friend and before that he'd been a friend of her husband, Julian's, but now he was more. A guardian. Almost a parent.

"Really." It was a statement more than a question.

He risked a glance at her. "What? What's going on in that sharp mind of yours, Margot Durand? You have me worried."

She smiled. "I'm just picturing you as a...guardian. That's really commendable of you."

"Now don't go putting me on a pedestal. He needed a place to stay and I had a spare bedroom. It was kind of like what you did for Taylor, just a little longer."

"How long?"

He took in a breath. "Two years."

"Two—!" She cut herself off, the exclamation clearly making Adam uncomfortable. Though he was the town's only detective and could take over a case with bravado, Adam was the furthest thing from a man who wanted attention drawn to his good deeds.

"It was the right thing to do."

"I believe that."

Silence rested between them but Margot's mind filled in pictures of Adam as a guardian. It was a pleasant picture.

"So..." He drew the word out. "Dex."

"All right," she laughed, shaking her head, "I'll hire him."

"Yes!" he said, sounding way too excited.

"But on a *trial* basis. He needs to prove himself to me first."

"Naturally. You know, when he was younger—" Adam's story was cut off by his phone. He pressed a button on his steering wheel and the sound crackled through the car speakers. "Eastwood here."

"Well howdy, Detective E," a booming voice said. Margot leaned back, as if to get away from the loudness of the voice, and Adam pressed another button. "It's Martin the M.E." The man laughed on the other end of the line but thankfully his voice was quieter now.

"He says that *every time* he calls me," Adam whispered to Margot. She grinned and pressed her lips together when the man spoke again.

"You got someone there with you?"

"Yes. Mrs. Durand from the bakery."

"Oh, great! I've been meaning to stop by, Margot. Wife's got a birthday coming up and—"

"Did you have something for me, Martin?" Adam interrupted.

"Yup, sure do. But I can call back..." His meaning was clear.

"I think it'll be all right for Margot to hear."

"Sure enough," Martin said. "I've got the tox screen results back on that fellow."

Margot's hopes soared. Would they reveal some way to clear George?

"Go ahead," Adam said.

"Looks like it was a lethal dose of Digoxin."

"Really," Adam said, pondering the results.

"But there was something else."

"Go ahead, Martin."

"Looks like there were trace amounts of insulin in the syringe. We wouldn't have seen it in the blood work but I of course sent off everything we found to The Big Guys."

"He always calls them that," Adam whispered, eliciting another laugh from Margot.

"So the syringe previously had insulin in it. Had it been used before?"

"Nope. My best guess here is that the culprit emptied out a diabetic syringe and filled it with a homemade killing remedy."

"Homemade?" Margot clamped her mouth shut. She hadn't meant to interfere but her curiosity had gotten away from her.

"Yes sir—er, ma'am. Digoxin is found in foxglove."

"Like the flower?"

"The very same."

Adam nodded as if he'd already known this.

"Anything else, Martin?"

"Not yet. I'll call when I know more."

"Thanks."

"Sure thing, boss. Bye, Margot."

He hung up and the car fell into silence again. A diabetic syringe filled with a homemade poison made from flowers found all over George's neighborhood—and even his front yard. Things were looking worse and worse for her friend's husband.

CHAPTER 8

DEXTER WAS WAITING at the door when Margot arrived at the shop early the next day. Startled, she took a step back when he emerged from the shadows.

"Sorry to scare you," he said with an infectious grin. "I just believe in being on time."

"Or early," she said, unlocking the door and typing in her code for the alarm system. "Welcome to your first day at the bakery."

"I'm looking forward to it."

"Just so you know, this is—"

"A trial period," he said, interrupting her, but not rudely. "I know. And I appreciate the chance."

Feeling slightly better about things and the reality that she would have help that morning, she put Dexter to work prepping the kitchen as she sat down behind her desk for the first few sips of coffee before the busyness began. She felt slightly guilty for making him work while she eased into the morning, but then again—that was what assistants were for, right? Besides, she was paying him well, even if it was a trial period.

Checking her email, she clicked on one that was marked from the library. Did she have a book she was late in returning?

When the email opened, she saw it was addressed to her from Barbara at the library. Margot had almost forgotten about talking with Wilhelmina and how Barbara had been gone on vacation.

She skimmed through the short email surprised to see that Barbara had cut her trip short due to a sprained ankle and that she would be at the library—on crutches—if Margot wanted to stop by that afternoon.

Margot wondered if Wilhelmina had told her what her questions regarded, but the scent of something burning drew her attention to the kitchen.

"What is—" She stopped short to see Dexter bent over an amazing creation of spun sugar.

"Sorry about that," he said, standing up after resting the spoon on the counter. "Some of the sugar got onto the element."

"What are you making?"

"I hope you don't mind," he said, looking sheepish, "but

when you said you were going to be making mini-cheesecakes, I thought about these spun sugar toppers. They are easy to make and it was something I could get out of the way now. I should have asked," he finished, looking nervous.

She smiled, impressed not only by his talent but his creativity. "I'm impressed. Though I will say you probably should have consulted me before using my ingredients. What if I wouldn't have enough for what we're making next?"

His expression fell. "I should have thought of that."

"It's all right. You did well with these and, thankfully, I'm fully stocked. Let's get to work, shall we? These desserts aren't going to bake themselves."

The rest of the morning flew by, and with Dexter's help, Margot was pleased to see that they were done well ahead of her planned schedule. Stepping back as the last of the cookies were pulled from the oven, she surveyed the kitchen. It was a little messier than when she worked by herself, but finishing nearly an hour earlier, and it only being Dexter's first day, seemed to make her choice to hire him obvious.

Then again, she wasn't going to tell him that just yet. Better to let him sweat it out just a few more days. Besides, the first day could be a fluke. Though she had a feeling it wasn't. He was a hard worker and a talented baker.

The front doorbell rang and Dexter popped his head out, a cheery greeting of hello welcoming guests. He sure was enthusiastic.

"Who on God's green earth are you?"

Margot pressed her lips together to keep her laugh in. Should she go out and rescue Dexter from Rosie's inquisition? Or let him sweat a little?

Deciding he'd already been through enough, she stepped into the front space of her shop. "Rosie, why are you giving my new employee a hard time?"

Rosie's chocolate brown eyes widened, the white stark against her brown skin. "New employee, did you say?"

"Yes. This is his first day." Margot crossed her arms, looking between them.

"He's not replacing me, child." She said it as fact, no question in her statement.

Margot let her laugh float out at the look on Dexter's face. "No, Rosie! Of course not! No one could replace you."

"That's right," she said, placing a hand on her hip. "What's he doing for you then?"

"He," Dexter said, breaking into the conversation, "is going to go clean up the kitchen."

He rushed off before Margot could tell him she'd help, but she turned back to Rosie. "Adam recommended him to me."

"Detective Eastwood?" Rosie perked up at his name. "Well then, in that case."

Margot rolled her eyes. "I could say Adam ran into your car and you'd still get that look on your face."

"He's a fine young man," Rosie said, her grin widening. "And I do mean *fine*."

"Oh, Rosie," she said, shaking her head. The two women gave into laughter just as Margot heard the kitchen sink turn on. "I should probably go back and help him. But what are you doing here early?"

"I came by to ask if I could get in a few extra hours this week. It's my granddaughter's birthday next month and I want to get her something special. A few extra hours would really help."

Margot smiled warmly back at the older woman. "Of course, Rosie. Anything you need. In fact..." She looked back toward the kitchen. "Maybe I'll leave Dexter in your watchful charge."

Rosie burst into a deep-throated laugh. "You know I'll teach him right."

"I do know that," Margot said.

After Margot explained what Dexter needed to do for the rest of his shift, she collected her items and stepped out into the fresh air. The library wasn't far from the bakery and she decided to take advantage of the perfect weather to walk.

When she reached the front door, she smoothed her hand over her hair and stepped inside. The quiet interior boasted only a few occupants, which at this time of day, she wasn't surprised. It was close to lunch and many in the senior community didn't leave their homes until later in the day.

She made her way to the front desk and was happy to find Barbara there. The woman reached for her crutches, but Margot held out a hand.

"Mind if I come to you instead?"

"Please," Barbara said, looking relieved.

They chatted pleasantly at first as Margot asked how Barbara's trip had gone and how recovery for her ankle was going. When there was a lull, Margot edged closer to her real question. She wanted to play it carefully knowing that, in their little retirement community, the library was quite a hub for gossip and Margot didn't want to be the one drawing attention to anything unnecessarily. At least not yet.

"So, Barbara, I was in here talking to Wilhelmina a few days ago."

"Oh, I know, she told me you wanted to see me. It's why I sent you that email last night. Almost forgot to. Had to log on right before I left."

"And I appreciate that." She hesitated. How would she word this? "So, there was a man researching something similar to what I was. At least that's what Wilhelmina said."

"Sure was." Barbara shivered. "Strange—and downright scary if you ask me—that he was looking into a man who ended up dead. Are you looking into the case? I know you solved that murder mystery at the beginning of summer. You going to do the same now? Seems like you've got a head for mystery."

Not the subtlety Margot was hoping for. "Not exactly. I'm just curious about this person. Could you describe him?"

"Well, sure," she said, her gaze traveling up to some distant spot in the ceiling. "He was white, tall, balding, medium build. Kind of average looking. I think he had light brown hair."

Margot groaned. It sounded a lot like George, but she couldn't be sure." Her hand flew to her pocket, but she realized with a grimace that she'd left her phone back at the bakery on her desk so there was no way to show Barbara a recent picture of George.

"He wasn't in here long. Sorry I can't be of more help to your case."

Margot groaned inwardly. "Not *my* case. The police's case." She forced a smile and stood. "Thank you for all you help. Hope your ankle feels better soon."

"Thanks, dear. And good luck. I know you can solve it."

Margot gave the woman a tightlipped smile and left. She

wasn't solving anything. Merely looking into leads. Leads that seemed to keep coming back to George.

~

"I DON'T KNOW, MARG," Tamera said, picking at her pasta halfheartedly. "I think someone is dragging their feet."

Tamera was surprised to learn that George still hadn't had his bail hearing. "Who's the judge?"

"Judge Castor. Something about him being sick and then the courtroom was double-booked. Does that even happen?"

Margot had no idea and merely shrugged, her bite of garlic bread melting in her mouth. "How are *you* doing with him being gone?"

Tamera looked off into the distance. "I don't know. I just keep thinking..."

"Thinking what?"

"That maybe I don't know him as well as I thought I did."

"Tamera..." Margot shook her head and reached across the table to grasp her friend's hand. "That is nonsense. You know him just fine and we both believe in his innocence. It's just a difficult time right now. What George needs is for you to be beside him. Remember the 'in sickness and in health' part of your vows?"

"I don't know if that applies here, Marg," she said, looking doubtful.

"Maybe not," Margot said through a grin, "but I think part of all of that is that it's in good times and in bad. These are the bad. So stick by him."

Tamera's eyes filled with tears. "You're right. Oh, Marg, I'm so sorry. This was awful of me. Of *course* I'm going to stick by him."

"Nonsense. You're being honest with me and I appreciate that. I know it's not easy. We all have our moments, but I know at the end of the day that you love him and will stick up for him."

She nodded and the waiter appeared with their check and to-go boxes. "No Antonio tonight?" Margot asked the young woman.

"No, his sister just came back from Italy so he's spending some time with her," the girl replied with a smile.

"Glad to hear she made it back." Margot paid for the meal and they left, getting into Tamera's car since Margot had left hers at Tamera's house.

"Need anything else before we go back to your place?" Margot asked. "You do have food at home, don't you?"

"Yes, mother," Tamera said with a smile as she pulled out onto the road.

Margot laughed and leaned back. Nighttime had fallen

while they'd eaten dinner and now it was dark, dim lights popping up in business, streetlights, and the porch lights of most homes they passed.

As Margot leaned back, bright headlights reflected in the side mirror and she held up a hand to block their penetrating brightness.

"Gosh, this guy is right on my tail," Tamera said, both hands gripping the wheel.

"Does he have his brights on?"

"Seems like it, right?" Tamera took the next turn onto Route 6, a road that ran parallel to Highway 1, and followed along the river. The road was narrow and winding, but for a longtime North Bank resident like Tamera, they were as natural as driving through town every day.

The lights behind them seemed to get brighter. "Wow, he must be in a rush."

"Tell me about it," Tamera said, her jaw clenching with each turn. "I'm pushing five over the speed limit as it is, but he's still getting really close."

Margot turned around in her seat, trying to shield her eyes from the bright light to see if she could catch the make of the car—or perhaps it was a truck?—but it was too bright to tell.

Then Tamera sucked in a breath as they went around a

particularly sharp curve and Margot whipped around to the front again.

"Margot!" she said as the sound of the vehicle's revving engine behind them was so close that Margot thought it was vibrating through her seat.

"Be careful, Tam—" Margot said just as they felt the vehicle hit Tamera's car from behind.

Tamera screamed but kept her eyes on the road. Margot reached up to grab the handle above her door to keep from flying forward just as the vehicle behind them struck again.

"I can't keep this up much more, Marg. This guy's going to push me off the road!"

"It's okay, Tam. You've got this. Just keep it steady." Margot's heart was racing but she forced her mind to calm down. They were coming up on one stretch of road with a bridge. Did the person behind them know about it? If he did, then they most certainly needed to make it past the bridge.

"Speed up."

"Are you joking? I'm already going ten miles over the speed limit."

"Do it! If he's at all close to us near Castle Rock Bridge, we could be pushed over the side."

It was all the encouragement Tamera needed. She pushed

down on the gas, creating distance between them and the man behind them.

"What about *after* the bridge?"

"You're going to take The Fork."

Margot watched Tamera's face for any sign that she didn't understand, but all she saw there was determination.

"I'm going to have to hit the brake, though."

"Wait until after we're past the bridge. If you keep enough distance, we should make it."

They waited in tense silence as the bridge came into view. As they had expected, the vehicle sped up, trying to get close to them again.

"Margot..." Tamera said through clenched teeth.

"We're almost there. Just hold on..."

Both women fell silent as they passed the entrance to the bridge. Halfway through, the vehicle sped up again but Tamera had anticipated the move and was already accelerating off of the bridge.

Now came the tricky part. She began to slow. The person behind them came up on them quickly but, at the last moment, she yanked the wheel to the side.

Margot had been prepared for the jolt, or so she'd thought, but the sudden change from paved road to gravel threw both of them forward then back as much as Tamera's ample pressure on the brake.

Eventually, they skidded to a stop on the long, graveled road. Both were panting and both had white knuckles.

"I think he's gone."

Margot turned and saw only darkness behind them.

"That was smart thinking, using The Fork."

Margot took in another breath. She and Tammy often hiked in the hills near the Potomac and they had lovingly name this road The Fork after the first time they'd agreed to meet here and Tamera had called Margot several times to verify its location.

"I'll never forget where this road is. Daylight, nighttime, it doesn't matter."

"And that's what I was counting on. Hopefully, they won't take the time to turn around and come back."

"You think they would?" Tamera's voice held a tremor.

"I don't know, but I'm calling Adam."

CHAPTER 9

"MARGOT, ARE YOU ALL RIGHT?" Adam rushed up the hillside, his lights shining up to where Tamera's car had finally come to a stop. Thankfully, the car was no worse for wear, but the women's nerves were frayed. Another officer, a friend of theirs, stepped into the light and made his way toward Tamera.

"I have never been so scared, Adam," Margot admitted. Her arms were wrapped around herself as if she was cold, but it was more to keep from shaking than anything else.

"I'm so sorry— I…" There was nothing for him to say. And there was no way he could have helped prevent the chase. But the question remained: why them?

"I…I just don't understand. Why us?"

Adam's jaw tightened. "I'm not sure either. I've had some news, but—" He looked around the scene. "If Drake takes

Tamera back to her place, can I take you home? So we can talk?"

"Of course, but let me make sure Tamera's all right with that first."

After explaining the situation to Tamera, she agreed and allowed Officer Drake to slip behind the wheel. Having him drive home would be safer than either of them driving the car. Then Adam got behind the wheel and headed off toward Margot's home.

She clasped her hands in her lap, knowing that they would shake and give away how she was truly feeling if she let them rest on her legs. Since they were close to the house, Adam didn't say anything and she instinctively knew that he would wait until they reached the safety and comfort of her home. It was a fact she was thankful for.

At her townhome, he saw her inside and seated on the couch, while he went to make a mug of peppermint tea. Only when they were seated on the couch, facing one another, and Margot had her mug of tea did he start the conversation she knew they had to have.

"What happened?"

She'd appreciated his earlier care for her, but now she felt overwhelmed by the details that she needed to convey to him. She started at the beginning, where she and Tamera had been and where they'd been planning to go—back to Tamera's place to decompress with a funny movie.

Then she described how the vehicle, now she was thinking it was an SUV, had come up quickly on them as if knowing the right time to approach.

"But wait," he said, interrupting her, "you said a few miles past when you turned onto Route 6 that the guy got close to you."

"Yes," she said, uncertain of why he sounded confused.

"But you also said that he knew the right time to sneak up on you."

"Yes, I could clearly tell that he was waiting for Castle Rock Bridge."

"Right." The lines on Adam's forehead deepened.

"What? I don't understand your confusion."

"I don't know if this guy—assuming it's a guy—knew about Castle Rock Bridge or not, but I do know that he had ample opportunities to run you off the road before that. I also know that he could have circled back to follow you up The Fork if he'd wanted to, but he didn't."

She reasoned through what Adam had said and then nodded in agreement. "I suppose I could be too close to the situation. I assumed he knew about the bridge, but maybe he didn't. Where does that leave us?"

"It leaves us with someone who may not be from the area."

Margot leaned back, her mug of tea reaching a drinkable

temperature. She took a sip, contemplating what Adam was saying.

"What do you know that I don't?"

His head jerked up and he met her gaze. "How do you do that?"

"What?"

"Know when I have information that you don't have." A corner of his mouth tipped up.

"Well...?" She waited, knowing he would tell her.

"I've been going over George's bank records."

Margot was suddenly suspicious. "What did you find?"

"I'm not sure, and it's *not* conclusive, but I have reason to believe that George was being blackmailed."

Margot felt her eyebrows rise. "By who?"

"No way to know."

"So...we're talking about cash then."

He nodded, obviously impressed.

"And I would assume similar, large withdrawals at a specific time interval."

"Yes and no. Over the past number of years, significant withdrawals of cash have been made, like you're saying, but they aren't at regular intervals, which is why it took our tech a while to pinpoint. They seem random."

"So maybe as needed?"

"It appears that way."

Margot put together what she knew of George and what she'd learned so far. He was a well-off lawyer in D.C. so he wouldn't be hurting for money. Tamera's business was not only successful in town and to upper class D.C. residents who liked to 'get out of the city,' but also online where she sold supplies on Etsy.

If she had to guess, she assumed they hadn't yet incorporated their finances since they'd only been married a few months. George could have easily hidden blackmail payments he was making if they weren't large enough to wipe him out.

"But, what's more—and possibly what's worse," Adam said, drawing her attention back from her thoughts, "is the fact that he made the largest withdrawal he's made right after he got back to North Bank from Hawaii."

"Oh, Adam..." Margot's mind raced back to the night when she'd spoken with Tammy. His eyes snapped to hers.

"What?"

"I'm so sorry, I meant to tell you this but forgot. Tammy says that she called his work and he didn't need to come back from his honeymoon for a work event."

"I already know." He looked pained. "And that's not even

the worst of it. He deposited the *same* amount of money the night we found Mark."

Margot's eyes widened. "What?"

"It's not looking good for your friend."

"But it doesn't add up."

"Murder usually doesn't."

"No." Margot set her tea down because she felt the need to talk with her hands. "I mean think of it this way—George is *paying* someone for all these years and then what? Suddenly decides to kill a star witness who seems to have no connection to George aside from George's company's involvement in his case? It makes no sense."

"Or George takes a payment to kill off the witness to replace the money he owes his blackmailer. A trade."

Stumped, Margot slumped back against the couch. It still didn't add up for her.

"It's late, and I should go, but I just wanted to make sure you were all right. I don't know who was after you ladies tonight, but I'll get to the bottom of this." He rested a warm hand on her shoulder. "And I want you to be careful. Promise me you will."

"Of course. I'm always careful."

"Careful to get into trouble." He gave her a rueful smile. "But seriously, Margie, I told you these things in confidence, not so that you'll do something foolish like take this case on by yourself."

She made a mental note of the fact that he hadn't forbidden her from the case, just taking it on by herself. Likely he'd just misspoken, but she'd hold him to it.

"I understand."

They stood and she walked him to the door. When he paused to look at her, she saw compassion in his eyes. His hand on her shoulder was warm as he leaned down and kissed her on the forehead. It was a sweet, caring thing and it helped ease the tension in her body from that night's frightening ride.

"Good night, Adam. And thank you for coming to my rescue...again."

He grinned. "Always."

~

MARGOT GRIMACED as her alarm shattered the silence of her room. It was still dark out, it always was when she got up for work, but after the car chase the night before, she hadn't been able to fall asleep as easily as she'd wanted. Tossing and turning most of the night, she felt like the car had hit her and Tamera instead of almost forcing them off the road.

Still, she showered, dressed, and made it to the bakery on time as usual. Dexter was there waiting for her and they got right to work. She questioned him on how things had gone after she left the day before and he gave her a rundown of what he'd done.

She was impressed at his skill not only in baking but also in the business side of things. He'd drafted a few proposals for her to look at regarding her website, current marketing she did, and improvements for special events she could host.

"Are you trying to take over my bakery?" she asked.

His hands stilled, one holding a wooden spoon and the other a metal bowl. "N-no," he said, eyes wide.

She broke in to a grin. "Don't worry, Dex," she said, using the nickname Adam used for him, "I'm just joking with you."

He let out a huge sigh. "You got me."

"But, in all seriousness, I really appreciate your proactive approach to working here. You're a good baker, but you also have great business sense."

"Thank you."

"Now let me ask you this," she said, leveling her gaze at him so he'd know she was serious. "Why are you really here?"

Was it her imagination or had he paled at her question?

"Uh, what do you mean?"

"I've checked into your credentials. Not only are you certified, but you've also got a bachelor's degree in business and you're just shy a few credits of having your master's in business management. I've called a few of your past references and they've loved working with you. Some even expressed regret over you leaving, as if they'd lost a vital part of their business." She placed her hands on the cool, stainless steel countertop and leaned forward. "Don't get me wrong, I'm happy you're here, but I don't want to start relying on you only to have you split a few months later. I think knowing why you're really here will help me decide whether or not I'll keep you on."

He blinked a few times in the silence that fell between them but then he slowly began nodding. He wiped his flour-caked hands on his apron and crossed his arms. His demeanor was in no way closed, just thoughtful.

"You're a smart woman, Mrs. Durand. Though Adam already warned me of that."

"He did, did he?"

"Yep." He grinned but then continued, "I understand why you want answers. I want a few myself, but I'll give you what I can. Though there are a few things I can't tell you...yet."

His response intrigued her, but she resisted pressing him for more information than he was willing to give—for the moment. As long as it didn't affect him working here, she didn't exactly *need* to know.

"I guess you could say that I see North Bank as a way to start fresh. I'm twenty-five and don't really know where my life is heading. To me, that seems like a waste." He grinned. "During a call with Adam, he talked a bunch about this place and…yeah, he happened to mention that you had a 'world class' bakery—as he put it—" Another grin. "—and he recommended me coming down here. I took him up on it."

Margot took in the young man's story with a nod. "Thanks for being frank with me. Do you want to own your own bakery someday?" She saw the question took him by surprise.

"I do." He sounded wary, like she'd just read his mind.

"I talk to Adam too."

"That dog." He laughed, shaking his head. "Nah, it's good. I would have expected you to check me out beforehand and I'm glad that Adam vouched for me."

"This is all helpful for me to know." She nodded once, then surveyed the kitchen. "Okay. Back to work."

"Mrs. Durand?"

"Yes?"

"Thanks for taking a chance on me."

"Sure thing, Dex. And one more thing?"

"Anything," he said, his face registering honesty.

"Call me Margot."

They worked hard through the morning and she showed him more of how her business was run. By the early afternoon when Rosie came in, they were ahead of schedule and she started to see the potential for having an assistant. Not so much that she could take time off, but more so that she could do the things she'd been putting off. Planning out further than just the next few months. Have more interaction with her customers. It all gave her a rosy glow to the day, until she got the text from Tamera.

THERE'S BEEN ANOTHER MURDER.

CHAPTER 10

MARGOT WALKED the few blocks to Grant Park where the body had been found. Despite the fact that the scene was closed off, she risked coming to the front of the onlookers where the bright yellow tape stretched across the entrance.

"Stay back, please," an officer said. He was younger, newer to the area, but if she remembered correctly, his last name was Smith.

She'd just made it to the front when she spotted Adam. He saw her and shook his head, a slight smile on his lips.

"Smith," he said, coming forward. The young deputy looked up to him.

"Sir?"

"Let that one through," he said, pointing to Margot.

"Yes, sir. This way, ma'am," he said, helping her under the yellow tape.

A few reporters tossed out questions for Adam but he ignored them, directing Margot to the shade of a large oak tree but not near where she assumed the body was.

"Why are you here, Margot? No, scratch that question. *How* did you find out about this?"

She grinned, knowing that he wasn't really angry at her for being there.

"Tamera was on a run this morning and saw the police cars. Heard from someone about what had happened. She messaged me. She wants to know if they are connected and, if so, if George will be released."

"And you just had to come by and see."

Margot shrugged, trying to look innocent. "I knew it couldn't hurt."

"Um huh." He shook his head, hands sliding to his hips as he looked back to where the body lay covered by a sheet. "I'm going to hazard a guess that this is not associated with the body found in Tamera's shop."

"What makes you say that?"

Adam roughed a hand over his jaw, the stubble there evidence that he had been called to the scene early that morning.

"The MO is way different and..." He trailed off and

looked down at her. "I shouldn't be telling you any of this."

She offered him a shy smile. "If it's any consolation, I promise not to mention anything you've said—or will say—to anyone else."

He narrowed his eyes in thought for a moment, then nodded as if in agreement with her.

"This scene was...messy. This was no murder by poisoning. And, while that's not conclusive evidence, it just *looks* different. In fact, it looks familiar."

"How so?"

"Remember how I told you I was working with my brother up in D.C. on a few cases?"

"Yes, I remember you had mentioned that at the beginning of summer."

"We actually worked a few that involved Victor Carow."

"Wait, the man who Mark Jennings was going to testify against?"

"You mean the *drug lord?* And yes, the very same man. Well, I should say his group. They have a certain way of... disposing of someone who has crossed them. It's part of the reason why I don't think Mark was killed by Carow's associates, but that remains to be seen."

"What do you mean?"

"This murder—it's got Carow's name all over it. Whoever he gets to do his bidding has a certain style. I won't say more, but the timing is odd. First Jennings is killed here and now this man? I don't like how all of this is coming together. We're in North Bank, for goodness sake. It's supposed to be Small Town America here."

Margot shivered despite the warmth of the sun and wrapped her arms around herself. "What do you think is really going on here?"

"I don't know," Adam said, his frown deepening. "But I've got to get back to the scene. Remember. Not a word."

She nodded in agreement and he saw her back under the yellow tape. As Margot walked away from the scene of the crime, she couldn't help but wonder what was going on in North Bank just like Adam had pointed out. This wasn't some hot bed of crime. It was a retirement community with a large senior population. Sure, they were close to the city, but why here?

The questions only managed to mount up in her mind, growing larger and larger until she couldn't think straight. The one thing she *did* know was that her friend needed her and she was going to be there for her.

～

AFTER MAKING a drive by of Tamera's house, Margot circled the large residential block and came back around to park far down the street. As she did, she noticed a dark-colored SUV she'd briefly seen on her first drive by. The outline of the driver was evident even from a distance. He looked to be a large man but she couldn't see more than that because of the tint of the windows.

The thing that was odd to her was that he had the windows rolled up and, in the ten minutes it had taken her to circle the block—due to a red light and a few pedestrian crossings—the person was still there.

At any other time, she may not have noticed the vehicle or the man in it, but her senses were on high alert. Not to mention the fact that the SUV looked like it could have been the one that ran them off the road the night before.

Her mouth instantly went dry at the memory of the headlights glaring and the speed at which they'd been driving over the massively high bridge only feet from flying over the side. If she could get close enough, would she see paint on the man's bumper?

Margot slid her hand into her purse and pulled out the mini-Taser she now carried almost everywhere with her. With her Krav Maga skills and this handy contraption, she felt secure. Armed with it in one hand and her phone in the other, she decided to approach the SUV. Chances were it was someone waiting to pick someone up and her fear was for nothing. She'd rather make a fool of herself. All she had to do was get close enough to get a good look at the license plate and maybe the face of the person in the vehicle.

She slipped down the tree-lined street, hiding behind bushes as they were available. Since she'd parked so far away, she had considerable ground to make up. But soon Tamera's house came into view as did the SUV parked only a few cars from Tamera's front door. Unfortunately, the person in the SUV had all but backed up into the car behind them, which made it impossible for Margot to see the back license plate.

She paused, covered by a large hydrangea bush, and peered through the leaves. She saw movement in the car and what looked like a flash of glass. Binoculars? Was he spying on Tamera? The feeling of foreboding increased. From the SUV's vantage point, they would be able to see all of the front windows of Tamera's house.

Making up her mind, Margot slipped from behind the tree and tried to duck-walk toward the car. She was almost to the car parked right behind when the sound of barking shattered the stillness of the neighborhood.

A light tan blur launched itself at Margot who, in her surprise, let out a cry as Mr. Puggles attacked her face with licks.

Lights blinked on at the same time the engine of the SUV roared to life. The next second, the sound of crunching plastic and metal accompanied the SUV's hasty exit from the tight parking spot. The driver had backed into the car and then rammed the bumper of the car in front of him in his hurry to escape.

The sound of screeching tires was the last thing Margot saw. She ground her teeth, angry at herself for not getting his license plate number, but she'd been so shocked at his hasty retreat from the parking space and the shock of having a dog in her arms that she hadn't been able to memorize it or even capture a picture of the plate. Some detective she was turning out to be.

"Margot, what is going on?" Tamera was running from the house to her, eyes wide in surprise.

Margot pulled herself off the ground and brushed off stray bits of grass. "What's going on is I think I just saw the person who tried to run us off the road yesterday. And I let him get away."

"What?"

Margot explained how she'd seen the man and how she assumed he had been spying on Tamera, to which her friend shivered and looked over her shoulder as if he could be right behind her.

"I don't like this one bit. Another murder and now this? Who is that man?"

"Did you see him?"

"Not really. He was wearing dark sunglasses and had dark hair—I think. He drove off so fast and there was a glare in the window."

Margot stared in the direction he'd driven in. "Well, at

least we can give a statement about the car. Want to go down to the police station with me?"

"Why don't you call Adam?" Tamera stopped and picked up Mr. Puggles, who squirmed to be let free again.

"I have a feeling he'll be busy at the crime scene for a while. Then you can stop by to see George. He's still not released?"

Margot saw the stormy look gather in Tamer's eyes. "No. And I've just about had it."

"Come on. Let's put Mr. Puggles back inside and head to the station." She surveyed the street one more time then said, more to herself than her friend who was already nearing her home, "I have a feeling there are more than a few puzzles going on here."

CHAPTER 11

A<small>FTER</small> M<small>ARGOT</small> and Tamera gave a revised statement about the vehicle from the previous night to a deputy on duty, they walked across the street to the jail where George was being held. It was adjacent to the courthouse and, while not high security, still had a sterile, cold feel about it. They were shown into a room with a metal table and three chairs, only a small window high on the wall and encased in bars and shatterproof glass giving off dim light.

As they sat, Margot turned to her friend. "Are you sure you want me in here? I can give you guys some time to talk."

"No." Tamera clasped Margot's hand. "I want you here. Besides, I think it's time I asked George why he came back early and I want you here with me."

When George was shown in, he sat down in the chair

facing the two women and reached across the table for Tamera's hands. "Tam," he said, his voice scratchy.

Margot saw tears enter her friend's eyes and she again realized how difficult this had to be for her. Not only was her husband *still* in jail, she had reason to believe he had lied to her.

"How are you, sweetie?"

Tamera sniffed. "Not good, George. I want this all to be over."

"I know, honey, me too. Me too." He patted her hand gently and Margot felt a wave of longing wash through her. She and Julian had had this kind of love. And though he'd been gone almost five years now, she could still almost feel his touch in rare moments of quiet when she closed her eyes.

But that was in the past and she needed to focus on the present. And if she was going to save her friend some of the heartache she was facing, Margot had to begin the difficult conversation.

"George," she said, hating to interrupt their moment but knowing it was necessary, "I've got some difficult questions to ask you."

He turned to her, surprise on his sharp features. "What do you mean, Margot?"

Margot glanced toward Tamera and then back at her

husband. "We know that you didn't come back for a work meeting."

The color drained from George's already pale features. "W-what do you mean?"

"I called your boss, George. When I mentioned the meeting, he didn't know what I was talking about."

The silence dropped heavily between them as George's gaze drilled into the metal tabletop. Finally, after a few moments, he took in a deep breath and looked up.

"I suppose I should have come out with all of this long before now, but I was...I don't know. I suppose I was hoping it wouldn't have to come up."

"What do you mean?"

His brow furrowed more deeply and he turned his gaze to Tamera. "I should have told you before we got married. I was going to...but then I thought it was behind me and it wouldn't affect our lives. But then...then it did and it was too late and..."

"George," Margot pushed into the one-sided conversation. "Start from the beginning. Let us know so we can help you."

He looked at Margot for a long time then nodded, turning his focus back to his wife.

"You knew that I was married before, but what I didn't tell you was that I had a daughter during that time." Tamera merely nodded, not wanting to interrupt the flow of her husband's confession. "She's a sweet girl. Her name is Sarah, and I would do anything to protect her."

Margot felt her stomach twist into knots. *Anything?*

"But by the time she graduated high school, I had been out of her life for a few years, estranged from her mother, and I'd barely seen her. I did hear stories of how she wasn't doing well, but I didn't even know how to find her." He let out a heavy sigh. "Finally, when my private practice was established, that was before I moved to Washington, D.C., I got an email from her. She was in some deep trouble and needed money. We met and, as I talked with her, I could see she wanted out. She'd been involved in all sorts of terrible things and just needed a new start. So, I helped. I got her out of the situation, moved her across the country to Virginia, and she started over."

"Wait," Tamera interrupted. "Sarah. As in...Sarah Newman?"

"You know her?" Margot wasn't following.

"That's where things get complicated." George seemed to deflate before Margot's eyes. "We hadn't been close and just because I helped her, didn't mean our relationship was healed. I was satisfied to know she was safe. But... then I was offered a job at my current company, a big step up for me, and came to find out that it was due to my daughter, who had married the head partner's son."

The pieces began to click. This was why Tamera had

known his daughter's name. Was it possible she had even met his daughter at an event? Margot looked to her friend and saw an expression of pain and confusion on her delicate features.

"When I came east, we met and decided it was best for us not to mention our familial ties. She had reinvented herself and taken another name before marrying Trevor— my boss's son—and she said that Trevor knew nothing of her past. I wasn't about to ruin what little relationship we did have, and besides, I wanted my daughter to succeed so I kept my mouth shut."

"But someone found out," Margot said, almost to herself.

George's eyes snapped to hers. "Yes. How did you know?"

"Because I'm beginning to see that there are several things going on here, and this is only part of it. You were—or are —being blackmailed, aren't you?"

"I am." George looked shocked that she knew.

Margot thought of the regular payments George had taken out of his account. "What happened when you came back early from the honeymoon trip?"

He sighed heavily. "Years ago, I had been contacted by a Harry Beakman."

Margot's mind flicked back to the email address she'd seen. *Beaky123.*

"He had gone to high school with Sarah and apparently

fallen in love with her, but she'd never returned the feelings. When he came on hard times years out of high school, he looked her up. Somehow he found who she used to associate with and followed her trail to Virginia. That's when he came to me saying he'd ruin Sarah's new life unless I gave him a little something to tide him over."

George ran a hand over his face, the weariness of all that had happened taking its toll on him.

"At the time, I wasn't really sure what to do. I wanted my little girl to succeed and I was afraid that Harry showing up on her doorstep and telling her new husband what she'd been involved in in the past would ruin everything. So I paid him. He went away and I thought I'd seen the last of him, but that was too good to be true. He started to show up every few months like clockwork. He never demanded so much that I couldn't pay him, but I knew he'd be coming back."

"Oh, George," Tamera said, grasping his hand. "Why didn't you tell me?"

"That's just it." He locked gazes with her. "When I met you, my life changed. Everything changed. I not only fell in love with you but I wanted you to meet Sarah and *know* she was my daughter. I wanted to tell you everything. I was going to—on our honeymoon in Hawaii—but then I got an email from Harry. I knew if I was going to tell you, I wanted to be able to say that it would never be a problem again. So I took more money than he'd asked for and went to meet him."

Margot thought of what Adam had told her about the larger withdrawal he'd made. The facts were lining up.

"I met with him and told him this would be the last of it. I was going to give him the money and then I wasn't going to give him any more. He threatened me, told me he'd go public with everything, but I'd already fessed up to Sarah and she'd agreed it was time. She was going to tell Trevor soon too. There really wasn't anything left for Harry to hold over me."

"What did he say?" Margot prompted.

"He got mad. We'd met at the park down the street from the shop, and he started throwing his hands up and arguing with me. Something snapped in me. I saw how foolish this all had been. I know that Trevor loves my little girl and I know that Tam loves me. There was no reason to keep secrets. So instead, I said forget it, pocketed the money, and walked off. That's when I stopped by the shop to get the glue stick since I was already in town. I went by the bank on my way back and deposited the money, then went home."

Margot leaned back. It fit. All of it. She needed to tell Adam that they were holding the wrong man.

STRONG HANDS CAUGHT her as she rushed from the room and straight into Adam's firm chest.

"Wha— Adam!"

He looked down at her, his gaze narrowing. "How did you know?"

She blinked. "Know? Know what?"

"About all of that?"

"Oh." She looked through the viewing window.

"I got your text," he said by way of explaining.

"I *didn't* know." She bit her lip, wondering what Tamera would think of her sending a text to Adam about meeting with George. "I just thought…well, I knew he hadn't told the truth about coming back to meet with his boss and—"

"Stop right there. Why didn't you tell me you were coming to talk with George?"

"I sent you a text." Margot bit her lip. She knew she'd messed up. She hadn't waited for him.

Adam shook his head. "If we're doing this—" He gestured between the two of them. She wanted to ask him to clarify exactly what *this* was, but he kept going. "—then we need to tell each other everything. Especially about important conversations like this." He pointed into the room.

"I didn't want to betray George's trust."

"I get it." He let out a sigh. "It's inadmissible but it's information I need so I can hone in on the *right* person."

"I know. And we'll persuade him to talk with you."

He stared off into space for a moment before he looked back down at her. "I put out an announcement to all of the patrol units in town and got a call from someone on the west side of town. Someone saw the SUV, right down to the paint on the front and back bumpers. Got a license plate number on it too. Seems like this Harry guy is the one who's been following you and Tamera."

"What?" Margot tried to reason through all of this and Adam's change of subject. So Harry hadn't gotten his money and now he was terrorizing Tamera? Was he doing it to send George a message? Seemed risky, but someone in need of money could stoop to something foolish like this.

"After this—" Adam motioned toward the two-way mirror into the room she'd just come from. "And your run-in with him, I think we have enough to bring Mr. Beakman in for questioning."

"I'm sorry, Adam," she said, resting her hand on his arm. "I really wasn't trying to keep anything from you."

"I know." He roughed his hand over his jaw again. "I'm just overly tired. This case—or cases, as it's turning out to be—are doing a number on our small staff."

Margot felt so sorry for her friend and the weight of responsibility that rested on his shoulders. They had to solve these cases—and quickly.

"We know George didn't kill Mark—"

"Or we're reasonably certain," Adam cut in.

"Right, so where does that leave us."

Adam huffed out a sigh. "I think it puts us back to a Carow sympathizer. Maybe a paid hit?"

"But it's clear the murderer wanted us to think it was George."

"Explain."

"Aside from the obvious—the body being found in the shop—I think Mrs. Henderson saw Mark go into the shop. Remember how Rachel said she loaned Mark her fedora? George almost always wears one, so it was as if Mark was being set up to look like George. Meanwhile, the killer waits for him in a darkened shop and attacks him."

"Making all leads point to George."

"Yes."

"So that leaves us with someone who knows George, knows he wears fedoras, and has access to the shop."

"That could be any number of people. Well, minus the access to the shop. That wouldn't be easy."

Adam nodded just as footsteps came down the hall toward them.

"Chief," he said, his voice sounding strained.

"Eastwood," the police chief said. He was a tall man in his mid-fifties with graying hair and piercing blue eyes that seemed to look through a person. He was rail thin and stood with his hands on his hips as he first looked at the two-way mirror and then at Margot before resting his gaze back on Adam. "Want to tell me what's going on here?"

Adam filled the man in with a concise wrap-up of what they'd just discovered. He finished by saying, "So we need to figure out what the link is between North Bank and Mark Jennings. Among other things," Adam trailed off, grimacing. Margot assumed he hated how vague it all sounded.

"And you, Mrs. Durand?" the chief said. He had only just transferred to North Bank around the time that Julian had been killed so her interaction with the hardened man had been limited.

"I was, um…" she fumbled for words.

"She was helping me." Adam stood a little straighter as if expecting lash back from this.

"In what capacity?" the man barked.

"She knows Tamera and George and was able to uncover the blackmail going on."

The chief's eyes narrowed again as he turned to look at her. "I won't underestimate the observations of an outsider. God knows our small staff could use a consultant or two. You run everything through Adam, you hear?"

"Y-Yes, sir," she responded. Had he really used the word consultant? Then again, he hadn't called *her* one…yet.

"Keep up the good work," the man growled over his shoulder as he turned back down the hallway.

"What…"

When Margot looked up at Adam, he had a strange expression on his face but it slipped away as soon as she rested her hand on his arm again.

"Does this mean you can take me back to the crime scene?"

He blinked. "What?"

"I need to see the inside of the shop again. I think we've missed something."

Adam let out a long breath. "Sure. But I'm making an executive order that we stop by The Coffee Kraft first or else I'm not going to make it."

CHAPTER 12

AFTER TELLING Tamera that they were going back to her shop, she handed over her keys and said she would wait there for George to be released. Margot tried to warn her that she could be waiting a long time, but her friend said she didn't mind. She told her that if they needed to get home, they could call a cab or another friend but that she knew Margot would need to check on her shop as well.

Reluctant but knowing her friend needed to stay, she took Tamera's keys and met Adam in the hall. He said he'd swing by The Coffee Kraft and get them both coffee and that they could meet up outside of the Craft Boutique in ten minutes.

The trip downtown took seven minutes, giving Margot just enough time to park near her shop and walk up the street to meet Adam in front of the boutique, the yellow tape still sealing it off from public entrance.

The scene had already been picked apart and documented, the tape only a precaution in case they needed to gain access again. Adam opened the door with his key and they stepped inside.

Everything felt—and looked—the same as it had when Margot had come in that night with Tamera. Everything except for the body, of course. Something she was grateful not to see again. A shiver at the mere thought made her wrap her arms around herself.

"You okay?" Adam asked. His penetrating gaze didn't miss anything.

"Just remembering the other night."

"I'm so sorry you had to go through that."

She gave him a halfhearted smile. "I would have preferred not to walk in on a body lying on the floor of my best friend's shop too," she quipped. "But thanks."

"So," he said, holding his hands behind his back and looking around. "What is it that the great Margot Durand saw that she can't put her finger on?"

His light tone made all of this feel more normal than it should have, but she ignored the second shudder that threatened to course through her.

"I'm not sure." She was still shocked that Chief Heartland hadn't dressed her down for poking her nose into Adam's case. Was it the fact that she had helped with the previous case at the beginning of the summer? Or was he so desperate to wrap this up that he welcomed her help? The moment she gave space to that thought, she dismissed it. John Heartland was anything but desperate. No, there was something else that she couldn't put her finger on but she wasn't going to spend time thinking about it. Not now when they were in the midst of an investigation.

She circled the area where Mark Jennings had been found. Nothing around him was disturbed. He had either fallen, or been placed, in one of the only areas where his large frame wouldn't hinder the already cramped aisles of the boutique. Coincidence? Or careful planning? But why was it so important that nothing be disturbed? If you had murdered someone, organization seemed to be the last thing you would worry about.

Margo closed her eyes and tried again to remember what had felt off about the space to her. She was certain it was a subconscious feeling that had seeped in to her conscious thought. Those annoying types of feelings that you *knew* existed but disappeared when you tried to put your finger on them.

She sidestepped and then stopped, standing up straight. "That's why," she uttered to herself.

"What? What's why?"

"I wondered why he had been placed here, but I think I know why."

"Care to enlighten this extremely tired detective?"

She looked up at Adam and noticed the deep bags under his eyes and the way his hair was ruffled on the side, probably from when he'd been dragged from sleep to come down to the park. He was guzzling coffee now, but she knew only true rest would make him feel better.

"Nothing is disturbed, and I thought that was on purpose —it may very well be—but look at the sight line." He joined her, looking where she indicated with her arm. "This aisle goes straight to the back door. Just that one rolling cart that Tam uses for go-backs is in the way. Move it, and you've got a direct path from the back door to here."

Adam nodded. "I can see that."

Margot stepped forward and knelt by the wheeled cart. "I'm not an expert, but it looks like the indentations are slightly off. Granted, it's a wheeled cart so we don't know if it's been moved recently or not. It's just at theory."

"So where does this theory get you?"

"To the back door." She stepped around the cart. "It wasn't forced, was it?"

"No."

"Then..." Her thoughts trailed off and she pulled out her phone.

"Who are you calling?"

"Tam. Hold on." She put the call through but her friend

didn't pick up. "Of course. She's probably got her phone on silent." Instead, she tapped in a quick text.

"What are you asking her?"

"I'm asking her who has keys."

"It's in the report," he said, scrunching up his nose in thought. "I believe she said herself, George, you, and her lawyer in case of emergencies."

"Well, I want to double-check. It's possible someone had a key—somehow. Or they are really good at picking a lock, but I just don't think they would have had time."

"You think they got in with a key."

"I do."

Adam shrugged. "Beats me how."

She nodded and did one more once-over of the room. It was still there. The feeling that something was out of place or missing persisted but without being able to put her finger on it, it was pointless to stand around waiting.

Adam's phone shattered the silence. He sent her an apologetic look as he slid his finger across the screen. "Eastwood."

BACK AT THE BAKERY, Margot slumped into her desk chair. It had been an incredibly long, confusing, and emotional day. Thankfully, when she stepped into the shop, the smells of sweets and the cooling air of the fans worked to calm her frayed nerves.

"Mrs. Durand?" a voice said from her door.

She looked up at her new assistant, a bit of flour covering his white apron but looking no worse for wear.

"Hey, Dexter. I'm so sorry for leaving so abruptly today."

He grinned, holding up his hands. "Not at all what I was going to say. I actually was going to ask if you wanted me to take care of tomorrow's baking on my own?"

His offer took her by surprise. He was a good baker, she'd seen enough in the last few days to know that she trusted his expertise, but she wasn't ready to let him take over completely. And certainly not as a temporary helper.

"Thanks for the offer. I really appreciate it—"

"But no thanks?" he said with a smile.

She reciprocated with a smile of her own. "It has nothing to do with your talent, just so we're clear. But I'll be in in the morning."

"Sure, just wanted to offer."

"Maybe I'll take you up on that someday."

He grinned and nodded. "I hope that you do."

"Feel free to head out. I'll close up."

He nodded and started to untie his apron as he left her office doorway. She checked her email quickly, replying to a few actionable notes, and then closed down her computer. She'd do a double-check of her inventory and then close up.

The silence of the bakery sobered her thoughts. She missed her days here. She hadn't seen Bentley nearly all week and, after getting used to seeing him almost every day, that was a big change in her schedule. She missed it. Missed the baking.

Right then she knew she couldn't go home yet. She would make something—anything—to give her hands something to do. She had a feeling it would help to calm her nerves and focus her thoughts.

Pulling out the ingredients she'd need, she set to work making her famous *religieuse*, which was two layers of choux pastry filled with white cream and topped with a dark chocolate icing and piped vanilla cream, emphasizing the look of the nun's habit for which the pastry was named. They were her favorite things to make and she tended to only make them weekly due to her detail-oriented focus and their time-consuming nature, but tonight seemed as good as any to splurge. She would freeze them and sell them at a discount the next day, but it would be worth it.

As she worked, her thoughts wandered back to Tamera's shop. What was out of place? It was driving her mad.

Her phone rang just as she was filling the pastry with cream. Pushing her hair back with the back of her hand, she rushed to where her phone was plugged into the outlet and used a knuckle to tap the answer and then speaker buttons.

"Margie?"

"Hey, Adam," she said, brushing the same unruly hair back again.

"You didn't go home yet, did you?"

When they had parted ways from the boutique, Adam had been heading to meet up with the M.E. about the body found in the park and she'd come to the shop.

"No, not yet. I'm here at the shop."

"Good. Wait for me to come get you."

She frowned. "Why? I've got Tamera's car."

"I'll escort you home. I'm sure you want to know what I found out at the M.E.'s office."

"You sure know how to entice a girl."

His full-bodied laugh sent a smile across her lips. "You know it. Be there in fifteen minutes?"

She looked over at the counter and grimaced. "Make it twenty and you have a deal."

"Got it." He hung up without preamble, but she was used to that. Julian had done the same thing.

Part of her felt bad for the feelings that were ever so slowly beginning to emerge toward Adam. It had been years since her husband had passed away, but that didn't mean that she could just pick up and move on. And what would Julian think of her and Adam? They weren't anything more than friends now...but was there something else there? Could there be? She was fairly certain Adam wanted there to be.

Sighing, she went back to working on her pastries and was soon drawn back to the boutique. As she switched out her pastry bag for the light purple icing she would use to add a small bouquet of flowers to the front of the nun-like pastry, she stopped, hand in midair.

Flowers. Purple flowers. That was it!

Piping on the rest of the flowers at lightning speed, she left one *religieuse* on the counter for Adam and put the rest in the industrial-sized freezer. Then she rushed to her phone and fired off a text to Tamera.

Waiting impatiently for the reply, she went about cleaning up the kitchen and getting everything ready for the next morning. She was just finishing up when she heard the ding of her phone.

Tamera's text confirmed what she'd remembered.

~

"Oh, I was hoping you'd been baking," Adam said as he

stepped through the back door into the kitchen and made a beeline to the *religieuse.* "These are my favorite!"

"You say that about every one of my pastries."

He gave her an impish grin. "Can't I like more than one?"

She laughed but grew serious. "Adam, I finally realized what was off in the boutique."

He paused mid-bite, his eyes growing wide. "Waa?" he mumbled around the pastry.

"I almost didn't see it because it had been changed, but then it was all so clear when I was piping on the frosting and—"

"Hold up," Adam said, licking that very same frosting from his lips. "What in the world are you talking about, Margot?"

Blushing, she realized she hadn't explained herself well at all. "Sorry. So, I remembered there used to be a painting of a foxglove field hanging on the wall right next to where the body lay. It didn't stand out to me—or Tamera— because that exhibit isn't curated by Tam, she lets the artist do it. But I *know* the foxglove painting was there when I checked on the shop a few days before Tam came back because I remember thinking I might purchase it for the shop."

"It's not there now."

"No." Margot thought back to their trip to the store that

day. "It was replaced by a sunset picture of the Potomac. It's lovely, but *not* the picture that was there before."

"So the killer took the painting?"

Margot hesitated. This was where she stepped into speculation rather than fact. "I'm not sure, but the painting was of foxglove—"

"The poison that killed Mark Jennings."

"Yes."

"And the killer didn't want to tip us off?" Adam said, though she knew he wasn't serious.

"What if the killer *was* the artist?"

"What would make you say that?"

"I don't know him well, but I did meet the artist, Mr. Jerold Bascom, at his opening. Everyone along Main Street came by to support him. He told a few stories about his works and I remember one of them being the large foxglove field behind his home."

"So this man has access to foxglove."

"Yes, but at the same time, why risk removing the painting? Unless you had one to replace it with and a valid reason to replace it? Jerold could have used the poison, seen the painting, and replaced it just in case it tipped anyone off to him. Since Tam doesn't keep tabs on what he has in the shop, no one would really notice it had been changed."

"It seems too circumstantial for my liking."

"Right," Margot said, walking toward her phone, "but I've got an idea."

"Uh-oh," Adam said, humor lacing his voice.

"See?" she said, holding out her phone for him to see. "That's him there. And, if I can take this to Barbara at the Library, she can confirm that it was *him* who was looking into the whole Victor Carow thing."

"That still is a long way from proving anything."

"I know," Margot said, feeling her shoulders drop. "But it's the only lead we have."

Adam nodded. "All right. Let's go talk to Barbara and see what she says. Then maybe we can do some research of our own."

Feeling bolstered by Adam's encouragement, she nodded and reached for her purse. "All right, Watson. Let's go."

"Nope," he said, narrowing his gaze at her.

"What?" she said.

"We both know that I'm Sherlock in this duo."

CHAPTER 13

WHEN THEY REACHED THE LIBRARY, Barbara had already gone home but Adam was able to flash his badge and convince Wilhelmina to give them her address. She opened the door, leaning heavily on her crutches, and looked surprised.

"What are you doing here, Margot?"

"Ma'am," Adam said, pulling out his credentials again. "I'm Detective Adam Eastwood with the police department. I'd like to ask you a few questions."

Barbara's eyebrows rose and she glanced at Margot again. "And she's here…."

"Because she's helping me with the investigation."

Margot pressed her lips together, trying hard not to smile knowing that admission had to cost him.

"Oh, I see." Her expression brightened immediately. "That's lovely for you, Margot! Come on in."

Barbara directed them to a small sitting area and landed with a grunt in an old recliner. Then she said, "How can I help you?"

Margot noticed, again with a barely concealed smile, that Barbara directed her attention fully toward her. "Um, well, remember when I came by the other day and asked about the man who you'd helped research Victor Carow?"

"Oh yes, I remember." Barbara's smile widened.

"I was wondering if you recognized the man you saw in this photo." Without indicating anyone specifically to Barbara, she handed over her phone.

The woman used her fingers to zoom in on the screen and peered very closely through everyone's photo. "Oh, you look lovely here. Turquoise really is your color, Margot."

Adam shot her a look that clearly said, *Can we speed this up?* But Margot merely smiled.

"Why thank you, Barbara." She was enjoying this too much.

"Well, I looked through the whole photo to be sure, but that's him."

Margot's heart beat more rapidly. "Which one?"

"The tall guy standing on the end there. He was the one who came in and who I helped. Nice man, but quiet."

"You're sure?" Margot silently berated herself for not having asked about the man's age. The major difference between Jerold and George was their major age difference, but Barbara wouldn't have known to clarify.

"Positive."

Margot met Adam's gaze and he nodded once, letting her know that he realized what this meant. After he took the lead, asking Barbara a few more questions, they excused themselves and headed back to Adam's car.

"She pointed him out. It's him—Jerold Bascom."

Adam nodded. "While she was looking, I shot off a text to a friend in D.C. He's doing some research on Mr. Bascom and should get back to me any minute now."

"I just can't believe Mr. Bascom would do something like this." Margot clicked her seatbelt and Adam pulled into traffic. "Where are we going?"

"My place," Adam said, his eyes on the road. It was nearing five o'clock and traffic was picking up. Though 'traffic' in North Bank hardly constituted that much worry. Still, the streets would clog soon and she was sure that, rather than going back across town to the police station, Adam's house would make a good staging ground for whatever they planned next.

Pulling into his garage, they entered through the doorway

that led into the laundry room and then the kitchen. A loud bark preceded scratching claws and then the impossibly large body of Adam's Great Dane, Clint.

"Hey, Clinty boy," Margot said, bending down. With one solid lick to the cheek, she jerked back with a laugh. "Well, that's a hello."

"He's got good taste in women," Adam said, wagging his eyebrows at her.

She laughed again and shook her head. "Well, if he was the *real* Clint Eastwood…"

"I know, I know," Adam said, holding up his hands. "He just happens to have two too many feet, eh? Hold on, let me take him out back."

The duo disappeared out the back sliding door and Margot made herself at home on Adam's large couch. She'd been in his home a few times, mostly for large BBQs he hosted due to the size of his back yard, but now she looked at it through a different lens. Through Adam her friend—maybe more than friend—lens.

He had several pictures of himself with his brother and parents on the mantle over an oft-used fireplace. Across from her, tall bookshelves were lined with everything from cheap paperbacks to large law tomes. If she remembered correctly, he had started off as a law student before changing focus. Now she wanted to hear more about that story and more from his past.

But her mind jerked back to the present when Adam's phone, abandoned on the kitchen counter when he went to take Clint out, started ringing. She bolted up from the couch and grabbed it just as Adam came in the door. The two nearly collided but he managed to catch her before she ran headlong into him while simultaneously answering the phone as if nothing had happened. He was smooth, she'd admit that.

Clint bounded up to her, looking to give another slobbery kiss, but he settled on a good, behind-the-ears scratching instead. She tried her best not to listen in on Adam's conversation, but it was nearly impossible since he was standing right next to her. As if sensing her dilemma, he beckoned her over to a barstool at the counter and pulled the phone away from his ear, tapping the speaker button.

"Can you say that again, Gary?"

"You got it, man," a man said, his accent immediately placing him from Maryland. "I ran the details on the name you sent me. Seems your guy has some very interesting ties to Victor Carow."

Margot almost gasped out loud but managed to cover her shock with a hand over her mouth. Her eyes met Adam's, but he looked back down at the phone as if to help himself focus.

"Go on," he said.

"I contacted a friend over at the DEA—"

Margot mentally filled in the initials: Drug Enforcement Administration.

"And he says that this Jerold guy is on a watch list or two."

"Why is that?" Adam's forehead showed his intense concentration. Margot wondered if he was kicking himself for not knowing that a man on some DEA watch list was living in his jurisdiction.

"Jerold Bascom is the grandfather of Thomas Bascom."

"Thomas," Adam said, "I recognize that name."

"I thought you might from your time up here. He's a low level player in the Victor Carow operation. No one that would especially draw your attention, but that's not surprising."

"Why is that?" Adam took the words right out of Margot's thoughts.

"Because he's not the important guy. Honestly, he's nothing. A dealer, but he's got no inside information. Nothing that would make you take notice—except for his family tie to Jerold Bascom."

Now Margot was confused. How would a simple drug dealer—though she feared that *no* drug dealer was truly simple—get wrapped up in a murder of this magnitude? Had he needed to prove something to his boss? Or had he been a fall guy? Or had he even been involved?

"The real interesting part becomes clear when you do a

little family history." Gary chuckled. "I feel like a regular historian."

"Must be nice," Adam said, "but get to the point."

"Okay, okay, hold your horses."

Margot glanced at Adam. She knew he wasn't an impatient man, but he was a man on a mission. He had a murder to solve and she could see that the stress, and lack of sleep, were taking their toll.

"Jerold Bascom, though not related in any way to Carow's drug ring as far as we can tell, *did* go to high school with none other than Archie Shaw."

Margot had no idea what significance that held, but Adam stood up from where he'd been bent over the phone and ran a hand through his hair. And, likely for her benefit, he said, "Victor Carow's grandfather."

"Ding-ding-ding, you've got it."

"So, what…" Adam started pacing now. "Jerold took the hit on Mark Jennings so that he could help his grandson? Bring him up in the ranks? What's DEA saying?"

"They've got a guy on the inside of Carow's ring and he says that a deal was made. Jennings for Thomas."

Margot stumbled back a step, hardly believing what she heard. Jerold Bascom had agreed to *murder* a man who had turned witness so that he could save his grandson. It was almost impossible to believe. Then again, she barely knew Jerold. The little conversation they'd held had centered around his artwork and that was it. He wasn't like the other retirees or those at the senior center who made a point to stop by the bakery and get to know her. He didn't go to any of the town's gatherings, as far as she had seen, and he wasn't active outside of putting his paintings up in Tamera's shop.

"And the recent victim?"

Gary sighed. "My guy thinks it was a warning, but unrelated."

The two men kept talking, but Margot lost track of the conversation.

What would Tamera say to all of this? And George? His involvement had to be accidental, didn't it? Or was he merely a scapegoat?

But the fact remained. Jerold had ties to Victor Carow and he had keys to the shop. Distantly, Margot knew that Adam had hung up with Gary and was now on the phone to the chief. He was relaying all of the information and getting men on tracking Jerold down, but all she could think about was how convoluted it all was. If what Gary said was true, he'd done it to save his grandson, but that didn't excuse his actions. He'd still murdered a good man, a man who could have sealed the fate of Victor Carow.

She slumped back onto the barstool and dropped her head into her hands. How could this possibly end well?

CHAPTER 14

"I NEED TO GO."

Margot looked up, her eyes locking with Adam's. "Aren't you going to wait for backup?"

His lips pressed into a thin line and he glanced to the side before answering. "I should have seen this connection earlier."

"How?" Margot placed her hand on Adam's forearm, hoping he would listen to reason. "You couldn't have known. You're not a mind reader."

"Either way, I still need to go. I need to make sure that Jerold isn't skipping town as we speak. Then again, he's had ample time. I doubt he's still even here."

Margot ran through the facts. If Jerold were certain that no one could tie him back to the murder, would he have left? Up until this point, the media had latched on to the idea that one of Victor Carow's men had murdered Mark Jennings. It made sense, knowing the importance of the trial and the violence Carow was known for—though not convicted of.

"He could still be here."

Adam paused at the sink where he was filling up a glass with water. "What makes you say that?"

"Look at it this way. Jerold isn't a spring chicken. He's lived in this community for many years and, while I don't know him well, I would assume he planned on living his days out here."

"He wouldn't wait around for us to find him, Margie."

"No, probably not, but he probably doesn't think he's even in the running as a suspect—and, up until a few hours ago, he would be right. It's such a new development that he could still be here. Besides, didn't you tell me that you thought the murder in the park was a Carow gang murder?"

"It was. I spoke with the M.E. and he confirmed the gang's mark on the body."

"See? That just fuels the idea that it was gang-related."

"There are a lot of holes in that theory," Adam said, though not unsympathetically.

"I know it, but to a seventy-five-year-old grandfather—or however old he is—it could be enough."

The first light of hope entered Adam's eyes at this. "Then I *really* need to go."

"Take me with you."

"Absolutely not."

"Adam..." She stood up and faced him, hands on her hips. "Do we need to review the facts here? He's not going to come after us with a gun. His weapon of choice was poison. Isn't that what most *women* kill with."

Adam grimaced but didn't reply.

"Besides, what will I do here?"

"Kiss Clint Eastwood?"

Margot rolled her eyes but had a feeling that was his way of agreeing. She waited, holding her breath.

"Okay," he finally said. "But there are ground rules and I want you to hear that you are *only* coming with me to stay in the car and *only* because I really don't think this grandfatherly Jerold Bascom—though a murderer—is going to come after us. Probably."

She smirked in triumph and handed him his keys.

Gary had transmitted Jerold's last known address to Adam's phone and, after double-checking with someone at the records office at the station, they set off toward Jerold's house.

Margot felt her stomach twist in knots. She wasn't exactly

sure why she'd decided to come, but she had a feeling it was something of the investigator in her. She needed to see this through. She needed to know that they had found the right man.

When they turned down the street where Jerold's house was located, she was glad to see that most of the neighbors didn't seem to be home yet. Less prying eyes were a good thing in this nosy town. Really, she was thinking of the neighbors' safety.

Adam parked down the street a bit then looked toward her. "Backup is on its way, though they are stuck in some sort of traffic accident. Of all the days," he said, rolling his eyes.

"You're not going in there alone," she said, incredulous.

"Like you said, you don't think he's dangerous."

"No, but still..." Then the front door to a house next to Bascom's opened and an elderly woman walked out, her tiny Pomeranian trotting beside her. She wore a pink tracksuit and looked to be around the age they assumed Bascom was.

"I've got an idea," Margot said and was out of the car before Adam could tell her not to leave.

"Excuse me," she said, walking up to the woman. Adam joined her, looking uncomfortable and scanning the area.

"Hello," the older woman said, her dog sniffing at Adam's feet, no doubt smelling Clint.

"I was wondering if you could help me. I'm looking for a Jerold Bascom?" Adam flinched when she said the name out loud but she persisted. "I wanted to buy a painting from him, but I haven't been able to get in touch recently. I thought he lived along this street and I wanted to stop by."

"Oh yes," the woman said, nodding rapidly. "Jerold is my neighbor. His paintings are very nice, aren't they? Say, you look familiar?" She leaned toward Margot with pinched eyes.

"I've just got one of those faces," Margot said, laughing uncomfortably. "Have you seen him recently?"

"Who?" the woman said.

"Mr. Bascom."

"Oh," the woman laughed and yanked her dog closer to her. "Haven't seen him out in a few days. It's not unusual, though. Some days, he'll be in there for almost a week straight without leaving. Just gets his mail now and then. I'm sure he could use the company, dear." She laughed again, the sound raspy.

"So, you think he's home?"

"I'm sure of it. Saw him get the mail this morning. Hasn't been out since, though. His car's still there. Besides, I'd know if he left."

"Why is that?" *Besides the fact that you're nosy,* Margot thought with good humor.

"Because his car is in desperate need of a new muffler." She winked and then tugged at the small dog again. "We'd better be off. Good luck with your painting."

Margot forced a smile then looked at Adam, wondering what he thought of her investigative techniques. His look was hard to read but he nodded. "Smoothly done, Watson."

"Let's go," she said.

"Ah, nope. Nice try, but—"

"Come on, Adam. You heard what she said. He's practically a hermit. He's not going to come at us with guns blazing or—"

The distant sound of sirens caught their attention.

"I told them no sirens." Adam ground his teeth. "Come on."

Now Margot wanted to know what made him change his mind. She risked asking, "Really?"

"Yeah, don't want him escaping out the back."

Margot almost rolled her eyes, but she was getting what she wanted and wasn't about to risk that.

"But stay behind me. Got it?"

She nodded and they approached the house.

CHAPTER 15

THEY BYPASSED the front door and walked down the driveway, ducking under the large bay window, even though the curtains were drawn, and coming to a stop at the corner of the house that led to where Margot assumed the back door was.

Adam turned back to her. "I'm going to go around first; you follow but stay directly behind me. Okay?"

Margot nodded.

"Okay?" he repeated.

"Okay," Margot said, realizing he needed to hear her agree with him.

Then he slipped around the corner, gun drawn. She still wasn't sure if this situation warranted as much fear as she was giving it, but then again, Jerold *had* killed someone. It was just difficult for her to wrap her mind around the reality that he was a cold-blooded killer. The nice man who painted such serene landscapes.

She almost walked into Adam when he stopped at the short row of three steps that led up to the back door. Only then did she notice that the door was open a few inches. Had Jerold escaped on foot? It seemed hardly likely knowing his age, but she supposed it *could* be possible.

Adam reached out at the same moment someone came rocketing out the back door. Margot shrieked, unable to help herself, and Adam went down. The man who had tackled him was unfamiliar to Margot. He looked like he was in his late thirties or early forties, though she only saw the side of his face.

Before she could do anything to help Adam, the man shoved up and off of him, somehow got to his feet, and he was off, racing around the other side of the house. Adam looked at her then at the man racing away.

"Go!" she said.

"Stay here," he commanded, then ran off after the man.

Margot's heart was thudding in her chest, trying to make sense of the situation. Who was the man? Had they somehow stepped in on a robbery? Had the man been watching the house and taken advantage of what he assumed was someone on vacation? But no, that seemed like too much of a coincidence. Then who was he?

Margot's mind raced back over the details of the case. Jerold had killed Mark Jennings for his grandson Thomas.

His grandson.

It was the only logical possibility, barring some random person just happening to be in this residence. And with that thought, her attention snagged on the now open back door.

She felt compelled to go inside, despite the fact that Adam had told her to stay. Hands trembling, she told herself that the police were already on their way and it couldn't hurt to poke her head in, right?

Taking a silent breath, she went up the steps and paused at the backdoor. It led into what appeared to be a mudroom type area; two coats hung on the pegs and one pair of rubber boots sat under them.

She slipped past them and through an entryway that led into a galley type kitchen. It was relatively clean, but she noted two coffee mugs on the sink. Had Thomas been staying with his grandfather? That was one question she hadn't thought to ask the nosy neighbor. Had the woman seen Thomas enter the house?

Taking pains to make no sound, she walked to the end of the kitchen. The doorway opened to a hallway leading toward the front door with a living room along the right side. The TV reflected back a Food Network show, though the sound was on low. Her heart pounded in her chest as she stepped into the hallway. She took another step and was considering checking upstairs, before heading back out before the police arrived, when a hand clamped over her mouth.

Her heartbeat pounded in her ears but she resisted the urge to scream this time.

She felt like a fool. She should have stayed outside.

"Don't move," the voice said, close to her ear. She immediately recognized Jerold's voice, though he sounded even older than she remembered. She held up her hands to show him she meant him no harm.

"I'm going to let you talk, but I've got a needle right here." The tip of a needle pricked the skin on her neck and everything in her body stiffened. She had to wait for the right moment. Mentally, she assessed how he was holding her, the leathery quality of his hand covering her mouth belied his age, and she knew in an instant she could easily get out of his grasp.

His hand slid down. "What do you want?"

She found it odd that he would ask such a question, but she wasn't going to take any chances.

"Jerold, it's me, Margot Durand."

She heard his quick intake of breath. "Wh-why are you here?"

Swallowing, she chose her words carefully. "I'm here with the police, Jerold. I think you know why we're here."

"Yeah? Well, where are they? Why'd they send you in? Last I heard, you were a baker."

He had her there. She affected a light laugh. "I'm working with them on this case," she fibbed, though it wasn't completely a lie. "But I wanted to come in to talk with you. To get your side of things. Why did you do it, Jerold?"

He stiffened but she thought he withdrew the needle, though she couldn't be sure.

"Do what?"

"I think you know."

She waited. She remembered Julian telling her that sometimes an interrogator's greatest weapon was silence.

"I had to."

Margot was shocked by this. Not just his admission, but the complete and utter sadness that now infused his voice.

"What do you mean?"

The next instant, he'd shoved her away and was hovering near a chair opposite her, the needle held up to his own veins.

"Wait—Jerold, stop!"

Tears filled his eyes. "You don't understand. I—I couldn't stand to see my foolish grandson running with that Carow gang. His father made a mistake and I let him...but not with Thomas. He has such a promising future and he was throwing it away on drugs. I knew Victor's grandfather—we grew up together—and I arranged a deal with him. I promised to help him if Victor would release Thomas from his hold. Archie promised—he promised." Jerold sniffed, large tears falling down his face.

Margot's eyes stayed glued to the syringe, its tip pressing against the man's sun-spotted sink.

"Jerold, it's okay. We can talk this out—"

"It's not okay!" he said, his voice raising. "But I knew it." He was regaining his composure. "I knew I couldn't trust Archie or Victor. I made sure I had insurance, but now..." He looked up at her, a moment of clarity showing in his eyes. "Now it's of no use."

Then without another word or even a moment's hesitation, he shoved the syringe into his arm and depressed the plunger.

THE NEXT FEW hours flew by faster than Margot thought possible. Unknown to her, Adam had come back from chasing Thomas, who was then safely in police custody, and he'd sneaked into the house behind Margot. He'd heard everything, capturing it on his phone's recording device, though he hadn't caught Jerold in time to stop the injection. It had happened too quickly.

Thankfully, the ambulance had already been called and

they were briefed on the situation en route. With Adam's quick thinking, they had bagged the syringe and any other paraphernalia in the house so the ER techs would have something to work with.

Now, Margot sat in the hospital awaiting some sort of news. Adam was there as well, though he hadn't spoken more than a few words to her in as many hours.

"Detective Eastwood?" a doctor said, coming out of two double doors leading back to the ER.

"Yes?" Adam said, standing.

Margot did the same but didn't speak. She was distinctly aware of Adam's feelings and yet she was glad he'd allowed her to stay with him.

"It looks like you're in for a bit of good news, or at least I think it's good news."

"What's that, Doctor?" Adam said. He looked even more exhausted than that morning when Margot had first seen him at the park. His shirt was wrinkled, his hair messed, and the lines at the corners of his eyes looking deeper.

"Turns out there was no digoxin in Mr. Bascom's bloodstream. Instead, we found a massive dose of insulin. He's a diabetic and I believe he was attempting to send himself into a diabetic coma. Fortunately, we were able to counteract that and he will make a full recovery. Though I am recommending a full suicide watch for at least the next few days, considering this information."

"Yes, yes, of course. We'll head up the security and watch for you. Thank you, Doctor."

The man nodded and left, and Adam went to speak with the officers who had stayed behind with him. He gave them instructions on what to do and then walked back to where Margot stood. The silence fell between them.

Margot looked up at Adam and saw relief along with exhaustion wash over him. It was over—or at least, mostly over. There was still one thing left for her to do.

"Adam," she said tentatively.

He looked down at her, but there was no anger there, merely exhaustion.

"I'm sorry. I shouldn't have gone into that house. It was foolish and—"

"It was," he said, turning to face her. Then he reached out and took her hands in his. "But I'm just glad you're safe."

She felt his forgiveness like a flood of cool water pouring over parched earth.

"I know you're inquisitive and I love that about you, but we've got to work on your listening skills."

She offered him a half-smile. "But I did get you your confession."

He rolled his eyes. "Good job, Watson."

"I still think I'm Sherlock," she said, winking at him.

"That remains to be seen." Then he stepped closer to her and she felt her pulse speed up. Thankfully, this time it had nothing to do with danger. Then again, was this danger of another kind?

"Margot, when all of this is over, could I take you to dinner?"

"Yes." Her response was immediate, but she wasn't afraid that she'd misspoken. In fact, she was certain she'd said exactly what she meant to. "I would like that, Detective Eastwood."

CHAPTER 16

THEY WALKED hand in hand through the gardens at *El Jardín*, a Spanish-style hacienda that offered its guests a unique dining opportunity near the banks of the Potomac. Rather than sit at a table and be served, guests made reservations in advance and, upon arrival, were given their own personal picnic meal, a bottle of wine made on the premises, and a blanket, then directed to a path that would take them through the gardens and to their reserved picnicking spot.

Margot had always wanted to visit *El Jardín*, but she'd never had the chance, until today and her first official date with the handsome detective.

While news of the high profile case that had come to North Bank was still circulating, it had been almost a month since Jerold's arrest. Though things were still far from being wrapped up, life in their small little town was slowly getting back to normal just in time for the fall season, but Margot wasn't sure if it would ever be the same.

"Here we are," Adam said, indicating a patch of grass under a sprawling oak tree. The weather was cooler, but Margot had come prepared with a heavier sweater and jeans. As she sat, sunlight spotting their blanket, she pulled the sweater on.

"Will it be too cold here?"

She shook her head. "It's perfect."

Adam held her gaze for a moment, as if assessing if she was telling the truth or not, then nodded once and unpacked the picnic basket.

They ate, discussing everything and anything, though she noticed he avoided his work and the case at all costs.

Finally, when she couldn't take it any longer, she put her wine glass down and narrowed her eyes at him. "Are you going to tell me what happened? Or do I need to drag it out of you, Detective Eastwood?"

"What are you talking about?" he said, coughing to cover his surprise at her direct words.

"I've hardly seen you since that day in the hospital and now you're avoiding any mention of the case. I'm curious. You know me better than that."

He grinned. "Not true. I saw you several times at the bakery."

"True," she consented, "but you spent most of the time talking with Dexter."

"How's that going by the way?"

"Well," she said, nodding. "He's a very competent assistant, though a little flamboyant on his desserts. A few years under my tutelage and he'll be a consummate professional, I'm sure." She laughed to show him she wasn't fully serious. "But really, he's a fantastic addition to the bakery."

"A permanent addition then?"

"I offered him a full-time position and he accepted. So yes." She took another sip. "But no changing the subject. What happened with Jerold and Thomas?"

"I can't imagine you haven't seen the news."

"I want the details. Nothing but the details."

"I knew you would."

She observed him but didn't see any disappointment on his features. It was more like resignation. He knew as well as she did that if this relationship was going to move forward, he would have to come to terms with the inquisitive nature of this French pastry chef.

"What I *can* tell you is that not all hope is lost."

"In what way?"

"Remember right before Jerold, uh—" Adam swallowed,

looking like he'd rather be discussing anything but this. "—injected himself?"

"Yes, of course. He mentioned 'insurance'."

"He did, and it's a good thing too. Now, you can't breathe a word of this to anyone—" Adam looked around then leaned closer. "—but he kept evidence he'd gotten from Mark before he killed him."

"What? How?"

"That's how he lured Mark to North Bank. He said he had more information for him and convinced him to come down to meet with him. Little did poor Mark know what he was getting himself into."

"But why wouldn't Mark just tell him to go to the police?"

"Jerold somehow convinced Mark that, at his age, he just wanted to live out a peaceful life. He said that Mark was already raking his name through the court system, why not take more information with him."

Margot nodded. It did make sense.

"Then comes George," Adam continued. "Apparently, before he went into painting full-time, Jerold worked at the bank were George used to make regular withdrawals. Add in some clever research and he had the perfect person to pin the murder on. With his access to Tamera's shop, it really was a good option—though thankfully, not error proof. We saw through the ruse pretty quickly, but some were almost convinced for a while there."

"Like you," she said, smirking.

He shrugged. "I go where the facts take me."

Then something else occurred to her. "Whatever happened to Harry?"

Now Adam leaned back and chuckled. "Poor Harry."

"You can't seriously mean that."

"I don't." Adam grew serious. "We caught him trying to leave town and have tried him for extortion, among other things. He'll spend some time in prison, that's for sure."

"I did talk with Tamera a few weeks ago and she said that George talked with Sarah and everything is out in the open now with no adverse effects. I suppose Harry is out of luck for blackmail in the future."

"Speaking of the future." Adam looked down at her and suddenly the stiff breeze did nothing to cool her heating cheeks. Something inside of her churned nervously and she looked down to fumble with the checkered blanket that they both sat on.

"Margot," Adam said, drawing her gaze back to his.

"Adam, I—"

"Would you like to go to the Fall Street Festival in D.C. with me next weekend?"

Immediately, her face filled with heat again. He was asking her to a street festival. Another date. Not...well, she wasn't sure what she'd thought he was going to say, but that wasn't important right now. Now that the danger was passed and her friend's husband was free, she could think of those *other* things.

And she did so now with a smile. "I'd love to."

He returned her smile as if he knew her internal struggle and was merely shaking his head at her leaping to conclusions, but all he said was, "Good. It's a date."

~

PASTRIES AND PILFERING

CHAPTER 1

Margot Durand stepped off the airplane and into the warm California breeze. It was hard to believe that just five hours before, she had been bundled up and running through freezing rain into the airport after Tamera dropped her off.

She made her way through the airport and down to baggage claim three where her suitcase would soon arrive. As she waited, she pulled out her phone and began to answer her messages.

One text came from Dexter Ross, her newly hired assistant of two months. He'd proved himself more than worthy to take over for her while she was gone for two weeks on vacation, but she was still like a nervous mother leaving a child in the hands of a stranger. Though Dexter wasn't a stranger and *The Parisian Pâtisserie*, her French style bakery located in North Bank, Virginia, was nothing like a child.

He sent a few pictures of the creations he'd made, along with her regular baked goods, and then a selfie with he and Bentley, the shop's daily patron and subsequent leader of the burgeoning senior community in town.

Her phone beeped and she saw it was a text from her sister, Renee, saying she was on her way to pick her up. Margot thought about how good it would be to see her sister and niece, Taylor. Despite the trouble that Taylor had run into in North Bank when she'd come to be an assistant for the summer at the bakery, she was now doing well and back in school studying to be a lawyer, to the shock of her parents *and* her aunt. Margot couldn't wait to hear all about it.

Then came another text from Adam Eastwood, North Bank's resident detective and a special friend of hers. Somehow he had managed to arrange attending a temporary assignment with the Long Beach police department during the same time she would be in town. Trying to hide her smile, she typed in a quick response to his request for dinner that night. She would have this evening free and then the next morning, it was off to enjoy a four-night cruise with one of her longtime friends and the residing French Pastry Chef on a Carousel Cruise.

Seeing her bag, Margot rushed forward and grabbed the handle of the rolling suitcase. Thankfully, she'd been able to pack light, the nice weather on the West Coast affording her the opportunity to wear light, flowing dresses and shorts. She was ready for a bit of relaxing, a bit of fun sharing the kitchen with her friend, and exploring the exotic locals of Mexico.

Stepping out into the traffic of the Southern California airport, the scents of the ocean mingled with exhaust in a distinctly Los Angeles smell. To complete the effect, tall palm trees waved back and forth in the breeze and a man sat on the corner playing a guitar and crooning out a Beach Boys's top hit.

Yes, this was Southern California personified. But after the last few months she'd had, it was time for some relaxation and a change in scenery. Especially after the more recent case against her friend Tamera's new husband George. He'd been suspected of murder and Margot had joined forces with Adam to clear his name.

But that was in the past and now—

"Margot! Over here!"

She spun around at her name and saw her sister hopping out of a sporty, silver BMW, arms waving. Taylor sat in the front seat, her head resting in her hand as if she wished she could disappear.

"Oh, it's so good to see you," Renee said, crushing Margot in her thin, tan arms. "It's been too long.

"We just saw each other a few months ago," she said through a laugh. "But you're right. It *is* good to see you. You too, Taylor," she said, bending down to look in the window.

The young woman grinned. "Good to see you, Aunt Marg. Want the front seat?"

"Nope, you stay there. I'll take the back and get the royal treatment."

Renee deposited Margot's luggage in the trunk and then took off as Margot sunk into the plush leather seats.

"New car?" she observed.

"Dillon," her sister said with an exasperated breath.

"He gave me their old car and got this one. Said he got a promotion or something. How cool is that?" Taylor leaned around the seat to look at Margot.

"Cool indeed." She saw her sister's grin all the way from the back and knew it was a welcome surprise.

"So what's the plan again?" Renee asked as she deftly wove in and out of traffic.

"Well, I was asked to go out to dinner tonight..."

"Oh, oh," Taylor said, "Aunt Marg has a date."

"Is that true?" Renee asked, her eyes flicking to the rearview mirror momentarily.

"It's with Adam and—"

"That cute detective!" Taylor injected.

"And he's in town for a temporary assignment. I don't have to go if you'd planned anything."

"We didn't," Taylor jumped in before Renee could respond.

"Actually," Renee said, giving her daughter a look, "that works out well. Dillon has some work party he has to go to, so you were going to be on your own anyway."

"Perfect," Margot said, feeling excitement bubble up inside of her.

"And then the cruise?" her sister prompted.

"Yes, I'll need to be at the docks by ten tomorrow morning. I'll be gone for four nights and then I'm here for the next week to spend time with you guys."

"Ugh, do you have to?" Taylor said, winking back at Margot.

Renee laughed and Margot felt relief to see the growing relationship between Taylor and her adopted mother. She was sure things weren't perfect, but they were doing so much better than at the beginning of the summer.

Confident that things were going as planned, Margot leaned back against the cool leather and took in the sights of Long Beach as they drove toward her sister's Spanish-inspired bungalow. Yes, this was going to be just what she needed; a relaxing vacation.

ADAM STOOD at the front door of her sister's house

dressed in khaki slacks, a brilliant white button-down shirt, and a sharp, navy blue blazer. He pulled off his sunglasses as she opened the door and she couldn't help the smile that slipped onto her lips, or the feeling of warmth that pooled in her stomach.

"You look like you just walked off the cover of Southern Californian Man magazine," she said with a light laugh.

"Is that a real magazine? Because I may want to forsake my job and move here. This weather is incredible."

"You couldn't be anything other than a detective and you know it," she quipped, grabbing her clutch purse from the hall table and waving goodbye to Taylor, who winked back.

"True," he said, placing his hand on the small of her back as he ushered her down the sidewalk. "But it sure is nice to get a little reprieve from the dreary weather back home. Your carriage, milady."

She gasped when he led her to a cherry red Mustang convertible parked at the curb, top down. "*This* is the rental car the department gave you?" Her eyebrows hiked.

"Well..." He shrugged. "When I explained to the nice woman at the rental office why I was here, she felt obligated to offer me something fun—since I'm here for work and all."

Margot rolled her eyes at his pouty face and slipped onto the leather seat warmed by the sun. "You're amazing."

"Why, thank you," he said, flashing white teeth her way. Was it just her imagination or did he already look tanner? "Hope you don't mind a little wind."

Her hair flew free and loose as he pulled into traffic, but she didn't mind. The warm breeze and feeling of freedom was worth a few tangles in her hair.

"Where are you taking me?" she asked, closing her eyes and resting her head back against the seat to truly enjoy the experience.

"You'll see," he said. She heard the smile in his voice.

A few minutes later, she felt the momentum of the car slow and opened her eyes. They were near the ocean, she could smell the salt on the breeze, but she also saw hundreds of boats in slips, their masts shooting up into the sky. Then Adam pulled the car to a stop in front of the valet station.

With a grin, he handed the keys to the valet and came around to offer her his arm. Margot took in the towering palm trees and the golden glow of the sun making its way into the ocean in the distance. There truly was nothing like a West Coast sunset.

They walked through an open courtyard area where a small band played festive jazz music and then he opened the door to The Bay View, a high-end restaurant from the looks of the exterior. Marveling that Adam was going to such an expense for her, she glanced at him sideways.

"You know I would have been happy with a burger on the beach," she said as they waited for the couple in front of them to be seated.

"But then I wouldn't have gotten to surprise and awe you with my expansive knowledge of—" He looked around the man in front of them. "—cob."

She burst into a girlish giggle, shaking her head. "Cob, huh?"

"Oh yes," he said, standing up straighter. "This restaurant had the best cob."

The waitress stepped in front of them before Margot could refute his claim and they were rushed to a small table on the deck overlooking the ocean. Wine and calamari appetizers ordered, they both took in the view.

"Thank you, Adam," she said, breathing in the warm, fresh air. "This is perfect."

"I thought you deserved a night off before going on that exhausting cruise."

She laughed again, loving the more relaxed side of the usually ultra-focused Detective Eastwood. "I do plan to work on it, you know."

"You do?" he frowned, taking a sip of his water.

"Didn't I tell you? One of my former students, Addie Petit, is the French pastry chef and principle baker on the *Carousel Luxury*. She's enlisted my help because she's receiving an award for her pastry work and they are throwing a large party in her honor. It's a bit of a thank you to me as much as I'll be helping her. I'm not complaining. It got me on for free, so I see a day or so of work for five days on a cruise as a good tradeoff."

He nodded slowly. "You can't just take a break, can you?"

"And when was the last time *you* took a break?"

He hunched his shoulders but was relieved from answering when their appetizer and drinks arrived.

"Well?" she pressed when the waitress was gone.

"I'll admit it, it's been a while. But this assignment here will be like a vacation, I'm sure."

"What are you doing, exactly?"

He averted his gaze. "Nothing too taxing. Just a few lectures and such."

"*You're* lecturing?"

"Yeah," he said, his voice coming out thin.

Was he hiding something?

"On what?"

When he looked up, she thought she saw a hint of apprehension on his features but then his gaze flicker over her shoulder and his eyes widened. "Gabe?"

Turning around, her gaze landed on a tall, handsome man

who struck an impressive profile in a dark jacket, designer jeans, and a button-up shirt with a few buttons left open. He turned at the sound of his name and she immediately saw the shock on his face.

"Adam Eastwood?" he said, coming toward their table, "I can't believe it. What are you doing in my neck of the woods?"

Adam stood and shook the man's hand then gestured to Margot. "I'm on a temporary assignment and..." He looked at Margot and his expression softened. "Having dinner with a friend."

"*Ravi de vous rencontrer*," Gabe said with a suave smile that was meant to convey his confidence with such an introduction.

"*Et vous aussi*," she said in reply, matching his look.

"She speaks French," he said to Adam. "I'm impressed."

"She *is* French," Adam said with a chuckle as he sat back down. "This is Margot Durand. Margot, this is Gabe Williams. One of Long Beach's finest."

"It's nice to meet you," she said.

"I haven't seen you in ages," Adam continued. "How have you been?"

Gabe kept his eyes on Margot an instant longer then turned to look at Adam. "Things are good. Just the same old, same old. Doing the daily grind and all. How are things going with the—"

"Sound's good," Adam said, interrupting the man before he could finish his sentence. "Busy, I'm sure."

Margot noted the awkward nature of the exchange and then saw Gabe's eyes narrow for a moment. "Right, well, what is life if you aren't busy?"

"Exactly." Adam laughed but Margot could tell it was forced. What was he hiding?

The waitress arrived with their entrées and Gabe stepped back. "I'll let you two get on with your dinner, but it was good to see you, Adam, and nice to meet you, Margot."

"We should catch up sometime. Maybe grab some coffee while I'm here?"

Now it was Gabe's turn to look uncomfortable but he forced a smile. "Sure. That'd be great. I've got a few things on my plate this week, but maybe next week if you're still around?"

"Sounds good."

Adam turned back to the table but before Margot could ask about what Gabe had been about to say, Adam interrupted her thoughts.

"This looks great! Let's dig in."

CHAPTER 2

THEY WERE BACK at her sister's home and Adam had just stepped out to walk her to the door when she stopped him with a hand on his arm. The bright moonlight warred for attention with the streetlights running down the street and, if it were possible, Margot thought the weather had gotten even warmer while they had dinner.

"Adam," she said, sliding her hand from his forearm down to this hand, "are you going to tell me what you kept Gabe from saying at dinner tonight?"

He feigned a look of confusion. "Gabe? What do you mean? Was he saying something?"

"Are you going to stand there and lie to my face, Adam Eastwood? Because if so, I'm going inside and you may never hear from me again." Though her words held weight, she kept them light. He was silent for so long she grew more frustrated and started to turn.

"Margot," he said, pulling her back and gripping her hand more firmly, "just hold on."

"I don't like secrets," she said. "And, maybe I'm foolish for thinking this, but I thought things between us were going...well. Maybe I'm just kidding myself and you can stop me right here if I'm wrong, but—"

"You're not wrong." His words effectively silenced her. "But..." He looked up, his gaze trailing down the street then back to her. "There are things that I won't—*can't* —share with you. At least not yet."

She understood the silence of his career. A detective held many things close to the vest, something she'd experienced firsthand with her late husband Julian, but this felt worse somehow. They weren't in North Bank, what could he be hiding from her here?

"Your buddy can know these things but I can't?"

He grimaced. "Look, I want you to trust me. Not just as a detective in your hometown, but as a friend and...maybe as more someday." He took a breath. "And believe me, when I can tell you, I will, but I can't. Not yet. I'm sorry."

"So you're not going to tell me?"

"Not yet." He grimaced but she could tell, despite his tightlipped response, that he *wanted* to tell her. At least it seemed that way.

"I understand."

He opened his mouth as if prepared for an argument but then closed it. "You do?"

"I do."

"Margot, have I told you how amazing you are?"

She laughed and shook her head. "You've resorted to flattery, Detective Eastwood? I thought that was below you."

"Never," he said, pulling her closer.

Her breath caught at his sudden nearness and she was aware of how warm and comforting his hand felt wrapped around hers. She craved that comfort more than she wanted to admit.

When they had finished the last case exonerating her best friend's husband from a murder charge, Adam had taken her out for their first official date. That had been just over two months ago, but she still wasn't sure what *they* were. A couple? Just dating? Even more? He'd called her his friend to Gabe Williams…

Her mind drew back to the present and the reality that Adam was drawing closer to her. Her heartbeat thundered in her chest but she didn't draw away. She didn't want to. They had only kissed one other time in a stolen moment after a street festival in DC. The festival had been interrupted by rain and they'd taken cover under an awning, drawing close to stay out of the downpour.

But now, after a romantic dinner and in the warm breeze

swirling around them, she wanted to experience that again. To feel his lips, soft but strong on hers. And the next instant, she did.

Her eyelids fluttered closed and his free hand wrapped around her, pressing gently against the small of her back. His fingers were warm through the silky fabric of her summer dress and the spicy scent of his cologne intermingled with the flowery scent of her perfume.

The kiss was short but not without its own type of passion. Tender, but firm; sweet, but short. His lips gone from hers much too quickly.

"Have a good cruise, Margot," he said. His breath fanned out warm against her cheeks.

"Have fun teaching, Professor Eastwood." His deep chuckle broke some of the spell and she stepped back to head toward the house. "I will. And, Margot—"

She looked up at him.

"I'll tell you when I can."

"You'd better."

THE NEXT MORNING dawned bright but subtly cooler than the previous day. Margot didn't mind, but knowing that it would be even cooler on the ship, she pulled a lightweight, striped sweatshirt over jean capris with comfortable, cushioned flats to finish off the ensemble.

Then, making sure she'd repacked everything she'd need on the cruise, she followed Renee out the door.

"Have fun and *relax*," her sister said when she dropped her off at the docks.

"Tell Taylor and Dillon bye for me. I'll see you all when I get back."

Margot pulled her large canvas purse higher on her shoulder and toted her rolling suitcase behind her as she made her way toward the large ship sparkling in the morning sunlight.

The *Carousel Luxury*, the finest in its fleet, rose up in front of her to a stunning height of fifteen floors for the cabin area with a length of over one thousand feet. The bright yellow and red flags stuck out against the gleaming white sides of the massive ship and flapped wildly in the wind. She felt like an ant the closer she came.

"Hello, ma'am," a kind looking older man said. He wore longer, white shorts and a white, button-up shirt with a badge that read "Jack" and held a clipboard in his hand. "How can I direct you?"

She showed him her ticket, uncertain of where she was supposed to go.

"Oh, you're here to help Miss Petit? Wonderful," he said, his smile widening, if that were possible. "Let me get someone to show you to the right entrance. Just one moment."

She nodded and watched as he keyed into a microphone attached to a radio. Soon a younger man came and led her to a gangplank that appeared to be the crew's entrance. "Right this way, ma'am," the young man said.

She followed him up the ramp and soon they were stepping into a room where a woman sat behind a desk looking slightly harried.

"Phillip, I thought I told you not to—" When she looked up, she stopped and pressed her lips into a smile. "I'm sorry, I didn't know you had brought a guest on board." Her gaze flickered to the young man at Margot's side and he rushed to explain.

"This is Miss Petit's guest for the week."

The woman flashed a forced smile at Margot and turned several pages in a thick binder in front of her. "Ah, Mrs. Durand?"

"Yes," Margot said.

"Welcome aboard." She looked to the young man, "You're dismissed, Phillip. I'll take Mrs. Durand to her room." Standing, she turned back to Margot. "I'm Sophia and I'll take you to your room if you'll follow me?"

Margot did, rolling her suitcase behind her as they turned down a long corridor.

"Your cabin has a lovely view of the water. I'm sure you'll be very happy with it."

"Thank you very much," Margot said, picking up her pace to match that of the woman.

They turned down one more hall before the woman pulled up short. "Ah, here we are." Retrieving a keycard, she opened the door and pushed it in. "Welcome to your suite, Mrs. Durand."

Margot gasped as she stepped past the woman into the ocean view room. She hadn't expected this. When she'd agreed to Addie's pleading to join her on a cruise, she'd thought the room would be in the interior and just big enough to fit a bed, but this room exceeded any idea she'd had.

It wasn't large by any standard, but it was bright and cheery, with an incredible view just as the stewardess had said. The sliding glass door led out onto a tiny deck with two chairs. Inside, a queen-sized bed took over the space of one wall with a small couch and chair at its foot. The tiny bathroom sat to the left with a closet next to it and then a desk next to that. Everything she needed —and more.

"This is lovely. Thank you."

The woman gave a brisk nod and handed her some papers. "Here is a map of the ship. I've indicated here, here, and here—" She pointed to the paper. "—where the kitchen and bake shop are located. You'll likely find her in the kitchen at this hour. This special keycard will get you there."

Sophia looked up and flashed another business-like smile before motioning to close the door.

"Uh, Sophia?"

The woman stopped, her mask of helpfulness firmly in place.

"Thank you, for all of this. I really appreciate the hard work you've done. I hope today isn't too stressful for you."

The woman seemed taken off guard but a real smile broke through. "One of our senior crew members is out sick for this cruise so things are a little...crazy," she said, breaking her business-like manner. "Thank you. I really hope you have a great time."

Margot watched her go then closed the door and sunk down onto the plush bed.

"Oh, I think I will," she said to the stillness of the room before she fell back against the cushions.

"I'M NOT sure what to do, Noah. I am one hundred and twenty percent certain I ordered more than enough, but I'm not seeing it on this inventory sheet. And where in the world are my other boxes?"

Margot smiled as she came around the corner into the commercial grade kitchen. She'd recognize that voice anywhere.

"Miss Petit," she said in her sternest teacher's voice.

The young woman, now in her early thirties, turned around, her dark brown hair pulled back into a tight French twist.

"Margot!" she screamed and rushed at her with open arms. "You're here!"

Margot laughed, hugging the woman back with equal force. "As if I'd miss this trip."

"I'm so glad you could come. Are you *sure* you don't mind helping me?"

"I am more than happy to do whatever you need me to. I'm at your beck and call."

The woman laughed, the sound like tiny silver bells, as she clasped Margot's hands.

"No, no! None of that. You are here to help me with the gala and awards ceremony, but in every other respect, you are our guest." The young man behind Addie coughed. "Oh goodness! I'm so sorry. Margot Durand, this is Noah Spence, he's my right-hand man."

"Pleased to meet you, Mrs. Durand. Addie has told me a lot about you."

The handsome young man smiled back at her, showing off deep dimples. He was handsome in a boyish way and when he turned his gaze on Addie, she wondered if they were more than friends. She filed the information away to ask her friend about later.

"It's nice to meet you too, Noah. Have you worked on board this ship long?"

"About three years now," he said, grinning at Addie. "Though this boss of mine has made it feel like more."

"Oh, don't listen to him," Addie said, laughing. "He's a great pastry chef in his own right and I'm lucky to have him on my team. So, are you ready to get the grand tour?"

Margot looked between Addie and Noah. "Can you get away like this?"

Addie laughed. "I'm a pastry chef, not a prisoner. And yes, we've been prepping early—baker's hours," she said with a wink at Margot, "and the guests won't all be on board for several more hours. It'll be relatively quiet. The perfect time for a tour."

"Great," Margot said, "lead the way, Chef."

Addie paused, closing her eyes and holding her hands out.

"What are you doing?" Noah asked, looking skeptical.

"Just basking in the moment that my most formidable, and most talented, teacher called me Chef. I have arrived."

The three of them laughed and Noah gave her a gentle shove. "Go on then."

They walked back out into the hallway and she turned to look at Margot. "What have you seen so far?"

"Seen?" Margot said, looking doubtful. "The hallway and my room."

"Got it," Addie said, grinning. "Then we'll head to the mezzanine and you can see what most people see first."

As they walked, Margot asked Addie to fill her in on the years since she had graduated from the institute that Margot had taught at. Filled with internships and jobs in well-known French bakeries in Paris, Addie then made her way to the West Coast where she gained employment with *Carousel* on their primary luxury ship.

"Will you be going back to France?" Margot asked when Addie had finished her litany of jobs.

She smiled. "I'm not sure. I'll have to wait and see how things turn out here."

There was something in the girl's smile that reminded Margot of how she'd acted when she'd been in love with Julian. "Addie, is there something you're not telling me?"

The girl's face blanched. "Not...telling you?"

"Is there—"

"Oh, *there* you are," said a loud, booming voice.

Both women jumped and turned to see a man dressed in dark pants, a white shirt, and a navy blue vest. He carried a folder with him and looked to be in a hurry.

"Please tell me you've made all of the arrangements for the gala. We set sail in less than five hours."

"Michael," Addie said, resting her hand over her heart, "I sent you a text not an hour ago telling you what I still needed. Somehow I've got supplies missing, though I don't know how that's possible. You replied that you were on it. Is that not true?"

The man stuttered. "I-I did?"

"Yes." Addie sighed then turned to look at Margot. "Would you give us a minute? The mezzanine is just that way. Feel free to look around, though I don't think any of the shops will be open yet."

"Take your time," Margot said and then slipped past them.

As she walked away, she heard them lower their voices as they compared notes. It was interesting that, on such a large ship with such limited access, Addie would find things missing from her kitchen. Or was it called a galley?

Margot smiled to herself but it soon turned into a gasp. As she pushed through two double glass doors, she was stunned with the beauty of the mezzanine. Against the far wall was a glass-fronted elevator that looked like it ran to the top floors of the ship. Then, in a circular space surrounding the open lobby-like area, Margot saw couches and reading nooks, small tables, and shop fronts surrounding the lower floor.

As she looked higher, she saw that at least three of the

lower floors were open, accessed by elevators or a staircase that sat at the far side. The décor was a gaudy mix of deep reds and golden yellows with accents of navy blue. Vibrant green plants dotted the sitting areas and the dim but plentiful lights sparkled off the gold surfaces. It really was a sight to behold.

"Sorry about that," Addie said, coming up behind Margot.

"That didn't take long."

She rolled her eyes. "He's taking over for one of our senior crew members—"

"The one who's out sick?"

Addie looked surprised. "How did you know?"

Not wanting to get the woman in trouble, in case that type of information was classified, she just smiled. "I heard a rumor."

"It's so sad, Alison is great—super organized and always on top of things—but she came down with something awful last night. When I got the text, I knew it was going to be crazy today. I just didn't expect this. Michael's been trying to slip into her spot for a while now—always showing up where he doesn't belong—and now this. I'm afraid the power will go to his head."

"How did you know she was going to be gone? She texted you?"

"We're friends," Addie said, smiling. "We do yoga together

in the mornings—there's a great class on board. You should totally join."

Margot merely smiled at this.

"But yeah, she was feeling fine then suddenly she's sick. It's bizarre. I mean, Michael's a good guy but he's... overzealous to put it mildly. And he's also nowhere near as organized as Ali."

"Do you have what you need? I heard you say something about missing supplies."

Addie shrugged. "He says he'll get it here. The thing I don't get is *how* I'm missing flour. It's not like anyone is going to use extra bags of flour. Maybe I just miscalculated. Anyway, let's continue the tour and then grab lunch. We have the *best* food on board the *Carousel Luxury*."

Margot had heard as much and agreed. "I'm ready to get to the relaxing part of this cruise. Lead the way."

CHAPTER 3

A NEW DAY dawned and found the *Carousel Luxury* cutting deftly through the vibrant, aqua blue ocean on its way toward Mexico and the port of Ensenada. Margot hadn't been to Mexico before and she was thrilled with the thought of exploring the touristy city. If she'd been traveling on her own and not with a cruise line, she might have considered a foray into the wilds of the land, seeing the true side of Mexico that she'd read about, but as it was, she and all passengers like her would be relegated to specific areas.

She pushed the thoughts of exploration aside as she strode out onto the wood deck and searched the area for a free chaise lounge. They wouldn't be in Mexico until the next day so she had no reason to think about what she would do until the next day. Wasn't that the luxury of the cruise? To relax, eat, and push worries to the side?

She'd donned shorts and a tank top, forgoing her

swimsuit seeing as how a slight haze still clung to the morning sky. It was warm enough in the sun, but she wouldn't be swimming. Instead, she'd packed a few novels. All thrillers, all involving crime, and all guaranteed to grip her attention no matter how distracting the activities of the deck became.

Fortunately, since it was still early, there were fewer people out and she was able to snag a chair overlooking the vast ocean as it slipped past. Reclining back and donning a floppy straw hat, she smiled to herself. *This* was perfection. The salty breeze played with the towel she'd tossed over her legs to ward off the nip in the air, but her attention was arrested by the horizon that met the sky in a gentle kiss. A perfect mingling of blues.

Reaching into her bag, she pulled out the newest Baldacci thriller and opened to the first chapter. She relished the feel of the trade paperback in her fingers; the thick weight of the book in her hand promising adventures one right after the other. She'd just started into the first paragraph when a shadow fell over her towel-draped legs.

"I'm fine, thank you," she said without looking up. She knew the stewards were good at their jobs. They were present and helpful, but at this moment they were being *too* helpful. She didn't want or need anything aside from silence and peace.

The shadow didn't move.

Closing her eyes and taking in a deep breath, Margot

fought the urge to continue to ignore the shadow. They would go away eventually, wouldn't they?

"I think you've mistaken me for someone else," a deep voice said.

Now she rolled her eyes. The action was hidden by her hat from the man whose voice she'd heard, but she was tempted to take the hat off and repeat the action. Instead, she remembered that there was no need to be rude —merely firm.

"I'm sorry, did I take your chair?" she said, still not looking up. "Or, perhaps, I'm in the way of your view?" Her tone wasn't exactly curt, but it was clipped and to the point.

"Nothing like that," he said. "But, if you were, I'd say you were entitled to it."

She rolled her eyes again and gave up the hope that he would go away. She should have expected this. A single woman with a book in her hands was supposed to be a clear signal: leave me alone. Apparently, this man had missed the sign.

"I'm sorry, but—" She looked up and stopped midsentence. Brice Simmons stood before her in all of his star-actor glory. He was tall, at least six feet, with broad shoulders, muscled arms and chest revealed beneath the deep V of his button-down Hawaiian print shirt, and a boyish grin that belied his forty years. To say he was tan was an understatement and it only helped to offset his bright white smile. The same smile women around the globe had lusted over for the last twenty years of his somewhat tumultuous career.

Margot closed her gaping mouth and tried to regain some of her composure. "Uh, what is it that you need of me then?"

He's just a man. But even as she tried to convince herself of that, she found it difficult to keep her thoughts straight with the exceptionally handsome man towering over her.

"I was wondering if this seat is taken." He indicated the lounge next to her in a row of five empty seats next to it. He was going to sit right next to her?

Her mouth went dry and her stomach clenched. She'd brought engaging reading because she wanted to be lost in the world of fiction, but not even one of her favorite authors could keep her distracted with Brice Simmons sitting next to her.

But that was ridiculous. She chided herself for her foolish, schoolgirl thoughts. She was a forty-one-year-old woman who owned a pastry shop. Not some teen with a star-crush looking for a ship romance.

"Sure," she said, her voice sounding pinched in her own ears, "feel free."

He grinned as if he sensed the underlying tension and the effect he had on her, then he slipped into the seat next to her. His long, muscled legs, just as tan as the rest of him, stretched out on the lounge. Then he began to unbutton his shirt.

She yanked her gaze back to her novel, feeling her cheeks heat, and desperately tried to read the rest of the first page. It was two short paragraphs but she kept reading the first line, hyper-aware of every move the man next to her made.

When he pushed the chair back a few clicks and laced his fingers behind his head, she let out a breath, closed her eyes for a few moments, then tried to refocus on the page.

"What are you reading?"

Heat rushed through her again. She knew she should tell him to mind his own business and get back to her book, but now the curiosity that was ingrained in her came to life. "David Baldacci's latest."

"He's good. Thrillers, huh?" His tone was conversational and her mind supplied an image of him in his latest action flick.

"Yep," she said, eyes still focused on the first page.

Finally, after several minutes, he spoke again. "My name's—"

"I know who you are," she interrupted then felt foolish.

"Then I'm at a disadvantage."

Relegating herself to the reality that she obviously wasn't

going to get any reading done, she closed her book, keeping her finger in her place, and looked over at Brice.

"Margot Durand." She leveled her gaze on him.

"Nice to meet you. Are you...traveling alone?"

The urge to roll her eyes was strong again, but she resisted. "In a way, yes."

His eyebrows rose above his dark sunglasses. "I'm not sure I know what that means."

Then she saw them walking across the deck. Two women in bikinis with light, see-through wraps draped over their impossibly fit bodies. They were, no doubt, heading this way.

"Well, I can see that *you're* obviously not traveling alone, so I'll just find another, *quieter*, area to read and let you have this extra chair. Looks like you'll need it." She forced a smile and stood, collecting her things just as the girls reached them.

"There you are, sweetie," one said, bending down to kiss him on the cheek, but he pushed her hand off his shoulder and sat up.

"You don't have to go. They aren't—"

"Who's this?" the other girl asked, her gaze hard on Margot.

"Really," he said, standing as she turned to walk away. "They aren't—"

"It's all right, Mr. Simmons. Your reputation precedes you."

And with that, she turned and left the handsome celebrity on the deck.

～

MARGOT FELT the heat of their exchange long after she had stepped into the coolness of the mezzanine area, but she would not be convinced by her fickle emotions. Sure, Brice Simmons was as handsome as they came and a talented actor too, but Margot was smarter than that. Smarter than to think his attention was anything other than a diversion to his otherwise planned out life. Wasn't that how most celebrities lived?

And then an image of Adam appeared in her mind and she smiled. Besides, when there was a man like Adam waiting for her back in Long Beach, and Virginia beyond that, Brice couldn't compare.

Pushing her tote further up on her shoulder, she trailed through the small shops and picked up a few small items for her friends back in North Bank. A crossword book with nautical terms for Bentley, a magnet for Rosie, and a postcard that she would send to the shop for them all. She intended to do more shopping in Ensenada, but for now, she enjoyed thinking of them as she shopped. A suitable gift for Dexter eluded her though.

Then she ordered a latte and sat down at one of the more

secluded tables on the main floor. Vibrant green plants sheltered her from those passing by and soon she was engrossed in the thriller that had proved so difficult to keep her focus on the deck. Occasionally sipping her coffee, she spent an hour reading before low voices broke into her concentration.

"I don't know. It's just what I heard."

"But...I didn't even know he was married," another voice replied, this one higher pitched and nasally, making Margot think of a mouse.

"Well, if it *is* true then she's going to know about it the minute we get back to Long Beach," the first voice said.

"What makes you say that?" Mouse said.

"For one, stuff like that doesn't just stay on the ship. And secondly, I mean—hello," the first woman paused for affect. "He's the captain. And if someone saw him with her...well, it's just going to get out. You'll see."

"That's so sad. I really liked her."

"Whatever. If she's messing up his marriage, it serves them both right."

The voices trailed off and Margot saw two crewmembers walk past. Finding it unsettling that she'd just been privy to a very private conversation about none other than the ship's captain, she closed her book and headed off to find Addie in the kitchen area.

Trying to shake off the sad thoughts of a man cheating on his wife, Margot nearly missed the entrance to the kitchen. She pressed the door open soundlessly but stopped just inside when she heard low but forceful voices. They were coming from the back of the kitchen, but she couldn't tell if it was Addie or not.

Then her friend's voice was clearly heard. "I just don't understand!"

Margot stepped forward, ready to go to her friend's aid, when she bumped into the metal prep table in the middle of the room and sent the spatulas, spoons, and other utensils clattering to the floor.

"I don't know how many times I've told you to—" Addie stopped when she saw Margot with her hands outstretched to pick up the utensils. "Oh, Margot. I thought you were Noah."

Margot offered a forced smile as she righted the canister at the same time she heard a door closing. So there was another way out of the kitchen.

"Is everything all right?" she asked, looking into her friend's eyes.

Addie avoided her direct gaze and fumbled with the edge of her apron. "Yeah. I'm just not...feeling well."

"Is there anything I can do?"

"For a headache?" Addie looked up, her wry smile unconvincing. "I don't think so. But thank you anyway."

She stepped back, untying her apron. "Hey, why don't I meet you for dinner tonight at The Acapella Room? I'll get us reservations and we'll catch up then. I think I'm just going to get some rest now. If you can fend for yourself?"

Every intuition Margot had told her that her friend was lying, but she wasn't sure that she should press the issue. Yet.

"All right, honey, you go on. I'll meet you there tonight, okay?"

"Thank you," Addie said, grabbing Margot's hand and squeezing for a moment. "I'll see you there tonight."

Margot watched her go, her suspicions aroused. Something was definitely wrong with her friend, but she wasn't sure what. And who had she been talking to in the backroom?

Her curiosity got the best of her and she made her way to the small office space at the back of the kitchen. There was another door. Margot opened it and popped her head into the hall, looking up and down it both ways. What corridor was this? She couldn't be sure unless she reached the end of the hall where additional directions were usually posted, but she had checked the door handle and it was locked from the inside. Without a key, she'd be locked out and likely more than a little lost.

Instead, she pulled the door closed behind her and went back into the kitchen. She was about to leave when she heard the office door open. A moment later, Noah came into the room.

"Oh, Margot." He stumbled back a few steps. "I didn't know you'd be here."

"I was just about to leave. I..." She fought for a good explanation but couldn't find one. "Were you here earlier?"

He frowned. "Earlier? No." He shook his head, looking genuinely confused. "I was, uh, making my rounds between the kitchens and our bakery shop in the mezzanine. Why? Did you need something?"

"No," Margot was quick to reply. "Sounds like you've been busy."

"I'm always busy. It's the nature of the beast," he said with a grin that didn't quite meet his eyes.

"You said you've worked here three years?" she asked.

"Yes, but before that, I was on a few different cruise lines. I feel like I practically grew up on a boat."

"Seems like it," she mused. "Well, I'd better get going. I'm going to do a lap or two around the ship—I hear that's great exercise."

"It is," he said, nodding with knowledge. "Enjoy it."

She left the kitchen feeling his gaze on her back. He probably wondered what she was doing in the kitchen without Addie, but as soon as she'd asked if he had been there earlier, she felt as if she'd locked herself into a bit of a trap. Since Noah hadn't been the voice from earlier—or he hadn't admitted to it—then if she'd said she'd seen Addie, he'd know Addie had been there with someone. Maybe she was being paranoid, but on a ship that put so much stock in gossip, she wasn't going to risk her friend's reputation.

Shaking her head, she mentally berated herself. She was doing it again. Meddling. Poking her nose where it didn't belong. Why couldn't her friend have just had a disagreement? Those happened all the time. There was no need to read more into it.

Besides, she was on vacation. It was time to start acting like it.

CHAPTER 4

MARGOT SLIPPED ON A LONG, cotton shift dress with tiny blue and white stripes. Accented with a golden anchor necklace and a lightweight grey cardigan, she slipped into her sandals and walked to dinner. The evening was cool, but not unpleasant, and she breathed in the salty air as she walked along the outside deck to reach The Acapella Room.

She'd read up on the menu and requested attire of this particular restaurant and looked forward to seeing the chef's creations. Her stomach growled in response and she secretly hoped that Addie was already there with their seat.

The walkway curved with the ship and, as she stepped past a young couple walking with their arms around one another, she caught a glimpse of a tall man in a dark blazer and jeans a hundred yards in front of her. What caught her attention were the jeans. They were distinctive

—a specific designer that liked to make flashy pockets on the back of all of his jeans—and she'd seen those jeans before.

Or, at least, she thought she had, on Gabe Williams.

But what would *Gabe* be doing on board a ship in the middle of the Pacific Ocean? Unless he was on a vacation, she reasoned. That was likely, seeing as he lived in Long Beach and he *had* said he would be busy this week and for Adam to call him the next week...but it seemed odd to her that he hadn't said anything about the cruise. She hadn't mentioned hers, but that was because she didn't know Gabe.

Frowning as she passed the hall that she needed to turn down, she took one glance in the direction of The Acapella Room and then kept walking. He appeared to be alone and in no hurry, but she followed at a discrete distance anyway. Still, she wasn't positive it was him. How could she explain following him if he turned around and found her standing there? Then again, she could have been going in the same direction as he was and then she'd play the surprised act about meeting a friend of a friend and what a small world it really was.

Could she pull that off though? Unlike Brice Simmons, she was no actress.

Up ahead, Maybe Gabe opened a door and slipped into the interior of the ship. After waiting a moment, she followed suit, hoping it wasn't going to be a long hallway with no place to hide, in case he turned around. But when she stepped inside the hallway, she was faced with an empty corridor in both directions.

Where had he gone? She hadn't even seen his face clearly enough to know if it really was Gabe either.

Feeling frustrated that she'd missed her opportunity, she was about to go back outside and make her way to dinner when she heard a door close down the hall to her left. Only after a moment's hesitation did she set off in that direction. She relaxed her shoulders and, rather than looking inquisitive, she tried to look like she was simply lost. That way, if Gabe did come around a corner or out of a room, she would be able to feign misunderstanding of directions. Though, if he were anything like Adam, he'd see right through that.

Why was she suspicious of him anyway? It was her nature to question and investigate, one of the things her late husband Julian had loved about her—or so he'd said. But it went back to his conversation with Adam at the restaurant and the fact that he looked as if he worked for a multimillion-dollar company, not the Long Beach police force. Or had she read into that? No, Adam had clearly said he was one of "Long Beach's finest," hadn't he?

The closer she came to what looked like a bend in the hall the more anxious she felt. Would she turn the hall and come face to face with him? Did he know she was following him? Was she being overly worried for no reason?

At the end of the hall, she read the sign that denoted what she would find if she turned in that direction. She was on the southeast wing, level five, or so the sign said. The arrow pointing around the corner indicated that it led to the sports equipment area. What did that mean?

Taking a risk, she did a quick peek around the corner to find the short hallway closed. Then the sound of something falling, muffled by the closed door, could clearly be heard. Someone was in the sports equipment room. But who? Maybe Gabe? And would they come back out this door? Her stomach clenched and she looked around. Aside from a very thin, very fake looking plant, and a door marked Housekeeping Closet, there was nowhere but back.

She heard another sound, this time something moving in the sports room followed by footsteps coming toward the door.

It was now or never. She was either going to pretend to be lost and risk whoever it was seeing through her cover, or she was going to...

Her gaze snagged on the housekeeping closet again and without thought, she pulled the door open. Thankful to see it was large enough to stand in, she stepped inside and closed the door, praying it wouldn't somehow be locked, not allowing her back out. Then she waited, holding her breath.

Moments later, she heard a door open then close and then

rapid footsteps heading back down the hall. Hoping to catch a glimpse of who it was, she went to open the door but it wouldn't move. Panic surged through her. Was she locked in to this small closet?

Taking in a steadying breath, she gripped the handle more firmly and shoved. The door burst open, taking her with it into the hall. Her first thought was relief at not being locked in the closet, but the second was whether or not she'd alerted whoever it was to her presence. She looked around and found that the halls were empty. It wasn't far back to the outside door, she reasoned, and the person had already made it outside.

Letting out a shaky breath, she closed the closet door and went toward the sports storage area. The door was closed, but when she tried the handle, it moved easily and opened out toward her. She stepped inside, the only lights that of an exit sign across the room and then the light flooding in from the hallway.

Margot pulled out her cellphone and tapped on the flashlight app, stepping inside the room but keeping the door open. She wasn't about to risk getting trapped in another room, even if only for a moment.

It looked like the room housed all sorts of sports equipment, hence its name, for guest's recreation while on board and probably even for when they docked in Mexico. In front of her she saw what must have fallen, alerting her to the person's presence in the room. A set of golf clubs lay on the ground, another set standing upright beside them.

She gingerly stepped over them then stopped, frozen in place. There, sticking out between a bin of beach balls and a wrapped up pool volleyball net, were a pair of ruby red high heels still attached to a pair of legs.

Slowly, careful not to disturb anything else, Margot stepped around the equipment and froze. It was a woman lying face down on the ground. She wasn't moving.

~

"You say you were lost?"

Margot swallowed. She didn't like lying and made a habit not to, but in this instance, she wasn't sure it was appropriate, or in her best interests, to point out she was following a man that she thought to be a Long Beach police officer…and she hadn't actually seen him go into the room. She'd only heard someone.

"In a manner of speaking. I mean, there are so many halls on this ship." She gave a light laugh even though that felt wrong in the presence of a dead body.

"Right." The ship's lead security officer, Harvey Pearson, was a grizzled older man with weathered features she'd expect to see on a man who had fished for a living, but he assured her that he'd been a cop before taking his 'cushy gig' on board the *Carousel Luxury*.

"And was it exactly that drew you to come into the sports storage facility?" His eyebrows rose at the question but she didn't feel as if he doubted her story, only that he was trying to understand it.

"I heard someone in there and then the sound of something falling. I assume it was those clubs." She indicated the fallen golf clubs.

"And you didn't see anyone?"

"No." She flushed and looked down. "I actually stepped into the, um, housekeeping closet."

His eyebrows shot up even higher. "And may I ask why?"

"I felt foolish," she said, embellishing on one of her feelings, even if it wasn't the main reason. "I mean, I was lost at the end of a hall and..." She shrugged.

He pursed his lips. "Look, if there's something you aren't telling me—"

Just then the door opened and a tall, handsome man strode in. He wore a navy blue jacket with gold braiding indicating he was the captain. Margot assessed him, her mind flitting to what she'd overheard that very day. He was good looking, probably in his early forties—maybe late thirties—and had a commanding presence about him. Then again, she knew she wouldn't be able to *see* unfaithfulness on a man. Though sometimes...

"Pearson, what is going on?" he said. His manner was

direct, if not a little gruff, and his voice reminded her of something but she wasn't sure what.

"Drugs. Looks like we've got an overdose."

The captain sighed. "Not again."

Margot's eyebrows shot up. "Again?"

"I'm sorry," the captain said, looking down at her. "Who are you?"

"I'm Margot Durand—"

"The pastry chef?"

She was surprised the captain knew about her presence on board with hundreds of staff to account for. "Um, yes."

"Pleased to meet you. I'm Captain Grayson Haus. And what exactly are you doing here? You're a long way from the kitchen."

"I was the one who found the...body."

He looked to the side where two of Harvey's coworkers were documenting everything. "Right. Well, I am terribly sorry for you. This is supposed to be a vacation and..." His eyes narrowed. "You're awfully calm about all of this."

"I was thinking the same thing," Harvey said.

Margot shrugged. "My late husband was a detective and I've...seen my share of dead bodies. Unfortunately." Both men looked surprised but she pressed on. "You've had drug overdoses on board before?"

The captain looked around as if he was afraid of being overheard but something in his expression softened. "Look, Mrs. Durand, this cruise goes to Mexico almost every week and there is an unsavory side to every town past the boarder, especially Ensenada. We've had our fair share of issues with recreational drugs being brought on board, though we do everything in our power to make sure that doesn't happen. Though, we've never had an overdose that was fatal." He ran a hand across the back of his neck. "Look, it's late. Once Harvey here has everything he needs from you, why don't you go back to your cabin to rest. I'm sure this has been trying."

She appreciated the captain's understanding nature, but she was more concerned by the fact that there was a dead body. What would they do? Contact the authorities? It would likely be the FBI that would investigate the case since it was on international waters.

"What do you plan to do?" she said, looking between both men.

"Don't you worry about it," Harvey said. She could almost hear the added, 'little lady.' "I'll be in contact with the proper authorities."

Margot wanted to take a better look at the woman, but she also didn't want to raise Harvey's suspicions any more than she already had. One more question couldn't hurt though, could it?

"Who is she?"

Both men turned to look at her. It was the Grayson who spoke first. "She was our sports and recreation coordinator. Kristen Chambers."

Margot nodded. "I see." At least that explained why she was in the sports closet, but it didn't explain why she was wearing a tight—and short—miniskirt, red heels, and a sequined top. "Are crewmembers usually allowed to…party?"

This time it was Harvey who answered her. "We discourage some…um, *personal* interactions between the staff and our guests, but we do encourage our staff to mingle when possible. She was well within her rights as a staff member to have a night out, just not with *this* type of recreation."

Margot understood. "I see."

"I think I have all that I need for now, but I may need to question you further or have you speak with the proper authorities when we reach port back in Long Beach."

"Yes, of course." She had assumed as much, but she knew the difference in pace between that of a drug overdose and a murder. Was this the former, or the later?

CHAPTER 5

MARGOT REACHED her cabin not long after she'd been released from the sports equipment storage area, though she had stopped to pick up a container of food to take back to her room. She'd also placed a call to Addie on the ship's phone, wondering if she was worried, but she hadn't reached her friend. She'd even stopped by her room but without an answer, Margot went back to her room.

Famished as she was, she placed the food on the small table and pulled out her iPad. It wasn't that she didn't trust Harvey and his security team, but if they were going to wait to contact the authorities until they were headed back to Long Beach, wouldn't evidence grow cold?

She paused, her fingers hovering over the small, attached keyboard. Evidence? Here she was treating this drug overdose as a murder—something Harvey didn't think it was.

Sighing, she rested her head on her hand, elbow propped on the tabletop. It wasn't that she *wanted* it to be a murder case so much as she was afraid that certain elements weren't lining up. Like the fact that she'd been following someone she believed to be a police officer only to find a dead woman where he'd lead her. Then again, she wasn't certain it *had* been Gabe—either at the end of that hall or even on board at all.

Adam's name glared back at her from the top of the email she'd started. Should she go through with it? Would he only worry? Then again, could she phrase her questions in such a way that he wouldn't be suspicious? Perhaps ask if he'd met up with Gabe? Likely not, he was a smart man, but just maybe...

Her fingers flew over the small, bluetooth keyboard and once she'd hit send, she leaned back. A picture of a large cake topped with éclairs and *religieuse* stared back at her. One of her monumental creations she'd done in her years of competing to be the best French pastry chef in the world. Or something like that.

A soft, memory-laden smile edged onto her lips but was soon replaced with the reality that a woman had died that night. Why? Was it as simple—and horrible—as a drug overdose? Or was it something else altogether?

Dressing in pajamas, Margot ate the now mildly warm dinner she'd taken with her and then climbed into bed. She was exhausted from the mental strain as much as from the reality that, yet again, she'd come across a dead body. Even on vacation she couldn't seem to get away from it. But that prodding at the back of her mind, the one that urged her to desire the truth in all circumstances, reared its curious head. It was the same reason she'd sought out the truth in both her niece's case and her friend Tamera's husband's case. The truth had to prevail, and if she could do anything to help that along, then she would.

POUNDING on her cabin door jerked her from fitful sleep and she stumbled out of bed, reaching the door as another fit of pounding began.

"Addie?" she said, looking at her through bleary eyes.

"I'm sorry, Marg, but I had to see you. Can I come in? I brought coffee."

The scent of bold French roast wafted out of the paper cup her friend was holding and, despite the restless night she'd had, Margot nodded and reached for the liquid caffeine.

"I just can't believe it," her friend said, hand going to her forehead as she paced the small space from the bed to the door then back again. "I mean, a woman is *dead!*"

Margot nodded, sipping the black coffee and grimacing when she burned her tongue. "I know. I was there."

"You were *what?*"

Margot frowned. "Don't you check your messages? I stood you up for dinner last night and then phoned to let you know I had been detained due to the—" She almost said murder. "—death."

"I... No."

Margot observed her friend through narrowed eyes. There were bags under her eyes and her hair was disheveled. In fact, it almost looked as if she hadn't gone to bed at all. She was also pacing again. Was she nervous?

"Addie, calm down." She reached her hand out toward the girl. "Come sit with me. Calm down. Did you know the woman?"

Addie shook her head, biting her lip before she answered. "Not really. I mean, I'm down in the kitchens almost all the time and don't have a chance to really do much recreation. I just— I guess I'm shocked."

"Of course, that's natural. How did you hear about it?"

"At a staff briefing this morning. It's so unorthodox. I mean, nothing like this has ever happened."

"Do you know anyone who knew the girl well?"

"Not really," she said. "I mean, from what I heard, there weren't a whole lot of people who *did* know her. Someone did say they'd seen her leave the club last night. I guess she was on her way to...I don't know, take the party to the next level?"

"But it was still so early," Margot mused.

"Right? I said as much, but one of the pursers in charge of that club said he saw her there often, never on duty or anything, so she was well within her rights as a crewmember to be there, but still…it *was* early."

"Was she ever seen with a man?"

Addie looked over at Margot with a confused expression. "What?"

"Sorry, I suppose you wouldn't know that. I was just wondering…maybe she 'partied' with someone on staff."

"Oh, that I wouldn't know." Addie looked down at the coffee held in her hands. "All of this is just too much right now."

Her friend's words alerted her to something deeper going on than just her upset over the dead crewmember.

"Addie," she said gently, "what's going on?"

Her friend looked up with wide eyes. "What do you mean?"

"You just seem out of sorts. Is there something I can help you with? It's a great thing to unburden yourself to a friend sometimes."

"Oh, uh, no." She shook her head and managed a feeble smile. "I'm fine. Really. I'm just…upset about all of this."

Margot had the distinct feeling that the girl wasn't telling her the truth, but she had no way to know if that was true or not. It also didn't feel like the right time to pressure her for a further explanation.

"I'd better get back to work. I'm just on a break. The pastries won't bake themselves as you well know, but thanks for listening to me."

"Of course. Do you need help this morning?"

"Absolutely not," Addie said with a stronger smile, "you're only on duty tonight. I hope you can get some relaxation time in. And I almost forgot to ask. Do you want to explore Ensenada today? I'll be done by early afternoon when we dock. I'd be happy to show you around."

"That sounds wonderful. Meet you in the mezzanine around one then?"

"Perfect. See you then."

"Oh," Margot called out to her friend. "Is it possible to see a list of passengers on board?"

The request shocked her friend and she rushed to find a reasonable explanation rather than admitting she wanted to see if Gabe Williams was listed as a passenger.

"I thought I saw Brice Simmons but I wanted to make sure before I made a fool out of myself asking for an autograph."

"Oh," Addie laughed, "well, there isn't guest access to it but I could check for you."

"No, that's fine. I'll take my chances."

Addie gave a little wave and disappeared out the door while Margot slumped back against the bed pillows. She felt bad about the fib she'd told her friend since she knew the egotistical man had indeed been Brice, but that also meant there was no way she could see the manifest. Well...no easy way at least. Maybe it was time she did a little digging of her own.

~

MARGOT DRESSED in white linen capris and a light blue tank top under a lightweight polka dot navy sweater. She tucked her canvas tote that would serve as her purse over her shoulder and headed out into the hall. She walked down the now familiar route to the mezzanine, but instead of veering off to the left and out the double glass doors that showcased the deep blue ocean waters, she walked down the steps and toward the customer service area.

It was still early, though not as early as she was used to waking up to get to the bakery, but that meant there was only one purser overseeing the computers. Thankfully, it was a woman. Her ruse would work with a man, but probably not as well. Margot had thought long and hard about what she was going to do and, when she stepped up to the waist-high desk, a computer monitor and keyboard the only things constituting the woman's work space, she put on a warm, slightly shy smile.

"Hello and good morning, ma'am. How may I help you?"

"Good morning. I have a question." She looked around, lowering her voice though no one was around. She bit her lip and did her best to look embarrassed. "There was this man last night…" Margot gave a girlish giggle. "He was the *sweetest*. I met him in the bar and he gave me his room number, we're going into Ensenada today, but I lost it somewhere between the bar and my own room." She looked sheepishly at the woman. "Is there any way to find out where he is?"

She pursed her lips and put on an apologetic look. "I'm so sorry, ma'am, but we're unable to give guests' room numbers."

"Oh, I completely understand but…" Margot huffed out a breath and played up her dejected look. "I *really* liked him and he was so respectful. That's rare these days. I don't need to see him exactly, but could you page him? Do you do things like that on the ship?"

The woman shook her head again. "No, we don't really page. Although…" She tilted her head. "I could leave a note for him and make sure he gets it before this afternoon." She smiled and Margot wondered if this was going to work.

"That might be all right," she said, trying to look hopeful.

"His name was Gabe. Gabe Williams." The woman clicked through her program and Margot added, "I think he's staying on the East deck. Fifth floor or something."

After a few more clicks, the woman shook her head. "I'm so sorry, ma'am, but there's no one here under that name."

Margot hid her dismay with surprise. "What? You mean he *lied* to me?"

The woman looked sympathetically at her. "I'm sorry."

"Figures I would meet a nice guy who wouldn't be that nice. Well, thank you so much for your help."

"Not a problem. Have a great day."

The woman's cheery farewell followed Margot through the mezzanine and out onto the deck as she made her way to The Acapella Room for breakfast. So she hadn't seen Gabe. Or, if it had been him, he was here under an assumed name. And she'd followed him to the room where a dead body had been found.

She was so preoccupied that she didn't even notice the handsome, tanned man blocking her path until she collided with his solid chest. Warm hands reached out and lightly cupped here elbows, setting her back on her feet.

Righted, she looked up into aqua eyes that rivaled the ocean outside the wall of windows that faced west.

"Margot Durand."

"Brice Simmons," she said, barely holding in her grimace.

His flashing white teeth told her he was more than happy to see her. "Let's have breakfast."

She didn't need—or want—his flirty attention. "That's all right. I'm sure you're busy. I'm…" She looked around for an excuse and spotted the two young women she'd seen the day before. This time they were wearing more than they had been on the deck, but only by a little.

"I won't take no for an answer. This way." He motioned for a waiter as the two women came toward him. "Tiffany, Haden, you're dismissed for the morning."

They nodded and turned away as if this happened often and Margot had a feeling it did. "Really, I'm fine eating alone."

"On a cruise? You already read alone, a waste of time if you ask me. Besides, you can go home and tell everyone you had breakfast with Brice Simmons." This arrogant smile nearly took all of the air from the room, or at least it felt that way.

Margot wanted to say that none of her friends would really care, but that wasn't fully true. She had a feeling Taylor would 'flip out,' as she was prone to say. But aside from her celebrity-crazy niece, no one else would care. If he'd been Frank Sinatra, it might have been another story.

Resigning herself that it was either breakfast with Brice or going hungry, she listened to her stomach and followed him as the waiter showed them to a table.

"Glad you decided to join me," he said, flashing her a brilliant smile before ordering a coffee with more qualifiers than Margot thought possible.

She ordered coffee with cream and then turned her gaze on the man sitting across from her. "You hardly gave me a choice."

There was that grin again. "Well, you looked lonely standing there. Besides, what I said was right, you can't go on a cruise by yourself."

She hiked an eyebrow. "You can, and I did."

"And how much fun are you having?"

"Actually…" She looked to the side, thinking of the body she'd found last night. "Not that much fun, but that's no fault of the cruise or being alone."

His gaze narrowed. "Are you talking about the body you found?"

"How did you know about that?" She was genuinely shocked.

"Oh, my staff likes to share information with me."

"Your staff?"

"Tiffany and Haden. They are my assistants."

They certainly didn't dress like any assistants Margot had ever seen. "Still, how did they know about it?"

"It's their job to be informed."

"I'd say that's more than staying informed."

"Think of it this way, if there's a threat that could affect me, it's their job to know."

That was interesting. The women looked like two pieces of arm candy, but she knew better than to categorize people by how they looked.

"They are your security?"

"That's Haden," he said with a grin, "Tiffany is my personal assistant."

"Interesting."

He leaned his elbows on the table. "I know it's unorthodox, but Haden graduated top of her class at the police academy and, once she'd had enough of being a public servant, she sought out something a little more profitable."

Everything about that statement made Margot recoil.

"What?" Brice said as their food arrived. He had insisted on ordering instead of choosing the buffet option and Margot had to admit the steaming bowl of oatmeal with artfully placed fruit on top did looked amazing. "I can tell something I said made you unhappy."

"My husband—my *late* husband," she added when she saw his surprised look, "was one of those odious 'public servants.'"

"And you don't like that she wanted to make enough money to pay off her school debts?"

Margot narrowed her eyes. "I take no issue with that."

"You said late. How did your husband die?"

His question shocked her and she almost choked on the bite of oatmeal she'd just taken. "You don't pull any punches," she observed.

"Sorry," he said, shrugging. "I've found that I can come across rather abruptly at times. I suppose it's just a fault I have."

That, or it was the reality that he could get away with asking whatever he wanted, whenever he wanted, due to his celebrity standing. Either way, she wasn't sure she wanted to open up about her husband's death with this total stranger.

"I only ask," he continued, popping a grape into his mouth and chewing thoughtfully for a moment, "because I've experienced loss as well."

Her eyebrows rose and she took a breath. What she would share with him wouldn't be anything more than what she'd share with anyone else. "My husband was a detective in our small town in Virginia. He was a casualty during a particularly dangerous case he was working. A wrong place, wrong time sort of thing."

"Oh, Margot," Brice said, reaching across the table and resting his hand over hers, "I'm so sorry."

She smiled but gently pulled her hand away. "It was five years ago. The wounds, though painful, aren't as fresh as they once were."

Brice didn't seem to notice her withdrawal and kept his hand on her side of the table as his vibrant blue eyes poured into hers. "My sister died of a drug overdose."

"I'm sorry to hear that," she said, genuinely sorry for him.

"It was terrible," he said, leaning back and shaking his head, lost in his own thoughts. "I can still remember what I was doing when I heard the news. Drugs. Terrible things."

Margot narrowed her eyes, trying to understand the enigma in front of her. He was gregarious, handsome, and charming, but there was something underneath all of that that Margot couldn't quite point out. A feeling. Something like an underlying current that felt off. Perhaps that was what celebrity did to a person.

They finished up their breakfast, the conversation remaining light and mostly revolving around Brice's considerable knowledge of Mexico. When Margot was done, she pushed her plate forward, took the last sip of her coffee, and made her excuses to leave.

"You're welcome to join us in Ensenada if you'd like. We'll be having a lot of fun." He grinned and winked.

"Thanks, but I've got plans. Thanks again for breakfast."

He merely grinned and she felt his eyes on her as she left the dining room. It had been the strangest breakfast she'd ever had.

CHAPTER 6

MARGOT WAS MARVELING at the incredible view when she rounded the corner and ran into Noah. Blinking rapidly in surprise, she stepped back but immediately noticed the young man's expression. Was it sorrow or anger?

"Noah, are you all right?"

He stiffened when he saw her and his expression changed to one of sadness. "I'm sorry... I just...sorry."

"Did you know the woman who died?" She blurted it out before she could couch her speech, but the words seemed to shock him out of his stupor.

"Yeah." His jaw clenched. "I knew Kristen."

Margot studied his expression, but he turned his gaze out toward the ocean. "I heard she was new to the ship?" She wasn't sure why she was asking exactly, but it did seem odd that the young man, who had been on the ship for three years, would know a new crewmember despite the fact that he was so busy working in the kitchens. Was he known to attend the clubs? Was that where they'd met? Or had they known one another off of the ship?

"I didn't know her all that well," he was quick to explain. "We'd just gotten drinks a few times off ship. You know. Caught up in Ensenada and did some touristy things together." He snuck a glance at Margot and forced a tightlipped smile.

"I'm so sorry to hear that she passed away as she did."

His eyes narrowed, "How did you hear about it?"

"I discovered the body."

"You did?" He looked completely shocked, but she also noticed that his face paled, the color all but draining from his features.

"Yes." She wrapped her arms around herself as the breeze picked up. She could just make out land in the distance and knew that within an hour, they would be docked in Ensenada.

"Yeah, and to overdose like that…" He shook his head and his expression hardened. "Pretty dumb if you ask me. But I've got to get going. Sorry."

"Oh, yes of course." She took a step back. "I'll see you tonight?"

He frowned. "Tonight. Right. Yeah, see you then."

She watched him walk away, surprised at the change in his demeanor. If Addie barely knew the young recreation staffer, how had Noah met her? Were they closer than he'd let on?

Pushing her inquisitive desire to the side, she went to the deck and took up a spot on an empty chaise lounge, planning on reading until they pulled into port. At least while she was here she wouldn't be tempted to look into the mysterious death of the young woman.

Then again, it wasn't *that* mysterious. Many people overdosed from drugs. It happened...but still, it bothered Margot for more than just the obvious reasons. The young woman had been dressed for a party, and yet she'd overdosed in the sports equipment room without anyone around. That didn't make sense.

Then a thought occurred to Margot. She put her book away and pushed off the lounge. Taking her cue from the sounds of shouting and cheering on the other side of the deck, she walked toward the recreation area.

Standing on the sidelines, she watched the organized game of pool volleyball. There were two crewmembers, a young woman and a young man. They both looked happy and enthusiastic with their job and the woman was cheering loudly for the players in the pool. The young man commented something to the woman and picked up a bag that looked like it was full of equipment and started heading toward the door leading inside.

This was her chance. Margot circumvented the crowd on the deck watching the volleyball game and met up with the young man just before he went inside.

"Excuse me," she said, putting on a warm smile. "I was wondering if I could ask you a question."

He looked surprised that she'd stopped him but characteristic of all of the crewmembers that she'd interacted with, he was only happy to oblige. "Yes, ma'am, how can I help you?"

"I know this may seem...unorthodox but..." She managed to look uneasy. "I was the woman who found...Kristen Chambers."

The young man's expression changed to one of shock and sorrow. "Oh, I'm so sorry to hear that. It's a terrible thing that happened."

She nodded, agreeing. "I just...I guess I wanted to know more about her. Maybe that sounds odd to you, but I just can't get that image out of my mind and I thought that, maybe if I knew more about her, I could...you know, move on?"

"Oh, I understand," he said, nodding. A look of sympathy overtook his handsome features.

"I was just curious about what kind of woman she was?" Margot schooled her features, looking interested but not *too* interested.

"She was great. Really good at her job. I know that

passengers really seemed to love her." His expression fell and he looked appropriately sad. "To be honest, I didn't know her well."

"Why not?" Margot looked openly curious.

"We worked different shifts pretty much consistently and she was new. I hadn't seen her around much so..." He shrugged to emphasize his point.

"Yeah, that makes sense." Margot scrunched up her nose. "So you never saw her...out? I mean, the heels and outfit she had on last night were pretty fancy."

"You could ask Carol over there. I know she likes to visit some of the clubs on board. She might know."

"Thanks so much," Margot said, offering him a warm smile, which he returned before heading inside.

Margot stood to the side and watched the game wrapping up. She still had an hour or more before she would need to meet Addie for their jaunt into town and she still had questions about Kristen. She was apparently liked by all but not really known by many—except for Noah. Had he met her at a club? If so, would Carol know?

When the game broke up, Margot watched as the woman collected the volleyball items and told everyone when they could expect the next tournament. She hauled a cloth bag with the balls and the netting from across the pool toward the same door that the young man had gone through.

"Hello," she said with a friendly smile when she approached the door where Margot still stood. "Can I help you?"

"Well." Margot again looked sheepish. "I was wondering if I could ask you a few questions...about Kristen Chambers."

The name shocked the woman but her smile only faltered slightly. "What type of questions? And, if I can ask, why are *you* asking them of me?" She asked in a kind, respectful way that Margot appreciated.

Margot explained how she had found the woman and that she was just trying to make sense of it all and get to know a little more about the woman whose life had ended. Just as the young man had, Carol softened immediately.

"I'm sorry you had to go through that—and on a vacation no less." She shook her head.

"Did you know Kristen then? The other young man who was helping you seemed to think you might know her better than he did."

Carol shrugged. "Well, maybe. She hadn't been with us very long and I really hadn't gotten a chance to get to know her well. I did see her at one of the clubs, though. In fact, it wasn't last night but the night before."

"Really? I noticed last night—" Margot grimaced. "—that she was dressed to go out."

"Yeah, I could tell right away she was a regular party girl.

Was dancing with this one guy. They seemed to really hit it off."

Margot's mind filled in the blank. "Was he tall and blonde? Good looking?"

"No," she said, shaking her head. "Tall, but he had dark brown hair, kind of curly I think? Looked like he was wearing some pretty expensive jeans. I know, terrible thing to notice, but that fancy stuff on the pockets sticks out."

Margot felt the breath leave her lungs. Jeans with fancy pockets. Gabe?

"Yeah, I know exactly what you mean."

"Sorry, but we really didn't talk much. She bunked with a few other women but I didn't see her around a lot. She kind of kept to herself when she wasn't on duty."

Margot nodded and thanked the woman. The new information filled her mind with questions. If the man in question dancing with Kristen *was* Gabe, how did they know one another? Did they even know one another? And was it a coincidence that Margot had been following who she thought was Gabe only to find Kristen dead?

The questions stacked up against one another but the timer on her phone went off, alerting her to the fact that it was time to make her way to the mezzanine to meet Addie. The questions would have to wait.

~

MARGOT ALMOST MADE a grave mistake as she made her way to the appointed meeting area. She almost ran into Brice. But, at the last minute, she slipped behind a large bank of leafy plants, sucking in a breath at how close it had been. He was a nice man, she'd give him that, but he was self-assured, arrogant, and no doubt wanted her to join him in exploring Ensenada. Something she wasn't going to do. Sure, she could turn him down, but when she'd tried that at breakfast it hadn't gotten her far.

Now, as she stood breathing shallowly so as not to draw any attention her way, she ground her teeth realizing that Brice and his *associates* had stopped just on the other side of her hiding spot.

"And you're absolutely sure, Haden? I mean we're talking about murder here."

Margot pressed her lips together so firmly she felt her teeth leaving impressions on the inside. Had he just said *murder*? It only made sense that he was talking about Kristen, but as far as she knew, it was an overdose. A sweet girl who'd partied too hard.

Still, that explanation hadn't sat well with Margot anyway.

"I'm telling you there's no connection. We're clean. But we have to go. He called."

The voice of one of his assistants was low but easy

enough for Margot to hear. So they had knowledge of the crime? What did this mean? And what did she mean they were clean? And who had called? How was Brice, of all people, involved with any of this? Or was he? Had Kristen known him or approached him at the club perhaps? That sounded like a place that Brice might go at night on the cruise ship.

It was all a big guess, though. There was no way for her to know more information...unless...

The sound of Brice and his assistants walking away drew Margot's attention. She checked the time and saw that Addie was already fifteen minutes late. Biting her lip, Margot surveyed the mezzanine. Not seeing her friend, she made a hasty decision. She left a note at the customer help desk, hoping that Addie would get it, and went in search of the handsome and potentially devious celebrity.

She rushed to the railing of the boat and looked out to the gangplank. Near the exit, she spotted Brice and his two female assistants. She'd have to hurry, but maybe she could still catch up with them and gain an invitation to tour the city with them as Brice had offered before.

Holding onto her canvas tote, she rushed down the steep slope toward the dock, careful not to let her sandals slide. At the dock, she skirted past disembarking passengers. The crowds were thinning, though there were still plenty of people around. Taxis lined up, their drivers waving their hands and speaking in broken English to attract any customer they could.

Brice stopped near one such taxi and she seized her chance. Trying not to look or sounded winded, Margot smoothed her hair and stepped up toward him.

"Hello, Brice," she said with a smile.

"Margot, fancy seeing you here." His smile was bright but there was something holding it back. Was it his thoughts of murder?

"Is your offer still valid for a little tour of Ensenada? I find myself with a free afternoon."

Now his smile definitely slipped. "Oh, I'm so sorry. You'd said you were busy and...well, something's come up. I won't be able to show you around today."

Odd. For someone who had seemed intent on having her join him, he'd sure changed his tune quickly.

"Oh really? You can't spare any time?" She fluttered her eyelashes, nearly making herself sick as she did.

"I'm really sorry." He widened his eyes trying to express the truth of his regret. His hand slipped to her arm. "Any other time..." He looked away as another car pulled up. It wasn't a taxi but an expensive black car. The driver got out and he was wearing a dark suit and white shirt. He opened the door and said, "Mr. Simmons?"

"Come on, Brice," the woman with blonde hair said. "Sorry." She flashed a fake smile at Margot that gave her the distinct impression she wasn't sorry at all, then ushered her boss toward the car, his hand sliding from Margot's arm.

"Rain check?" he said, a hopeful light coming into his eyes.

Margot said nothing and watched as he slid into the dark interior, one of the assistants with him and the other into the front seat.

She watched as they pulled slowly into traffic. The urge to follow him was so strong that Margot didn't even try to ignore it. She found the next available taxi and nodded to him. "Let's go."

The man, short with a dark moustache, grinned and hopped into the front seat. "*Si, Senora*. Where to?"

His English was better than she'd expected, but for a tourist town, she knew she shouldn't be too surprised. "Can you follow that town car?"

She pointed ahead to the black car and the man turned to look at her. "Follow?"

How was she going to explain this?

"Is he...you know, your lover?"

"Uh..." She bit her lip.

"I got it. *Silencio*." He grinned and swerved into traffic despite the blaring horns of those behind him.

Margot slumped back into the worn leather interior of the older car. She knew this wasn't the brightest idea she'd had. Even as she thought it, she heard Adam's voice in her head berating her for taking a chance like this. Then again, she was in a cab. She was just following the man to see where he went in a city he seemed immensely knowledgeable of. If it looked like they were driving into a bad part of town, she'd have—

Frowning, she peered up at the name on the dash. It said Juan. Well, then she'd have Juan turn around and take her somewhere in town where she could do some sightseeing. A stab of guilt struck her as she thought about Addie. She had come on this cruise as a favor to her friend but also to spend time with the woman. Then again, it seemed Addie had things she needed to attend to that had kept them apart as well, but still… Should she have stayed around and waited for her friend rather than follow Brice?

Just then Juan pulled over.

"Why are we stopping?"

"They stop. You stop. *Si?*"

"Yes. *Si.*" She peered up ahead and saw Brice and the two women get out of the car. They were on a side street but she'd noticed the larger main thoroughfare a few streets over. They were still in what appeared to be a good neighborhood and Margot knew if she got out here, she was only a few blocks' walking distance to touristy crowds and shops.

"Thank you, Juan," she said, tossing a 500-peso bill at him.

He grinned, appreciating the tip. "You need me to wait?"

She shook her head. She wasn't planning on crashing his party, but she did want to see what was so important that Brice would rescind his offer. Not that she was such an important person to him, but he'd made it clear he wanted her company that day but something had definitely changed.

"*Adios*," Juan said, then drove off.

Stepping into the shade of a nearby building, she donned a floppy hat she'd kept in her tote, shoving her shoulder-length hair up into the hat and leaving her neck and shoulders bare. Then she put on a large pair of sunglasses that hid a good portion of her face. And, for good measure, she took off her sweater and shoved it in her tote, which she carried by the straps instead of over her shoulder. It wasn't a great disguise, but she also didn't look like she had when she'd seen Brice last.

Then she strolled along the street, happy to see others walking around at a similar pace. When she got to the front of the building, she saw that it was a restaurant with a patio space out back. Rather than go in, she circled around to the back through a narrow alleyway just past the building. From there, she peeked out and could just see Brice and his assistants sitting down at a large table near a rock fountain.

The man seated at the table with them wore a blazer of a light blue, his pinstriped shirt opened much too low in the front to reveal gold chains mingling with his dark chest hair. His black-rimmed glasses gave him a distinguished, expensive look.

Who was this man? Why was Brice meeting with him? It obviously was important enough that he blew her off or couldn't take her with him. But more than that, she wanted to know what they were saying.

That was when she saw her opportunity. A mariachi band was making the rounds singing at each table and they had just finished up a song. They were coming toward the table that Brice was at and everyone's attention as on the band.

She took a breath and prayed for invisibility even as she jetted out toward the waterfall.

"Hey!" a voice cried out.

CHAPTER 7

"PLAY SOMEWHERE ELSE!" the voice said.

Margot stood with her back plastered to the large rock waterfall structure that sat at the corner of the patio. There were tall palm trees jutting up into the sky, which provided natural shade but the water also acted as a cooling agent under the hot Ensenada sun.

She held her hand over her abdomen, her heart still pounding. She'd assumed they'd seen her make a dash for the relative cover of the waterfall, but apparently she had gone unnoticed while Gold Chain told off the mariachi band.

"I'm glad you could meet on such short notice," the man said.

Margot tried to move closer but was afraid of being seen, despite the lush foliage covering the rocks. The rushing water created a barrier to the sound and it was difficult to hear everything being said.

"I didn't feel like I had a choice." Brice's tone was clipped.

"Life is full of choices," the man said. His words were followed by a raspy laugh.

"Choices to cheat me?" Brice said.

"Cheat? What? What is this cheat?" Gold Chain sounded incredulous.

"I've given you what you asked for and you've consistently under-delivered."

"You don't know what you speak of, I—"

One of the women with Brice interrupted Gold Chain's tirade and said something but her tone was so soft that Margot missed it.

"Well, that is a lie. All of it is a lie. I had no hand in it. You come down here on your fancy cruise or shooting a movie and you think we are all barbarians. That's not how I do business." Gold Chain sounded angry now.

"We shall see," Brice said, sounding unconvinced.

Margot frowned. What was going on? What was Brice involved in and what had the man under-delivered on?

The woman was speaking again and Margot kicked herself. She knew if she moved any closer she would give away her position.

"Down to business—if you still wish to partner with me," Gold Chain finally said. His tone held anger but Brice didn't interrupt again. "I'm sending Andres here to run a very important errand, one you know that is very crucial to our...business. And we're going to have a Mexican feast. No more talk of cheating or murder."

So one of the women had mentioned the death on the ship—the *murder*. This filled Margot with curiosity, but she also honed in on the man's words. Who was Andres? If he was the one doing their bidding, then she needed to follow him. Especially if they were just going to sit and eat all afternoon.

Sending someone to do their bidding would make complete sense. Brice, though American, was still a well-known actor. If he'd shot a movie in Mexico as well, then more than just tourists could recognize him. There was no way he could be tied to...

Her thoughts came to a skittering halt. What? What *was* all of this?

"Andres, *llevar esto a* Ramone, *por favor*."

Risking a peek, Margot snatched a glance of Andres. He was tall, lanky, and dressed in a faded brown t-shirt with dirty khaki pants. He almost didn't look like he belonged in the restaurant, but she watched as he took the proffered envelope from Gold Chain and shoved it into his waistband at the front of his pants. No risk of pickpocketing that way.

She ducked back down behind the rocks when he turned to leave and contemplated her exit. There was no more mariachi band for her to count on for distraction. She glanced around and her gaze alighted on a large, black cord. Smiling to herself, she waited only a moment before yanking the cord.

Suddenly, the large fountain dripped to a stop. As expected, Gold Chain made a fuss at the fact that the cooling water had stopped and, seeing her opportunity, Margot slipped past the table that was focused on a harried waiter coming to the loud, jarring calls of the demanding man.

Smiling to herself, she slipped back down the alley and out toward the front of the restaurant just in time to see Andres at the end of the block. Thanking God that she'd worn comfortable sandals, she picked up her pace and reached the end of the block just in time to see Andres turn down a narrow alleyway. She was careful to keep her distance, and thankful that there were enough pedestrians to hide behind when Andres did a cursory glance behind him.

He stepped from the alley into the street and, after a few moments, she did the same. They had passed what she assumed was the main thoroughfare and were now on another side street. The dilapidated condition of the buildings made her stomach clench in unease but she kept on.

Then, as the foot traffic began to dissipate, Margot began

to worry that he would notice her. How could he not? She was a white, obviously American woman and stuck out like a store thumb. She hid behind a stack of old crates as he rounded another corner then came out just as two young men stepped into her path.

"*Hola, chica,*" one said with a sly smile.

She came to a halt and clasped the straps of her purse. She should have known better. The minute he left the more heavily populated areas, she should have gone back. But it was too late for 'should haves' and time for her to figure out her next move.

"Excuse me," she said and tried to walk around them.

"Hold on. Not so fast." The other one spoke and put a hand on her arm.

She immediately stepped back and sized them up. She had reached the Black Belt Level in Krav Maga and was confident of her ability, but she really didn't want to fight these men.

"Let me pass," she said, looking both of the men in the eyes.

"No." He reached out and went to grab for her, but she maneuvered past his grip with lightning speed.

The other man laughed at his buddy's inability to get a hold of Margot but she was already prepared for his attempt when a hand clamped down on her shoulder.

"There you are, honey," the voice said. Her stomach lurched and her attention jerked to the side to see who had come up behind her. Her shock nearly made her gasp.

Gabe.

She swallowed, blinking up at him. "These fellows weren't bothering you, were they?" He looked between the young men who started to back up when he appeared, seemingly out of nowhere.

"Nah, mister," one said, then they both turned and ran off.

"Honey?" she said, looking up at him, a million questions vying for her attention.

"I figured it was better than any other line I could come up with. Fancy meeting you here…Margot."

"Same to you, Gabe Williams."

"You've got a good memory."

"You've got good timing."

He gave her a cocky half-smile and shrugged. "What say we got back to the nicer parts of Ensenada?"

She agreed and let him lead the way. He seemed to know exactly where he was going and, when they reached the busy streets, he stopped near a vendor that sold fruit juice. Passing the woman a few pesos, he handed Margot a cold drink.

"Here, this'll help take the edge off."

She resented the fact that he thought he knew her, but she accepted the drink anyway and took a long sip. It was good.

"Are you on the cruise?" she asked, her eyes never leaving his face.

"I am."

"Do you know Kristen Chambers?"

He hesitated a moment too long, his weight shifting from one foot to the other, before he said, "That name doesn't ring a bell."

He was lying, but she had no way to prove that. Though she did think she caught a hint of something that passed behind his eyes. It was there and gone so fast she couldn't be sure, but it looked like sadness.

"Well, I trust you'll be all right to get back to the ship."

"I never asked you how you found me?"

He grinned. "Just lucky, I guess."

A loud noise drew her attention down the street and when she turned back, he was gone.

RATHER THAN CHANCE another unpleasant encounter with young men looking to scare foolish tourists who'd lost their way, Margot took another taxi back to the ship. She was cutting it close as it was and rushed to her room to change into her baking attire. Then she made her way to the kitchen.

When she arrived, she recognized Michael Bowers there, directing two burly Mexican men hauling in crates.

"Oh, Mrs. Durand," Michael said, his smile looking tight. "I didn't know you'd be here. I hope we're not disturbing you."

"No, I just came to get a head start on the desserts for the gala tonight."

"Ah yes," he said, looking down at his clipboard. "And Miss Petit?"

"I'm not sure where she is. She'll probably be along soon."

"Good." His curt reply matched his tight nod. "Just a delivery of flour. The workers will be gone any minute now."

Soon, the men had left and Michael gave her a slight bow before leaving as well.

Faced with a quiet kitchen, Margot let her mind wander. She needed the calming effect baking would have on her and was happy to get started without Addie, but her mind wouldn't let go of the strange events of the day. Where had Andres gone? Were the young men associated with him or were they just opportunistic? Where had Gabe come from? Had he been following Andres as well?

So many questions and yet nowhere near enough answers.

Rather than muddle through it all, she opened one door of the gigantic refrigerator and pulled out butter. Butter was always the perfect start to any recipe.

And then she set to work.

When Addie came in an hour later, she took in the work Margot had already done with surprise. "You've been busy."

Margot looked up and smiled. "Thought I'd make up for leaving you earlier today."

"Leaving me?" Addie tugged an apron on then turned to wash up at the sink. "What do you mean?"

"We were supposed to go into Ensenada today."

"Oh my gosh." Addie turned around, hands still dripping. "We *were*, weren't we?"

Margot was shocked. They had only made plans that morning and the girl had already forgotten? What was going on? She had never been so forgetful in school, Margot knew that for a fact. She appeared flustered and after the argument Margot had overheard, she wondered if there wasn't something seriously wrong going on.

"Addie," Margot said, resting her hands on the cool metal top of the counter. "What's going on?"

"Wh-what?" she said, toweling off her hands and turning

to the list Margot had made on the white board next to the bank of ovens.

"I've known you for years now and, though we haven't seen each other much of late, I know you're not some flighty school girl who forgets things like trips into town with her friend. Something's got you preoccupied and I wish you'd just open up to me about it."

"You're right," she said, her tone clipped. "I'm not *some school girl* and if there is anything wrong, it's *my* business, not yours. You've always been nosy, Margot, but seriously —cut it out."

Margot blinked, taken aback by the girl's cruel words. Then, an instant later, Addie's eyes welled with tears.

"I'm sorry—I didn't mean that." She let out a long breath and propped her hand on her hip, shaking her head. "I'm...I'm just under a lot of stress right now. And yes, there are some things that I really can't share with you right now. Not with anyone really..." She looked over her shoulder as if someone would come in the door at that exact moment. "But I'll tell you when I can, okay?"

Margot felt her sympathies return and nodded with a small smile. "Addie, I wouldn't force you to tell anything you didn't want to. I just want you to know that I'm here for you no matter what. If you need a listening ear, okay. If not, that's just fine."

Addie held her gaze as if assessing if Margot really meant

what she said. Then, finally seeing what she needed to, she nodded. "All right."

"What do you say we make some amazing French pastries?"

Addie gave her a small smile, agreed with a nod, and they went to work. Halfway through their list of baked goods, Noah showed up. His face was red and splotchy as if he'd gotten a sunburned from being outside for too long, and he looked tired.

"Sorry," he said, slipping on his own apron. "I overslept on the beach."

Margot narrowed her eyes and noticed the line at the back of his neck. There was white skin next to beet red skin as if he'd gotten sunburned from above. That didn't usually happen on the beach since most men didn't wear shirts when they were lying out. Then again, maybe Noah did. Still, to be late to one of the most important baking times seemed extremely irresponsible.

He stepped to the whiteboard. "Want me to update?"

Addie gave a curt nod, no doubt unhappy at his tardiness, and went back to the dough she was working with. Margot watched as Noah took inventory of what they'd already gotten done and what was left to finish up. He put lines through the pastries they'd finished, wiped out a few pastries, and reorganized based on baking times. His writing was extremely neat and Margot smiled to herself thinking of Dexter and his chicken scratch.

When they were finally finished, Margot was shocked to see that they only had an hour until the gala was set to begin.

"You'll have enough time to get ready, right?" Addie asked, looking worried.

"Yes, of course." Margot took off her apron and tossed it on top of Addie's and Noah's in the bin near the back door. "I'll see you there?"

"Definitely. And Margot—" Addie stepped toward her. "I'm really sorry. About earlier. I...I was way out of line. You have always been a good friend to me and this— Well, it's killing me, but I really can't talk about it. Yet."

Margot wrapped her arms around her friend and squeezed lightly. "It'll be fine. And apology accepted. Now go get ready and I'll see you at the pastry table."

"Deal."

Margot watched Addie disappear into the back hall and turned toward the hall that would lead to her quarters. There was definitely something that Addie was hiding. Until this point, she hadn't considered it had anything to do with Kristen Chambers's death, but was she wrong to rule out her friend because she knew her?

Of course Margot didn't think Addie capable of murder, but that shouldn't negate the fact that her friend was definitely hiding something.

The only question was: what was she not telling Margot?

CHAPTER 8

Margot hastily swiped sparkling eye shadow across her eyelids, biting her lip in the process and worried that she wouldn't be ready in time. The baking had taken longer than she expected, but she wasn't usually the type of woman to spend an exorbitant amount of time on her appearance. Instead, she did what she could to make her eyes pop with thicker eyeliner and an extra coat of mascara, and then she slipped into the sapphire blue dress she'd purchased just for this cruise. A woman had to treat herself every once in a while, didn't she?

After stepping into a pair of three inch, navy blue heels, she looked at herself in the full-length mirror on the back of the door. The dress hugged her curves and flowed out at the bottom in a mermaid style, and the sweetheart neckline sparkled with tiny, silver speckles that glittered in the overhead lights from the cabin. She felt elegant and allowed a small, ruby-lipped smile before turning to her iPad to check her emails before she left for the gala.

The smile appeared again when she saw that Adam had emailed her back. She immediately clicked on it and read his short reply. He told her not to worry and then wished her an exceptionally fun night, making sure to tell her that he hoped it would be full of surprises. Then, before the sign-off, he said he hoped she was wearing his favorite dress. She laughed out loud at this and shook her head, envisioning the dress he was talking about.

After they had attended the rainy Washington D.C. street festival, Adam had come to her pleading for her to join him at a fancy dinner to be held in D.C. He'd explained that his brother Anthony, a detective in D.C., had invited him and he needed to bring a plus one. He'd begged her, fighting off her halfhearted excuses with his charming smile, and she'd caved.

It was that night that she'd worn her fancy red dress, the one that had left Adam speechless for a full minute when he'd first seen her, and the same dress that had caused him to be distracted more than once during the party. She remembered his sweet smile even now.

Well, he wouldn't know it, but she had a feeling he'd like this blue dress just as much as the red.

She closed the case of the iPad and looked once more in the mirror before stepping toward the door. But then she hesitated. She wished Adam was there. He wouldn't stop until Kristen's death was properly investigated. He would have gone with her to trail the man. He would have— No, what was she thinking? He would have given her a stern talking-to if he even knew she'd gone out of the tourist safe zones in the city.

But there was one thing Adam definitely would have known—why Gabe Williams was on the cruise. Odd that he hadn't mentioned him in his reply email since she'd discreetly asked about him. Maybe she was making more of it than she should be, but it was too much of a coincidence, wasn't it? And the fact that he'd shown up to help her now had her asking even more questions than before. Had Adam sent him to watch over her? No, that made no sense either. She'd barely seen Gabe around, something a good tail would be able to accomplish, but that would also mean she'd never have been able to follow him like she had. Besides, why would Adam have her followed? He wasn't *that* paranoid.

Releasing a sigh, she pulled the door open and stepped out into the hall with determined steps. It was time for the gala and she and Addie's creations to be announced. She wouldn't let thoughts of conspiracies or investigations cloud her excitement for the night.

The dinner was fabulous and she found her tablemates to be intriguing. Sadly, Addie was nowhere to be found, but just as the time was arriving for the award to be announced and the desserts introduced, she spotted her friend on the other side of the room. Making her excuses, she slipped around the dining room and dance floor and joined Addie.

"There you are. I was starting to think *I* was going to have to take all the credit tonight."

Addie gave a halfhearted laugh but it did nothing to change to pale look on her face. She shot a glance over her shoulder nervously. "Are you all right?" Margot asked.

"F-Fine. Yes, I'm—I'm fine."

Margot wasn't convinced but the lights dimmed and a spotlight highlighted the table in the middle of the room. It illuminated a masterful display of pastries to tantalize the guests.

"Where's Noah?" Margot asked. "Isn't he supposed to be here to accept the award as well?"

"I-I don't know." Addie answered one question but was too distracted to register both questions, her gaze unfocused in front of her.

Margot fought the urge to place her hands on either side of the woman and give her a firm shake to bring her out of the daze, but she was afraid it would do no good. Besides, now wasn't the time or the place.

They were called up on stage and she stood next to Addie, impressed at her friend's forced smile. It was fake, but it would be hard to tell from the audience. It was obviously something she'd perfected in many competitions before.

The lights were bright and the announcer, one of the performers who took on the role of MC, began to highlight Addie's many accomplishments and the various awards the ship had been given because of her expertise.

Margot found her attention wandering around the room. She tried to look interested in what the man was saying about her troubled friend, but then her gaze caught on Noah. He was slowly, almost sneakily, making his way around the back of the room. Was he trying to avoid being seen so they wouldn't bring him up on stage? He was as much a part of this as Addie, and certainly more so than Margot.

Then, as she glanced back to where she'd seen him last, he stopped behind one of the furthest tables. He stood against the wall and looked to be waiting for something. But what? Then, as Margot watched, keeping her gaze moving over the room but always coming back to Noah's location, she watched in astonishment as Brice walked past and unobtrusively passed something to Noah, pausing for the briefest of words before he continued on. She thought she caught Noah's imperceptible nod.

She jerked her gaze away, hoping they hadn't noticed her watching them, but when her eyes landed on another area of the room, this time she actually gasped, though thankfully it was quiet.

There, in the back of the room wearing a tuxedo and looking like he belonged in a James Bond movie—or the gala night—stood Detective Adam Eastwood.

~

"WHAT IN THE *world* are you doing here?" Margot demanded.

"I'm not sure if you're pleased to see me or...angry? And can I just say that dress..." He shook his head, expelling a breath. "It's better than the red one."

She grinned, knowing he'd think as much, but soon the grin faded. "Seriously, Adam, why are you here?" She didn't know why, but her heart was pounding. She was sure it had something to do with the ramifications of all of this, but at least a small part of the palpitations was due to how handsome he looked in a tux.

Something she didn't need to notice right now. She couldn't afford to be distracted. If Adam was here, something was going on. She had a gut feeling and those were almost never wrong.

"It's a long story."

She placed her hands on her hips and he took it as an invitation to admire the dress again.

"Really, Margie, that dress..." He shook his head.

"You're doing it again. Getting tongue-tied over a dress. It's *just* a dress."

His grin widened. "You're right. It *is* just a dress, but you make it look amazing."

417

Now Margot blushed, unable to let his comments slide off. She liked the fact that he thought her beautiful and wasn't ashamed to say it. It did a woman well to be complimented. Yet, his timing could have been better.

"About what I said in my email—" she began.

"Will you dance with me?" he asked, his eyes locked on hers.

She let out a sigh. "You're not going to give this up, are you?"

"Nope. Not until you agree to one dance. Just one?" He looked at her with sparkling hazel eyes and a boyish grin she'd found she had trouble resisting.

"All right," she gave in, accepting his proffered hand.

In her mind, a dance just meant she could explain the situation to him in close proximity, which would better ensure no one overheard them.

They slipped into an easy rhythm and she let them sink into the dance first, finding that she enjoyed being in Adam's arms more than she should. Then again, it *had* been five years since she'd lost her husband. It didn't mean she'd lost her love for him—she wasn't sure she'd ever stop loving him and she'd come to terms with that —but she had gained an appreciation for the fact that her heart could feel again. She certainly felt things toward Adam, though at the moment they were overshadowed by her curiosity as to why he was here and the reality that something was going on—she just didn't know what.

"There was a murder—" she began.

"Oh, Margie," he said in a disappointed tone, "are you really going to ruin our dance with talk of murder? And wasn't it ruled drug overdose? Not murder?"

She gaped at him. "How did you know that?"

"Just call me...informed.'"

"What are you up to, Adam Eastwood?" she asked, her eyes narrowing.

"I may or may not have done some digging before coming out here."

"What type of digging? And why *are* you out here?"

"Is saying I missed you too cheesy?"

She rolled her eyes. "What's the real reason?"

He was about to answer when a commotion at the back of the dining room drew their attention. A young purser came rushing into the room, tears streaming down her face. She rushed blindly forward, making her way toward the captain. A few crewmembers moved to intercept her but she shook them off, only stopping in front of the stoic man.

They watched as the woman explained something with frantic hand motions and then burst into tears. As her news was conveyed, the captain shot to his feet, a look of concern washing over his handsome features. Then he motioned to two men who Margot knew were part of the security team, and they left the room. The third security team member ushered the sobbing woman out after them as well.

"I don't know about you, but I don't think people are supposed to cry like that on cruises."

She glanced up to see a look of genuine concern on Adam's face despite his sarcastic tone. He wasn't one to make light of troublesome situations, though his humor in all areas of life was one of the things Margot appreciated most about the detective. She could see on his hardened features that his detective sense was kicking in. "What do you say we go see what's up?"

Margot was stunned at his suggestion but leapt at the chance. "I thought you'd never ask."

They made their way off of the dance floor and then, as discretely as possible, slipped out of the same door the captain and the men had. Adam slipped his hand around hers and she felt the warmth sink past their hands to her heart. She'd missed him.

The hallway they had stepped into extended in both ways but they heard hushed voices coming from the right. Looking at one another, they set off toward the voices. The hall curved and they pulled up before coming into view of an open door ahead. A sign above it indicated

"Security Office." Margot's stomach clenched—this didn't look good.

"This was not an accident."

At the words, Adam's hand squeezed Margot's.

"This was clearly thought out. Murder."

"But he's not—"

Adam released her hand and stepped forward. "I heard murder. Can I help?"

Margot suppressed a smile at Adam's direct approach, but followed him to the entrance of the office.

"And who are you?" Margot recognized Harvey Pearson, the ship security officer.

"I'm Detective Adam Eastwood." Adam took out his credentials and showed them to the man.

Harvey's brow furrowed. "Detective? From *Virginia?*"

"And liaison to the FBI," a voice said behind them.

Margot and Adam both turned around.

"Gabe?" Margot exclaimed.

"We meet again," he said, smiling at Margot. "You just seem to be everywhere, don't you, Mrs. Durand?"

Margot noticed Adam's intent look at her but thankfully Gabe continued.

"I'm Gabe Williams with the FBI," he said, flashing an official badge at Harvey. "I've asked Adam to join me here."

Now Margot shot Adam a look that demanded an explanation, but she knew now wasn't the time or the place.

"What is going on?" Gabe asked.

"I—" Harvey began.

Just then they all heard footsteps pounding down the hall and they turned to see the captain with the crying woman at his side, another security guard as his escort.

"Captain," Harvey said, standing straighter.

"What is going on here?" the captain demanded.

"Gabe Williams with the FBI."

"And…" The captain's eyebrows rose and his gaze moved to Adam and then Margot, frowning.

"Detective Adam Eastwood and Mrs. Margot—"

"Durand. Yes, I know of Mrs. Durand, but I don't know *why* she's here."

"Mrs. Durand and I are…acquainted," Adam said with a forced smile.

"Yes, but I don't think having a *guest* here during this, um, time is appropriate."

"And can you tell me exactly what's going on here, Captain?" Gabe said, ignoring the Captain's hesitance about Margot.

"At the moment, I—"

A young crewmember wearing a medical coat ran down the hall toward them, his gaze solely focused on the captain. "Sir, he's dead."

Margot felt the stab of the words, her stomach clenching at the reality that another death had occurred on board the *Carrousel Luxury*.

"Who is?" Gabe said, stepping forward.

The young man looked to the captain and then back to Gabe. At an almost imperceptible nod from the captain, the young man cleared his throat. "Michael Bowers."

CHAPTER 9

MARGOT SAT on the deck attached to her cabin looking out over the lights of Ensenada. They would depart later that night and begin their travel back, but her mind was overloaded with the events of the evening. First, finding out that there had been another death, then discovering it had been the somewhat stiff but organized Michael Bowers, it was almost too much to take in. What was going on?

Margot had faded into the background as details were demanded and credentials shared, but soon the captain put his foot down and demanded—albeit politely—that Margot go back to her cabin as they dealt with the details of the death. Begrudgingly, she'd purchased a coffee and made her way back to her room, waiting for Adam to come knocking on the door. That had been hours ago.

The sound of a light tap made her jolt forward, the wrap

draped over her knees slipping, and she rushed to answer it.

"Adam," she said, relief flowed by concern rushed through her. He looked exhausted with dark circles under his eyes and his shoulders slumped, but he offered her a soft smile.

"May I come in for a bit?"

"Of course," she said, ushering him into the small space. "Do you want me to order you something?"

"No, I grabbed a bite to eat with Gabe before coming to see you."

"The balcony is nice," she offered.

He smiled and nodded, following her out. They sat in the chairs that angled toward one another and she resisted the urge to demand what he'd discovered. For a few minutes, he just stared out at the city, the lights blinking and the faint sounds of music coming from somewhere, probably one of the many restaurants still open to tourists. The breeze was warm, though by no means hot, and the scent of salt hung in the air.

Finally, he shifted and leaned forward, elbows on his knees. "I probably shouldn't do this, but I'm going to fill you in."

Margot felt the sense of apprehension fill her. What was going on? What would Adam tell her about what had happened? Would they know what was behind it?

"You don't have to," she began, knowing she desperately wanted to know what was going on but that she didn't want to put Adam in a bad position for sharing things with her.

"I asked Gabe, told him of our history, and he agreed. He also hinted that you may already know more than you should." She heard the humor in Adam's voice and part of her relaxed.

"So, as you heard, Michael Bowers died. The woman we saw rush into the room tonight was a friend of Bowers and had just been informed from local authorities that he'd been the victim of a brutal stabbing in Ensenada. They rushed him on board and the woman came to notify the captain, but...as you saw, it was too late."

Margot's mind jumped to several things at once. Stabbing. That meant murder. But when had it happened? Where?

"What time was he stabbed? Where?" Adam's eyebrows rose and she felt ashamed. "I'm sorry. It's awful that he's dead, terrible, but I'm wondering..." She didn't finish her sentence because she wasn't sure that she could. She didn't have all of the necessary information yet, but there were several things that weren't adding up. Like Noah. She pictured him at the back of the gala tonight. What had he given Brice?

"WE'RE NOT SURE. His body will need to be examined by a

M.E. The best the doc could say was it was recent, and not too far from the ship."

This caused Margot to frown. "But all of the less friendly neighborhoods are further away from port."

"I know." Adam leveled his gaze on her.

Had Brice paid off Noah for killing Michael? But no, there was no way he would have had time to do it. It was pure conjecture and there was no evidence...then again, she *had* followed Brice to that restaurant and it did sound as if things were going on. But Noah? What part did he play in all of this? If any at all.

"Before you go piecing things together, wait until you hear this."

"Are you finally going to tell me why you're here on my cruise ship?"

"*Your* ship, huh?"

"You know what I mean," she said with a smile.

"Well, like Gabe said, he asked me to come. Or...maybe what's more accurate is that I demanded for him to get me on board. Among some other strings I pulled, I was able to get down here quickly."

"But why? What about your assignment? Your lecturing?"

He shrugged. "Why? Because of your overly innocent little email digging for clues. I know you better than you think, Margot Durand." He offered a tired smile. "I wasn't about to let you have a mysterious adventure without me. Besides, I wanted to make sure you were safe."

Warmth surged through her at his words and she felt a light blush color her cheeks, thankfully hidden by the darkness. "Thank you, but I wasn't sure, until now, that it *was* something mysterious. Clearly, we have a murderer on our hands."

"We?"

"I suppose it's you and Gabe then. Did you know that Gabe was FBI?"

"About that…" He shifted back in his seat and she saw him shake his head. "Turns out Gabe has been running an undercover operation dealing with some pretty interesting things. Even the woman who was murdered—"

"So it *was* murder?"

"Definitely— Well, we can't say for sure until the M.E. confirms, but Gabe assures me she never would have taken drugs. She was an undercover agent."

Margot gasped. "She was?"

"Yes, she's been working with none other than Michael Bowers. Apparently, he's involved in some pretty terrifying things, including but not limited to drug and gem smuggling from Ensenada."

"Really," she said, leaning back in her chair and trying to

piece it all together. She hadn't interacted with Michael much, but he hadn't looked like a smuggler. Then again, what did a smuggler really look like?

"Yes. Kristen had been working closely with him but there was another piece to all of this: a contact who works on the ship but didn't reveal his—or her—identity. They would leave notes in certain locations for Kristen and Michael. It's the only reason she was staying undercover, she wanted to nail all of the components in this ring. She'd been working on the local side of things until this silent partner got her a job on board the ship recently."

"But then she was murdered. Was she suspected then? Is that why she died?"

"That's unclear at this point."

"I can't believe it." Margot leaned forward, her elbows on her knees. She'd known something was going on, but she never would have imagined smuggling.

"That's the thing, there are more things involved than just a simple smuggling operation—if there even is such a thing."

"What about Brice?"

Adam hesitated a moment. "Brice? Brice who?"

"Brice Simmons."

"The actor?"

"Yes." Margot stared at him, surprised he didn't know what she was talking about. "What's his part in all of this?"

"I, uh… Gabe didn't say."

Margot's heart pounded. They didn't know of Brice's involvement? Surely he was involved in *some* way. There were too many things going on to not have him as part of the operation, now that she knew there was an operation. Then again, was he involved or had she merely seen a man hand something to a crewmember? But that seemed like too much of a coincidence, especially after what she'd overheard at the restaurant that day.

She filled Adam in on what she'd done that afternoon and what she knew of Brice.

"Sounds like he's definitely mixed up in this then—at least in part. I'll need to discuss it with Gabe. But you…" He shook his head. "You know better than to go off on your own like that, Margie." He looked worried but she assured him she'd been fine.

"But still—" he began.

Then another thought occurred to her and she interrupted his next lecture fueled by worry. "Addie isn't mixed up in this, is she?"

"Your friend, the pastry chef?"

"Yes," Margot said, nervously twisting her hands together. "She's been acting so strange and, I don't know, almost looking guilty."

"Gabe didn't mention her, but he didn't mention Brice either. All he said is that he's certain that there is at least one more member of this team to consider—and there could be more."

The reality sunk into Margot's chest and she felt despair take root. Addie acted guilty. She had been moody, gone often, and distracted. Was it possible? Were those signs of guilt or was she hiding something condemning like being involved in a smuggling ring?

Margot didn't want to believe it, but she knew that the only way to clear it all up was to have a conversation. Something she would do the very next morning.

THE NEXT MORNING, Margot woke to bright sunlight streaming through the thin curtains she'd pulled closed the night before as Adam left. He'd promised that they could trace down leads in the morning after breakfast with Gabe, but her mind had been set on seeing Addie. She didn't want to believe that her friend could be involved with something like a smuggling ring, but there had to be some explanation for her evasive behavior. But what could be so important that Addie wouldn't have shared with Margot?

She pulled the drapes aside and saw nothing but ocean stretching out before her. It was a stunning sight, the water registering a deep, azure blue. She could stare at this view for hours, but the press of the case was too persistent. She showered, dressed, and was out the door early.

Cringing, she knocked on Adam's door.

After a few shuffling footsteps, he opened the door wearing a bright blue polo with khaki shorts and a sleepy grin. His hair was adorably mussed and she resisted the urge to reach up and smooth it down. They needed to focus on the case, not the fact that she wanted him to remind her of the sweetness of his kiss.

"Ready?" she said, hands on hips.

He just shook his head. "Give me a moment to at least run a comb through my hair."

Grinning, she followed him into his room and looked around. Clothes were strewn everywhere and the top of his small desk was covered in papers.

"Didn't you just get here last night?"

"Yeah," he said distractedly from the bathroom.

"Then how is it possible you made this big of a mess?"

He didn't answer right away but, when he came out of the bathroom with slicked down hair and a big grin, he shrugged innocently. "I'm usually tidy, but there's something about being away on a trip—vacation or not— that makes me feel like I don't need to constrain myself to tidiness norms."

"You goof," she said, smiling.

"So, to breakfast?"

"Yes."

His grin widened and she led him down their hall and out the door into the early morning air. It was cooler, the breeze from the ocean coming in stiff gusts, but soon they were back inside and heading to a buffet.

Gabe met them at the entrance and led them to a table in the back. Once they had their food, they ate in silence for a few moments before he jumped in.

"What can you tell me, Margot?"

Her eyebrows rose. "And what makes you think I know anything?" Her coy response made Adam smile and Gabe shook his head.

"Look, I saw you around the ship the first day. I was going to say something, but it could have compromised my situation. I'm registered here under the name Josh Wilkes and I couldn't have you coming up and saying you knew me as Gabe."

"I understand," she said, nodding. "But I have one question."

"Shoot," he said, taking a bite of light green honeydew.

"Why were you near the sports storage area where Kristen was found?"

He grinned, chewing and then swallowing before he could answer her. "So it was you following me."

She inclined her head.

"You're quicker than I anticipated. Nice catch," he said to Adam with a wink. "I was looking for Kirsten. We were supposed to meet that night. I'd seen her in the club, acting like we didn't know each other. She said she'd been called to a face-to-face meeting with her contact. It was supposed to be our big break. We'd arranged to meet at the storage area.

"I'd just gotten there and slipped inside, hoping to avoid whoever—well, now I know it was you—but then I got a text from her saying that the meeting had been canceled so I left and the passage was clear on my way back."

"I hid in a laundry closet," she said with a shrug.

"Clever."

"She couldn't have sent that text though, could she?"

He pressed his lips together. "We believe her contact found out about who she really was. I think they were the one to message me, likely thinking they were buying themselves time before Kristen was discovered."

"But then I heard something—or someone—else in there after you'd walked past, which drew my attention."

"And you found her," Gabe said, his expression pained.

"Yes. Do you think that whoever killed her left out the back door? No one passed by me after you left."

"It's possible." Gabe broke a piece of bacon in half. "Or they were already gone."

"I've got a question," Margot said, her forehead wrinkling. "Do you have *any* idea who her contact could be? I mean, there have to be some suspects."

"There are a few people I've been keeping an eye on, but whoever it is is very careful and covers their tracks well."

"You should tell him what you saw," Adam said, finally speaking up after spending considerable amount of time working through his eggs and toast.

"What do you mean? What did you see?" Gabe leaned forward, elbows on the table cradling a cup of hot coffee in his hands.

She explained seeing Brice pass something to Noah as well as the conversation she'd overheard between Brice and his assistants and how she'd followed him to see what was going on. She recapped the conversation he'd had with Gold Chain but also how the trail had run cold when Gabe had rescued her.

"Why were you there, though?" she asked Gabe. "If you didn't suspect Brice, why were you following Andres?"

"We *don't* suspect Brice...at least not yet, but I have had my suspicions about José Luis Martinez—the one you call Gold Chain," he said with a grin. "He owns that restaurant you were at and many other businesses catering to tourists. He's done well for himself, no doubt, but we think he's done a little *too* well for the operations he has going. I've been down to Ensenada quite a bit recently and I'm usually staked out by whatever restaurant he's in. I saw you sneaking around and, when you came out to follow Andres as well, I knew something was up. I had no idea you were following Brice, though."

"So you think the restaurant is a front then?" Margot asked. Her mind started to piece things together.

"We can't definitively say, nor does it affect us. What's really our problem is anything that goes on on board the ships that come into port and anything affecting U.S. Citizens." Gabe looked over to Adam. "You know how it is. We've got leads everywhere but nothing solid. Though we have some cooperation with the officials in Ensenada, we need proof. Martinez has covered his tracks well and whatever happens on U.S. soil is covered up just as quickly."

Adam nodded, his lips pressed into a hard line as he thought through the situation.

"What if Brice *is* involved though?"

"We'd need evidence. Besides—what do you think? He hired *Noah* to kill his own partner? It doesn't add up. Noah isn't even on our radar."

Margot thought this through. *Should* Noah be on their radar? She thought of him coming in late and his lie about where he'd been. People lied all the time though, and for various reasons. Then again, the reality of two murders was enough to bring anyone into question.

"If he is involved and he's working with Noah, it's possible Kristen was found out. Or perhaps..." She paused. "Then there's Michael Bowers. You say he's a part of this...so is it possible whoever is behind this is eliminating partners for a reason?"

"It's possible," Gabe said, steepling his fingers. "Kristen said she hardly interacted with Bowers. They worked independently of each other though they did know about one another. She made it clear their instructions were that they weren't to be seen together—at all." Gabe sighed, leaning back in his chair. "I'm so frustrated. I've been working this case for over a year now. The drugs are coming into the U.S. and we've all but pinpointed the *Carousel* cruise line, not just this ship but several of them, but there is never any concrete evidence. And why drugs *and* jewels?"

Margot didn't have an answer for this but something Gabe said made her think of another angle. Addie. She had signed on to the *Carousel* cruise line a little under a year ago.

Something wasn't right there and she had to find out what exactly was the problem.

"Sorry." Gabe tossed his napkin onto the empty plate before him. "I need to go. I've got a ship to shore call set up and it's imperative I make that. I'm afraid it'll be hard for me to get straight answers around here now that my cover is blown. I'd appreciate it if you keep your eyes and ears open to anything."

"Of course," Adam said, shaking his friend's hand.

"Margot," Gabe said then strode away.

She watched him go, wondering what was next. Someone had killed Kristen and now Michael. They had no suspects and no tangible leads. How was that possible?

"I know that look," Adam said. "Where to first, Watson?"

She smiled, standing up and tossing her napkin down. "We're going to see a woman about a pastry. And it's Holmes," she added with a wink.

CHAPTER 10

THE MIDMORNING CROWD was in full swing, those who had slept in late making their way to the buffets and restaurants for breakfast. Margot wasn't interested in anyone else at this moment. She only had one person on her list to visit. She had a feeling that, once she was able to clear her friend and find out the truth, she would truly be able to focus on the case at hand and, with Adam by her side, help solve the murderous mystery.

They turned down the hall that led to the crew quarters and Margot stopped in front of Addie's door. She let out a breath and turned to look at Adam. He smiled at her and she felt her spirits renewed. It was nice to have someone with her.

She raised her hand to knock but the door swung inward. Curiosity and worry got the best of Margot and she pushed it further in, stopping only when she got a clear view into the room.

"Addie?" she gasped.

In front of her, embracing a man whose back was to them, Addie was locked in a passionate kiss.

At the sound of Margot's surprised exclamation, Addie jerked back from the man, stepping a full two feet back and covering her lips with her hand. Her flush made her look sixteen years old instead of thirty-two.

"M-Margot?" she stammered.

When Margot finally pulled her gaze from her friend to that of the man, she gasped again. "Captain?"

He stammered something but fell silent, his gaze jerking to Addie then dropping to the floor. Margot thought of the first day when she'd overheard the crewmembers talking about the captain having an affair. Was it with her friend?

"I'm new here, but I've got a feeling you don't kiss all of your crewmembers like that," Adam said, gently pushing Margot into the room and closing the door behind them for privacy. She was almost too shocked to register what was happening, but then she realized that Adam was being discrete for her friend's sake.

"Oh my," Addie finally said, shaking her head. "This is it. I can't take it anymore, Grayson. I just can't."

He gave her a pained look but then his features softened and he smiled at her, reaching out to take her hand. "Let me." He turned to look at them. "Margot, Detective Eastwood, we're engaged to be married."

It took a few moments for the words to sink in to understanding. "You're not married?"

It was the captain's turn to look surprised, then realization dawned and he sighed. "There are those on board who like to make up stories. I am not, nor have I ever been, married. I *do* like to keep my private life just that—private. I'm afraid that leaves too much room for minds to wander and imagine."

Margot burst into a wide grin. "That's fantastic!" Then she laughed. "I mean, that you're engaged."

Now Addie beamed, looking back up at the handsome man beside her. He was several years older than she, but Margot could see instantly the love they shared. "I'm so happy Marg."

"I suppose we owe you an apology. Or, rather, *I* do." The captain shook his head. "I've been captain of this ship for two years now and I've never looked at any of my crewmembers with anything more than leadership in mind...until I met Addie." He sighed and took another moment to study her face before looking back at them. "But, in my position of leadership, it's a tenuous thing for the captain to be in a relationship—of any kind—with a crewmember. It's not against company policy, just so we're clear, but it can affect how the crew perceives me as well as Addie."

Margot was beginning to guess what had happened. "You're hiding the engagement."

Addie nodded. "I would have told you, Marg. I wanted to and it's caused no end to arguments between us. I understand Grayson is trying to protect me, but you are one of my closest friends... It's just that I couldn't risk someone like Noah overhearing. It's been murder on me to keep it from you."

Margot felt the relief of her friend's confession at the same time she felt the reminder of how serious their true mission was on this ship—not to uncover secret engagements, but to catch a killer.

"Then I wish you both happiness and can assure you that neither I nor Adam will share your secret—right?" She grinned up at Adam, who nodded.

"Did you need something?" Addie said, shyly looking back at the captain.

"No," Margot said smiling as she walked to the door, pulling on Adam's arm. "I'm so happy for you both."

"That was a dead end," Adam said once they were in the hallway. "Though I can't say they aren't inspiring."

Margot's stomach clenched at his words. Did he mean their engagement? But no, she couldn't allow herself to think about that—not now. Besides, that couldn't have been what Adam was talking about...could it?

Pushing the thoughts from her mind, she tugged on Adam's sleeve. "Come on. I've got an idea."

~

THEY SEARCHED through Kristen's room after getting permission from Gabe. Clothes of all colors and styles cluttered the small cabinet that was hers in the four-person room. All the other crewmembers were on duty, which gave them a window of privacy.

"I've got nothing," Adam said, standing up and stretching as best he could in the cramped space. "You?"

"Nothing." Margot dropped the sequined pink miniskirt that matched the one Kristen had been wearing when Margot found her. Sighing, she ran a hand over her hair. She'd been sure there would have been something for them to find, anything that could tie Brice to the whole thing, but there was nothing.

She stepped toward the door but stopped, looking back over the area. If she were Kristen and she was working undercover, where would she hide something she didn't want any of her roommates to find—either accidentally or on purpose? The logical place would be under the mattress, but most people would check there first so Margot hadn't been surprised when it was empty.

Adam stood from where he'd been examining the empty space below the drawers under her bottom bunk when he hit his head.

"Ouch!" he cried out, his hand reaching up to rub a spot on the top of his head.

"Careful, you're not exactly made for this space." She smiled but then froze. He wasn't made for this space. No tall person was.

"What?" Adam said, recognizing the look on her face. "You've got an idea."

She stepped to the tall dresser to the end of the ladies' beds. One side held one girl's clothes and the other held Kristen's. She looked down at the bottom and noticed the woman's shoes.

"She was tall, wasn't she," Margot said to herself, holding up a size ten shoe. "Taller than her crewmates." She looked through the other women's compartments, careful not to disturb anything. "Adam, look on the top of the closet! Is there anything up there?"

Adam reached up, his nose wrinkling at the effort. He was tall, but Kristen would have been even taller in her four-inch heels. Then his eyes shot open. "I've got something."

Margot waited patiently as he pulled out a handkerchief and stretched to reach whatever it was. Finally, with a grunt, he pulled down a stack of written notes. Excitement bubbled up in her.

"What are they?" she asked as Adam riffled through.

"Looks like they are written in some sort of code. Probably nothing too complicated. I think..." His voice trailed off as he read through a few, careful not to touch any of them. "I think they are pick up and drop off locations. Though it's difficult to tie these to Kristen exactly. I'm assuming they're hers, but…"

Margot leaned forward. "May I see one?"

He angled one toward her, holding it open with the handkerchief, and she gasped. "I know that writing."

"You do?" He was shocked.

Margot stepped back, blinking. "It's Noah's. Noah Spence."

"The guy who bakes? The *same* guy who you saw talking with Brice?"

"Yes!" She frantically ran through all that she knew about Noah. He had seemed upset about Kristen's death, but was it sadness or anger? Had he been the one to kill her? And what of Michael Bowers? Had he also been involved with that? And what about Brice? How was he involved with any of this?

"Talk to me, Margie," Adam said, his gaze intent on her. "Tell me what's going on in that brain of yours."

She blinked rapidly. It was all starting to come together, but in order to crack the case, they would need the involvement of the FBI and a few well-placed visits in Ensenada. "Is the FBI really working with the authorities in Ensenada?"

Adam frowned. "If Gabe says so, then yes, he'll be in contact with local authorities."

"Then I need to talk with him. And I need to talk with someone else too."

Adams eyebrows rose. "Are you going to fill me in?"

She smiled up at him, brushing off a swatch of dust from his shoulder. "Always."

CHAPTER 11

MARGOT CLUTCHED her canvas bag with one hand, the strap slung over her shoulder, and her floppy hat with the other as she made her way across the crowded deck to the more private deck at the back of the ship. The moment she turned the corner, the wind died down somewhat due to the partition, and she let go of her hat.

There, reclining in a blue-cushioned chaise lounge, lay Brice Simmons. His chest bare and tanned, shining with a recent application of some type of tanning oil, no doubt applied by one of the bikini-clad women on either side of him.

Margot fought the urge to roll her eyes as she approached, hoping she got what she wanted out of this meeting.

"Hello, Brice," she said with a bright smile.

Brice moved, his hand reaching up to push the dark and expensive sunglasses onto the top of his head. He looked surprised to see her, but in a pleasant way.

"Margot. It's good to see you. Will you sit?"

He looked to the side where one of his assistants was already getting up.

"Actually, I was wondering if we could talk...just you and I?"

His surprise grew, but so did his smile. "Absolutely. Ladies, will you give us a few minutes?"

The former police officer, Haden, looked ready to argue with him but then she looked at Margot. Likely assuming Margot was no threat to her boss, she followed the other woman down the deck.

Brice smiled again, patting the lounge next to him. "Please."

She sat, leaving her legs on the ground and propping her elbows on her knees to look at him. "What I have to say may not be pleasant," she began.

He replaced his sunglasses and his eyebrows hiked, but he didn't say anything, allowing her the room to explain.

"You see, I followed you into Ensenada. I saw where you went."

He tried hard not to let his emotions show but she caught a glimpse, the quickest flutter of movement, in response to her words.

"I heard what José Luis Martinez said to you. I also know that you know Kristen Chambers's death wasn't an accident. It was murder."

Brice sat up, more like jerked up, and yanked off his sunglasses. "You don't know anything." His gaze drilled into Margot but she didn't flinch.

"But I do, Brice. I think you are working with people on this ship to smuggle drugs into America."

"Drugs? No. Absolutely not. We do *not* smuggle drugs," he said, the color in his tanned cheeks flushing red. "I would never—" He ground his teeth and looked out to the ocean. "I would never do that. Not after my sister."

She remembered his story about his sister. So he had been telling the truth. That meant it was time for Margot to take the next step.

"Look, the FBI is on this case. They are going to finger you in the smuggling. It's no use for you to deny it. They'll find the drugs."

"There are no drugs!"

"Don't deny it," Margot pushed. "I know you met with José and the FBI are already looking into his business. They'll find your drug connection and that'll be it."

"I'm telling you, Margot," he said, leaning toward her with fury in his gaze. "No drugs."

"Then what aren't you telling me, Brice? Because the

police are going to find all the evidence they need. There was an undercover agent. It's over. And, from where I sit, your sister would be disgusted with you." It was a low blow, one she was loath to make, but she had to push him to a certain point

"I would never do that! Not drugs. Never. Not for anyone." His features fell and he looked out to sea again. "It's gems."

Margot leaned forward, her gaze flicking over Brice's tanned shoulder. "What do you mean?"

"I smuggle gems into the U.S. without paying import taxes."

"Gems?" She had suspected this, but she wanted to be certain. "You met José when you were here filming *Green Flames Rising*, didn't you?" She needed to dig further, to get him to open up more.

"You know a lot for not knowing the truth," he shot back. "Yeah. I met José when he catered some of our meals. He said he had a way for me to make some extra money on the side. It was during that time in my career when my gambling debts were plastered all over magazine covers. He said he could help. That he knew a guy. I was certain I could get them to the right people and sell them for a lot more than they could here in Mexico. There's a hot market in underground Hollywood circles." He sighed, rubbing a hand over his face.

"But not drugs, Margot. Never drugs. I wouldn't..." He

broke off and she saw the pain on his features. "I know what they do to people, to families. I'd never be a part of that."

She watched him, looking for any signs of deception, but while he kept his gaze on the ocean in front of him, he gave no indication that he was lying. Lost in painful memories, yes, but not lying.

She nodded slightly and Adam, Gabe, and two of the ship's security officers stepped out from behind the wind partition where they'd been listening to the conversation.

"Mr. Simmons, you're under arrest."

He looked from the men to Margot. "You're with them? What? This whole time?"

"No. Not at first." She shook her head, unsure why she felt the need to explain herself to this arrogant man.

"It's a shame, you know," he said with a rueful grin. "You and I could have made a pretty great power couple. Besides, I love good French pastries. Then again, who knows? I've got access to some great lawyers and I'm sure you'll find that my hands are clean. Friends in high places and all." He winked at her.

She felt the urge to slap him. As if sensing this, Adam stepped beside her and wrapped a protective arm around her shoulders.

"Good thing I've got friends in high places too."

His hands now cuffed behind him, Brice turned his attention to Adam, his eyes dancing between the man and his arm around Margot.

"Ah, I see. You prefer the more law-abiding type. Well, to each their own."

"Come on, Simmons," Gabe said, rolling his eyes. "Let's go."

Margot watched him go with a mix of sadness and justification. She was glad he had been caught, but now they had to wrap the more pressing—if not more important—angle of how drugs were getting into the U.S. when they weren't tied up in Brice Simmons's operation.

Or were they?

Margot leaned into Adam, letting out a sigh as her mind raced through details. If Brice wasn't involved with drugs, it was a stretch to think he was involved with the murders. She wouldn't rule it out, but she couldn't bring herself to see him complicit in something so sinister. At least the smuggling of gems was purely from a monetary motivational standpoint. But murder? That fell more in line with the drugs, at least in Margot's mind.

"What's on that beautiful mind of yours now?" Adam said, smiling.

"I was just thinking that—if Brice wasn't involved with drugs, what if his contact was involved with them *and* the gems."

"I think I know what you're getting at, but do we have enough proof to arrest him?"

Margot's eyes narrowed as her gaze flew to the water in front of them. "Maybe not yet, but I have a feeling I know how to catch him because I think I know where the gems *and* the drugs are. But it'll require a little bit of planning. Are you up for that?"

"Absolutely."

"Good, because it's crucial we don't make a mistake. I have a feeling this was their last cruise."

∼

"I'M SO sorry about all of this," Addie said as she and Margot sat on the private deck attached to Margot's room. "If I'd had any idea…"

Margot laughed. "You can't guess when murder is going to happen. It's in no way your fault."

"What's next then?" Addie's brown eyes peered at Margot over her steaming cup of coffee.

As much as Margot trusted her friend and wanted to share what was going to happen next, she knew that the less people that knew, the better.

"I'm afraid I can't say, but I wanted to take a few minutes before we docked to chat with you and make sure everything was all right. We've barely seen each other on this cruise—for good reason—but first and foremost, you're my friend and I care about you and what's happening in your life. I know you couldn't open up to me before, but if there's anything you wanted to share now, I wanted to let you know that I'm here for you. I was once your age and in love—" Margot smirked at how old saying that made her feel. "—and I relied heavily on my friends during that time."

Addie sighed and turned her gaze out to the ocean. Land was just visible in the distance and, with their arrival, plans would be set in motion that would end everything. At least Margot hoped so.

"It's just frustrating," Addie said, looking back at Margot finally. "I love Grayson so much and I know he's the right guy. Like, he asked me to marry him and I had no doubts, but sometimes he's just…so frustrating."

Margot chuckled. "I understand. Men look at things very different."

"Very."

"But you guys are talking about it, right? That's the important part. To keep communication lines open."

"Oh yes." Addie nodded emphatically. "We talked a lot after you and Adam left. I think it was good. After this nightmare of a cruise is over, things should settle down. Again, I'm so sorry."

"Really, it's okay."

They both looked off into the distance until Addie spoke up again. "So, Adam..."

Margot smiled, knowing what her friend was getting at. "He's a good friend."

"More than a friend?"

"Maybe."

"Sure," Addie laughed. "I saw the way he looks at you, though. He definitely cares for you. How do you feel about that? After Julian and all."

Margot let her friend's question sink in. How did she feel? Then again, it was hard to pinpoint her own feelings when, in the back of her mind, she was still cycling through the logistics she'd worked out with Gabe and Adam. But, didn't that count for something? The very reality of her reliance on Adam and her trust in him spoke volumes.

"He's a good man. Similar to Julian in some ways but very different in others. I..." Margot felt the faint flush and chided herself for reacting so childishly about it all. "I really care for him."

"Good." Addie reached across and gripped her hand. "You deserve happiness. Especially after..." Her words trailed off but Margot didn't need her to say any more. Julian's death had been unexpected and mysterious, a shock to Margot as well as anyone who had known her husband.

Then again, his job had been dangerous and she'd known that. But still...

"Margot?"

Drawn from her thoughts, Margot looked up and met her friend's gaze. "Thanks again for coming. It was only fitting that I received this award with the person who helped me become what I am today."

"You had a lot of amazing teachers."

Addie shrugged. "But you were the one who taught me to love being a baker, not merely the art of it." She stood, letting out a sigh. "I'd better get back to the kitchen. Noah will be cleaning up in preparation for disembarking. We've got a week off of this ship while it undergoes some new construction so that means vacation for the crew, but a massive move for certain areas—the kitchen being one."

Margot sat up straighter. "Oh? What does that mean?"

"Nothing too major. We just have to get any extra supplies off when usually we'd let some sit. Our food overflow gets donated to a charity in the area, which Noah oversees, but I want to make sure things are flowing smoothly. They'll officially pull everything off tomorrow, but I have the day off so I'll just check in now."

"I understand," Margot said, following Addie to the door. "Let's see if we can all do dinner—Grayson included— toward the end of this week then."

"I'd really like that. I'll let you know."

Margot watched her friend walk back down the hall as more pieces fell into place. She had to update Adam and Gabe.

CHAPTER 12

Night had fallen across the dock, the sounds of water traffic much decreased at the late hour. There were still workers going back and forth, but they were confined to the warehouse areas instead of near the gangplank that led to the aft entrance for the crewmembers.

Margot walked arm and arm with Brice as they made their way up the gangplank. Her heart pounded in her ears, but she continued to remind herself that they would be safe. No matter what, Adam would watch out for her and she knew that.

"This isn't a good idea." Brice swallowed hard, not even looking at her.

"You're making the right choice, Brice. I think at heart you're a good guy, but you've made some poor choices. Think of your sister—she'd want you to do this."

He nodded almost imperceptibly and kept going. "You're right. She would. You kind of remind me of her."

Margot wasn't sure how to take that. His sister had been a drug addict and eventually overdosed.

"I mean, before the drugs," he added quickly. They were almost to the outside door where a dim light shone out from the hall inside. "She was smart, observant, and wouldn't take no for an answer."

Margot smiled despite the situation. "Thanks."

They approached the door and Brice reached out.

"Easy," a voice said into the earpiece she'd concealed under her hair. "You're doing great, Margie."

She resisted the urge to react to Adam's nickname. Instead, they walked inside and Brice led the way toward the kitchen.

"Okay," Adam's voice whispered in her ear, "time to put on the act."

Brice wasn't wearing an earpiece so she whispered to him. "Here comes the act." He nodded and she let out a peal of feminine laughter as they came up on the kitchen door. "Oh Brice, you're too funny."

He pushed the door in and she stepped into the kitchen with him.

There, at the back by the pantry door, Noah stood

surrounded by bags of flour. "What in the—" He pulled out a gun, aiming first at Brice then at Margot. "Margot? What is *she* doing here?"

"Noah?" Margot said, trying to sound pleasantly surprised. "You're his contact?"

He frowned, his gaze flying to Brice's. "What is going on? What does she know?" he demanded.

"Dude, chill." Brice patted Margot's hand woven through his arm. "She's with me now."

"I'll repeat myself," Noah said, still leveling the gun at Margot, "What is *she* doing here? Where is Haden?"

"She's my new partner," Brice explained. "And please, man, put the gun down. This is a civilized operation."

It lowered a fraction of an inch. "I don't get it." His gaze rotated to Margot. "What are you doing here?"

"I want in on the action," she said with a smile. "I've gotten to know Brice here on the cruise, and he let me in on the sweet deal you guys have going on down here. I wanted in."

The gun rose again. "Absolutely not."

"Oh come on," Margot said. "I may run a pastry shop, but that's not all I do." She flashed a cunning grin his way.

Noah looked interested for a moment before his mask slid into place again.

"I'm in the import-export business, if you know what I mean," Margot said, rehearsing what Gabe had told her to say. "I'd be a valuable asset to this organization. I took this opportunity to see if I could do some networking in Ensenada."

"But you're friends with Addie."

"Sure," Margot said, shrugging, "but she hasn't seen me in a while. People change. Desperate times call for desperate measures."

He wasn't buying it, she could tell, but she had to do something to convince him. Then it came to her. She slipped her hand from Brice's arm and stepped forward, trying not to let the gun barrel frighten away her courage. "Look, I know this guy—" She pointed over her shoulder at Brice with her thumb. "—isn't daring. I have a feeling you're the type of guy who sees an opportunity and goes for it. I'm not afraid of getting into…other things. If you know what I mean."

Now Noah looked confused, his gaze going between Margot and Brice. "What is this? Some kind of setup?"

"No," Margot said.

She looked back to Brice, who now looked appropriately angry and she thanked the Lord she was working with an actor.

"Dude, I don't know what she's talking about."

"Drugs," Margot said, putting her hands on her hips.

"Plain and simple. I mean we *are* talking about Mexico. If you aren't dealing, you should be, because as nice and clean as gems are, they won't make half the money you could get through dealing. Am I right?" She shot a hardened look at Noah.

She waited, knowing silence was her friend right now. He looked from her to Brice then back to her. He broke into a smile, his gun lowering. "You're kidding. How did you know?"

"What?" Brice exploded from behind Margot. "You're joking, right? You are *not* bringing drugs in. Tell me you aren't, Noah."

She did all she could not to admire Brice's masterful acting job and kept her gaze on the man in front of her.

"You had everything worked out, didn't you, Brice?" Noah said, his laugh cynical. "But you didn't get it. You still don't. So what, your sister overdosed. That's sad, but grow up. Gems do well, but I couldn't live on that. No one could—unless they were some world famous actor." He shook his head.

"What are you talking about?" Brice asked.

"I'm talking about being sick and tired of being your peon. I mean, seriously? Did you think I was going to work for you forever? I started importing drugs almost a year ago and have made double what we made last year."

"Noah—"

"Stop it," Noah yelled, the gun going back up but this time pointed at Brice. "You have *no* idea what it's like. Day in, day out, saying yes to all these customers demanding things. Working at a job I hate. All of it just so you could have access to Mexico and José. Well, forget that. I have my *own* network now."

"The missing gems, you took them, didn't you?"

Noah grinned again. "Ah, I see someone has started to pay attention. I told you that José wasn't able to deliver as much so that I could keep some back for startup money. Worked like a charm—until you came on this cruise to check up on me. I knew my gig was up."

"Wait a second," Margot said. "You're done? Just like that?"

He looked at her with boredom. "For this cruise line, but I've already got new people lined up on another while *I* retire. But don't worry, I've got a place for you." She hated the way he said it, but was glad to see he was still talking. Now she needed him to admit to what happened on board the ship. To the murders.

"What about me?" Brice asserted.

"I took care of everyone else, I'll take care of you."

Margot backed up, as if afraid. "What are you talking about?"

"Don't worry," Noah said, "I usually take very good care of my partners—as long as they aren't double-crossing me. I found out Kirsten was planted by a rival gang." Margot recognized the undercover story Gabe had told her they'd created. "And I couldn't leave any loose ends so Michael had to go too, thanks to a few gang members in Ensenada that respond well to cash. You see..." He looked back at Margot. "I take care of my own business. I don't force others to do it." Now he looked back at Brice, who looked appropriately shocked.

"But, what about our deal?" Brice stammered.

"Speaking of my own business, there *is* one more thing I need to take care of." He lifted the gun at Brice and pulled the trigger.

MARGOT SCREAMED, covering her head with her hands and cowering in front of Noah. She looked back at Brice, but he lay on the ground.

"Get down!" a voice screamed into her earpiece.

She obeyed and dropped to the floor just as a barrage of men in swat uniforms flooded the area. Shaking on the floor, Margot cowered on the other side of where Brice had fallen.

"Put the gun down!" a burly officer shouted at Noah. He looked around him, at the officers who all had guns trained on him, and finally moved to put the gun on the floor.

One officer moved forward and secured the weapon and

then two more came in and took hold of him as Adam raced into the small kitchen directly toward Margot.

"Are you all right?" he asked, looking down at her with his hands on both sides of her face.

She nodded. "B-Brice," she managed.

"I'm okay," came a voice from the other side of the island.

As Adam helped her to stand, she saw two officers helping him stand as well. One had pulled away his shirt to reveal the sturdy Kevlar vest that had caught the deadly bullet. She breathed a sigh of relief and nodded at him even as one officer put the handcuffs back on him. His negotiation to help them tonight would help him with his sentence, but he'd still need to do some jail time. She hoped that it would give him some time to think about what he'd done and to make his sister proud in his future decisions.

Adam wrapped his arm around Margot and pulled her toward the door just as Gabe came in.

"Great job, Margot," he said, nodding at her. He now wore a jacket with the initials DEA on the front. She narrowed her eyes at it and he shrugged. "So maybe I'm not FBI, but I used to be." He winked at Adam then took her hand in both of his. "Thank you again for what you were willing to do. You gave us the time we needed to gain the evidence to put Noah away."

"I'm glad. I also have a feeling you'll find all the other evidence you need in the flour sacks."

"What?" Gabe looked over his shoulder to where Margot was pointing.

"When I came on board here in Long Beach, Addie had it out with Michael Bowers about the fact that her flour hadn't been delivered. He said he took care of it, but then when we were in Ensenada, I came in to find more flour being loaded. I have a feeling it's either not flour or the drugs and gems are hidden in the flour."

"We'll check it out," he said with a nod. "Thanks for the tip. Now you guys go enjoy Long Beach. I hope it's restful and you can put this whole thing behind you."

Margot laughed. If only she and Adam could have a normal vacation experience, but she had a feeling that would never be the case.

They walked down the gangplank to the waiting Mustang convertible.

"You still have this?" she said, incredulous.

"Of course," he said with a grin. "I may have come down to Mexico for a few days but I wasn't about to give this beauty up just for that."

"By the way," she said, looking at him when they were seated, "how *did* you manage to get to Mexico, and on such short notice?"

Adam looked at her for a moment then turned his gaze back to the road. "It's a long story."

"Does it have something to do with how you know Gabe?"

"Um hum," was all he said.

She knew he was holding something back, the same thing he'd been holding back when she asked him what Gabe had meant at the restaurant. What was it about Adam's past that he didn't want her to know?

"Adam," she began, trying to find the right words, "I understand there are things you don't exactly want to share with me, but sometimes..." How could she put it? "Sometimes I feel like there is a whole part of you that I just don't know."

They drove in silence for a long time, the blare of an occasional horn the only disruption to the windswept quiet, but when they pulled up in front of her sister's house, he turned off the engine and turned toward her.

"Margie," he took her hand, holding it between both of his, "I care for you a lot. I hope you know that. I hope that you can *see* that. But..." He pressed his lips together in thought for a moment. "But there are some things I can't tell you. At least not yet. I hate that—I really do—but you have to trust me that I'll tell you when I can."

She nodded slowly. She understood, and yet she didn't. What was so important that he couldn't tell her about it? Was he working undercover? Was it something to do with his job? His past? His present? What was so important that Adam Eastwood had to keep it secret? He hadn't said it was classified, so aside from that, she didn't know what else it could be that he couldn't share.

Letting out a sigh, she gently pulled her hand from him. "I'm just disappointed you feel like you can't share this with me, that I'm not trustworthy enough. Good night, Adam."

He watched her go, his hazel eyes following her all the way up to the front of the house. When she turned around, she saw that he hadn't moved, his eyes still on hers. Then she stepped inside the house, closing the door on him.

CHAPTER 13

THEY ALL SAT at a large table on the patio of the *La Playa* restaurant. Margot, Adam, her sister Renee, her husband Dillon, and Taylor. Even Addie and Grayson had come for the farewell brunch. After a week of shopping, visiting Disneyland, going to the beach and trying to surf with Taylor and her friends, Margot was ready to head back to the East Coast.

She missed her shop and, though she was kept in the loop from Dexter and assured that everything was going well, she wanted to be back to her regular schedule. Vacations were good, but they weren't real.

She thought back on the debriefing meetings she'd had with Gabe and Adam as well. Noah was being charged with two counts of murder along with his drug and gem smuggling, and she felt better knowing that his contacts on the other ships had been found and removed. Brice had also been sentenced to five years in prison with hopes of getting out earlier on bail for good behavior. She hoped he would turn his life around.

The notion that the gem and drug smuggling had ended, along with cooperation with the Mexican officials in Ensenada, filled Margot with contentment, but the fact that lives had been lost saddened her. There was no end to crime and destruction in this world, but she was glad she could have played a small part in ending some of it—even while on vacation.

Renee had just told a joke but Margot didn't laugh. She hadn't heard it and she could tell that Adam knew she was lost in another world.

"Hey," he said, leaning close, "let's take a walk."

Margot was torn. Looking around the circle of friends and family, she didn't want to leave them alone, but she desperately wanted to clear up the stuffiness that had descended between her and Adam.

At the same moment, Addie looked her way. "I'm sorry," she said, leaning forward, "but Grayson and I need to head out. We're meeting his mom tonight in Oxnard and we want to leave ourselves enough time to get out of the city."

"Of course! It was so good to see you." Margot embraced her friend as Adam shook Grayson's hand.

"He's a good guy," Addie whispered into her ear, "whatever it is that's going on, talk to him about it."

She leaned back and looked at her friend. "How—?"

"It takes one to know one," Addie said with a laugh. "All relationships are rocky, but I think you guys are suited for one another. I hope things work out."

Margot found herself hoping they would as well. She said good-bye to Grayson and then told Renee that they would meet her back at her house later. Then, slipping off their shoes, she and Adam set off on the beach.

They walked for a short time before he spoke up. "I was worried sick when I got that email from you."

"How did you know something was going on?" In the back of her mind, she was suspicious. She hadn't said anything particular to tip him off—or at least she hadn't *thought* she had—but now she was wondering if he'd known more about the situation. If he'd known Gabe—

She stopped herself. She *knew* Adam. Knew he was a good guy. Knew that he wouldn't do anything to hurt her. And yet here she was questioning his every move. She huffed out a breath and turned to look at him as they walked along the water's edge.

"I just had a feeling. Honestly..." He gave a humorless laugh. "Any time you ask me questions about things, I get the sense you're trying to pry information from me without coming out and telling me the truth." He eyed her with a look and she dropped her gaze.

He was right. Here she was, demanding that he be honest

with her—which was a good thing—and yet she hadn't come out and told him the truth either.

Sighing, she reached over and took his hand in hers as they walked. "I'm sorry, Adam. At the time, I only had suspicions. I didn't know for sure that anything was going on."

"I know. And I didn't think too much about it until I found out what Gabe was doing."

"What?"

"I just had a feeling." He shook his head with a faint smile. "Gabe's always been a slippery one."

Margot laughed. "What does that mean?"

"He's a good guy, but he dips into a lot of different things and sometimes that's gotten him in trouble in the past. I should have known he was working on something undercover. It just fits."

Margot pressed her lips together, knowing what she needed to say, but fighting against saying it. She cared so much for Adam, but her own independence, something that had grown in the wake of Julian's death, was sometimes stronger than she knew what do to do with. When they reached a set of swings looking out toward the ocean, Adam led them over and they sat, swaying back and forth.

"Margot," he began, but she cut him off.

"I'm sorry, Adam." He looked surprised. "You've done nothing but help me and believe me in all situations. I...I know I ask too much of you sometimes. I know you don't mean to keep me in the dark about things. I suppose I just need to have more patience. If you say you'll tell me when you can, then I need to believe you. Will you accept my apology?"

He smiled back at her, reaching out and clasping her hand in between the swings. "Of course. Just know that I care—very deeply—about you. There are things I want to share, but...I just can't yet. I will when I can. I promise."

Despite the desire to demand answers and her tendency to grow frustrated, she took a deep breath and nodded back at him. The look on his face was genuine and filled with care—for her.

She turned her gaze back to the ocean as they swung in tandem, hands held between the seats. She felt like a school girl again, if only for a moment, and she relished the innocent nature of what life looked like from the simple viewpoint of sand, sea, and sky.

∿

Thanks for reading the *Margot Durand Cozy Mystery Boxed Set*. I hope you enjoyed reading the story as much as I enjoyed writing it. If you did, it would be awesome if you left a review for me on Amazon and/or Goodreads.

If you would like to know about future cozy mysteries by me and the other authors at Fairfield Publishing, make sure to sign up for our Cozy Mystery Newsletter. We will send you our FREE Cozy Mystery Starter Library just for signing up. All the details are on the next page.

At the very end of the book, I have included a preview of the next book in the Margot Durand series as well as a preview of a book by a friend and fellow author at Fairfield Publishing. First is a preview of *Muffins and Murder* where Margot has to solve a mystery that goes back decades to a treasure hunt gone bad. Second is a preview of *Up in Smoke* by Shannon VanBergen - it's the first book in the Glock Grannies Cozy Mystery series. I really hope you like the samples. If you do, both books are available on Amazon.

- Get *Muffins and Murder* here:
  amazon.com/dp/B072MLXF4K
- Get *Up in Smoke* here:
  amazon.com/dp/B06XHKYRRX

FAIRFIELD COZY MYSTERY NEWSLETTER

Make sure you sign up for the Fairfield Cozy Mystery Newsletter so you can keep up with our latest releases. When you sign up, **we will send you our FREE Cozy Mystery Starter Library!**

FairfieldPublishing.com/cozy-newsletter/

After you sign up to get your Free Starter Library, turn the page and check out the free previews :)

PREVIEW: MUFFINS AND MURDER

MARGOT DURAND gently packed the second box into her canvas bag, the bright colors of the lightweight cardboard popping against the tan of the tote. She donned her bright green rain jacket and palmed her purse-sized umbrella as she made her way to the front door.

"Be back in an hour," she called behind her.

"Okay," a voice answered from the kitchen. Dexter was working on a new creation—one she had agreed to oversee but was now having second thoughts about.

"Don't burn down the place," she called.

"I won't," he called back with a laugh.

Pressing her lips to keep from calling out more warnings, she pushed the door open and took a moment under the stoop awning to pop open the umbrella. Her grey Hunter rain boots would protect her feet from the downpour just as she was trusting in the umbrella to keep the rest of her relatively dry on the way to the senior center. That, and her precious cargo.

The Parisian Pâtisserie, her French bakery located on a historic, cobbled street that ran parallel to the Potomac in the small town of North Bank, Virginia, hadn't been the same without its star patron, Bentley Anderson.

A retired lawyer and avid crossword player, Bentley had come in to the *Pâtisserie* every day for the last few years, until last week when he'd thrown his back out. Under doctor's orders of rest, Bentley had stayed in his small, senior living apartment not far from the Senior Center, but she'd gotten a call that morning that he was seriously contemplating coming down to the bakery or else he might face going insane from lack of 'mental stimulation,' as he'd put it.

Rather than risk another potential injury, Margot had made a deal. She would bring the bakery to him if he'd tell her an interesting story or two to pass the time. He'd readily agreed.

Getting there without soaking today's delicacy, French breakfast muffins, or spilling the coffee was a challenge, but soon Margot was headed to his door under the covered walkway of one of the senior complexes that dotted the riverside in North Bank.

"It's open," he called when she knocked on the door.

Bentley sat in his favorite chair in front of the double sliding glass doors that looked out over a stunning vista. The town of North Bank stretched out below the senior facility situated on a hill and they could clearly see the winding and slightly muddy waters of the Potomac stretching out in front of them. The rain beat down, dotting the glass and making the waters choppier than they normally were, but it was still a stunning view.

"I'd say you got the best of both worlds today."

"How's that?" he asked, turning to peer up at her.

"You get the view *and* the pastries."

He grinned and eyed her tote. "You bring me some breakfast?"

"Of course. And coffee to boot."

"You're my angel," he said, stretching his hands out toward her. "Now hand it over."

Laughing, she made her way to the kitchen and placed

three French breakfast muffins covered in icing on a plate, pouring a large mug of coffee as well. Then she placed her own pastry on another plate and carried it all into the living room. "Here we are."

They ate in silence for a time, the only sounds the pitter-patter of the rain against the glass and scraping forks on plates. As soon as Bentley was done, Margot leaned forward. "You promised me a story."

Bentley licked the last of the icing off his fork, smacking his lips together in pleasure, then nodded to her. "I thought of a good one, but I think you've had enough of death and sadness to last for a while. Am I right?"

She frowned, thinking about that. In recent history, she'd stumbled across more than her fair share of mysteries. Granted, working the cases with handsome Detective Adam Eastwood was a bonus, but that didn't mean it hadn't affected her. Then again, her last mystery had happened in California during a vacation to Ensenada, Mexico, where, with the help of Adam and his friend DIA agent Gabe Williams, they'd ended a drug and gem smuggling ring. Despite the happy ending, the events along the way had weighed on her. The reality of the depth of human greed was a difficult thing to comprehend.

Then again, it had almost been five months ago and she had moved easily back into the rhythm of life at the bakery while occasionally dating Adam. If he hadn't been so busy recently—

She cut those thoughts off where they started and refocused on Bentley's statement. "Oh come on, Bentley," she urged with a smile, "give me something good."

They had started the tradition of storytelling when she had gotten back from Long Beach. Over the course of several days, she'd told him the story of what had happened on her trip and, seeming to enjoy it, he had in turn shared a story from his past with her.

As a trial lawyer, among other odd jobs Bentley seemed to have had, there was no end to the amazing tales he could tell about his past. She also had a feeling he enjoyed opening up to her about the past, seeing as he had no family that visited him—or none that Margot was aware of.

"Oh fine," he said, nodding, his eyes unfocused on the pane of glass in front of him. "I'll tell you the tale of the sunken treasure."

~

"I WAS IN MY EARLY TWENTIES," Bentley began, his eyes scanning the distance, "but it was the best summer of my life, spent out on a boat for twelve to fourteen hours a day. I came back so tan, my mother thought I'd fallen into a vat of brown paint." He rasped out a laugh.

Margot smiled to herself, imagining a young, tanned Bentley out on a boat and looking as though he owned the world.

"I was making pretty good money that summer, all of it would go to my schooling, and that made the experience all the better. I mean, I had to pay for my law degree somehow." He laughed again. "You see it was that summer that I went hunting for treasure."

Margot laughed. "Treasure? What, is this story about pirates?"

He flashed a wicked grin. "Not exactly."

"That's a little disappointing," she joked.

"Let me tell the story, girl." He gave her a fake warning look and continued. "I worked on the boat with my friends Russ Gorssi and Harrison Douglass. We were all certified scuba instructors and took out small groups of people to see fun attractions on the Florida coast. It was a sweet little operation and the administration portion was run by the prettiest girl I'd ever laid eyes on. Melinda Kaufman." Bentley sighed and Margot almost giggled but kept quiet, not wanting to interrupt again. "Her younger brother Sean would ferry people back and forth from the main boat. He was a little bit of a brat, but you couldn't blame him. He was still a teen and we were obnoxious college students."

Bentley took a sip of his coffee. "One day, after we'd come back from a long day of instruction, I was relaxing on my bunk in the small apartment we'd rented for the summer. When I looked through my mail, I was shocked to see I'd gotten a letter from our mutual friend Tony

McLaren. At the time, he was studying international law in France."

"Were you all studying to be lawyers?" Margot asked.

"In one way or another, we were all studying law, but in different veins. Harrison had political aspirations and Russ was more interested in finding a wife than a degree. But law was what bonded us. Anyway, the exciting part—" Bentley eyed her. "—was that Tony found an old map in an antique store in Barcelona while he was there for a break from school. As a joke, he cut the map into four halves and sent it off to me, Harrison, and Russ."

"You're joking," Margot laughed.

"Hardly!" Bentley shook a finger at her. "The only reason he sent it was because it was in the area that we were diving. He thought it quite the coincidence and thought it would be a good laugh for us all. He kept part for himself but it was the inconsequential part. With our three portions, we were able to piece out where this supposed treasure was buried."

"Did you dive for it?"

"Eventually, we did one day after work was over. And you know what?"

"What?" Margot leaned forward in her seat, interested now.

"We found it."

"You did!?"

"We did, but that's when the trouble started."

"Trouble?"

Bentley shook his head. "I was studying to be a trial lawyer and I liked to study up on various laws along the way. Kind of like my affection for crosswords. Anyway, I had looked into what would happen if you found treasure where we were diving—since I think I was hoping we'd find some—and I knew we were required to report it, but the other guys immediately objected. They said that they didn't want the treasure snookered away from us. Talked about selling it on the side and such."

"What happened?" Margot asked, afraid to know what had really become of the treasure.

"When I finally convinced them that my way was the best, most honest way, they agreed to do things as the law dictated. We left it where it was, intending to come back a week later when we knew more about how we could accurately claim it, and swore ourselves to secrecy. But when we did go back...it was gone."

"No," she said in disbelief.

"Yes." Bentley shook his head with a sad expression. "We never did find out what happened. Maybe someone had overheard us talking about it or we were followed out there. We couldn't be sure, but it was gone."

"I'm so sorry," she said when her phone beeped. She

looked down to see that Rosie had texted to ask a question regarding the shop. She was way past the time she'd told Dexter she'd be back. "And I'm sorry again, but I've got to get back to the shop."

"Of course," he said, waving dismissively.

"Bentley," she said, standing, "why did you pick that story?"

He looked out the window again. "I found out that Tony died last week. I guess our adventures—given to us by him—brought it to mind."

Margot frowned and walked toward the television. "I'm sorry to hear that, Bentley. Do you want the TV on?" He usually did when she left. He nodded.

When the screen came to life, Bentley gasped as the picture of a man flashed on the screen. The anchor was speaking.

"...was found dead in his Chesapeake Bay home late last night. And so ends the Grossi family business. It's rumored that the Grossi Market was bought out but we won't know until further—"

"Wait." Margot looked to Bentley, whose mouth was wide open. "Is that *Russ* Grossi? Your friend?"

Bentley nodded and looked up at her. "And now he's dead too."

THANKS FOR READING a sample of *Muffins and Murder*. I really hope you liked it. You can read the rest at: **amazon.com/dp/B072MLXF4K**

PREVIEW: UP IN SMOKE

I COULD FEEL my hair puffing up like cotton candy in the humidity as I stepped outside the Miami airport. I pushed a sticky strand from my face, and I wished for a minute that it were a cheerful pink instead of dirty blond, just to complete the illusion.

"Thank you so much for picking me up from the airport." I smiled at the sprightly old lady I was struggling to keep up with. "But why did you say my grandmother couldn't pick me up?"

"I didn't say." She turned and gave me a toothy grin—clearly none of them original—and winked. "I parked over here."

When we got to her car, she opened the trunk and threw in the sign she had been holding when she met me in baggage claim. The letters were done in gold glitter glue and she had drawn flowers with markers all around the edges. My name "Nikki Rae Parker" flashed when the sun reflected off of them, temporarily blinding me.

"I can tell you put a lot of work into that sign." I carefully put my luggage to the side of it, making sure not to touch her sign—partially because I didn't want to crush it and partially because it didn't look like the glue had dried yet.

"Well, your grandmother didn't give me much time to make it. I only had about ten minutes." She glanced at the sign proudly before closing the trunk. She looked me in the eyes. "Let's get on the road. We can chit chat in the car."

With that, she climbed in and clicked on her seat belt. As I got in, she was applying a thick coat of bright red lipstick while looking in the rearview mirror. "Gotta look sharp in case we get pulled over." She winked again, her heavily wrinkled eyelid looking like it thought about staying closed before it sprung back up again.

I thought about her words for a moment. She must get

pulled over a lot, I thought. Poor old lady. I could picture her going ten miles an hour while the rest of Miami flew by her.

"Better buckle up." She pinched her lips together before blotting them slightly on a tissue. She smiled at me and for a moment, I was jealous of her pouty lips, every line filled in by layers and layers of red.

I did as I was told and buckled my seat belt before I sunk down into her caramel leather seats. I was exhausted, both physically and mentally, from the trip. I closed my eyes and tried to forget my troubles, taking in a deep breath and letting it out slowly to give all my worry and fear ample time to escape my body. For the first time since I had made the decision to come here, I felt at peace. Unfortunately, it was short-lived.

The sound of squealing tires filled the air and my eyes flung open to see this old lady zigzagging through the parking garage. She took the turns without hitting the brakes, hugging each curve like a racecar driver. When we exited the garage and turned onto the street, she broke out in laughter. "That's my favorite part!"

I tugged my seat belt to make sure it was on tight. This was not going to be the relaxing drive I had thought it would be.

We hit the highway and I felt like I was in an arcade game. She wove in and out of traffic at a speed I was sure matched her old age.

"Ya know, the older I get the worse other people drive." She took one hand off the wheel and started to rummage through her purse, which sat between us.

"Um, can I help you with something?" My nerves were starting to get the best of me as her eyes were focused more on her purse than the road.

"Oh no, I've got it. I'm sure it's in here somewhere." She dug a little more, pulling out a package of AA batteries and then a ham sandwich.

Brake lights lit up in front of us and I screamed, bracing myself for impact. The old woman glanced up and pulled the car to the left in a quick jerk before returning to her purse. Horns blared from behind us.

"There it is!" She pulled out a package of wintergreen Life Savers. "Do you want one?"

"No, thank you." I could barely get the words out.

"I learned a long time ago that it was easier if I just drove and did my thing instead of worrying about what all the other drivers were doing. It's easier for them to get out of my way instead of me getting out of theirs. My reflexes aren't what they used to be." She popped a mint in her mouth and smiled. "I love wintergreen. I don't know why peppermint is more popular. Peppermint is so stuffy; wintergreen is fun."

She seemed to get in a groove with her driving and soon my grip was loosening on the sides of the seat, the blood slowly returning to my knuckles. Suddenly I realized I hadn't asked her name.

"I was so confused when you picked me up from the airport instead of my Grandma Dean that I never asked your name."

She didn't respond, just kept her eyes on the road with a steely look on her face. I was happy to see her finally being serious about driving, so I turned to look out the window. "It's beautiful here," I said after a few minutes of silence. I turned to look at her again and noticed that she was still focused straight ahead. I stared at her for a moment and realized she never blinked. Panic rose through my chest.

"Ma'am!" I shouted as I leaned forward to take the wheel. "Are you okay?"

She suddenly sprung to action, screaming and jerking the wheel to the left. Her screaming caused me to scream and I grabbed the wheel and pulled it to the right, trying to get us back in our lane. We continued to scream until the car stopped teetering and settled down to a nice hum on the road.

"Are you trying to kill us?" The woman's voice was hoarse and she seemed out of breath.

"I tried to talk to you and you didn't answer!" I practically shouted. "I thought you had a heart attack or something!"

"You almost gave me one!" She flashed me a dirty look.

"And you made me swallow my mint. You're lucky I didn't choke to death!"

"I'm sorry." As I said the words, I noticed my heart was beating in my ears. "I really thought something had happened to you."

She was quiet for a moment. "Well, to be honest with you, I did doze off for a moment." She looked at me, pride spreading across her face. "I sleep with my eyes open. Do you know anyone who can do that?"

Before I could answer, she was telling me about her friend Delores who "claimed" she could sleep with her eyes open but, as it turned out, just slept with one eye half-open because she had a stroke and it wouldn't close all the way.

I sat there in silence before saying a quick prayer. My hands resumed their spot around the seat cushion and I could feel the blood draining from my knuckles yet again.

"So what was it you tried to talk to me about before you nearly killed us?"

I swallowed hard, trying to push away the irritation that fought to come out.

"I asked you what your name was." I stared at her and decided right then that I wouldn't take my eyes off of her for the rest of the trip. I would make sure she stayed awake, even if it meant talking to her the entire time.

"Oh yes! My name is Hattie Sue Miller," she said with a bit of arrogance. She glanced at me. "My father used to own most of this land." She motioned to either side of us. "Until he sold it and made a fortune." She gave me a look and dropped her voice to a whisper as she raised one eyebrow. "Of course we don't talk about money. That would be inappropriate." She said that last part like I had just asked her when she had last had sex. I felt ashamed until I realized I had never asked her about her money; I had simply asked her name. This woman was a nut. Didn't Grandma Dean have any other friends she could've sent to get me?

For the next hour or so, I asked her all kinds of questions to keep her awake—none of them about money or anything I thought might lead to money. If what she told me was true, she had a very interesting upbringing. She claimed to be related to Julia Tuttle, the woman who founded Miami. Her stories of how she got a railroad company to agree to build tracks there were fascinating. It wasn't until she told me she was also related to Michael Jackson that I started to question how true her stories were.

"We're almost there! Geraldine will be so happy to see you. You're all she's talked about the last two weeks." She pulled into a street lined with palm trees. "You're going to love it here." She smiled as she drove. "I've lived here a long time. It's far enough away from the city that you don't have all that hullaballoo, but big enough that you can eat at a different restaurant every day for a month."

When we entered the downtown area, heavy gray smoke

hung in the air, and the road was blocked by a fire truck and two police cars.

"Oh no! I think there might have been a fire!" I leaned forward in my seat, trying to get a better look.

"Of course there was a fire!" Hattie huffed like I was an idiot. "That's why Geraldine sent me to get you!"

"What?! Is she okay?" I scanned the crowd and saw her immediately. She was easy to spot, even at our distance.

"Oh yes. She's fine. Her shop went up in flames as she was headed out the door. She got the call from a neighboring store owner and called me right away to go get you. Honestly, I barely had time to make you a sign." She acted like Grandma Dean had really put her in a bad position, leaving her only minutes to get my name on a piece of poster board.

Hattie pulled over and I jumped out; I'd come back for my luggage later. As I made my way toward the crowd, I was amazed at how little my Grandma Dean—or Grandma Dean-Dean, as I had called her since I was a little girl— had changed. Her bleach blonde hair was nearly white and cut in a cute bob that was level with her chin. She wore skintight light blue denim capris, which hugged her tiny frame. Her bright white t-shirt was the background for a long colorful necklace that appeared to be a string of beads. Thanks to a pair of bright red heels, she stood eye to eye with the fireman she was talking to.

I ran up to her and called out to her. "Grandma! Are you

okay?" She flashed me a look of disgust before she smiled weakly at the fireman and said something I couldn't make out.

She turned her back to him and grabbed me by the arm. "I told you to never call me that!" She softened her tone then looked me over. "You look exhausted! Was it the flight or riding with that crazy Hattie?" She didn't give me time to answer. "Joe, this is my daughter's daughter, Nikki."

Joe smiled. I wasn't sure if it was his perfectly white teeth that got my attention, his uniform or his sparkling blue eyes, but I was immediately speechless. I tried to say hello, but the words stuck in my throat.

"Nikki, this is Joe Dellucci. He was born in New Jersey but his parents came from Italy. Isn't that right, Joe?"

I was disappointed when Joe answered without a New Jersey accent. Grandma Dean continued to tell me about Joe's heritage, which reminded me of Hattie. Apparently once you got to a certain age, you automatically became interested in people's backgrounds.

He must have noticed the look of disappointment on my face. "My family moved here when I was ten. My accent only slips in when I'm tired." His face lit up with a smile, causing mine to do the same. "Or when I eat pizza." I had no idea what he meant by that, but it caused me to break out in nervous laughter. Grandma Dean's look of embarrassment finally snapped me out of it.

"Well, Miss Dean. If I hear anything else, I'll let you know.

In the meantime, call your insurance company. I'm sure they'll get you in touch with a good fire restoration service. If not, let me know. My brother's in the business."

He handed her a business card and I saw the name in red letters across the front: *Clean-up Guys*. Not a very catchy name. Then suddenly it hit me. A fireman with a brother who does fire restoration? Seemed a little fishy. Joe must have noticed my expression, because he chimed in. "Our house burned down when I was eight and Alex was twelve. I guess it had an impact on us."

Grandma Dean took the card and put it in her back pocket. "Thanks, Joe. I'll give Alex a call this afternoon."

They said their good-byes and as Joe walked away, Grandma Dean turned toward me. "What did I tell you about calling me 'Grandma' in public?" Her voice was barely over a whisper. "I've given you a list of names that are appropriate and I don't understand why you don't use one of them!"

"I'm not calling you Coco!" My mind tried to think of the other names on the list. Peaches? Was that on there? Whatever it was, they all sounded ridiculous.

"There is nothing wrong with Coco!" She pulled away from me and ran a hand through her hair as a woman approached us.

"Geraldine, I'm so sorry to hear about the fire!" The woman hugged Grandma Dean. "Do they know what started it?"

"No, but Joe's on it. He'll figure it out. I'm sure it was wiring or something. You know how these old buildings are."

The woman nodded in agreement. "If you need anything, please let me know." She hugged Grandma again and gave her a look of pity.

"Bev, this is my...daughter's daughter, Nikki."

I rolled my eyes. She couldn't even say granddaughter. I wondered if she would come up with some crazy name to replace that too.

"It's nice to meet you," Bev said without actually looking at me. She looked worried. Her drawn-on eyebrows were pinched together, creating a little bulge between them. "If you hear anything about what started it, please be sure to let me know."

Grandma turned to me as the woman walked away. "She owns the only other antique store on this block. I'm sure she's happy as a clam that her competition is out for a while," Grandma said, almost with a laugh.

I gasped. "Do you think she did it? Do you think she set fire to your shop?"

"Oh, honey, don't go jumping to conclusions like that. She would never hurt a fly." Grandma looked around. "Where's your luggage?"

I turned to point toward Hattie's car, but it was gone.

Grandma let out a loud laugh. "Hattie took off with your luggage? Well, then let's go get it."

THANKS FOR READING the sample of *Up in Smoke*. I really hope you liked it. You can read the rest at:

- **amazon.com/dp/B06XHKYRRX**